"With *The Inconsolables*, Michael Wehunt expands the idea of what horror can and should do. The supernatural and the deeply human blend seamlessly in this unsettling collection, rife with subtle terror and unexpected tension. You'll never look at the world around you in quite the same way again." —A.C. Wise, author of *Hooked* and *The Ghost Sequences*

"No one does slow, creeping dread and unease like Michael Wehunt. *The Inconsolables* contains stories that ask you to remove your tear salt-seasoned heart and then consume it. And you'll do it. Gladly. For anyone seeking stories that lodge themselves inside the meat of you, this collection is a triumph." —Kristi DeMeester, author of *Such a Pretty Smile*

"These stories exist in the liminal space between elegy and the uncanny and prove beyond all doubt that Wehunt is one of our modern day masters of horror." —John Hornor Jacobs, author of *A Lush and Seething Hell* and *The Incorruptibles*

"Michael Wehunt is one of my favorite, trusted guides navigating stories of grief and loss, sadness and regret. My reader's heart left standing in *Greener Pastures* so eager to welcome that unique, familiar voice ushering me toward a new strange path twisting through Wehunt's garden of eerie, weird, beautiful things—*The Inconsolables*; what a gift." —Sadie Hartmann, author of *101 Horror Books to Read Before You're Murdered*, Bram Stoker Award®- nominated editor

"Michael Wehunt is one of my favorite authors writing today. This collection is haunting, moving, unsettling, and visceral. These stories drill down to my core, undoing me as they go, leaving me spent and shaken, searching for solid ground. And just when I was ready to throw in the towel, to surrender, there was a ray of hope, and it was heartbreaking in its brilliance." —Richard Thomas, author of *Spontaneous Human Combustion*, a Bram Stoker Award® finalist

ALSO BY
MICHAEL WEHUNT

Greener Pastures
Everything is Beautiful and Nothing Bad Can Ever Happen Here

THE INCONSOLABLES

STORIES

MICHAEL WEHUNT

BAD HAND BOOKS

The Inconsolables
Copyright © 2023 by Michael Wehunt
Print ISBN: 979-8-9881286-1-8

Front Cover Artwork by Michael Wehunt
Illustrations by Trevor Henderson
Cover & Interior Design by Todd Keisling | Dullington Design Co.

Foreword copyright © 2023 by John Langan

"Vampire Fiction" is original to this volume; "Holoow" first appeared in *Darker Companions: Celebrating 50 Years of Ramsey Campbell*, edited by Joseph S. Pulver, Sr., and David Aniolowski, PS Publishing, 2017; "Caring for a Stray Dog (Metaphors)" first appeared in in *Black Static* #62, edited by Andy Cox, 2018; "The Pine Arch Collection" first appeared in in *The Dark* #36, edited by Sean Wallace and Silvia Moreno-Garcia, 2018; "The Tired Sounds, A Wake" first appeared as a limited-edition chapbook by Dim Shores, edited by Sam Cowan, 2017; "A Heart Arrhythmia Creeping Into a Dark Room" first appeared in *Miscreations: Gods, Monstrosities & Other Horrors,* edited by Doug Murano and Michael Bailey, Written Backwards, 2020; "The Teeth of America" first appeared on www.michaelwehunt.com, edited by Michael Wehunt, 2020; "It Takes Slow Sips" first appeared in *Lost Contact*, edited by Max Booth III and Lori Michelle, Perpetual Motion Machine Publishing, 2021; "Is There Human Kindness Still in the World?" is original to this volume; "An Ending (Ascent)" first appeared in *Gamut* #11, edited by Richard Thomas, 2017.

Bad Hand Books
www.badhandbooks.com

Dedicated to Joseph S. Pulver, Sr.

In Memoriam, OVERmoon,
    We will always see where you just were
    Because
When the lantern that burned differently flickers out,
All the light changes.

TABLE OF CONTENTS

DISSECTING WEHUNT:
A PARTIAL PHYLOGENY

I t's there in the title: to be inconsolable is to be unable to be consoled, which is to say, unable to receive comfort after a loss or disappointment. The "s" appended to the word transforms adjective into noun, modifier into category. In so doing, it frames the stories in Michael Wehunt's excellent second collection. The characters in these pages live in the wake of deaths literal and metaphorical, of frustrations big and bigger. Wehunt has short-handed his work as Robert Aickman meets Flannery O'Connor, and while there's certainly truth to the comparison, the writers who lurk in the background of this collection feel more like Updike and Cheever, Raymond Carver and Richard Yates, those unsparing chroniclers of mid-twentieth-century anxiety. For these writers, the past is a promise dead on the vine, the future a steadily narrowing pathway to no good ending.

Not terribly promising material for a group of horror stories, you might say. Sounds as if the characters' lives are already plenty horrific without the addition of a vampire or werewolf. And indeed, it's difficult to write well about disappointment and loss of this stripe within the literature of the fantastic. That Wehunt succeeds in this challenge, and so well at that, testifies to his ability as a writer. As I see it, his particular strengths are located in his prose style, the inventiveness of his monsters, and his willingness to dive deeply into his characters' psyches. They're all wrapped around one another,

DNA style, but let me tease each one out for a moment so we can consider it.

The prose, first. Horror fiction has had its share of stylists, many of them greater and lesser degrees of baroque. (Think H.P. Lovecraft.) The field has also seen plenty of writers who steer in the opposite direction, towards a kind of restrained, even minimalist, approach. (Think Richard Matheson.) Michael Wehunt's writing falls somewhere in the broad territory between these poles. Lean without being starved, it's direct and clear. It's unafraid of metaphor, of figurative language in general, and the figures Wehunt weaves into his sentences are both surprising and inevitable, as the best tropes are. Indeed, part of what propels the reader through his stories is watching its style unfold, its tropes open. His language does not stray too far from whatever it's engaged with, riding its protagonist's perspective like a boat on the waves, rising and falling with the character's perceptions. It's in his use of language—his attention to it—that I think you see Wehunt's debt to Robert Aickman and Flannery O'Connor, as well as to recent stylists such as Laird Barron, most clearly. There are readers—and writers—who opine that style is the frosting on the cake, a decoration more pleasing to the eye than the tongue. As do these other writers, Wehunt demonstrates the way(s) in which a writer's language choices are a crucial part of the recipe.

As is his use of monsters. At the heart of every horror story worth the name is the monstrous, the departure from the everyday which calls into question our fundamental assumptions about our lives. More often than not, the split from the normal is embodied in the form of the monster, most of whose forms are familiar to us. Stephen King describes them in terms of a Tarot deck with five cards: the vampire, the werewolf, the thing-without-a-name, the bad place, and the ghost. The challenge for a writer of horror fiction is to deploy these monsters in fresh ways. Wehunt achieves this in two ways. The first has to do with context. In the collection's opening story, "Vampire Fiction," he uses the vampire in a narrative whose protagonist's lifelong obsession with the undead escalates when his wife and daughter leave him. His reflections on the vampire tradition, combined with abundant metatextual references to contemporary horror writers, destabilize the vampire's lengthy history and associations, moving out of focus a monster whose every feature had appeared dreadfully familiar just a minute ago. By the time we've reached the story's end, all we can say for sure about the vampire is that it is something you call to yourself.

Wehunt's second strategy with the monstrous is to use something seemingly ridiculous as its avatar. This is the case in the collection's longest story, the powerful "The Tired Sounds, A Wake," in which a wife and husband experiencing a combined mid-life crisis find themselves subject to repeated, unexpected appearances by mimes in their daily routines. At first, Wehunt's use of the mime appears deliberately absurd, a willful effort to flout generic convention. (Though there are clowns and the like in the work of Thomas Ligotti and Jon Padgett, not to mention the one lurking in the sewers under Derry.) With each encounter, however, the mimes lose their absurdity and gain in sinister resonance, their fundamental silence symbolic of the couple's inability to communicate with one another, while the mimes' encounters-with-invisible-objects routines embody the unseen barriers keeping husband and wife apart from each other. Those repeated appearances also give the mimes an emotional heft, which transforms them into surprisingly effective examples of the monstrous. (For what it's worth, I see them as forms of the ghost.) Much of the best horror fiction risks ridiculousness in order to achieve something startling and memorable: this is the case, here.

His close attention to his characters' psyches is, as I see it, the third ingredient to Wehunt's fiction. In a story such as "Holoow," for instance, he guides us into the perspective of an older woman recently relocated to a senior living facility after her adult daughter decides her mother is no longer able to live on her own. From the window of her new residence, Claudette, the protagonist, witnesses strange figures performing strange tasks in the street below, and sees weird shapes in the room across from her. As the story proceeds, Wehunt maps the parameters of his Claudette's psyche through a mixture of memory, conversation, and perception with a deftness reminiscent of Katherine Anne Porters' "The Jilting of Granny Weatherall." At first, the immersion in Claudette's consciousness appears to explain and contain the bizarre things she observes as projections of her interior life. The story's end, however, confuses this interpretation, as suddenly the distance between what is within and without Claudette collapses, and it seems as if it might be as fitting to describe her as a projection of the bizarre things she observes. It's another way in which Wehunt's debt to Aickman is showcased.

I know that Wehunt has identified himself with a group of Atlanta-based horror writers including Kristi DeMeester and Anya Martin. Given his works' frequent use of North Georgia settings, the association makes sense. I also see connections between his writing and the considered weirdness of Matthew Bartlett and Jon Padgett, on the one hand, and the lyrical horror of Nathan Ballingrud and Glen Hirshberg on the other. When all is said and done, though, Michael Wehunt is his own writer, and a damned fine one, at that. Rumor has it, he's written a novel. I'm looking forward to it.

—John Langan

THE
INCONSOLABLES

STORIES

VAMPIRE FICTION

The weekend his family left him, Fulton started thinking about vampires. He hadn't considered them in so long, but the house was different now in such a stark way, empty and full of cold spaces. It had become a container vulnerable to dark imagery.

Kat and Laney were going to Michigan, to stay with Laney's grandparents, to think. Kat said these immense things as Fulton stood in the mouth of the dining room, struck silent in the slanting fall light from the picture window. She clamped their daughter's wrist in her hand. Their suitcases had been secreted inside her hatchback since the morning.

She said, looking back once, "I don't know what we are anymore." The front door opened and closed with a deep hollow knot of sound, as though the furniture had been removed with them.

He sat in Laney's bedroom that night, holding her old picture books in his lap and turning their cardboard pages. She was reading a little on her own now but still liked it when Fulton acted out the stories or pretended he was having trouble with the "baby" ones.

His hands looked clumsy holding the books without her. But their presence on her low shelves, the leaving behind of them, made this feel like a short pause, like they would come back, and he would invite them in.

When he was a boy, there had always been a book in his hand, in his school bag, under his pillow. Sitting on Laney's narrow bed and thinking of invitation, the warmth of welcome and faith and reconciliation, first brought the memory of vampires.

He had loved them once. But decades had passed since he wedged himself into his own narrow bed with those old library books. The sodium lamp in the lot just outside the apartment would stretch his shadow up the wall while his brother Owen snored on the other side of the room they shared.

Later, living on his own for the first time, cigarettes had spilled out of ashtrays and the world had taken place more at night. There had been something about vampires then, too. He began to wonder what, other than growing up, had made that something go away.

Laney hadn't wanted to go. He could still hear her voice, each "Daddy" farther away than the last, like echoes decaying in the sunlight. Like vampires dragged out of their coffins. It had been bright that day, but since Kat's hatchback faded down the street, the fall had turned wet under the gray lid of clouds without them.

When he wasn't sitting in his daughter's room the first weekend, he followed himself through the house, never quite catching up and never quite letting himself see anything other than glimpses: Kat's half of the couch without her curled up on it, Laney's collection of capes that weren't pooled on the hallway floor, the crayons that weren't scattered across the dining room table, half of them broken.

The rooms swelled with their missing sounds. It was something like pretending, which brought him even closer to vampire fiction.

Sunday evening, his eyes burning for sleep, he could almost hear his brother's snores as he sat cross-legged on Laney's bed. Owen had died the day before he turned twenty, in a car accident that had been his own fault. Alone on a mountain road, drunk after a party, while Fulton had been fifty miles away at school, maybe in the same moment reading about a fictional character dying in the jaws of a monster. Soon, in a couple of years, Owen's death would be as old as his life.

He looked out Laney's window, where the moon had been wrapped in wool and put away. The air held a fine hint of rain.

The nearest streetlamp down on Underwood Road wasn't close enough to the house to read by, but still something brought the wisp of memory through some crack. There was a reason he imagined Owen in the house.

But he didn't think of ghosts. He thought of vampires then, and the distance of the streetlamp, a hundred and twenty or more feet from this side of the house. The bedtime game he had played at his grandmother's came back to him, strong and vivid.

She had lived three short miles from Fulton's family, and he would stay with her often, for days at a time, without his brother. He would sit with her on the front porch, watching cars go by and listening to the quiet close itself back up when they were gone around the curve.

Owen hadn't liked vampires, or anything scary, so Fulton had done what any big brother would do. He warned him that awful things would come suck his blood in the night. It helped stoke Fulton's own fear.

At his family's apartment, the light outside had been much too close, washing the lot into glare. Perfect for reading, but useless for the game. Alone in his room at Grandma Alma's house, the distant streetlamp had hung in the darkness, and he could focus on scaring himself.

He peeked outside and watched the light by the curb. It was set in a tapered glass-walled box, a Victorian lantern, so that its yellow-white cone spilled to the ground like a faded dress.

These few seconds brought so much back to him. The streetlamp at Grandma's, off a road that wound through hours of rural towns dreaming of suburbia, had stood at a similar distance. A perfect distance. Her light had been a naked thing on a utility pole. On damp nights the lamp had worn a bleached gray corona around its head, and Fulton would imagine it fizzing down there at the edge of the yard, right before the long clutch of trees. Its light, like the one he watched now, had come nowhere near him, eroding in the first few feet of his grandmother's grass.

At eight years old, all the way to fourteen or so, Fulton would put off sleep and pretend a vampire was standing under that pale light, looking up the grade of the yard and through his window with its dead eyes glittering in its white face. The vampire and the boy would stare at each other for such interminable moments.

It was little more than a shape, always too far away to make out any details, and this was the first part of the fright. Not knowing what it looked like took the tension Fulton gave breath to and turned it up, like a hand on a dial.

This necessitated the next part—bringing the vampire closer.

"You can come in," Fulton would whisper, and tap the windowpane. He would close his eyes then and lie back on his pillow, letting the bedroom's dark soak him. After he counted to twenty, the vampire would now be standing beside his bed, looking down on him, its arms hanging at its sides, fingers that were too long curled below the hips. Its face—almost a man's face, but not quite—was surely distorted and full of a strange texture.

But Fulton would keep his eyes closed tight. The delicious seconds had weight and seemed to pull the heat from his body, drawing it upward into his face, pooling all his body's blood into his ripening neck.

Chills would crackle along his skin, bringing his arms to a crawling life of their own. When the anticipation crested, a feeling he now thought had been like an ocean wave folding over in its exact moment of gravity, he would open his eyes at last.

Nothing was ever there. His imagination couldn't live up to what it saw before he looked. The world outside couldn't live up. But the build of expectation was a sublime, chemical thing. A soft gasp sometimes escaped his mouth. The thrill might almost have been sexual, he realized all these years later, or something that anticipated it.

How he had loved the game, those creatures, chasing this bright fear. Nights at Grandma Alma's had been his only contribution to vampire fiction, these isolated terrors he wove around himself in private.

This old thrill—just its memory awakened a flush of goosebumps along the tops of his arms. He twisted into a brief dance as a cold trail stuttered up his spine. A hint of metal on his tongue, so brief he had swallowed it before a true taste.

He looked down. Laney's bed was small. It could help bring back the childish awe of the game. But the more he thought about it, the less he wanted a simulation. He wanted to experience these same things from this side of his life, with all the attendant experience he'd gathered along the way. The decades of not pretending anything. It couldn't be about him if he ignored everything that had come after.

By the time he got to the bed he had shared with Kat and saw the impression of her head still in her pillow, his appetite for old games began to sour into this new regret. He lay down on his back. Even though the sky was banked with clouds and the neighborhood lights were quaint and distant, the room held little real dark.

For twenty seconds he squeezed his eyes shut anyway. He imagined Kat standing there instead of a vampire, and when he looked, there was only the bedroom door in the dimness, half-open like a slack mouth.

Fulton began his week as he did all the others, in his cubicle on the eighth floor of a sand-colored block, extracting what his clients wanted for their websites and parsing those desires into what the team he facilitated could actually do.

White noise exhaled from the speaker above his head. In the lulls between calls, his mind filled with vampires again, and around noon he had to speak with a divorce attorney about her ad campaign, worried the whole time he would bring up his family.

These suppressed things hummed in him. He got a fresh notepad from a drawer and wrote WHY VAMPIRES and underlined it. His thoughts were too cluttered to begin. Was it the vampire's turning away from light and warmth that had always entranced him? It had surely started before this, with the fear itself, awed and implacable. The way it had in primitive cultures throughout history. The atavistic came first. Fear of the unnatural and the dead.

He finally wrote *Terror* beneath the underline.

But as a boy he had imagined what it would be like to open his eyes in a dark no good churchgoer could ever want to know, soil packed around the coffin he had been buried in, the faintest trickle of water and the creeping of worms. He had tried to see himself lying dead and recalling the act of breathing now that he couldn't work his lungs, lifting his hands and wondering at the movement of their fingers, using his strange new sight to see what they looked like with all the blood gone.

His parents, up on top of the earth, would cry over pictures of Fulton, asking God why He took their child. Owen would still snore in the room he had all to himself now, but the close parking lot light would slide between the curtains and show the tears drying on his cheeks. Under all that dirt, what would Fulton do if he found out he couldn't cry with them? What if he realized he didn't want to?

In the safety of his grandmother's guest room, warm thriving blood going in circles through him, he had sometimes teared up at this thought, but he had smiled, too.

Fulton would outlive the three of them, as it turned out. Blind luck and nature. Owen had haunted his parents' home instead of Fulton, like an extra shadow pinned to them as they went to the same places on the same days. Eight years ago bone cancer had come and eaten his mother between her birthday and Christmas. Dad had let himself go until the heart attack.

Vampires had to be made. This had excited him as a child. And they lived such long, long lives. These points had led to him, when he was eight or nine, asking the only expert he knew, *Who made God?* Pastor Langan, who had bent over to Fulton with his hands on his knees waiting for the question, rocked back as though pushed, his blue eyes wide for an instant.

It had never really left Fulton, the grownup's lack of a satisfactory answer. "Well, no one, little man," the pastor had said. "He's always been there, waiting for us." Fulton had asked how anything could just *be*, all the way back to the beginning of time and even before then, but the forty extra years Pastor Langan had lived bore down on Fulton until he grew quiet. Forty years—a blink of God's eye, an hour in a vampire's life, but so long here, under the sun.

Even so, he had never spent much of his time wanting to *become* a vampire, not really. It was closer to the truth that he had fantasized about making contact with something so inscrutable, to have it reach for him with its powerful dread throbbing around it in the air. The cold bones of its fingers. Reading had fueled his imagination, until he could produce something no haunted house attraction or film could approach.

But to think of it as thrill-seeking cheapened it, and he sighed in frustration, irritated that he couldn't articulate the old feeling.

He added *God* and *Immortality* and *Death* to the list, and his mind turned to all the different types of vampires he had encountered as a kid, because was there any other mythology that had been painted with as many different brushes? His stomach hurt and he couldn't remember the last time he'd eaten, so he took the notepad to the cafeteria set off the lobby of the building, bought a sandwich and a carton of milk.

He turned to the second page and made a new heading, TYPES. "Blood types," he said, and laughed until it struck him how odd hearing his voice had already become when he wasn't speaking to a client. A woman two tables away glanced over at him, and he went back to his list.

The Romantic/Sexual (Lestat)
The Classic (Dracula) (so many rules)
The Creature (this is the closest)

He started with the romantic vampire because he wanted to move past it quickly. The tortured noble souls of Anne Rice had never interested him much, not even when the prose so often dripped into the erotic and he was caught in the amber of puberty.

He remembered in his teens being drawn into the pained history of her stories—ancient Rome and the manses of New Orleans—but a hundred slow pages seemed to elongate between each lowering of shadow.

He'd wanted as many of those shadows as he could get, in which the unknowable stain of the vampire would infect the words.

Her undead often grew disenchanted and existential, sick with their unendingness, to the point where many walked into the sun to turn willingly to ash. For all the rich tapestry of those stories, Fulton wanted the vampires of tombs and wet dark and rot.

Most of all, he wanted to *not know* the vampire until it was there, above him, too late. That it was impenetrable was its horror. Rice's vampires were the protagonists, telling their stories and their emotions and coloring themselves with elegant nuances. He wouldn't accuse her of watering down the mythology—his experience was too confined to childhood—but he had never felt those wonderful chills on his arms.

Still, he found he might want to give her idealization another chance, and decided to stop by the library and check out the first of her *Vampire Chronicles*. The one with the Tom Cruise movie. It would be interesting to see how a middle-aged man who had loved and lost so much might react to the Gothic emotions, even if he worried they would read like romance novels now.

Kat had missed Fulton's sensitive mooning phase, the narrow window in which he might have bonded with Lestat and all the other Rice vampires whose names he couldn't recall. They had met when Kat was twenty-three, not long out of college, and Fulton could see thirty on the horizon.

The years in between vampires and Kat felt the most like fiction, the half-blank kind that faded as soon as he lived it. He didn't read much after school. Horror films had never found a strong foothold with him. Then, finally, Kat became his story and the uncanny hadn't mattered anymore. And after four miscarriages, Laney had come and given them their happily ever after.

Early on, in the years before her birth, they would take weekend road trips at the drop of a hat, drive up to places like Cloudland Canyon and pretend they were lost in the woods. There was a lot of sex back then, with birdsong and cicadas, or the percussion of a just-finished rainstorm.

How many nights of fresh green dark might he have lain cocooned, letting himself imagine vampires creeping toward their tent? What a powerful iteration of the old game it would have been.

Fulton should have climbed out of his sleeping bag and gone walking in that blackness, near-blind and listening for snapping twigs. What he couldn't figure out now was why he hadn't—whether it was as simple as love, jobs, nights with friends, tiredness pulling the wonder from him. The drabness of real life. Or it could have been his brother who closed off his childhood, the reality of death without the invitation.

He wished he knew. It felt important.

He thought of their four lost babies before Laney. They could have been conceived in those dense woods. None of them had made it far enough for burials to be considered, but he felt that the long weeks of mourning that followed each time Kat lost the baby had—had what? Brought him nearer to or further from the boy who wanted to meet a vampire?

Even with the fear of no children, he and Kat had been a beautiful creature of their own, for a while. What if he were to live a thousand, or a thousand thousand, years into the future, making new Kats that would grow to loathe him just the same? Countless nights crawling through windows to taste the next lover.

What if the emptiness expanded until he couldn't hold it inside, would he stay in the woods a little too late one morning instead of hurrying to his cursed sleep? The sun would rise screaming through the foliage, its voice finding him there in dusty bands and confetti pieces cut by limbs and leaves, burning him to ash. And in the last moment he would understand the romantic thing he had become.

But again it struck him that becoming a vampire had not been the whole point, or even half the point. He wanted the dread. It felt strange to remember all these things. To wish he had never forgotten them.

A man came into the cafeteria and unmuted the television up on the wall. A talk show host erupted in a blur of noise. Fulton pretended the ceiling lights buzzed and flickered with her voice.

S toker's *Dracula* had been his first vampire and the origin of the streetlamp game. He'd found it in a box of his mother's worn paperbacks when he was seven, the only scary thing among dozens of what she called bodice-rippers. Two or three years later, he'd broken the spine enough to need tape to hold it together.

The famous name, scrolled in silver, caught his eye in the library's fantasy section. He forgot about Lestat. The book was warm in his hand, as though forgiving him for straying, and he tried to remember its details. There had been rats in Dracula's castle, and wolves, some line about creatures of the night. A bat flapping against a window.

The hint of a shiver touched him, and suddenly the empty house didn't seem such a terrible thing to return to.

Even at the height of his vampire obsession, he'd always been restricted to his hometown library, so his education had been only partial. This one didn't have a horror section, so he affected a hunching sort of walk, head tipped to the right, and skimmed over titles promising dragons and swords, hunting one of the unknown number of vampire stories that had been written in the last twenty-five years.

He was nearly crawling on the floor like a creature himself by the time he gave up. There weren't many. He only managed to find a collection of short stories titled *Dead People's Things* by someone named Kirsten Mester, two fangs bracketing the title on the spine and a backwoods vampire among the subjects highlighted in the jacket copy.

This brought Stephen King's *'Salem's Lot* to mind. He found it in the general fiction section. The novel was another wonderful part of his childhood, and part of the reason windows had figured so heavily in his imagination. He added it to the stack in the crook of his arm and called it a good start.

At the counter he asked the clerk, a man around his age and with almost the same amount of balding on the crown, if he knew of any other vampire fiction. The man glanced at the three books Fulton put down on the counter. "I'd say that's enough of that stuff for one Halloween!" He laughed and Fulton just stared at him. A button on his shirt read BALLINGRUD GA IS SPOOKTOBER COUNTRY.

It took a moment for Halloween to fit into Fulton's own context. He hadn't even made the connection. Until Laney had turned three and wanted to dress up like a pickle she named Paul Tremble, the holiday had been yet another thing relegated to his past.

A moment of panic touched him: What had Laney wanted to be this year?

He had a library card—Laney could spend an entire Sunday afternoon carefully selecting a book to read—so he was in his car five minutes later and calling Kat for the first time since she left. He didn't let himself think about what he was doing. After a dozen rings it went to voicemail and he began to speak, the words coming out of his mouth with not enough life or tone.

"Hi, it's me. I wanted to say I don't care about that guy. You wouldn't admit it but—I don't know, it feels obvious. If you're really in love with him, it's all right. But I love you and if you still love me, too, I'm—" He paused and the word *inviting* was there on his tongue, dark. It clung too close to his new thoughts. "And I miss Laney, she never told me what her Halloween costume was going to be," he finished instead.

At home a few patches of sky had torn clear. Stars watched him through the holes, but he couldn't find the moon. Deep in the woods north of town, far from ambient light, the dwindling numbers of wolves would be silent and perhaps lethargic. Fulton looked out toward them, in the direction of the mountains, which even on the clearest of mornings were visible as mere suggestions, too far away. Appalachian, Carpathian, they both felt similar in his mouth.

He brewed coffee and took a mug and the pot into the back yard, to the garden table beside the shed. It was cold but he hung a camping lantern from the shed eave and watched the half-acre of trees hunch together in the dark beyond the pale reach of light. No eyes gleamed at him from their canopy. For a moment he fantasized about digging a grave for himself.

With the coffee to warm and fuel him, he read *Dracula* until the lantern's batteries, last used in the old sanctioned wilderness before Laney was born, began to give, the light dimming in weak strobes.

He had forgotten how much of the story flirted with romance: Dracula's ability to charm and stir a sexual chemistry that was only half-hidden in the nineteenth-century language. But there were enough pockets of dread to keep him turning the pages, and the epistolary newspaper clippings and journal entries made the story transcend its age, somehow.

One thing stood out enough to dampen the rest of the story: the rules and religiosity of the vampire myth as Stoker had interpreted it. Fulton's phone told him it was one in the morning, but the caffeine still sang in his blood. He pulled the two lists from his back pocket and wrote a third heading, RULES, then switched the lantern off and went into the house.

At the dining room table, he jotted his thoughts down under the new heading—*sunlight, crucifix, garlic, moving water is a barrier, shapeshifting, stake,* and a few others. These things put the vampire in a box, more restrictive than a coffin, and seemed to neuter it into something a hero could study and fight. Dark powers had counterbalances. He understood this, but he'd never cared for comic books.

The rest of the novel trickled into the foreground of his memory— Van Helsing and the others racing the sun up the Carpathians. He would keep reading to the end, maybe, but only in search of the small moments that would let him remember the old thrill. For now his eyes were hot with fatigue.

In the bedroom he sat in stillness until he could hear the memory of Owen's snores across the room. The lamp sent his shadow reaching up the wall behind him, elongated and strange. He stripped down to his boxers and let the air simulate fear all over his body.

After a moment in which he almost laughed at himself, he pushed the bed against the far wall, the top of the mattress a few inches above the windowsill, and switched the lamp off. He lay down and curled himself toward the window.

Through the parted curtains the streetlamp was farther removed from the house than it was from his daughter's room, and when he imagined a vampire standing in its veil of light, the silhouette could have been cut out of the dark, indistinct as it was. Its eyes were lost in the distance, but Fulton trusted that they could pick out every detail of the wedge of Fulton they saw across the side yard, through the double-paned window and the gap between the curtains.

His family felt very far away. The vampire stood in the cone of light as though rooted or carved from stone. "You can come in," Fulton exhaled onto the glass. The invitation bloomed fog on the pane, and he tapped twice on the glass around it. He lay back on the pillow, wriggled his way toward the outer edge of the bed, and clenched his eyes shut.

He decided to count to thirty, give the vampire time to glide across the longer stretch of grass and into the swollen quiet of the house, down the hall past Laney's room to this door parted like the curtains. Or like lips, he thought, and his tongue came out to wet his own.

At ten it happened—anticipation prickled his naked torso and exposed arms. Eleven, twelve…sixteen…twenty-one, twenty-two, the weight of regard pressed down. The vampire stood over him, and Fulton did not let himself peek.

As he neared thirty in his mute count, the entire illusion began to dissipate, more soluble than it had ever been as a child, and he knew the visitor was gone, had never been there even in his thoughts, before he looked. The space between the door and the jamb was still six or seven inches. To the left, Kat's print of some Maine island tried to brighten the dark with sunrise. The air did not press in to fill a space where something had moments ago stood watching.

His skin couldn't writhe with awe or cold atavistic impulse, but he had felt a breath of it, enough to remember by. He could imagine a tang of grave dirt in his lungs, crumbs of it clinging to the slick body of a worm uncoiling on a floorboard below, and never mind that these things were not there. The caffeine let go of him and sleep was easy.

W as their hunger for blood anything like his hunger? The first of the last fights between Fulton and Kat had started in late spring with Laney, when he had pulled her too hard by the wrist to get her out of a mud puddle. Asking her twice then telling her once hadn't worked, and Kat watched out of context from the dining room window as he yanked their daughter, just five years old, Fulton, what were you thinking?

Laney had done more than cry, she'd screamed until he was terrified he had dislocated her shoulder.

He'd never hurt her before, not even by accident, and he said it wouldn't happen again and it hadn't. His temper had always had an even keel. But still a space had been levered open between him and Kat. It let new things in. It ate at the both of them as they lay in bed those nights, under their skins but also external, somehow, a feeling that might have stained the ceiling like water and dripped endlessly onto their wakeful faces.

He supposed their marriage, not plump with passion anymore but still a fine and warm enough thing, had begun to rot. The air had been hot and wet all summer, the town soaked in unseasonable rains.

Were they fenced in by the rules and turned tame? Could they circumvent them? In July, Fulton started collecting Laney from preschool on his lunch hour because Kat worked from home less and stayed at her office later and later. When Laney started kindergarten two months ago, there was no one home to meet the bus. Fulton struck a deal with Ms. Barron two doors down—a hundred dollars a week to watch Laney until he got home.

The arguments with Kat deepened. Trenches were dug.

Sometimes Kat would smell too clean when she came home at dusk, like soap, her dark hair damp. He thought of faith, and tried to have it.

She started leaving the house some Saturday mornings. Laney would ask him when she was coming back so Fulton took her to the library, then on to Bulkin Park to play hide and seek in the stand of pines there, pretending he couldn't see the bright green of her favorite jacket when it was his turn to count. After dinner, Kat still gone, they would sit on Laney's bed and he would read her books out loud until she fell asleep in his lap. She never failed to drool on him.

The end of summer was when the house began to lose its sounds. Maybe it had already become a sort of tomb.

Now he pictured a trail of garlic bulbs along the edge of the driveway, leaning against the grass, garlic hanging from the front porch. Holy water drizzling from the clouds. What chemical change occurs in a vampire when confronted with a religious icon, one that's imbued with the faith of its bearer? Does the stolen blood bubble in its gut, does whatever fluid still swimming in its eyes begin to blacken? Is faith a kind of sunlight?

He waited until October, last week, to ask her if she was having an affair. "No," she said, and studied the Maine sunrise on the wall over his shoulder. A few nights later he brought it up again and said he didn't understand how a single thread of his fatherhood—a fleeting moment when he was too stern with the most precious thing in his world—could change the fabric of their marriage and push her into another man's arms.

"There isn't anyone." She looked at him this time. "And it wasn't that. I've snapped at her myself. You changed when I saw you with her in front of the house. The way the light touched you. The way the sun was setting, the way dinner was getting cold. It felt like the way you've always hidden some of yourself from me. I don't know. I didn't know who you were."

She came home late the next night and the night after, and the scent of soap clung to her. Then she left. He wondered how clean she smelled in Michigan, what her parents were saying about him, if Laney was crying without her books.

Tuesday his first call was with the owner of an HVAC company outside of Baltimore. Both men were still on their first cups of coffee. Less than fifteen minutes into the consultation, the owner asked Fulton if they should reschedule, if anything was wrong.

"Well, my wife and child have moved out," Fulton told him, "and I've gotten back into vampires to fill the hole they left behind. I think I've been scared to be scared, you know?" Following a considerable silence, the HVAC man said he had a lot of work to get to, they'd talk again some other time.

Somehow the clouds thickened further in the throat of the sky, and the sun had to leak through. He finished *Dracula* and read *'Salem's Lot* over the rest of the week, staying up late until the streetlamp game. The compulsion of the words, all the pretending, kept him away from his phone.

Kat hadn't called him back, and even opening his alarm app every night made him want to text her, email her, call and wake her up. Winter was approaching Ann Arbor much faster than it was down here, shaving off autumn, and with longer teeth. She and Laney would be bundled up against the cold early nights.

Fulton was glad *Dracula* had faded from his mind over the years. The capes and red lips got in the way by bringing the vampire into the romance of society. They diluted the bestial terror of him. And the transformation into bats and wolves rang hollow to him. Even as a child it had felt too wizardly, like a werewolf tidied up by smoke and mirrors.

But King's vampires brought his childhood back with a force nothing else had approached yet. There was blackness and mold and evil decay in the story, and when he reached the chapter where Danny Glick appears, suspended in the night outside Mark's window, tapping, Fulton was a child again. He could imagine, for a bittersweet moment, that he had never met his wife or thought of a daughter.

Many of the rules were locked in here, too, but at least King gave them twists, such as the fallibility of faith. And the power of the invitation custom—the complicity of it, the shared role—spoke to him. Its breath trickled over his skin.

The trees in the neighborhood began to turn the vivid colors of death. The weather began to lose its warm blood.

Barlow came a little closer to being the creature Fulton had listed under TYPES, but the novel and the old TV movie from the seventies kept getting mixed up in his mind. King's creature had been rendered inhuman by time, something that mixed with Count Orlok from *Nosferatu* to suggest some strange otherness in the template of Fulton's own personal vampire.

But Barlow had Straker to Dracula's Renfield, which humanized both villains too much. He didn't like how the vampires needed human aid and even worship, and he found it a little harder to care what happened to them in their ends. They were wonderful stories, he could hardly believe he had gone so long without them, but he wanted to strip the myth down, closer to its bone and tissue.

Each night before sleep, he looked out at the street and pictured the vampire under the lamp, and he lured it to his room. The chills came a little stronger now, and he lay with their gentle eruptions of dread all over his body, until he at last opened his eyes to the empty room, the absence of the vampire, looming over him.

As a child he had gotten closer to some imaginary line. It wasn't belief that was missing because he had never believed, how could he really have? But he was still grateful to feel some release on these new nights.

If not belief, he wondered if what he was trying to do could be an occult process, somehow, a summoning or a ritual best undertaken with arcane markings, symbols that were the antitheses of holy water and crucifixes. There had been stories of demons and witchcraft and vast tentacled beings in his childhood, but the deeper seeking, the strange current of bonding, had never matched that of the vampire.

Looking at these possibilities from the encroachment of middle age, he wished even less for an occult solution. It would be yet more restrictiveness, another religiosity. A black mass was still a mass.

He kept adding disjointed thoughts to his WHY VAMPIRES list: *autonomy/separateness, like an animal, the smell of sour dirt, solitary, something deeply personal and corrupted.*

Several times he typed "vampire mythology" into Google, but his resolve held. He cleared the search bar. Education would muddy the water. Just as he wanted no black magic, he avoided context outside of his own memories and his own inclinations. These were still forming, or reforming, like the weaving of a chrysalis.

W hen Laney was born, he had experienced a sickness of spiritual terror, a gasping weight in his chest that lingered for days and loosened in him for weeks before it was gone and he opened up to the joy of her. There had been a fear that he was not capable of being a father, much less one who could protect his child from the world.

Every daddy of a little girl felt it, but hadn't his been so stark? He had pictured her dead and broken at the playground, in the street, opened up in the trunk of a man's car, too many times, his gut twisting with the images.

What would the inside of a vampire look like? Sinew, of course. Dried strips of ligament like jerky hanging in the basement of a house that has burned. Muscles kept inflated by some unknown biology, while the organs have withered to peach pits, flaky with old blood. Except the heart, if the stories had it right.

And missing Laney and Kat, his life now seemed to lose its own vital fluids, like watching a vampire in the moments of its becoming, growing parched and assembling an obscure anatomy. All he could do was reach back to the other version of himself, his childhood, rich with blood and passion.

Was a vampire allowed to keep its soul? He wondered if it went out somewhere, or if it remained, reduced to yet another cinder in the body's new ruin. Or did another of the many rules dictate that it was siphoned into hell? As with Pastor Langan's clutching at an answer all those years ago, perhaps the reader was meant to question the fact of the soul itself, no matter its vessel.

His thoughts separated into all these strands. He tried to connect them together as each followed the one before it, and it seemed to him that he was almost writing a story, full of things connected by signifiers like this spiritual terror.

A little piece of his own vampire fiction, except it had no vampire, so the story would have to be about finding out what he wanted. Who he had been and who he was. It would force him into metaphor. And this not knowing crawled over his skin, too, with the chills of his nights.

B ut over the weekend he read a story from the Kirsten Mester book and knew things would change. For the first time since Kat went to Michigan, he felt a kind of hope.

He scanned the table of contents early Sunday evening, looking at the story titles for clues. None suggested a vampire directly, so he chose "The Pine Arch Creature" and settled into one of the sun-worn

Adirondack chairs near the tree line behind the house. He turned the chair to face the oaks and pines he knew, their pleasant bitterness breathing out at him as the light began to drip below the horizon to the left and clouds poked through rifts in the sky like tufts of cotton.

In the story a man desperately wanted to survive lung cancer and so sought out a vampire on the internet. It pulled Fulton in at once, the quiet way in which the man loved his young son, the broken marriage. The catalyst came from a different place than his own, it was more decided and relatable, but here was a character outside of the old archetypes, just an average man who reached out for the dark. A kindred spirit, almost. Fulton pulled his coat tighter around himself.

The protagonist found an online group claiming to know a swath of Kentucky woods in which a vampire lived, presumably in the rotten heart of a ruined oak tree. Pine Arch Research had documented their findings for more than a year, allegedly verifying, through the hanging of various items on the tree during daylight hours, that religious icons and folkloric totems had no effect on the creature. Perhaps it feared only the sun's faith.

The tension coiled and loosened as grainy video footage was described—group members at dawn remotely filming an indistinct figure loping through the woods and diving toward a smudge of dark at the base of the oak. But the images were blurry and nothing the protagonist could call affirmative. After days of sifting through posts and video clips, he inevitably drew the location of the woods from the anonymous users and drove there himself, three states away, weakened by chemotherapy and coughing blood into paper towels from a roll.

Shortly before the car pulled off the road, the trees showing their bones against a clotted sunset, the author revealed that the protagonist had brought his young son along with him. *"Daddy,"* the boy said from the backseat, *"are we going to play in the woods,"* and the small unexpected voice rose like a jump scare from the page.

The father poured chloroform on a rag and pressed it against his child's face until he went limp. The shock of the act was brutal. Fulton tried to believe Mester had done something unfair, but still it resonated. It worked at him.

The protagonist carried his son deep into the scrub woods and laid him on the leaves beside the dead oak tree, then waited for the dark. Fulton felt his eight-year-old self again, his eyes feeding on the plot with impatience but wanting to stop and savor the dread of each sentence.

And the vampire! When it crawled out of its hole on the story's eighteenth page, a lump rose in Fulton's throat. It was a nasty thing, very like the creature he had been holding in the back of his memory, a relative of what he had willed beneath the streetlamp outside his grandmother's house. It had been human once, of course, and was nearly so now, but years of living like an insect in spoiled wood and beneath rocks had shifted its physiology out of true. Its features were like many thinly sliced faces laid over each other, the alignment so close to perfect.

Or perhaps it was an elegant blend of species, something new, with its unknowable intelligence. The point was that he (and the author, and anyone happening across the considerations of "The Pine Arch Creature") could only guess.

"I brought my son as a gift," the protagonist told the crouching thing, the corrupted god. "My only child, so that you might turn me." And whatever rung of evolution the vampire crouched upon, it swung down from it now, and fell onto the boy with a liquid grace.

When it was finished, the child tossed a few yards away with his throat torn open, the vampire asked the protagonist to let it in. Half its face was slicked with blood. Its eyes held too much of the dying light, like the flat lamps of a deer turning to find a trail camera's lens.

"But I came to your den," the protagonist said, and Fulton smiled at the use of den instead of home. "Let me in," the vampire repeated, pressing its tented fingers to the man's chest. Fulton smiled again. He thought the sentiment was a nod to the romanticizing of older vampire fiction even as it committed a sort of blasphemy against it.

Fulton found himself pleased when the vampire sipped a mouthful of the man's blood and turned to vomit it onto the forest floor. *"This is soured blood."* It gestured toward the dead boy. *"Soured as your love."* It felt like an honest way to imagine the creature's palate, this overlap between the humanity it had left behind and the cells that now thrived in its body. The protagonist still did not reveal his cancer, but the vampire knew disease by its taste.

It slithered back into its hole, and the man wept by the remains of his son for a long time. Until with a last cry of despair, he, too, slipped into the dark under the tree. Which couldn't end well for him, but the story stopped there with a lovely shiver.

Fulton was fascinated by how the author had sketched the vampire so clearly without using specific words of curvature or lineation. Such a creature could not be scrutinized as other things, but it could be felt as a sensation, half under the skin. There were no rules except the only ones that mattered: those of light and invitation. And the voice of the story—even the conflicting notes of anguish and motive called to him.

There had been nothing like the purer anticipation Fulton lay with on his bed, but the story carried a trace of something that made him feel as though it had been written for him. This author might have anticipated that Fulton's thoughts would turn to vampire fiction. The cancer was a device, a symbol. The family dynamic in Mester's story had begun as a mirror of his own, but in the end, it might have presented him with a significant choice—Fulton as pure self or as father and husband.

He would never harm Laney, he knew that. The horror of the protagonist's decision, the chloroform and the rag, stayed with Fulton until his resolve crumbled and he called Kat a second time. It rang through to voicemail.

"I figured it out, honey, all the rules were in the way but there's only one that means anything." He spoke in a rush punctuated more by gasps than commas. "I'm inviting you back into my life. Hell, I'm inviting myself back into my life. I know this is your house, too, we've both been invited in since the day we closed on it. Do you remember all that rain? A day like that, even a vam—" He clipped the word in half, beheaded it, banished it. "I still love you. And Laney. I want you both to come back."

He hung up, shaking, and got ready for bed. The moon had ripened to a thick wedge, and under the streetlamp the vampire gazed up the gentle slope of grass at him. They watched each other for longer than before. The details of it were a little clearer, a little closer. He did not whisper the invitation because there was no need, there were only recognition and resignation. The vampire was all he had.

When he finally lay back, eyes closed, he felt it above him already. It leaned over and the air changed between it and him, pressing down. And for the first time he could smell it, a handful of earth cut with the hidden stench of gone meat. The blend was a floral, maddened perfume.

The chills were amazing, wave after wave of cold wonder rasping and crackling over his skin. He knew if he opened his eyes, the vampire would not be there. So he kept them closed and dwindled into sleep.

The clouds dissolved and left a brilliant, shocking blue laid out like fresh paint in a tray. A flood of sunlight burned out from it, but Fulton felt little of it in his cubicle. He worked late Tuesday and when he came home, half an hour past dark, Kat was sitting on the porch in one of the rocking chairs, trying out a smile.

She held a pumpkin in her lap and for a single fleeting second, she seemed more like a Halloween decoration he had forgotten about than a woman, much less this specific woman, this wife and this mother of his child.

"Your birthday's tomorrow," she said. "I didn't wrap Laney up but she's waiting inside."

He had forgotten his birthday. He pulled her to him and held her there. A different kind of chill touched him, something that felt much further in the past than a couple of weeks. "You brought some of Michigan back with you," he said. "It's freezing. Let's go inside."

His daughter's face rose up in the gloom when he pushed the door open, and he had just enough time to stoop before she leaped at him, her arms tight around his neck, repeating "Daddy, Daddy" in a bright stream. He asked her if she'd brought some of her Grammy's weather back with her, too, and if she needed warming up.

But it turned out Kat never went to Michigan. She told him later that she and Laney had been staying at the Sleep Inn out on 20, less than a dozen miles away, while she decided what she wanted to do. "I heard what you said in that last voicemail, and you told me everything I needed to know, love," she said, slipping her arms around him. "It was *you*. Really you. I could feel it in your voice."

She had cheated on him, with someone from her office. She had made his faith a fallible thing. But he forgave her in an instant, wouldn't hear another word, and it was a simple thing. There was no questioning the rightness of it.

He left Kat in the bedroom and went to tuck Laney in. "What are you reading these days?" he asked her, pained only for a moment that he had no idea.

"Just something about a boy and animals," Laney said. She smiled, not quite looking at him. Her eyes were bright and young.

Fulton brushed crumbs of dirt from her hairline, where it curled behind an ear, and thought about the day she wouldn't get out of the mud puddle. How close he had come to really hurting her. He hugged her and she went still, her cheek cold and dry against his neck.

"Let's get you and your animals warm," he told her. She smiled at something behind him, but the room was empty when he turned to look.

He lay next to Kat, horrified that his two selves, his two eras would meet. She wanted this to happen because she didn't understand how the story went. The streetlamp game would have to go, but he wanted so badly to check the part in the curtains, this time with a new dread.

His wife's body was chilled and thick with warmth, her own two selves, the temperatures meeting in a front that created a strange, exotic weather in the room. He couldn't quite reach over and touch her yet.

Whatever might be standing down there under the light—it didn't exist, it was only in his imagination, yes, but he had invited it in already. The nearly religious fear crystalized in him again. He had to keep Laney safe.

He slept late the next morning, deciding to celebrate his birthday by calling out of work and fortifying their home. Just in case. Kat had left a note saying she'd pick Laney up from school and see him later with a surprise for his big day. *Next year is the big 4-0, but that doesn't mean today shouldn't be special!* It was more legible than her usual leaning scrawl.

He drove into town through a mass of sunshine. At the grocery store he bought four ropes of garlic and tried to cover his question to the cashier with a laugh: "Know where I can buy a crucifix?"

She looked from the garlic to him and shared his joke. "Halloween, huh? Well, there's a Christian bookstore over on Bartlett Road."

Fulton went straight to the bookstore and bought three crucifixes from a balding man who wanted to talk to him about his church. He stopped at the library and slipped the three books into the overnight box, then hurried home as though the sun had already begun to die out in the west, and hung garlic from the front porch and back door. He nailed the last two ropes above the two bedroom windows. Inside the house he placed a crucifix under each of their pillows.

A weight rolled off him, then, even if he had never had faith in these rules. The house had been purged and would now be filled back up with what he wanted in it.

Then the daylight did creep lower, staining the trees and the distant worn teeth of the mountains. He began to worry he'd dreamed his family back the night before. When the dregs of the sun faded and the deep green black swelled in the pines, he saw the flat eyes of animals gleaming like coins within the dark. Just a few, watching him from between the outlines of rough pine trunks. He stepped back toward the house. Bats wheeled low through the yard—just a few of these, too—though surely there were no mosquitos left for them here at the end of October.

He went inside, peered out through the small window above the kitchen sink, breathing and letting his courage mend itself. Then back outside, and the eyes and the bats were gone.

He pulled the sheets of paper out of his pocket and by the kitchen light behind him read the three entries under TYPES. Which of these had smelled of dirt and spoiled meat two nights ago in his bedroom? It seemed such a desperately important thing, maybe as vital as WHY VAMPIRES.

All the dozens of questions he had asked himself crowded in on him, the ones about his life and the ones about vampires, but none of them lined up properly. It was hard to find parallels or rhyme or reason.

The thought of some emotional self-vampirism fluttered around him, too, but he brushed it aside with distaste. He was no closer to wanting to be a vampire, but he could be a better husband. Kat could be a better wife. Their family could be a better creature.

Kat's little car pulled into the driveway on the other side of the house, half a beam of headlight catching the back yard. A high chirping screech filled the night before he heard the engine cut off. She needed power steering fluid, but she wouldn't want him to tell her.

He met them halfway, in the kitchen, and hugged them both at once. They felt a little cold again, but so did he, and Kat's hair did not smell of soap. If anything, she needed a shower. Laney could use one, too, and he doubted his own cleanliness. They were all where they belonged.

"What took you two the whole evening?" he said, sitting down at the table. "My birthday's almost gone."

"Sorry, Daddy." Laney hopped onto the chair beside him, almost swallowed in her green coat. "It took forever to find you a good present."

Kat held out a brown paper bag. Fulton took it, removed the pink tissue paper, and pulled out a thick book with a pebbled black cover, imitation leather, like the Bibles he and his brother had as kids.

"What's this?" he said, flipping through the blank unlined pages.

"It's for you to write your own stories in." Kat grinned at him. Her eyes were dark in the glare of the ceiling light.

"But I'm not a writer, honey," he said. "I've never been one."

"You can write one about me, Daddy!" Laney placed something on the table and began digging her nails into the flaky skin. It was one of the garlic bulbs.

"Don't play with that, sweetie," he told her. "It's yucky." He took it from her. She held her fingers under her nose and made a face.

Kat sat down across from him. The night wove itself black outside the windows. Safe from it in the warmth and light of the kitchen, his wife and daughter smiled. Fulton smiled with them. Something wasn't right, and he looked at the flakes of garlic skin around the bulb, wishing they could be broken crayons instead. And he kept smiling.

He woke in the deeper seam of night, two hours into his next year. A subtle stink hung in the room. Kat was gone from the bed, and the curtains were wide open even though he'd closed them as tight as he could before turning out the light. He couldn't see the moon anywhere outside as he listened for whatever had brought him from sleep.

His ears strained until he began to imagine Owen's snoring, but the real sound came again, from the other side of the far wall, in Laney's room. She was giggling. His breath left him and his eyes wanted to drag toward the window, so he let them. The streetlamp down at the road dripped its gown of light toward the asphalt, but nothing stood within it, nothing moved.

He managed to breathe in and lay back against the pillow. He shut his eyes and pulled the sheet over his chest. But the old game settled over him, too. The chills crept along his body. He felt the vampire watching him beside the bed.

This time he didn't count to twenty. He opened his eyes.

Kat stood at the edge of the mattress, looking down at him, and her face had changed to something almost her face, the alignment so close to perfect. "You finally did it, love," she said. "You found out why." That fertile, turned smell of earth. Her eyes now the flat lamps of a deer in dark trees. And her smile, it was somehow tender and cold at the same time.

They had not come back. Kat was up in Michigan right now, with Laney curled into her because there was just the one guest room.

Instead, the vampire had become his family. Instead, Fulton had made both choices. Somewhere, long behind him, an eight-year-old boy was still telling his seven-year-old brother that things would come drink his blood in the night.

Caught in the awful chill that came in waves over his skin, painful now, Fulton managed to reach back and under his pillow with his left hand. He brought the crucifix out and thrust it at this new wife. Laney giggled again, closer, and he saw the hinted shape of her in the doorway, the gleam of her eyes, below the print of the sun coming up over the little island in Maine.

Kat wrapped her hand around the crucifix, squeezing Christ against her palm. Her fingers met each other like a dying spider on the back of the cross. "You said there was only one rule that mattered to you," she whispered. "Right?"

She crawled onto the bed. She crawled onto him. Her smile opened and he saw the long teeth leaning at him from the hole behind it. "Right?" Her voice had changed to something almost her voice. Something in it had spoiled.

He told himself, *Terror, God, Immortality, Death*, and wondered which.

HOLOOW

Once the waxy dusk went black, the color rotting away behind distant mountains Claudette might never see again, the men in red coats came to work down in the narrow road. This was the third night they had done so. They huddled there between the decaying building and the newer one, around some obscure task.

Claudette had yet to glimpse what the five of them were so intent upon, or even what they looked like, and the dark seemed to mute their noises. Occasionally, one of them would stop and glance up toward her fourth-floor window. She told herself she was too far away to be looked at in any real sense, but had started switching the near lamp off.

She sat at the window and watched their red coats shifting together, her hands heavy in her lap. Knotted things, her hands, hardly more useful than bundles of sticks. Her piano played on inside her head without them, hard stabs and vigorous tempi that kept the dust off her memory.

Looking outside had nothing to do with her hands and how they had betrayed her, so it had become the lesser of the evils. She could lose herself counting the windows in the disused apartment building across the way, clouds knitting into half-shapes above, pretty young mothers on phones below.

It was only an alley, really, a shortcut between Emery St. and another she still hadn't learned the name of, but it had a niceness to it during the day. The way the buildings held a rail of sky like a vise. It made a person want to pass through it.

From her vantage point in the dark, the fabric of the workers' coats seemed a porous wool, much too hot for late summer, with no logos or utility to them she could see. They would toil at their mystery until some point after she crossed off another day and eased herself into the low-bellied bed.

She never managed to see where they came from. There was no arrival of cars, no echoing of pre-work voices in the walled space, no preface. They were just there, and only appeared or disappeared when she wasn't looking. She wondered if the Thousand Oaks facility had any reason to spruce up an alley, when what graceful façade it showed the town was on the other side, luring people in with their old folks trailing behind like resigned pets.

It's not a facility, Mama. This was one of Lidia's favorite mantras. *I promised you we wouldn't do elder care yet. It's an apartment, just like anyone else in town has. Only difference is the hospital's close and you got this cord you can pull if something bad happens.* Claudette had grimaced at that *yet*, a little word that held everything big in it.

There had come a day, in the house she and Harold had owned half her life, when Claudette had to stand up from the piano. The pain had been something alive crawling up her arms after half a stubborn hour on the bench. Her fingers wouldn't straighten for some time.

She had called her daughter in a rare moment of weakness and broken down in tears, confessed that she'd been going to bed with throbbing fire in her hands for months now. And her fingers, her long lovely fingers that could span six keys like a bird's wings, had begun to curl and bunch into things like claws. The arthritis had finally defeated her.

A week later, Lidia had put a shockingly small portion of her mother's life in boxes—she might as well have taped Claudette up in one, too—and taken them away to a "senior apartment" in Nashville, where she could check in on her every other day.

The house in Leipers Fork—*too much room for one, Mama*—was sold and would be divvied up between Lidia and Jason. The piano went into storage, a useless ghost hunched under a bed sheet. Two months on and she missed it more than she did all that space that had held her family within it.

And Harold. He had been dead too long to miss with any real tenderness. Four quiet years since the car crash, and it almost made her ashamed, that it could be like a scab falling off and the scar it left behind wasn't at all dreadful.

A light went on in the apartment building across the alley, the fourth-floor window respective to her own. She'd never seen a light in any of those dozens of blank closed eyes. It had no curtains, she hadn't noticed that before, and the room within was streaked with a blurry gloom.

A tall wardrobe stood against the far wall, nearly centered in the frame of the window. It could have been the twin of her own, the one that Lidia had now because it had been two feet too tall to bring here.

Claudette had adored that piece, the smoked rich oak. It felt like an insult to see one so like it now. Part of a bed was visible to the right, but she couldn't tell where the shadows began or ended, or what might be casting them. Below her in the alley, the men did not pause, did not look away from their hidden work, but somehow they assumed more watchful postures.

She pressed her forehead against the pane to reduce a few inches from the hundred feet between the two windows. A figure lay on the bed, but she couldn't see its face, couldn't decide if it was in fact a figure. It could have been lumps in a blanket.

The light brightened then dimmed. The shadows grew furry. She noticed that the bottom edge of the room's window seemed inconstant, as though something were crouched just below it, trembling to lift into her sight.

She sat back in her chair, her hand lifting to clutch at the meeting of her blouse collar. Her curtains dropped shut. Her lungs hitched and her heart squirmed inside her. "Lord God," she whispered, and for a moment thought to peer back down at the men in red coats. But instead she struggled up from the chair and shuffled toward the bed, where her pain pills were, her bones full of gravity.

L idia came and took her downtown, bought her a new nightdress and some bracelets with stronger magnets than her current ones, as though they could make a difference. They had brunch in a café whose name Claudette forgot while they were still in it, so troubled was she by the fact that her dead parents were in the kitchen, watching her, the bustle of waiters and cooks passing around them.

They peeked at her through the cutout window, furtive, wary, the first shocks of true white in their hair. It could have been 1976, the day before the stroke took her mother and surprised everyone.

"What is it, Mama?" Lidia asked, shaking Claudette's arm. Gently, always gently, she treated her like glass these days. "You see somebody you know?"

"I don't—" There was only a line cook at the window, clipping sheets of paper to a metal wheel. She turned back and gave her daughter a false smile, the light from the front windows too bright in her eyes. "It's nothing. I just wish I could go ahead and dry up. Get it over with."

Lidia paled and began to cry, as blandly as she did everything else. "I worry about you, Mama," she said. Going on fifty years and Claudette had never grown accustomed to the depths of love in those green eyes. "You don't ever make space enough for anybody. I think we need to get Jason and the boys out for a visit. It'll do you good."

"Well. I guess." She pushed her plate away with the heel of a hand. Claudette hadn't seen her grandsons, Kelton and Twain, in more than a year and hadn't particularly cared to. She was glad Lidia had chosen to be with a woman. Less noise in Claudette's life.

She stood as Lidia paid the check, peering around toward the kitchen. A face that might have been her father's watched her through the round window in the kitchen door, its nose flattened against the greasy acrylic pane.

———

It hurt her hands to grip the photo album, to turn its cardboard pages. But she felt any reason she would have to dream up her parents was too obscured in her mind, as though things really were slipping away from her. Sixty-eight was well on the early side for dementia.

Night fell outside and made her artificial light a deeper yellow. She didn't notice the ripening colors of the evening—to her the warm gray clicked over to blue-black like a shutter. She heard the faint stirring of the men below but needed to put things right in her mind before she looked.

But there was nothing in the pages that stirred a dark memory. These were all prosaic remembrances. The children hardly remembered their grandmother, but her father had doted on them in his gentle way until the cancer got him in '83. Claudette couldn't remember the last time she had seen him.

She felt guilt for that, but not enough to dredge up anything by hallucinating the two of them at breakfast. If she was being honest with herself, she rarely thought of her parents. Her mother had been a warm stranger, and Claudette's bond with her father had been difficult in ways she had never articulated.

She parted the curtains and let herself see the lighted window. Slowly she noticed that it was the apartment directly below the one that had been illuminated the night before. This one was on the third floor. The shadows were thicker now, more lethargic. It was harder to see inside at this new angle, but she thought the same wardrobe, the sister of hers, stood in the rear of the room.

And the bed seemed tilted up toward her now, so that she saw it was stained with mold. The same man-shaped lump lay under the blanket. She kept her chin raised, to block the bottom of the window from herself, prolonging the moment before she finally saw that there was a figure hunched below the sill, after all, its back clothed in pale green.

It looked to be on all fours, but seeing only the edge of it she couldn't be sure. The way it trembled, perhaps someone was injured and slumped against the wall. Perhaps the window was lower than she assumed, and the figure was sleeping. It was none of her business.

The fourth floor window was dark and covered now. Why was the tableau recreated below? Or had it been? If she could pretend her long-dead mother and father were watching her from a restaurant's busy kitchen, couldn't she pretend anything?

In the alley, she noted almost as an afterthought, the men in coats stood farther from her tonight. They were strung out in a line, bent over something she could see no more clearly than before. She stared at the window and its spoiled glow for some time, daring it, but the figure remained in its position until her breaths grew steady and shallow, her pulse fluid.

S he dreamed less often and less vividly now, but assumed that deeper in her mind she still spent the nights at her piano, playing one of hundreds of things but most often "Hollow," the allegro molto from Rachmaninoff's second piano sonata. Harold had come up with the nickname for the piece because it was all scales and fireworks but had none of the delicate passion of a Chopin or Beethoven.

Claudette had always kept a special cold look reserved for when he said things like this, as though piano music should serve only candlelight. *It's an allegro. Don't be so dense. It means briskly. And even Beethoven could get feet tapping, how many times do you need me to tell you?*

She couldn't bear the thought that her music had been stolen from her dreams as well.

A week before her thirtieth birthday, in the spring of 1978, a spotlight had switched on and bathed Claudette in a kind of adulation, a singling out of her. It was her Moment and the whole of her life withered into the background of it. Nearly two hundred people had listened to her play that night, only a third of the Presbyterian church's seats but it felt like a cavernous amphitheater under a silent slow lightning storm. She was no longer a part-time piano teacher.

Her fingers had danced through Shostakovich and Tchaikovsky. She had finished with "Hollow," then Pärt's "Für Alina," a modern piece she had come across in a moment of serendipity. It was the slowest, most elegiac thing that had ever been written, and she heard not one cough in all the pregnant gaps between the notes. It had been the first of many nights for Claudette, the nascent prodigy on her way to thirty-one years of this light, some of them in the Nashville Symphony.

She wept off and on most of the day, not calling her daughter, not changing out of her nightclothes. Her hair loosened from its bun and fell around her shoulders, and her hands were too useless to wind it back up. A box of crackers sat on the windowsill for what little hunger she had.

Every few minutes, she checked the facing windows to verify that each from the last two nights was covered. The second-floor window below them was, too, with canvas drapes nearly the color of the surrounding brick.

Again there was no evidence below that the men in the red coats had been there in the night. The sun already glared and her fingers twitched, their old ghosts busy on a distant keyboard. She watched each end of the alley for figures that lingered, dreading to see her mother or father loitering behind a corner. Still the question nipped at her: Why had she seen them?

Claudette had always thought of seventy as only the first portico into darkness. But here, two years shy, she felt something like true grief, and she realized it was her first taste of it. If she could have her hands back she could play all of this far off to the rim of the earth, beyond import. She could play until age found her and her skin sagged and sloughed off her bones. They'd pull her off the piano bench and bury her next to Harold out behind the church where they'd married. It would be enough.

The afternoon whitened like an overexposed photograph, too blind and sheer, and Claudette kept her vigil. Sometime in the afternoon, she thought she saw Harold on top of the old building, only a glimpse as the sun slid just behind the figure and placed it in a corona. The day burned slow into rose and orange and her head eased onto her breast.

When she lifted it, dark had adhered to everything in the room. The lamp next to her had died. She stood, an ache coiled deep in the small of her back, and watched shapes crouch and almost shuffle two, three inches to the side before settling back into a sofa, a chair at the small dining table, a coat that had fallen from its hook by the door. These shapes were too dark to be silhouettes, but she stared at them until they admitted they were only her things.

She waded into the dark. Her fingers brushed something hanging in front of her face. She choked back a moan—only the emergency cord. A thought touched her, *Pull it. Tell them to get Lidia out here, put me somewhere.* But she bared her teeth at it. The light switch was there on the wall, a button she could press with a palm and spare her fingers.

She reached for it and the door moved once in the metal frame, as though something had gently pushed it from the hallway. Claudette held her breath for a long time before pressing the heel of her hand against the button. In the warm light she took one of her pills, dry, feeling it catch in her throat.

"Let's see the show, then," she told the room, and shuffled back to the window. Tonight the second-floor room across the alley was washed in a light less constant than her own, the same dull gloom the room above had been smeared in, and the room above that before it.

The wardrobe was lost from view now, but she could see a Persian rug identical to the one that had lain next to her piano the past four decades, a pale gold with a distinct orange diamond in the center. Too rare a design to pass off as coincidence. Her father had bought that rug for her mother before Claudette was a thought.

The steeper angle gave her only the eight feet or so closest to her, closest to the man—or a broad woman, she supposed, she'd never been thin herself—hunched on all fours below the window. The figure was shaking, shifting now as though in discomfort from the sustained position. Shadows bent and curled around it.

Claudette's face itched, a delirious heat rising to her skin, and she looked down toward the street where the men in red coats, such benevolent things in comparison, stood around a large obscure lump, their backs to her, curved so that their coats formed one long bloody smile in the dimness.

She squinted her eyes and saw it was something beneath a tarp, surrounded by smaller objects under smaller tarps. Closer, a longer, darker shape lay perpendicular to the alley walls, nearly bridging the two buildings.

When she looked up, the person on the bed—it had to be a person, bound up and tortured, likely—writhed briefly. The figure under the window lifted its back, lowered it, then began to raise its head. Claudette saw half an eye appear, crowned by a wisp of white hair, and gaze up toward her.

A chill of half-familiarity touched her and she found herself seeing both her father and her husband in that cold look. She snatched the curtains shut, crying out with the pain that gripped the fine bones in her hand.

Enough of this. She would not let them scare her. That would have to be the important thing. A derelict in a condemned apartment building wasn't anything to do with her. Workers in cheap Santa Claus coats weren't anything to do with her.

Even as she thought these things, she peeked down—one of the men adjusted the larger tarp, and in the moon's sudden brief glimpse she saw the keys of a piano before the object was covered again.

"I don't feel up to it," Claudette said into the phone, furious with her daughter for being in Knoxville for her job and with herself for forgetting. "You should be here to take me."

"Mama, I'm sorry." She could hear the hurt in Lidia's voice, the I've-let-you-down quiver that had never quite left it, not really. "We talked about you taking a cab. Dr. Kelley's eight blocks away. It's just physical therapy, but it's fine if you're not feeling right. I'll be there Friday evening, soon as I get into town."

"I'm tired. And tired of being cooped up in here. But you go do your work. The bridge club will be here in a minute. We're hitting the town tonight, dancing the tango." She bit her lip. *Stop this mewling, Claudette. You look a fool.*

"You can't give up on yourself, Mama. Your hands aren't you." In the background Claudette could hear a sudden swell of quiet as the TV was turned off. "And I talked to Jason. He wants it to be a surprise, but he and the boys are coming. Today or tomorrow, depends on if they stop off. Now don't you tell them I told."

"Well. Come see me when you get back. I need fresh groceries." And she pressed the end button. The dread fell back over her then, knowing the ground floor window would be full of that diseased light tonight, and not knowing what might come after that. Only that she had to see.

The tarps and what they had covered were gone. All the windows she could see in the facing building had curtains or blinds or drapes, save two that were boarded up. The only difference was a slack cable, two stories up, running from one window on her side across to an opposite window, above a battered steel door. She wondered if the men had installed it there. She felt she knew nothing in the world.

Her parents and husband weren't lurking anywhere she could see. The ends of the alley emptied onto their streets and not one of the occasional pedestrians slowed or paused to look in or up at Claudette. Life outside stumbled forward and left her in her box.

Could she have seen things in the café because she had not attended her father's funeral? Some nascent complex a shrink would stroke their chin over? The children had still been a little too young, and she had stayed home with them while Harold went. She could almost remember the look he'd given her, sidelong as he put his hat on. Not wanting to say the wrong thing and so saying nothing, as was his way.

But surely there had been a reason for her refusal. Such a cruel thing, not to say goodbye. Had her father angered her near the end? No, she couldn't think of a single harshness from him, except—

You always were stingy with your love, Poppet.

Poppet. She'd let herself forget his pet name for her. He had said that to her on her wedding night, after most of the guests had left, the strung lights reflected in the wet grass outside the Parthenon, Nashville's silly little replica. She remembered that small green galaxy now, what was left of the rain that had threatened to ruin the ceremony in the park. The humidity of the night dampening her dress.

He had said something else, too, before her mother joined them. *I can't help but hope you'll be kinder now.*

The words stung more all these years later than she could remember them doing then. She pawed the curtains open again and looked to either end of the alley. The sun had started to tire in the distance. Guilt flushed her cheeks and she told herself it was the warmth of the fading day against her face. He'd been a foolish old man, never thinking of himself.

Don't speak ill of the dead, Claudette. Who thought of one's own father like that? And Harold. Who spent the last thirty years of a marriage forcing a man into a separate bedroom? Lidia and Jason had still been children the last time she'd made love to her husband.

She didn't want to think of these things and so she didn't.

Later she stood and walked to the door and unlocked it, just so she could feel the bolt slide into place when she twisted it back. She cried out at the bloom of pain, but it was a necessary thing.

She put on a light green sweater against a new chill. Back at the window, she looked down and saw a vertical segment of the room on the ground floor. The drapes had been drawn back a foot or so. A deep red shifted away from them, out of sight. In the coat's place she saw a row of white teeth—piano keys.

One of those damned men had put a piano in the room, was pushing it back into the gloom. She thought of the wardrobe, the rug. Had someone raided Lidia's storage unit?

Just the idea of her actual piano—an Estonia she'd saved for years to buy—in a condemned building right in front of her made her blood seethe. The emotion ran stronger than even the fear of ominous figures playing a morbid joke on her.

Someone she couldn't see tore the drapes down in the ground-level apartment. She watched the exposed room, its one large shadow heaving its bulk as it drew in the dark, until the light came on. The piano was hidden but she thought she could make out the edge of her bench's brocade covering, whose lemon-yellow had made a strange harmony with the rug in her music room. A sliver of that rug was visible below it.

She stood and moved toward the door, turned right toward the phone, but hesitated, unable to wring her hands like she wanted. She made herself sit back down. Her patience was wearing thin. Her children would have to do something about all this.

She prayed it wasn't senility. Such an indignant ruin, but she'd never known how to talk to an entity she considered a myth. God had no ears. Down in the alley, having crept or scuttled in during her moment of indecision, the men in red coats stood in a line, those on either end pulling on a rope.

Something huge lifted off the ground and she saw it was a black sheet. Soon it halved the alley. Claudette wouldn't have known it was there without the sickened light of the apartment below, or if she hadn't caught them in the act.

Inside the ground floor apartment the window was half-open, another new difference. The space below the window was empty, but the bed held the same uncertain shape. It took two painful minutes to get her own window ajar. As she watched, a sound drifted out, a few plaintive, syrupy piano notes.

She straightened in her chair, recognizing it at once as Rachmaninoff's allegro molto. Harold's "Hollow." But it was all wrong. It couldn't have been more *off*. What idiot fingers could make such an ugly sound? The player had training, which made it worse, which made the stretching out of the piece unbearable to Claudette. It sounded like someone had allegro confused with adagio.

It was clumsy, derivative tripe, but it captured her, sitting by her window in her hated little apartment, it reached up and lifted her out of her diminished life for a long, strangely transposed moment. It nearly burst with a liquid sentiment, a cheap romantic poignancy.

For an instant she wished Harold were in the room to hear this, to tell her he'd told her so. It was still wrong, though, all wrong, she wanted to scream the fact of it down to that window.

Then the piano went silent. The light around it snapped off. The shadows clouded in to take its place, and Claudette heard a voice call out, "Hello!" Low and wet, a thick voice full of phlegm stretching the *o* into an *ooh*. It repeated the word again and again, until she realized it was saying something else—"Hollow!"—and she went cold. But it was as wrong as the sonata movement and sounded more like "Holoow, holoow." A haunting, dying owl or an old man playing at being a ghost. Yes, but more than anything there was a profound sadness in the voice, carrying in it the same timbre of the piano.

The men in red coats had vanished while her attention was distracted. A minute, two minutes of dense silence, that malformed word still hanging in the air like a decaying echo, then the squeal of metal near where the men had raised the black sheet and cut the alley in half. Claudette stared and was just able to see the sheet ripple as something brushed against it, closer, marking its progress toward her building.

It was coming for her. It would crawl up the stairs—she could only imagine it on all fours, loping up and around and calling out that owlish word against the concrete walls.

She couldn't bear to have it outside her door, pushing, moaning at her. She stood and crossed her living room, unlocked the door with a whimper. She passed down the hall toward the elevators, away from where she thought the stairwell was, not thinking yet. There was only an image of her things in a room that for the moment was unoccupied. Her piano filled her mind, crowding out the entirety of her life.

She jabbed the down button at the elevator, relishing the pain of it, and stepped inside. As the doors slid closed she heard the rumor of a voice, the possibility of that elastic "Holoow!" leaking into the fourth floor. The lobby was cold and sterile and empty, the front desk vacant, and the night outside was twenty degrees warmer.

Claudette hurried around the building, pain twinging in her knees, and into the alley. The thick metal door of the neighboring building hung open, a deep black shape pasted onto the night. The dark sheet was completely hidden unless she squinted at it.

Trash lay strewn inside the old building, along with dust and a silence that got into her ears, thick and pressing. But the dark was not as complete as it should have been. She walked forward until she reached a hallway, while ahead a much larger space opened up, from which she picked out the dim shapes of columns and a long counter.

Down the hallway to her left, a wavering light struggled out of a doorway. It looked like candlelight, and she wondered why she hadn't figured that out before.

Claudette approached the room, a part of her reaching back to the first time she ever walked onto a stage. It was the only point of reference that felt true to her. The light flickered, her hands gathered at her throat, and the whole of the building seemed to hold its breath like a great lung.

She could already see her piano, a wedge of it through the open doorway. The rug on the floor, the half-forgotten way its delicate pile had felt between her toes. A strange memory pushed into her mind, an insignificance hiding just beyond the frame of the door: the birdhouse Harold had built with Jason and Lidia, the robin that had taken residence there. This let in flashes of Harold asking her to help plan birthday parties for the kids as they grew up so fast on her periphery. The arguments he would never quite start with her. She could almost hear the robin's song.

But as she drew close, the one thing the room felt bereft of was music. Hers. How could that be?

She entered with no hesitation, though her eyes went to the window and the empty floor below it, the bed and the blanket upon it. Lumps were arranged beneath the blanket, approximating the shape of a man but with too much of the anatomy. There were no candles to match the quality of the light, after all, just a wide dome in the ceiling littered with crawling bugs inside, the light shifting around their carapaces.

It really *was* her piano, her Estonia, its lid propped open in welcome. The gouge a young Jason had put in the side of it was there, faded into the character of the wood over the years. How long had she gone without speaking to him after that?

She closed the door, turned the lock in the cheap doorknob, and sat down on her love-worn bench. A light filled her, and she could nearly imagine it not suffusing her but falling on her from the ceiling and the sky, picking her out of the great crowd of the world.

She had never made it to the concert halls of Manhattan, or even Atlanta. She supposed she could admit now that she hadn't been quite that good or that young. Yet she had felt that hot light on her. The hush and the almost spiritual awe, and what did it matter where it had been? It was worth all the sacrifice.

Claudette sighed and straightened her fingers as best she could. The pain when she splayed them, testing their span, was exquisite. The music had once leapt up from the keys into her hands, the tight strings humming inside their box. But when she brought her fingers down, tapping the key bed with the heels of her hands, a deformed noise arose.

She tried again, biting her tongue to tamp the flaring ache down and racing into "Hollow," her mind three measures ahead of her ears when she realized that what emerged from the belly of the piano was a dripping slow dirge, just as she'd heard float up to her own window earlier.

So she sought that strange yearning depth and it came perfectly, unbidden to her, swelling with the stabs of pain in her fingers and wrists and forearms until she felt the marrow would burst from the shells of her bones.

She fell from the bench with a cry, the rug absorbing the shock, and she lay there panting, shuddering. An object shone faintly at her from under the window. She crawled over to the edge of the rug and picked it up, a photo of her parents holding her children, fitted together like a complete idea, and Harold leaning into them like an afterthought.

No, he was rushing into the frame because he'd set the camera timer, she realized. Which meant Claudette hadn't been there.

Snow coated the trees and the eaves of her childhood home in the background. The five of them wore matching red coats, and a vague memory of some Christmas pageant came to her. Lidia or Jason crying because Mama was supposed to play the piano but had decided to stay home with her own music.

The sharp, bolting aches crept up her arms. She crouched, trembling, and something inside longed to get out of her. Whether it was a wail, or the kind of cleansing sob she had never voiced, or something more significant and whole, the cold that had always rooted in her, she didn't know.

A terror slowly clutched her as she realized she was on all fours beneath the window, without the strength to get up. Something had given out in her back. She raised her head a few inches. With her right eye she saw her warm bright window on the fourth floor, draped with her creamy curtains. A silhouette sat there, cut out of the yellow light, the same loose bun of hair in the back as Claudette's own.

She hadn't locked the door behind her when she left the apartment.

It was such a lonely shape, she thought, until another figure was framed in the light. Then another. Small shapes, and the shadow with the bun lifted its hands up—fingers that flexed and wriggled freely in the light—and grabbed the head of one of them.

Claudette gasped as the shadow pulled one of her grandsons into a hug, then gathered the other one in as well. A man's silhouette stepped near the window—Jason—and together the four of them made one amorphous blur that rose against the curtains.

Claudette opened her mouth to yell something, a warning or a plea, but only the low keening "Holoow" crept out. Her eyes went back to the photograph. Where had she been that day? The other days? Where had she been?

A noise came from the bed beside her. Something rolling, shifting back and forth, thumping against the mattress. She lifted her eyes, the picture still pulling at her from between her useless hands, and saw the lumps drop to the floor, pulling the blanket down with them.

Claudette glimpsed a squirming red mass, like a tangle of coats, before the corner of the bed blocked her view. She could only listen as something tried to say "Poppet," but the sound carried such a contrasting weight. The voice she remembered had been so patient and kind and indulgent.

The next words came quickly, other voices low and liquid as an unplugged drain. The sounds of movement increased, and she heard her life dragging itself across the rug.

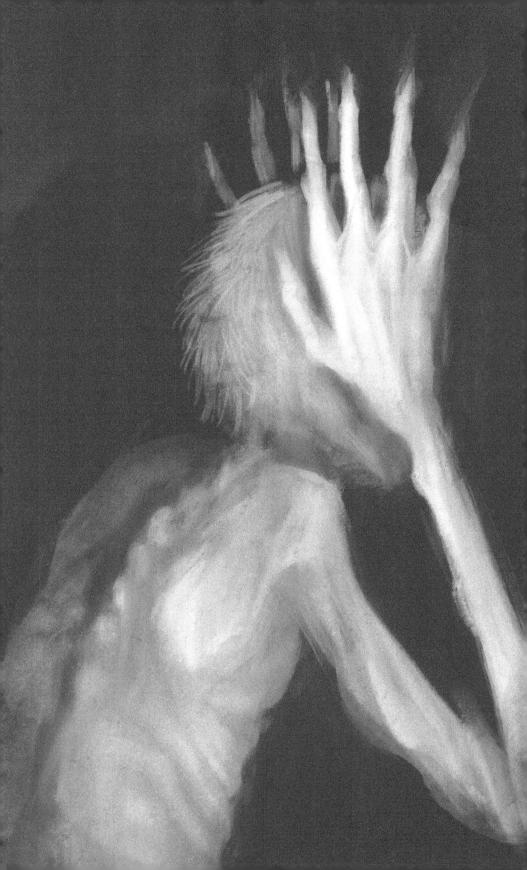

CARING FOR A STRAY DOG
(METAPHORS)

1. GRACE

Once Kent opened himself up to metaphors, they were everywhere.

The dog, stopping for the dog in the first place, was such an obvious one, he told himself that night as he washed her in a motel bathtub. He was already thinking of what he might call her, names Lissa would have asked for, his fingers scavenging for ticks under the dog's thick white fur, where it was easier to spot them, and under the brown fur, where it was not.

Dozens of names came to him. His knees hurt from kneeling, but he worked the motel shampoo into the matted tangles, digging his fingers in and massaging. The filth slowly loosened, swirling into a milky gray around the drain. She trembled the entire time but stood still and resigned for him. The soft half-words he murmured seemed to help.

He accepted the metaphor without much thought or reservation. Of course the dog would be a stand-in for his daughter, who had been dead—he did the pseudo-math—just over five dog years. There was a warmth and almost a peace, that he would embrace it in the same way Lissa would have, unthinkingly, with the earnestness of a child.

The dog's ribs stood out, stark against the wet fur, and Kent ran his hand along her side. "Let's get you dry and have some more dinner," he said to her as he turned the water off. He braced himself for a vicious shake that would patter his face and soak his shirt, but she only turned her head toward him and yawned, her jaws opening and her tongue unrolling between the yellow teeth. He lowered his head toward hers and her lips peeled back, turning the yawn into a warning.

Grace, he decided, that would be her name. It wasn't something Lissa would have picked, probably. She had only just turned four when the angry man walked into her pre-K classroom with an AR-15. Her casket had been closed. He closed his eyes tight. Opened them and ran his hand from the dog's head down to her back. Lissa would have chosen something like Puppy or, he was suddenly sure, Pappy, and giggled for days about it.

Grace, though. It felt like what he was looking for, stumbling around in the new dark of his life, so why not be obvious about that, too?

He lay on top of the bed in the motel room that first night with the dog curled up between his spread legs. The love in his life had bled out and she fit into the hollow of it. Her tail was a damp brush over her nose, as though she didn't quite trust him yet. That was okay with Kent. He had too much time.

"Grace," he said into the stale air, pushing the silence away for a moment. But it sank back down on him. It was too cool for the rattle of the air conditioner. He'd spotted the dog that afternoon, crouched by a gap-toothed fence, on the upper lip of a ditch running along Highway 92 on his way out of town. Half-starved and much warier than she was now, seven hours later.

There had been only a sliding glimpse before he pulled over. He wasn't sure if something in her posture, miserable and defeated, had tugged at him, or if the metaphor of what he was doing had already taken hold when he left the house.

The parking lot light prying at the curtains outside seemed too yellow and sickly. He stared at the ceiling and listened to the air brakes of tractor trailers out on the road. A faint thread of studio laughter flared in and out from an adjoining room's television. Occasionally other sounds, whether forced or ambient, brought the noises of gunfire to his mind.

Although he'd been twenty miles from Lissa when it happened, coding in his cubicle, he'd still seen too many movies to avoid having an idea of what the gun would have sounded like there in the small rooms and hallways. In the worst moments, his mind added the children's screams.

The day she died, her class had been rehearsing a play about forest animals. They would have performed it the following week. Lissa practiced her deer for days at home, making antlers with her hands against her forehead. She only wanted to eat lettuce and things found in the woods. "And a garden, because deers like to steal food sometimes because they get hungry," she added. Ellie corrected her grammar and told her this particular deer would eat her ravioli, too. There was spinach inside, so that would be all right, wouldn't it?

All those soft felt animal masks must have looked stark and bitter and so heavy on the floor, in the aftermath of the shooting. Some of them speckled or soaked with blood. The curled shapes of small bodies. Kent squeezed his eyes shut and pushed his thoughts toward Grace.

She must have been a pretty dog, even striking, not long ago. Her eyes were a rich brown, the left with a flawed rind of blue along the lower rim. The blue of Lissa's eyes. Some of that beauty had returned now that he'd cleaned her up, but she still had a journey back to health. He thought this was another metaphor, one that held hands with the first.

She had clearly been on her own for months. She had no collar. Her nails needed trimming. A fever nested in her skin, and she couldn't have weighed much more than twenty pounds. Even when she shifted against his legs in her sleep, he could feel the ridges of her bones. He'd want to double her weight at the least. They would start with a trip to the vet tomorrow before the two of them hit the road for points north.

Growing up in Jasper, the mountains close enough to look like things arriving, stepping down onto the interstate at any moment, his next-door neighbor had owned a border collie with a splotching of black and white. He remembered hugging him when he could, burying his face in the fur and smelling something sweet and primitive.

That breed was what Grace reminded him the most of, only with brown instead of black and a more squared face like a pit bull. Her coat carried a similar soft wildness, lush and and a little shaggy. The brown was too rusty to remind him of his daughter's hair, but taken with the trace of blue in the dog's eye, it was close enough.

Lissa would have lost her mind if Kent had brought a creature like Grace into the house. He could hear her voice squealing with joy and clung to it in his mind, willing it to always stay so vivid and close to recall. She would have helped him wash her, but at a short distance in case the dog lashed out in fear. Go easy, honey, he would have said. You have to earn an animal's trust.

The world was all trees and strip malls here outside Athens. They would cross into South Carolina tomorrow and ride the hypnosis of the interstate and figure out the rest later. He reached down and stroked the dog above her haunches. She trembled for a moment, a low growl stirring in her chest, then went still. He lay back and listened to her wet breathing. He pretended it was rain against the windows.

It had snowed on Lissa's last Christmas, the first snow she had ever seen, and that, too, must have felt like a metaphor at the time, this ferocious little three-year-old making her way through every new experience, learning the world, giving it back her bright cackling laughter.

He and Ellie had bundled her up and set her down in the back yard, watching her gaze at the blanket of what passed for a snowstorm in Georgia. She had turned to them, her nose already running in the cold air, and pointed up. "Look, popsicles!" The snowmelt from the roof had frozen into a row of uneven teeth that strained toward them from the eave above the kitchen door.

Lissa had turned back to the snow, this new thing to discover, and promptly fallen into it and cried. So Kent had taught her how to make snow angels.

The memory had seized him yesterday and wouldn't let him go. He'd walked out back of the house and stood in the first fall morning under forty degrees, late November clearing its weak southern throat. For the first time it meant Christmas would come, then next year, her birthday in January, the anniversary of the shooting four weeks later.

And he just couldn't do it. He and Ellie had gone as cold as those icicles toward one another since February. Nine months, enough time to grow the replacement child they'd never have. The house was pregnant with black silence. They never fought but he wished they would at least do that. He stood in the back yard, looking at the place where Lissa had fallen, the place where they'd built a sad little snowman. It was all covered in dead leaves now.

He had packed the first bag he saw in the hall closet. Then emptied out his half of the checking account. Ellie was at work and he didn't even tell her he was leaving her and the house and his job and everything else in Keeseville.

G race woke before he did. She waited for him by the door so he carried her around the building to a grassy island in the parking lot where she could relieve herself. She didn't like to be carried so he needed to get a leash as soon as possible. She squatted over some pine needles and he looked away demurely, smiling.

It was amazing that he'd gone thirty-one years without a dog. His father had been allergic, which seemed to have programmed Kent to be without pets. But he would have gotten Lissa one before much longer, he was sure of it. He and Ellie had started talking about the right time. The smile held on another moment before fading.

He fed the dog some more of the kibble he'd bought at the Publix down the road, spreading it on the floor because he didn't have a bowl. She ate too quickly, and when he reached down to add a last handful, her teeth flashed and she bit him. He fell back and onto the bed, but she simply returned to her breakfast, her bushy tail switching back and forth.

The skin on his hand was broken in two places, like a vampire bite, the bone bruised. But he laughed. He felt almost good, somehow, loosened in some inscrutable way, and the wound was nothing he didn't welcome. You have to earn an animal's trust.

He got his own breakfast at a drive-thru, bought some gauze and Band-Aids for his hand and two plastic bowls for Grace's food and water at the same Publix, then found a vet on his phone and drove into Athens. No, he hadn't adopted her yet but he was going to, he told the doctor in the examination room. He'd found her on the side of the road. If the dog didn't have a microchip through which her owner could be traced, he and his daughter would nurse her back to health. They'd take her on two walks a day unless it was raining.

He smiled at the right moments, worried that Grace would soon be taken from him and this would all be over. If he had been a different man, he would have prayed.

But she had no chip. They tested for worms and rabies, clipped her nails, told him to feed her an extra meal a day but not too much. The doctor speculated that she was maybe six years old, a mix of pit bull and border collie, and Kent said that was exactly what he'd thought. She was weak and had a bit of a respiratory infection, but with the short round of antibiotics they were prescribing, it was nothing to worry about.

Kent paid for the antibiotics, heartworm medication, dental chews, a harness and leash and collar. Finally he walked Grace out under a graying sky and bent down to scratch her ears, telling her they both felt better already, even if they were nearly four hundred dollars poorer.

Thirty miles up I-85 Kent began to think about metaphors again, how closely he wanted to be guided by them. To not plan ahead. What did he have to lose, he countered every argument. His mother lived with his sister up in Virginia. They were both healthy, but the map in his mind had no other pins pushed into it yet.

Grace lay across the backseat, her muzzle between her front paws, and he called back to her every quarter hour or so, using her name so that she would get used to hearing it.

If caring for the dog was a metaphor for his daughter, there should be something to protect her from, a way for him to earn the grave he had dug himself into. He needed a risk, a conduit, a dark weight to balance this new thing in his heart.

Soon he passed out of Georgia into South Carolina. The sky whitened. His hand throbbed with a pleasant pulse under the gauze, his cells busy repairing the wounds. He drove with the radio on, turned low so that the DJs and commercials and songs were all the same handful of ghosts, murmurs that weren't quite silence.

He wondered out loud to Grace as the Civic droned north. What had her life been like before, did her old family have kids, had she been on her own for too long to remember? He told her she would have loved his Lissa. They would have been best friends, but he got only a few sentences into this before he had to change the subject.

The dog would sit up and assume an interested posture, watching cars and sliding tree lines, the gaps where neighborhoods or industrial parks crept up toward the highway. The rhythmic ugliness of billboards like commas marking their passage. Then she would lie back down with a sigh, her breathing too ragged for comfort.

Sometimes she lay in the space where Lissa's car seat had once been, and Kent let his eyes drift again and again to the rearview mirror, to the images overlaid there.

The world further emptied out and the miles lengthened between exits. A compulsion rose through all the sameness, an itch to leave the highway, and the trees seemed to lean toward him from their low western banks and away from him to the east.

He took the next exit, a town called Taylors with nothing but old farmland spread out from the ramp, the suggestion of vacancy and endless forest ahead. None of the usual small cluster of industry huddled at the interstate to lure travelers. He sat at the end of the ramp for a minute, alone on the earth. Looking for a gas station would ease the tedium.

But the first thing they passed was a small church, two stubborn miles down the road, and it pulled at him as Grace had. He might have invented the sensation, he knew, and the dog only picked up on the energy he put out into the closed space. But she got to her feet as he slowed the car and barked at the church, a dirty white wooden thing crouched behind its tongue of gravel lot. It was the first time he'd heard her bark, and it was rougher, deeper than he had expected.

He turned into the lot, the gravel muttering under the tires. He stopped and the church loomed. Dusk seemed to be arriving in a sudden swing of the sky.

To the right and behind the church, a little overgrown graveyard lay in a pocket beneath several oak trees, hints of tombstones folding into shadow. Kent looked for a sign by the road but there was none, only the words TAYLORS CORSE BAPTIST painted in black over the narrow white doors of the building.

The steeple rose ten, twelve feet above the roof, and it bothered him that it was a cone without any sides. It bore no cross. He didn't know if he had ever seen a steeple like it anywhere. Its paint was cleaner or newer, a more perfect white, and he wondered if, without corners, it could have possibly been made of the same wood as the walls below it. It seemed somehow an occult thing, or a symbol of another place used in the wrong way.

He sat in the car for several minutes before getting out, staring through the windshield at the church, the dog staring with him and whimpering. He turned his phone on for the first time all day and was relieved to see no texts or voicemails. Ellie seemed to agree with his decision.

It was foolish to deny the reason he had stopped here. Nothing had guided him off the interstate other than his bladder. There was only the simple fact that the man who had walked into Our Hands Daycare on that February morning and killed five children and two adults had been the pastor of a Baptist church.

The media had devoured his backstory, and so had Kent. Andrew Butler Perry, forty-two, an electrician and man of God, separated from his wife, father of a seven-year-old daughter who went to her unblemished elementary school an hour south of the lives her father had ended that day.

Perry had turned his gun on himself in the end, but Kent wished he hadn't. He wished he could have seen his eyes with their light still in them. That cold lump in his chest was what had stopped the car here. It was waiting to feel echoes of the man decaying out of this worn white church that wasn't even in the same state.

There was nothing of the sort, but he left the car and approached it anyway. He turned back once, saw the uneasy silhouette of the dog in the backseat, and almost went back for her. But if this was to be another metaphor, he preferred that she stay there, safe.

2. Corse

The doors were not locked and led directly into the nave of the church, which ached with cold, its air still sour with the bodies that gathered within it to worship, as if they had just slipped out through the back at his coming. What daylight remained struggled through the windows and turned to a milky gloom, so that the pews huddled in the dark center.

What here could represent the man who had killed Lissa? Or the composite idea of all men like him? How could God allow such emissaries? Kent had not been in a church in close to ten years—his wedding—and before that not since he was a frightened and uncomfortable boy. He could only be a stranger here, and his old fear touched him now.

In the moment these thoughts came to him, each attached to the other, he heard a rustling of fabric or wings, then a scraping sound from the end of the aisle, that of a heavy object dragged across the floor. Slowly, out of the dimness, he saw that the altar had been pulled away and a figure stood beside it, watching him.

The figure's hands might have been raised above its face, palms facing one another against the forehead—otherwise it was indistinct, a part of the greater dark that had nearly filled the church to its windows.

It was so cold in here. It had gotten inside his thin coat. He told himself the figure was a statue of something—an effigy of Christ, strange in a Baptist church—just as its head tilted to the left.

"Hello?" he called out but the single word was absorbed in a well of silence halfway across the room. He pulled his phone from the pocket of his coat, tapped the flashlight on, and turned it toward the front of the church. The nearer pews rose and leaned toward him, doubled by their new shadows. But the figure stood too far from Kent, so that only a rim of the light reached it, enough to show the raised hands were growths or horns of some kind extending erect from its head. It lifted its arms from its sides as though to confirm this.

Would you be marked? something asked him, far from a voice and more like a woolen texture in the air, and Kent raised the phone again, this time with the camera engaged. A soft thud was followed by footsteps.

He tapped the shutter button repeatedly as he backed toward the exit, the flash erupting in the dark, stuttered glimpses of the figure's long shape. A chorus rose of wood shrieking against wood. Kent's shoulder slammed against the door and he wheeled around and outside.

In the car Grace was barking in one continuous blur of fury or terror. Her freshly cut nails clattered on a back window. He kept walking with his back toward her, knowing those were not words he had heard or felt, knowing the metaphor had taken them from his mind and given them back. He reached the car, still looking toward the church, but nothing emerged.

Grace calmed down by the time he had backtracked to the interstate and headed northeast again. He got it into his head that one of the gravestones in the cemetery had his name etched into it. *Marked* into it, and no amount of distance, or coffee at a gas station three exits up, or pulling over on the shoulder to hug the dog, burying his face in her fur, would shake the thought.

He stopped off in Gaffney for the night, not far from North Carolina, walking Grace twice around the motel before they settled into their room. She ate her second dinner with her usual speed then curled up between his legs again, the front half of her body turned a little more toward him tonight. Kent lay there and thought of what he had seen, or dreamed, in the church.

Some part of him wanted to return to Taylors Corse Baptist and examine the headstone of every grave until he found *Kent Alden* cut into stone above the question of his death. He remembered the strange cone of the steeple, its perfect corrupted shape.

Eventually, as the dog shifted herself into more comfortable angles between his legs, his memory began to claim there had been a gap in the letters painted over the church's doors, as though the P had flaked away from TAYLORS CORPSE. Or the gap had been to the left, and an A had decayed from COARSE BAPTIST.

Neither of these was true, he told himself. Nor had his grave been dug yet outside of metaphor. There had probably not been a gap at all in that middle word, and even so, COURSE was as likely as the others, so he and Grace would continue theirs toward the vague north in the morning.

Grace was hot to the touch when he woke, her breathing still a little loose and wet. He wedged her morning dose of antibiotics into a treat and fed it to her, then stroked her head between her ears for a few minutes, listening to the world, remembering the vet saying it was probably nothing, she would be fine.

Outside the box of the motel was a gray heavy rain, trucks spewing fans of dishwater in their wake. The streetlamps still burned on their high stalks.

In some other version of Kent's life, he would have been in the morning stand-up meeting on Zoom by now, sketching a userflow on the virtual whiteboard app. A wind of chaos roaring in the empty cavity of his chest, where his heart used to be, the subtraction of Lissa from the world, a thin scream of confusion. His teammates averting their eyes as he hunched over and spoke into the camera and they saw the fear and blank grief on his face yet again.

He wondered if Ellie was still working, still logging on in the morning, still directing her staff. Still letting them all see Lissa's death in her eyes.

The church had followed him through his sleep. Taylors Corse Baptist yielded almost nothing on his phone screen when he searched for it along with several variations of its name. He even tried the strange word *corse* by itself and wasn't happy to learn it was an archaic spelling of *corpse*.

But he did find a website that looked to date from the early days of the internet, a lurid yellow background with the pixelated heading *Our Church Page* in a burned orange font. The name and denomination were absent. A sidebar contained a half-address, *Taylors SC 29686*, and two lines of text hung orphaned in the body of the page:

"Unless you are educated in metaphor, you are not safe to be let loose in the world." Robert Frost

He knew Frost, the poet who stopped his horse by the woods on a snowy night. For years he had hidden a hundred-dollar bill next to that poem in a thick paperback for emergencies. As he stared at his phone screen, it seemed that Frost had hidden something in him.

Kent had let himself loose, hadn't he? Or Andrew Butler Perry had. Or a cruel and useless God. He didn't know which had broken the last latch holding his life. The quote burned too powerfully for him to think. The very presence of it on a site connected with that church unnerved him. He remembered the trees seeming to bend toward the Taylors exit on 85.

Would you be marked? Something, if only his mind, had asked this of him. He decided he might as well accept it as truth and as metaphor at the same time. A link at the bottom of the page, beneath an expanse of yellow, read WORSHIP WITH US, but when he clicked it, nothing happened except the Frost quote falling an inch down the screen.

His finger touched the molding around the camera lens on the back of his phone, and he remembered taking photographs inside the church. The memory felt secondhand, as though he had heard the story in passing somewhere.

He opened his photos and seven gray squares waited. Whatever they would show him, it was probably best left behind, in his and Grace's past. Dozens of Lissas stared up at him below, rows of her, and he realized the photos from the church were the first he had taken since February.

He briefly considered deleting everything on the phone. Instead he tapped the first of the new images.

Light and dark had blended, or crashed together in an attempt to blend, the dark pushing back. A washed-out exposure was all he could see, a yellowed gray, with what could have been two eyes shining like coins high in the center. The next three were the same, except that he was sure the eyes grew larger in each.

But by the fifth, a shape was coming forward, melting into the camera flash and the foreground, the broad distorted figure of a person that could have been traced in pencil by a child or a left hand, its face a smudge smeared by a thumb.

And in the sixth, the pews had been shoved away from the aisle and the figure flared out at its bottom, a mass of black, robed or with long legs crouched to leap at the camera. He could see the horns now, broken antlers tipped forward like stains in the light, rooted in the eyes and breaking through the skin of its forehead. The figure's hands gathered at the waist.

Kent swiped to the final photo. The pews were restored to their rightful places. The figure was gone, the aisle a dim stripe of non-color, but a dark blurry bar bracketed the photo on each side. He stared for a minute, peering between the bars so he could avoid thinking about them, and noticed something in the background. Zooming in broke the image into pixels, but he thought it was Grace, lying stretched out on the floor.

He bent over and hugged her. *Educated in metaphor*. He had no picture of his new companion, so he took one of her curled up, her tail meeting her nose to complete the circle of her body. At the sound of the shutter, she jumped down off the bed at last, a spring in her that put his mind at ease. She lapped at her water and made quick work of the breakfast he poured into her bowl.

He debated finding another vet anyway, for a second opinion, just to make sure. But he felt a final metaphor was needed. This one would be a place, a ghost of home, and he supposed a clean slate, if that could ever be an option. And last of all, an ending. Finished with her food, Grace jumped up on him, her paws digging in above his hips. He squatted down so she could lick his face. Her tongue was cold and smelled of rich powdered meat.

He deleted all the new pictures except the one of Grace on the bed. This moved the last photo of Lissa next to the first of the dog, and he could almost hear his daughter laughing from the phone, her arms spread for a hug that he was pretending to refuse her. He pretended she wanted to hug her new dog.

He didn't need to enlarge the photo to see every detail of her the day before she died. There were three pale blue jewels in the plastic tiara she was wearing. A unicorn reared at the sky on her orange shirt. Her teeth were bared in a grin. He had memorized it all, how the pose that meant a hug was almost exactly the same as when she played her monster game, growling as she chased him around the house.

Kent knew the photo by heart, but he tapped on it anyway. It was easier to look with Grace beside him.

In the afternoon, a hundred and fifty miles of North Carolina behind the Civic, Ellie texted him: *how can you run away from her?*

South of Greensboro, they picked a motel far off the interstate. Kent gave the dog two chicken legs for her second dinner. Kent bought them raw because he read once that cooked bones could splinter and cause internal damage, and the thought of hurting her made it harder for him to breathe.

She seemed to be feeling better so he thought they should celebrate, and as the first bone broke in her jaws, it struck him that tonight was Thanksgiving. The irony, the forgetfulness, these went on the list of metaphors.

Outside was warm and damp as spring. They walked a mile down a tree-lined street, a sense of calm around them, and he felt that they had escaped the gas fumes and grime of all the industrial hubs that grew like spores along the highways. Splotches of red and yellow appeared in the oaks, a few maples. They passed a Bradford pear on the lawn of an abandoned house that could have been dipped in blood.

After several blocks, a tall child appeared and began to track their pace across the street, hunched forward with his hands over his eyes, or rather forming blinders so that the fingers extended together above the forehead. The child wore an orange long-sleeved shirt, and Kent stared until he was sure it was a boy and nothing on earth like his daughter. He couldn't tell if there was anything printed on the shirt.

The boy looked young, somehow, even with his face half-hidden, not much older than Lissa had been. But he was horribly elongated to the length of a ten-year-old, his arms folded into impossible thin triangles, his legs unsteady stalks. He took exaggerated steps, as though creeping after something ahead. The way his hands were positioned resembled horns, just as the horns of the thing in the church had at first resembled hands.

Kent felt the child watching from the corner of his eye, from under the heel of his hand. He thought again of Lissa's class that final day, the little drama about forest creatures she and her friends had been acting out. This boy could have been a deer following a hunter with a wide blank grin.

Grace growled deep in her chest, and they turned right at the next street, back toward the motel. Kent looked back over his shoulder every twenty feet, but the boy was gone.

H e was close to sleep when a TV came on in the room behind his head. Violins swirled like syrup and he drifted toward sleep in spite of them, the dog a little oven against his legs. He wasn't sure how much later it was when Grace barked a soft warning.

Kent lifted his head and saw a shape standing outside the window—through the left curtain, which was made of a heavy and half-opaque material, he thought, the word *coarse* already in his mind—a silhouette cast by the hazy light of the parking lot. The TV noise was gone. Something like horns stretched above the shape's long head, and when it leaned toward the window, he heard dull taps against the glass.

He lifted his legs from around Grace and swung them over to the floor. The dog whimpered as he stood and approached the window, the silhouette still facing him, its arms hidden. He stood there with the lip of the curtain in his hand for a long time before pulling it to the left.

Someone with long hair stood with their back to the window, leaning forward with their forearms on the railing as though to take in the view of a dozen cars bathed in muted sodium lamps. A pair of plush antlers were clipped atop their head. The way the person leaned, away from him, was an inverse of what he had seen through the curtain. And though he had heard something tap the window, he tried to find relief in such a harmless answer.

For a moment he was sure that if they sensed him, if they turned around, it would be Ellie with her nose a circle of brown greasepaint. It was too early for Christmas, and he couldn't remember a single moment of Halloween. Just that they had stayed in, kept the front porch light off.

Smoke curled up between the antlers, then a hand lifted and he saw a cigarette. Only a smoker. He let the curtain drop. Back in bed the shadow took on the shape of an indistinct hump, and finally it moved away, out of the window.

He dug his fingers into the dog's fur and massaged. Her skin was warm, but not much more than he thought it should have been.

He woke with their destination lit up in his mind, as though he had dreamed an atlas, so after breakfast he took I-40 and began driving east instead of north. They would be in what felt like the right place long before dusk.

They passed through Durham and Raleigh, the tree lines denser with ragged pines mixed with oaks and maples a month past their peak foliage, their candle flame colors mostly gone, leaving their skeletons behind. The Outer Banks, a chain of islands off the North

Carolina coast, pulsed in him like blood as he and Grace curved toward them. They would have the beaches to themselves, beaches he and Ellie had always meant to visit, before and after their daughter.

He drove across the state, stopping only once for gas and lunch off of 64. A faded sign on the road at the edge of the Shell station lot pointed into the trees, away from the interstate. Beside the arrow were the words MOMEYER CORSE BAPTIST.

"Course," he told Grace, who stood behind him in the back seat, at attention. "Not *corpse* or *coarse* with an A. Isn't that right, girl? Course it is." He laughed but still sat there another minute, at the mouth of the lot with his turn signal unengaged.

He imagined a great magnet pulling at the car, the fillings in his back teeth. In the rearview someone was coming out of the gas station with their fingers like horns over their head, a plastic bag dangling from one hand over their face.

Kent's eyes found Grace's. He could see the Lissa-blue flaw interrupting the soft brown—it had moved to the dog's right eye in the mirror's reflection. "Give me a kiss if you want to go check out this church," and he shifted his head back toward her. She turned away from him, so he got back on the highway.

The sky widened, reaching down like a palm over the land, which thinned as they neared the end of it. The greater masses of trees fell behind them, and eventually they reached the two bridges that took them over the water to Nags Head.

The Outer Banks—the name alone suited everything he wanted. It had metaphor built into it. The open air, its salt and grit, would file away his broken edges. He would be eroded into a rounder, more manageable shape. He would be mended as far as mending was possible.

The horizon laid itself out in an unreachable seam behind a great sheet of grayed blue. It was a thread he had never known to look for, and it settled a question he had not known to ask.

"This is where we're going to be, Grace," he said. The town was empty and overcast and breathtaking. "This is where we're going to be let loose."

3. COTTAGE

He was right. They had the beaches to themselves. Half the year this place was surely flypaper for tourists, but as December neared, he saw only handfuls of locals scattered around. It felt like a diorama. He ate nearly alone in restaurants as TVs played on the walls with no one to watch them.

It was good to miss his dog, even to worry about her. The world had a lonely ambient hum here, the rustle of Roanoke Sound on one side and the foam of the Atlantic on the other. All his senses were lulled.

Whatever sickness had been simmering in Grace broke apart at last, and she fell in love with Kent. He had earned her trust. Something in the way she looked at him could not help reminding him of his daughter, and he gave himself to it. They went everywhere together.

She got a piece of glass stuck in her paw on a walk their third day in Nags Head, and Kent wept for the first time in years for something other than Lissa. He disinfected the wound just to be safe and fed her steak for dinner.

He bought a bottle of red wine and started smoking cigarettes. Sand got in his teeth. He opened a checking account. And he bought a matte black handgun, a Ruger, a profoundly ugly thing that would stay in a box until February seventeenth, the anniversary of Lissa's death.

The first time he took Grace to the ocean, their first full day, a mile of shore extended in both directions, south to north. He unclipped her leash and she ran until she was a speck along the hem of water, and with a single call of her name, she ran back and then past him the other way.

The wind was cold and textured against his face. His eyes watered. He felt his mouth smiling and wondered if this could go on.

In the spring he would get a job, he thought, something that existed out in the open and far from computers. A beachfront restaurant, he'd learn to be a fisherman, an artist, he didn't care. For now he was content to take a four-month lease on a cottage just a minute's walk from the ocean—a three-room thing of weathered boards that would need a lot of work to earn any name grander than cabin, but it kept the bulk of the sand and wind out and the rent was five hundred dollars.

Soon he had found the perfect trails for him and Grace to wend their way through the dunes down to the beach, where she could run and chase tennis balls without a threat in the world to find her.

In some ways Lissa drifted from him, as though she could not thrive on the salty air or the scarcity of rich earth, or abide her father in a new climate. Sleep was difficult with thoughts of her, in a way it hadn't been before, and he felt that something more than grief had crept into him. He worried that he was profaning her memory. Exorcising her spirit. Letting time do its work and scab over his heart.

Some of the first nights in their new home, he left Grace in the cabin, briefly detaching the metaphor from her as though it were a leash, and walked down to the ocean wrapped in a blanket. He didn't try to picture Lissa there, in the dunes or splashing in the surf. He talked to her instead, the wind snatching the words from his mouth, and he listened for her closeness in his voice.

The sound of gunfire was gone. It was something he could not have done just days ago, and that was all right with him. He hoped Ellie was finding her own way.

At the end of the second week, they took the car out to explore in the afternoon. He wanted to find a smaller beach, watch the light slant onto the high tide.

The next town north was called Kill Devil Hills, but to his great relief, there was nothing he could find to the name. It was rather the opposite—a more populous section of the island, with resorts and tourist traps. There were more townies here, too. He turned around and headed south, the more promising direction, over a short bridge to where the land further narrowed to a thin needle of asphalt and dunes bearded by sea oats.

He lost himself in the overwhelming presence of water, the sense that civilization had rotted away to bare nature, climate change had been fast-forwarded here, until Grace began to bark. Up ahead was a small abandoned church, its steeple rising in a dunce cone just like the one back in South Carolina.

Kent slowed the car beside it, then stopped. The place might have been left behind decades ago. The ocean had been merciless with the paint, stripping its walls to the wood. There was no sign out front, just the words SALVO CORSE BAPTIST painted over the doors in familiar black letters. This paint looked much more recent. There were no gaps between the letters in CORSE, but somehow this made him more certain that there had been on the Taylors church.

Grace barked again and jumped against the window, clawing the glass. He didn't try to hush her. He simply sat there and tried to figure out why this was his second metaphor. What was a *corse*? The dog made sense. The Outer Banks made sense. But Lissa had not needed to be protected from a church, had she? Only something that had partly lived inside of one.

He watched the two bleached doors and began to admit to himself that he had allowed his own fear to leak into his choice, or whatever had chosen him. When he was ten he had told his parents he didn't want to go to church anymore. He had rehearsed the conversation, but it had backfired, as it always would have. They interpreted his nightmares, his sullenness, as Kent finally reaching the age of accountability in the eyes of God. That his fear was of hell, that he needed to be saved and baptized.

The truth had been bigger, harder for a child to put into words: The entirety of God's wrath had frightened him. The imagery of their little church haunted him, not so much the terror of hell and its lake of fire as the pushing of it onto him. The tending of pastures and homesteads by the congregation, God's honest work, the dirt under everyone's fingernails. The old deacons looking at him from the corners of their eyes. The women waving their hands in the air, transported to a place of light. The hymns melting together into one long drone, slipping in and out of harmony, the thin timbres of all their voices collected. The way the pastor—a new one every year or two, none stayed long—shouted about damnation, his face red, then dropped his voice into a false serenity, the slack in his line luring the sinners in.

Every Sunday had the same rhythm, to scare and shame him into repentance.

Kent's parents had taken him to church more after his plea, not less, until he was thirteen. The deacons had squeezed his arms and asked if he was right with the Lord, if his sleep was troubled, if he would go to the right place if he died in the night. The kindest sort of terrorism. God had stayed in his nightmares, the vastness of His dark complete enough to leave no room for a devil. He had His own horns.

And Kent had grown up. He had never been washed in the blood of Jesus. He had outlasted Him.

He got out of the car. Grace's barks fell into a deeper, hoarser pitch. She tried to jump into the front seat and out the door with him, but he shut her inside and walked toward the dead church. Its doors were not locked. He pushed his way inside, and the late afternoon sun filled the interior like a bowl, the way light sloughs into a forest clearing.

Pews were scattered like kindling. There was no altar and no pulpit and nothing stood back in the few shadows watching him. If anything waited here at all, it was an accidental peace.

"Course," he told that peace from the middle of the aisle. "With a *u*. I have to move on. It's okay." He filled his lungs with old air and breathed it out with something possibly new in it.

Either the dog barked louder or the church's silence diluted enough for it to reach him. Outside the sun was bleeding behind a dune. In its glare several figures surrounded the car, pressing against each other to get through the open back doors.

It was hard to guess their ages. Like the boy who had followed Kent and Grace back in South Carolina, each of their bodies seemed to have been lengthened through some unnatural process. They weren't much shorter than Kent's five-nine.

Grace was a blur through the windshield. She snarled and yelped. Kent ran to the car, and the group of children fled into the liquid of sunset, their silhouettes horned with their raised hands, elbows cocked as they crossed the road and vanished toward the beach.

The dog lay on the seat now, her chest pulsing with shallow breaths and blood leaking from crude wounds raked into her sides and belly. The church had lured him away from his purpose of protecting her. Never before had the dog seemed so perfect a metaphor, and this time Kent was able to be here for her. He got behind the wheel and turned back north. Even a place like this, at the end of his world, had veterinarians.

H is phone woke him late that night, rain brushing the roof. The dog fidgeted between his legs, a wide plastic sheath around her neck so that she couldn't tear at the bandages wrapped around her belly. Something tapped at the eastern window, and he looked across to see a shadow standing outside, a tall black shape that pulled back into the dark as soon as it had his attention.

Ellie had texted him again, *I see her sometimes*, followed a few minutes later with, *I am going to church now, it helps.* He and his wife, these inconsolables, grasping ahead in their separate throes of worship.

G race was soon herself again, never far from him now. She learned a few tricks and taught him a few of her own, such as how to know when she wanted her special spot scratched, his fingers digging into the scruff of her neck.

He bought her a litter of plush and chew toys for Christmas, a pair of soft antlers for himself. He wore them into January, smoked cigarettes in cold sunsets and thought about the person he had seen at the Greensboro motel, checking to see what his weak shadow resembled across the sand.

Sometimes he wondered why Ellie got to see Lissa, or whatever approximation she meant. If it was a haunting, he supposed he had removed himself from it before it began. It was Ellie's story. He was stuck with puzzles and hints of other children making horns at him from the windows of beach houses as he walked Grace or in the alleys between shops as he drove to the supermarket. These echoes of a daycare play that was never performed. These metaphors.

But he contented himself with hearing his daughter in the things he said to her at night by the water, Grace trawling the beach in a perimeter around him. The dog weighed thirty-three pounds now.

He painted a name for the cabin above its door, in black paint, the letters huddled close together: GRACE COURSE COTTAGE. It felt like naming a boat, so he bought a bottle of champagne and smashed it against the hull.

N ags Head stayed a ghost town without a ghost story. The whole of the Outer Banks was bare. There were no New Year's fireworks, only the still and cold stars fastened to the black sky.

He stayed close to home as the weeks unraveled into February. One morning he gave in and searched for Salvo Corse Baptist on his phone. He found the same website as before, the same Frost quote suspended in the queasy yellow—only the address had changed to Nags Head, and this time when he clicked on the WORSHIP WITH US tab, a new page loaded a grainy image of an empty beach with a black smudge emerging from the water. Near the extreme foreground was what could have been the back half of Grace's body, with either the brown splotches of her fur or blood edging into the frame.

They came for her again that night, as though having waited for him to see the photo. Kent stood in the moonless dark behind the cottage, near an Eastern red cedar, while she attended to her business. A cold breeze cut its way up to them from the shore, and for a moment he couldn't find her when she growled.

He turned and the awful stretched-out children came out of the low woods to the north with the blades of their hands against their foreheads, breathless and silent as they gathered around the dog. Her growls turned to moans and he stumbled toward the children, knocking them aside and not quite registering how hot their skin was, how they warmed the air around them.

Two of them had lifted Grace between them, struggling with the weight of her in their strange long limbs. They dropped her as he screamed and lunged at them, and she gained her feet and fled around the side of the cottage. Still the children made no sound as they ran back into the trees, flickering through the shadows like worn film. Their heat flushed on Kent's skin like sunburn as he called Grace back to him and checked her for injuries.

And the cold soothed them back inside, where he kept a vigil for her with the Ruger beside the bed on the floor. There wasn't much point in putting it back in the closet the next day, so he left it there, in the open.

Ellie didn't contact him again until the anniversary of the shooting, the seventeenth: *there's a graveyard somewhere with my name in it I can't see her anymore.*

He wrote back this time: *I thought the same thing but our graves haven't been dug yet. You have light left in you. A lot of that light is hers. That's where you can see her. I love you and I am so sorry.*

Kent deleted his wife from the phone. He hated himself for it, that he had nothing to add to what they had been. That he couldn't love her now. He pictured Grace curled up between Ellie's legs, but the image had no truth. It threatened the delicate symbolism he had constructed.

He let the anniversary of Lissa's death pass, shut inside the cabin with Grace, but went down to the beach late the next day, the first sunset of the true new year. He took the gun, the last of his metaphors. His only hope was that Grace would find a family somewhere, locals with a little girl who would treasure her.

Along the shore smaller metaphors washed toward him, were pulled back toward the seam of the horizon, lazy and relentless with static. Metaphors salted the air, wheeled over his head with white wings, fell behind him with the light to the west. The world had been stripped of its textures and literal meanings, leaving their symbols behind, all with the same import of somehow moving forward. He saw the world in imagery.

The ocean was deeply cold but Grace stood at the foamy hem of the surf, holding a vigil for Kent. The two of them had their own language now. Kent looked back toward the cottage, drawn by the sound of distant streaming gunfire, and saw something thin and tall rise up over the ridge of a dune.

The sunset cast it as an inkblot from behind, slowly resolving into detail. Its head was long and its jaw pushed outward. He saw its horns but waited for arms to appear, to know if its hands were pretending the horns or if it was the corse.

He still didn't know what *corse* meant, but perhaps this, too, was a metaphor, like everything else, the thing itself as well as his lack of understanding. Children spilled out from behind it, around the dune, five of them, and in the glare they all could have been Lissa. They were her size now. For a moment they wore soft orange shirts and plastic strips atop their heads with toy jewels catching the light, and Kent was terrified and filled with hope that he would see her come across the sand toward him.

But none of them could maintain the illusion when they ran toward Grace at the water's edge, the sides of their palms lifting to plant against their foreheads, the too-long fingers hooked into horn shapes. Their legs and arms had elongated again below the cherubic faces. The orange shirts were gone, swallowed by gray sheets like faded ghosts.

The dog stood her ground, snarling, even as spumes of wet sand began to lift around her, the sound of the gun shaking the air.

Kent reached the water before the children and took Grace into his arms, folding her in so that his back faced the dune and shielded her. A dull hammer struck his left shoulder. A fire lit up inside it. He slapped at Grace to drive her away, farther down the beach, and he watched her run until she was a sweet mote of brown and white.

Pain blossomed around his heart. He fell onto his back.

The children gathered over Kent, their faces blurring into wide hungry mouths, but a wordless keen pulled them back to the dune. They streamed toward the corse, whose arms had raised from its sides to open its black robe.

It could have been God and it could have been Andrew Butler Perry. It could have been the last twelve months, circling back to him from his earliest fears to his freshest. It could have been every school shooting that was forgotten until the next one. It was the perfect chaos of metaphor, in its way.

Something in the cold wind, in the foam of water, gave him a question: *Would you be let loose?*

The children passed between the folds of the robe, into or through. But he didn't see what was exposed there. He was tired of reading into it. He wanted to be a man with a dog, healing by the sea.

The corse watched him from the dune, its black robe pulsing and twitching with the children inside. "Let me loose," Kent told it. "It's okay." He pulled the gun and his phone from his pockets, tossed them away. He lay back and watched the sky turn to blood orange. His hand fumbled to his shoulder and came away a brighter red.

He turned his head to the north, where Grace had passed out of his sight down the beach, so that she could have been a grain of sand. He called her name and settled his head back again. Eventually the tide would come and baptize him, or something else would.

His shoulder throbbed, but fainter now, and when he searched for the wound he could not find it for a moment. The ocean crept toward him. The dune was empty in the course of the dying light.

Kent hoped that Ellie's story would have a happy ending, and he called the dog's name again, with more strength. He closed his eyes until he felt a tongue lick his face, opened them to see Grace lowering herself to the sand beside him, her own eyes expectant, the left traced with a rind of blue like morning.

THE PINE ARCH
COLLECTION

From: x_ <pinedemon@x.x>
To: Aly Duarte <alyalyoxenfree@gmail.com>
December 18 2017 3:36 am
Subject: The Pine Arch Collection

—Play the attached video and you can see, almost from the start, that something isn't right. But you don't know what. A sort of—familiarity. The trees are gasping in the fog. All you can make out for two and a half minutes are their thin trunks sliding through the white breath of a fallen cloud. There is no lamp on the camera. No night vision.

—At 2:17 a voice whispers, deep and thick. Increase the volume, reverse to 2:17: "She is sleeping." You are welcome to think it whispers something else. But there is a—familiarity. What could almost be light approaches ahead, through the thinning screen of the trees. The camera is expelled from their mouth onto a bare patch of lawn. There is the moon. Pause the video at 2:38 and see the back of your house, at a distance of perhaps 80 feet. Something huddles against the wall, a heavy black lump with arms reaching up toward a window. Your low bedroom window a closed eye. You beneath its lid, warm.

—Resume play. The arms of the heavy black lump reach closer to your windowsill. The arms stretch up with a dreadful slowness. Zoom in but the resolution decays and you can't tell if the arms have fingers, or hands. The camera holds for 43 seconds, then moves back into the mouth of the trees. The pines gather. The cloud folds around the shot again and the wall of your house recedes. The heavy black lump and its arms reaching.

—Do the arms reach the window? But the video ends at 3:59.

—We have chosen you.

—Pine Arch Research is a group of filmmakers based—locally. As the title of the attached .avi file tells you, this is *The Pine Arch Collection*. When you complete your segment, send it to demon@pinearchresearch.com. Tap your own personal terror, real as blood. Breathe it into the camera with authenticity. Recommended length is 3-7 minutes. Finished product will be uploaded to YouTube (on a channel that does not exist at the time of this writing). Complete running time unknown. Cult status guaranteed.

—Welcome.

From: Aly Duarte <alyalyoxenfree@gmail.com>
To: Bobby Power <bpower@gsu.edu>
December 18 2017 10:03 am
Subject: Shoot this weekend

Hey B. Texted you but wanted to elaborate. So something weird happened and I don't know if I can do the shoot Saturday. I might have a new project, but..........I don't know. Got an email overnight from an encrypted (I'm assuming) address. Like a chain letter but for a cheap found footage horror movie? That's what it seems like anyway. They sent the video clip with a sort of narration pasted in. Strange and pretty grim. I guess I got the most recent clip (and most recent director, if I'm right that it's being passed along like that old typewriter story game), so it's hard to say. But THEY FILMED MY HOUSE. I'm a little spooked at the moment. No, I haven't responded to the email.

But IF I do a segment for their project and I need staging help, extra eyes, whatever, would you be down with rescheduling our shoot and joining forces on this too? I think *Hamlet on Tape* can wait another week. Pretty sure you'd be into this project, if it's not too guerilla style.

Anyway, talk later?

-A

From: Bobby Power <bpower@gsu.edu>
To: Aly Duarte <alyalyoxenfree@gmail.com>
December 18 2017 11:39 am
Subject: RE: Shoot this weekend

Mysterious dudes in the woods filming your house at night? Um, that's a red flag, don't you think? You know how those movies always end. It sounds even worse in real life.

I'm cool pushing Hamlet back, but you have to sell me on this. "Doubt thou the stars are fire" and all that.

How about you come to my place after work and we'll talk about it. Your call but I'm not sure I'm super comfortable with you going back home.

Bobby

From: Aly Duarte <alyalyoxenfree@gmail.com>
To: Bobby Power <bpower@gsu.edu>
December 18 2017 12:08 pm
Subject: RE: Shoot this weekend

Sure, it's red flaggy, but it's just…the boldness of reaching out to me this way, not to mention the fact that they must have seen some of my work. I like it. I love the outré element this has and there's just something about the way it's filmed that's got my head filling with ideas, angles. I sketched something for it. Picture the woods, a pile of tree limbs shaped like a mound, with an opening at the bottom. [shivers]

I'll let you know about coming over tonight. But for now, are you in? I only need a couple of nights. Sorry to bail on you AND ask for help basically in the same breath. I'll be fine on my own with something simple if need be, but…..see aforementioned spookiness.

Also, there was this really tall Chinese guy in your surrealist film class back in school. He came out with us once. Blanking on his name, but that was, what, 6 years ago? He told me he was in this blog group that would go camp out at filming locations of cult horror movies. His face lit up the whole time he was talking. Can you put me in touch with him? I want to know if he's heard of Pine Arch Research. They are ghosts online. Can't find a thing and the URL I was given (pinearchresearch.com) doesn't exist. It would be nice to know who sent this clip where some person/creature/prop was REACHING UP TO MY BEDROOM WINDOW.

There was nothing outside this morning, don't worry. I peeked. I told myself to actually go back there and check the ground against the wall, give the woods a good stern look, but I had to get to work early, haha. It's totally fine, I promise. It's my turn now so the only creep hanging around in the trees would be me, right? Although...this clip they sent is messed up. Just wait.

Let me know!
-A

From: Bobby Power <bpower@gsu.edu>
To: Aly Duarte <alyalyoxenfree@gmail.com>
December 18 2017 5:52 pm
Subject: RE: Shoot this weekend

It would be cool if you answered your phone.

Okay, fine. I'll help...even though if some blood cult stuff goes down, you'd be better in a fight than I would. But you've won my interest, I admit it. Pine Arch Research rings zero bells for me. Big surprise, I know. ☺ But hey, unacceptable recruitment strategy aside, it's totally possible they've seen some of your stuff and were impressed!

And the Chinese guy's name is Wes Cheung. Or was. I haven't talked to him in forever but a mutual friend told me earlier today that Cheung disappeared a couple years ago while investigating…wait for it…a creepy YouTube video. Him and the other guys who ran that blog. I have no idea how much of that is true. You've seen the video, but maybe refresh your memory before you go shaky cam. *Under the House*, the one where the men are sitting outside and staring into the camera until you want to yell at your monitor for them to stop, then they go into that freaky basement with the loud humming noise. It went pretty viral for a while. Anyway, see a pattern here? Yeah, probably not, but be careful.

I wish I could ask Brit. She lives in this wheelhouse. You remember her, unfortunately. She's deep into this stuff (anything occult in film, really) but I didn't exactly deal with her well when you came along and we became an "item." And, well, you might remind me that I did inadvertently get her kicked out of school (and a festival!) when I let slip that she'd plagiarized that horror author for her final project.

How about we do your shoot Thursday and Friday nights? I can make that happen. I'm assuming your place? In the meantime, I hope you're still coming over.

Send me the video clip?

From: Aly Duarte <alyalyoxenfree@gmail.com>
To: Bobby Power <bpower@gsu.edu>
December 19 2017 7:42 am
Subject: RE: Shoot this weekend

Don't get mad but I worked late and was tired…then I went ahead and did some filming last night. And I don't know how to describe it. Let's meet up tonight after work and I'll try. That way we can both watch together. But to tide you over I'll attach the Pine Arch clip and mine, too. (The latter of which is rough as hell. No editing. Hint: It's not what it should be.)

-A

From: Bobby Power <bpower@gsu.edu>
To: Aly Duarte <alyalyoxenfree@gmail.com>
December 19 2017 5:23 pm
Subject: RE: Shoot this weekend

Aly. Why won't you answer your phone or text me back? And why did you shoot thirteen minutes of darkness? Is that the woods behind your house? It's just that I don't remember it being foggy last night. What the hell is with all the breathing and that laugh? And the clip these people sent to you. The way theirs ends and yours begins. How did you manage that continuation…editing? Or you met up with them? Come on, we need to talk. That THING under your window is the creepiest shit I've ever seen.

I'm sitting at home. Tre is out with friends. A bad feeling here. Come sit on my couch, let Sebastian purr on your lap, and let me see that you're okay. For solidarity I've got my camera right here. It's waiting to lend a hand.

B

From: Aly Duarte <alyalyoxenfree@gmail.com>
To: Pine Demon <demon@pinearchresearch.com>
December 19 2017 10:12 pm
Subject: The Pine Arch Collection

I need to bow out. I don't know what your game is here but this is too out there for me. Yes, I'm stubborn. Yes, I've tried shooting this scene four times now, even in the morning when the daylight fills the trees, but in playback it's still night with thick fog and someone (plural?) that's not me breathing just off camera. There's a cold sort of gleam on everything, but it's underneath the dark, somehow, I can almost see the pile of limbs the shot is approaching back in the woods. I saw it fine when I was shooting it in, you know, the DAYTIME.

It's like a hut that's collapsing. Did you Pine Arch people build that? It's basically what I had in mind for my friend and me to put together this weekend specifically for my segment. I have the story notes. SO...how is it there already?

There's not much land behind my house. At this point, where the stick pile is, you're not far from the creek, then the slope down to Camp Mile Road and up again toward the old nature reserve. I picture your crew with a black van parked down there on the ribbon of road, hiking up the hill in your dark clothing with a fog machine and a roll of twine to lash all those limbs together. I mean...at the very least wait until I say yes before you go into production design on my property.

Bear with me. We're parting ways at the end of this email.

Four times I filmed this. Night, day, morning, evening. Each was a little different but not different enough. I did a test shoot of my kitchen and on playback it's my regular kitchen, morning light streaming in, like the bland establishing shots at the beginning of a found footage movie.

"I'm a normal person with a normal life, look at me before I start this fateful day," said the doomed filmmaker, whose disappearance has been a mystery until this video was found, etc.

So it's not the camera, is it? You can kind of see things happening on the screen, out in the woods, you can hear those long half-whistle breaths I should have felt on my skin they're so close, but it was just me in the milky daylight walking through the woods with nothing but leaves crunching under my shoes.

And then that fucking laugh. Christ. I didn't actually hear that, so how did it get into my camera? How did the fucking night get into my camera, for that matter?

I kept trying, and on the fourth attempt I figured I'd turn the night vision on even though it was 4 p.m. and it was business as usual. I get back to the pile of limbs and everything's quiet, no creepy laugh, only the sun corroding out to the west and this calm cold.

Except in the footage. In the footage there's the laugh and when I approach the pile of limbs something is crawling out of the hole in it. It's low to the ground, a green-dark shape, another lump with the night vision failing to stick to it, as ridiculous as that is to say. Not so ridiculous when I watch it now though.

So this time I play the role, I've got the night vision on in the sunshine. I turn and run and I give up. You can hear me whimpering and saying, "Oh God, oh God" as the camera bounces and the trees whip by as I run. Everything has that night vision phosphorescence. The streaking and the panic. You've got your staples. I ticked your boxes, so good work, although you know the *Blair Witch Project* guys already did that way back when, right? Kept their actors in the dark (literally, hahaha ha) and tried to scare them into this authenticity you're looking for? I'm sure you know that. The word "research" is in your name.

AND. Not to mention the worst of it, that every time I play the footage back that THING, your "heavy black lump," is pulling itself up into my bedroom even though I didn't film the window. You see it glitch out and then supposedly it's IN my bedroom. My back was to the house. I was walking into the woods when I started recording. THE CAMERA WAS FACING AWAY FROM IT. So I guess I have to move or never sleep again. At least in *Blair Witch* their cameras were actually allowed to film, you know, what they pointed them at. They had some autonomy.

Anyway, I'm attaching the .avi of all my takes with the request that you go ahead and move on to the next person. I am a filmmaker, not an actor. I am not a test subject. There is no pinearchresearch.com so who knows if anyone will read this. Either way, don't worry about an explanation. This isn't working out for me. And please don't shoot any more footage at my home. Don't come anywhere near my home.

Sincerely,
Aly Duarte

From: Aly Duarte <alyalyoxenfree@gmail.com>
To: Pine Demon <demon@pinearchresearch.com>
December 20 2017 1:21 am
Subject: RE: The Pine Arch Collection

Please stop this. There is something in my house waiting for me to film it. Is it the lump? It won't show itself until I turn the camera on. Please call this off and

Ok what if I do a scene going through the house checking all the rooms until it finally reveals itself? I'll use my camcorder with the fold-out screen and watch it as I go, so I can see it. I can give you heavy breathing and gasps I can frame the shots well then cut to black when the camera finds the lump and it's rising up at me and I leave and send you the file and we're done. give me a few minutes I'll be back. will you tell everyone to stop and will you reply so I know you're even getting the email?

From: y_ <pinedemon@y.y>
To: Bobby Power <bpower@gsu.edu>
cc: Aly Duarte <alyalyoxenfree@gmail.com>
December 20 2017 3:40 am
Subject: RE: Shoot this weekend

—Play the video and you can see the arms reach her window. They lift the sash and move into the house. The heavy black lump slides up the wall to follow its arms. At :51 the image pixelates and freezes. At 1:08 it clears and the heavy black lump is no longer on the screen. It is understandable for you to wonder if the pixelation is a digital trick, to make you think the heavy black lump has entered her bedroom.

—The open window stares at the camera for more than one minute. It gapes. It resembles a mouth more than an eye now. A voice whispers at 2:24, deep and thick. Increase the volume, reverse to 2:24: "Where is Bobby?" You are welcome to think it whispers something else. But there is a—familiarity.

—Distortion rolls across the screen and the house is gone when it has passed. The shot is moving in perhaps the opposite direction, through the woods at—night. Pine trunks puncture a ground fog, pull it into threads. Thin musical breaths seem to stretch out from both near the microphone and farther from it, breaths that take 10 seconds or more to exhale. Too long. The camera stops, the sound of leaves crackling and shifting stops. The shot tilts down then gathers a white-green tint as it lifts back up, and visibility is increased. Something laughs. Someone, you tell yourself. Not something. You think it must be her, though it is pitched low and distant.

—And the shot continues forward until, at 4:08, a shape pulls itself from the fog. The shape resolves into a mound. It is difficult to see. You think it is constructed of oak and birch limbs, the latter of which is a species of tree that is sparse in this region, which could mean the maker spent time finding material. Perhaps the birch was transported here. A hole has been crafted at the bottom of the mound, like a mouth, or a window. Pine boughs curve over it.

—A figure crawls out of the hole, not unlike a spider the way its arms are elevated to show the sharp silhouettes of its elbows, the way its legs jerk and drag along the ground. It moves out of the mound with such slowness, such inevitability. It could be the same heavy black lump. It could be another. This is unclear in the dark, and the night vision does not reveal the figure to you as it should. You hear only the sound of leaves rustling in a soft storm of movement. The shot turns and flees, a wild sense of motion. The strange breaths have ceased and are now her breaths, quick and rasping.

—You think of how everything you have seen happens in a straight line. The line does not deviate into the trees. House to mound. Mound to house.

—The scene cuts out then returns inside her house. An hour has passed, there is a timestamp now that reads 1:26:41. :42. :43. :44. The quality of the image has changed, the screen is shaped more like a square box. There is more grain. There is yet more—familiarity. You recognize this frame, her kitchen, the small table with her pale green backpack, her dim hallway as the view turns and slides into it. It is her camera.

—Watch her hand reach into the shot. Light floods the sink, tub, toilet, the empty narrow bathroom. You see a wedge of her reflection in the mirror, dark curly hair, the fine bones of her face. Her wide frantic eyes.

—She says, "Please, no." The shot retreats and continues down the hall, unsteady, her hand pushing doors into rooms and fumbling inside to flip the light switches on. She leaves the lights on in the rooms, in a breadcrumb trail. Until her bedroom is the last dark thing.

—The door at the end is partly open. The door is incomplete and you wonder why. Pause the video at 6:13. You think these are the same reaching arms from her outside wall, creeping out around the door as they crept up to her window. Zoom in but the resolution decays and you can't tell if you are in fact seeing those arms, whether there are fingers, or hands. Behind them, in the dark bedroom through the gap of the door, is a shape.

—Resume play. But the video ends at 6:16. The timestamp ends at 1:29:08. You think of how you could almost draw a straight line from kitchen to bedroom.

—We have chosen you.

—Pine Arch Research is a group of filmmakers based— locally. As the title of the attached .avi file tells you, this is *The Pine Arch Collection.* When you complete your segment, send it to demon@pinearchresearch.com. Tap your own personal terror, real as blood. Breathe it into the camera with authenticity. Recommended length is 3-7 minutes. Finished product will be uploaded to YouTube (on a channel that does not exist at the time of this writing). Complete running time unknown. Cult status guaranteed.

—Welcome.

From: Bobby Power <bpower@gsu.edu>
To: Aly Duarte <alyalyoxenfree@gmail.com>
December 20 2017 8:05 am
Subject: WHERE ARE YOU

Hey this is not cool. Called you, texted you, DMed you, went to check on you, nothing. I just got back from doing three laps around your house. Your lights are out. Your car is gone. I'm freaking out a little over here. Just tell me you're okay.

Speaking of not okay, I got one of those Pine Arch emails. With a new clip. With you in it. And my name. And that creepy thing. I took a lot of deep breaths and with each one I told myself that this is your segment. You're just helping them make a movie and I'm the idiot here. I'd love that. I'd love for it to be just really effective marketing and I'll accept their invitation and join in the fun. Just PLEASE TELL ME I'M THE IDIOT HERE.

But the email they sent was in our "Shoot this weekend" thread, so either you're in on the joke and cc'd yourself or something is very very wrong.

Got my phone on me. Blowing off work today. Will be back at your place again. JUST CALL ME.

From: Aly Duarte <alyalyoxenfree@gmail.com>
To: Bobby Power <bpower@gsu.edu>
December 20 2017 8:42 am
Subject: The Pine Arch Collection

—It's fine B. I'm fine. This *Pine Arch Collection* thing is really interesting.....it's sort of all about asking you to decide what "found footage" really is, what you can trust, perception, etc. Like anything that doesn't involve hearing my voice or physically being in my presence in real time. And what is horror as fiction if it's not horror without proof? So you'll forgive me, pretty please, for not giving you those two undeniable signifiers, my voice and presence. There can't be too much—familiarity.

—I can't believe we haven't been making horror movies this whole time. You'll see.

—Give my love to Sebastian and tell him he'll see me soon. I miss being coated in his fur.

—Aly

From: Bobby Power <bpower@gsu.edu>
To: Brit Evenson <evenson.song@gmail.com>
December 20 2017 11:32 am
Subject: Help! Need info

Hey Brit, long time no anything. I'm sorry. This is urgent but I don't have your phone number anymore. I know I dropped out of your life and you're probably not my biggest fan, but you used to be into occult stuff and you did your thesis on folklore in British horror films (I think it was British). I need your help if you have any expertise closer to home.

There's a supposed group of DIY filmmakers around here (assuming metro Atlanta) that call themselves Pine Arch Research. They're fucking with my friend Aly. Yes, that Aly. I'm really sorry but they're inviting her to take part in some weird found footage movie. Everything feels off and I think she might be in real trouble. I'm attaching the clip they sent her to build off of, along with the first bit of footage she shot for her own piece. This was from yesterday morning, I think.

Aly and I are only friends now but I'm still just as worried. She won't answer her phone or her door. I don't think she's home. She did email me back to explain why she won't answer but she wrote something that the real Aly never would: she called my cat Sebastian and she NEVER does that. She always calls him Seba. She always tells him and my roommate to not let me call him Sebastian. It's not much. It could be her going along with their project, like a performance piece or something. But I don't think so. I think they have her computer and are reading my emails with her and then posing as her. I know it sounds crazy.

I'll be going back to her house later and I'll break in if I have to, but in the meantime, I really really need to know about these Pine Arch people. I'm sorry but this is important. I could be filing a police report tonight and I'll be refreshing my email on my phone. If possible, please call instead at 678-392-4006.

Thank you so much, Brit. I can explain the rest later when there's time. And I'm sorry about everything back then.

Best,
Bobby

From: Bobby Power <bpower@gsu.edu>
To: Aly Duarte <alyalyoxenfree@gmail.com>
December 20 2017 9:42 pm
Subject: RE: The Pine Arch Collection

Still not convinced I'm the idiot here. Still hoping I am. If so, I'm just glad you're okay. I'm coming over again. *Hamlet on Tape* can be shelved a couple of weeks. Hell, a year. Sebastian misses you, too. Almost as much as I do. I don't want to type this sentence but why did you call him Sebastian you never do that?

Love.

From: y_ <pinedemon@y.y>
To: Bobby Power <bpower@gsu.edu>
December 21 2017 2:17 am
Subject: The Pine Arch Collection (new .avi attached)

—Seba. Seba. Tell Seba we miss him.

—You see yourself knocking on her door. The viewpoint is from the eastern corner of the house. Her car sits in the driveway, the front third of it in frame. You ask yourself if you have been allowed to return to your own home so you can sit there now, warm, reading this, watching yourself knocking on her door.

—What color is Seba?

—You pound on the door, shout her name. 1:47 into the video you come down off the short porch and walk toward the camera, which withdraws toward the rear of the house until it is enclosed in the darkness of the first trees on the edge of her property. It watches you walk, almost run, behind the house and stop, scanning the back wall. Farther down is the door leading into the house, into the kitchen. You do not even try the doorknob, you break a pane of glass and reach through with your hand to unlock it.

—Just before you enter the house, there is a laugh, somewhere behind you, from the trees. You turn, thinking it must be her, but it is pitched low and distant.

—Inside the kitchen you turn the light on by the door and see her pale green backpack, the cluster of her keys on the table beside it. You watch yourself do these things through the door you have just opened. The camera has followed you. A spear of broken glass floats on the right side of the screen as the shot moves close.

—A scream strains to find you from the rear of the house. It slows into a long groan that sounds fuller, watery, somehow closer. You watch yourself shout her name and step forward into the hallway and disappear into the gloom there.

—The shot cuts to a gloved hand closing the kitchen door. At 3:52 the camera follows you into the hallway and makes the short turn toward the last room. Wide bars of light fall from the doorways leading to it. Her bedroom door is fully open, a narrow mouth.

—You are standing halfway between the camera and the end of the hall. You say her name twice. The same low laugh from outside comes out of the room and the dark line on the floor at the opening of the bedroom begins to push out into the hallway, into the light, across the fine old wood boards. The arms, pause the video at 4:11, they are perhaps the same arms but they have hands, and fingers. There is no need to zoom in and decay the image resolution. You see a face follow the arms out of the dark. Her face is underneath the face smiling.

—The POV shifts to the side, enters the bathroom, anticipating your turn and sprint back up the short hallway. For a half-moment, the mirror is there on the right edge of the screen. You see an ear obscured by dark hair, a gloved hand bisected by the strap of the camera, which blocks the rest of the profile.

—The sound of your running feet. The shot turns away from the mirror and into the kitchen as you roughly open the door. You are gone, your scream pulling apart and fading in the night.

—What are you saying as you struggle toward your car? Has anything crawled from the woods to meet you? You have a camera in your home. The authenticity would be more chilling if you had brought it, as you were asked to contribute. But in footage that will be presented as "found," the discerning viewer will criticize the camera operator/ protagonist for continuing to film in scenes of great personal duress. Though limited in this certain way, here are a colder eye and a steadier hand.

—Tell Seba we miss him.

—The shot moves back into the hallway and turns. The heavy black lump pulls itself along the floor. Her face lowers with a wet moaning hum that lasts until the scene goes black.

—And returns to an empty hallway. And goes black.

From: Bobby Power <bpower@gsu.edu>
To: Brit Evenson <evenson.song@gmail.com>
cc: Pine Demon <demon@pinearchresearch.com>
December 21 2017 4:10 am
Subject: RE: Help! Need info

I don't know who else to reach out to. The police went to Aly's house but it was empty. I got silence when I asked to file a missing persons report. An uncomfortable laugh when I asked for help. Do you know anything about Pine Arch Research or a kind of...I don't know how to describe it. A crawling shape like a person something that's like half tar. I think it got her. I think it might BE her.

There aren't actual woods behind my house, just some huddled trees before the next street, but there's a mound made out of limbs just like the one Aly saw at the back of her property in her video…their video, I'm not sure which anymore. It has the same "pine arches" curved above its mouth. They made a mound for me and put it just inside the trees where I can see it from my bedroom window. I filmed it. I didn't go up to it but I filmed it. Nothing came out of it and nothing is climbing up my wall either.

I'm attaching the video I made so you can see. If you noticed a cc on here it's because I'm adding them to this email, if you're reading it Pine Arch please just leave Aly alone. Leave me alone it's enough I did a clip for you. It's not my fault nothing is happening.

I searched for Pine Arch Research again and this time I found a short story on Google books that has a film group with the same name. It's fiction though. Seemed like a vampire story. Do you know Kirsten Mester? I know you had a friend named Kirsten back then. I used to call her your cult buddy.

I think I was jealous of your film, Brit. It was an amazing work and I wouldn't have knowingly let it slip that you'd plagiarized that writer. I didn't even think it took enough from Ligotti to actually really be plagiarism. I didn't know then you'd taken whole chunks of text and plot wholesale.

And telling Ken—I don't know, I didn't think of him telling Wes, I didn't think of Wes being in that "film haunt" group and taking offense and what a mess that all turned out to be. It was just a stupid thing I did.

Please tell me you know how to help my friend. I'm scared. I've never been so scared or so tired.

Bobby

From: Bobby Power
To: Pine Demon <pinearchresearch.com>
December 21 2017 10:52 pm
Subject: please

Attaching an hour of the mound out back. I was outside, sitting there. Waiting for it to come out and whose face would it have? Aly is this you? Let me help you. Nothing happened outside but at the end of the hour I get up and turn back to the house and you can see the creature at my wall reaching up to my window. What the fuck. My window is higher than Aly's so I don't know if I'm supposed to give it a boost? Leave the window unlocked? Leave. Please leave me alone. Just leave me alone.

From: Brit Evenson <evenson.song@gmail.com>
To: Bobby Power <bpower@gsu.edu>
cc: Pine Demon <demon@pinearchresearch.com>
December 22 2017 12:28 am
Subject: RE: Help! Need info

—I shouldn't respond, but it is precious of you to reach out. The clips you sent are interesting, rough. From what I gather, Pine Arch Research is a group of filmmakers based—locally. They seek authenticity. These days, I do as well.

—You mentioned expertise. And folklore in horror films. That is one way to put it. You might think it's not my place to say, but perhaps you and your Aly should take your lumps.

—It is also interesting that you don't recall the name of my film you ruined. *A Birch Coffin*. Birch. Huh. Not a particularly southern tree. However, I thank you for at least the semblance of an apology. But ask yourself something—what IS a horror film? It provides you with ingredients. As someone recently mused, it asks you to decide what you can trust. You want to decide. And what is horror as fiction if it is not horror without proof?

—I'm happy to say I haven't thought of Cheung in some time. He met up with his own monster, I hear. Time to move on. And Kirsten is typing away in the next room, in fact. She has her own concerns. I will tell her you said hello.

From: y_ <pinedemon@y.y>
To: Bobby Power <bpower@gsu.edu>
December 22 2017 12:44 am
Subject: The Pine Arch Collection

—Click here to watch a live video feed.

—Blackness pales to darkness and movement. The quality of the image has changed dramatically, vertically oriented, a widescreen tipped onto its side. The shot turns to display a hole framed by woven tree limbs, the hole it has come out of, then rises and moves until the entire mound is in the shot. Oak and the rare birch again. The camera swings back to face your house. Your woods are shallow. You have so few trees.

—You can see the arms, stretched so long now, reach your

window. They lift the sash and move into the house. You did not lock the window. The heavy black lump slides up the wall to follow its arms. The image pixelates and freezes. Several seconds later it clears and the heavy black lump is no longer on the screen. It is understandable for you to wonder if the pixelation is a digital trick, to make you think the heavy black lump has entered your bedroom.

—Seba is black with white fur around his neck like a scarf. His front paws are white.

—On the live feed you see yourself from behind. You are seated at your desk, the pale glow of your monitor bleeding onto you. Your bedroom doorway frames you on the screen. Zoom in but the resolution decays and you can't tell if the arms reaching across the room for you have fingers, or hands. The discerning viewer will criticize you for remaining seated in a scene of great personal duress. It is time to decide.

—Someone laughs. You think it must be her, though it is pitched low and close. You turn to face the camera with authenticity.

—Welcome.

From: z_ <pinedemon@z.z>
To: Pine Demon 2 <demon2@pinearchresearch.com>
December 25 2017 9:47 am
Subject: merry xmas (footage is over)

—Hello Evenson. We collected their computers and cameras. We collected their remains. See forwarded threads and attached clips.

—The footage has been edited. Upon your review, we will upload the finished film to a Pine_Arch channel on YouTube. As you can see, we have taken the liberty of incorporating several shots scanning ("reading") the email threads from each of their computers. (We see instances of your name and email address due to your surprising decision to involve yourself. You are welcome to excise/obscure these.)

—The email threads are cut into the film as an ongoing narrative between the two subjects you chose. We believe our own contributions, as curators, add to this narrative as well. The questions that are raised, we find them to be key to the film itself.

—Their heavy black lumps have been released into the woods. Perhaps to your birch trees. But at least to the pines, so prevalent here. *The Pine Arch Collection* is complete. Cult status guaranteed.

—You're welcome.

THE TIRED SOUNDS, A WAKE

The Tired Sounds

Lorne has been paying attention. His wife used to ask him to be better about that, to listen, to notice things. Before she started painting and became the distant one. But he's been trying, anyway, though it's not for her, exactly. It's even less for himself. He supposes it's for them, that separate third they make where they overlap, but even with the word *divorce* hanging all summer like a leaden cloud, his new alertness seems a discrete part of the whole.

The word came from his own mouth, after all. It was a stone he had to spit out, and he's been looking at it since, its fluids long dried. *Divorce.* Wanting to swallow it back.

He sits bowlegged on a public toilet, pants up and belted, and his thoughts loop and land again on the way a husband and wife fit together, rub against one another, pull away, look askance. Nothing with urgency, all this subtle motion. The complacency and the hesitance. It must be like getting your sea legs, some long voyage with the same ovals being walked into the salted wood of the deck, while the far green thread laid down across the horizon draws closer with a sort of agony.

But you do arrive. You're not quite where you thought you'd be. And these frictions, when they are gone, reveal a great island of tedium, smooth and ordered as a fresh calendar. Their absence reveals lesser sounds.

Lorne is in the restroom because there are kids everywhere outside it, a pestilence of them. He's shut away from the birthday party, and the way his wife feels in his head just now is strange. Out of true, in a way that reminds him of repeating a word until its meaning turns to mush and a brief surreal ecstasy drops over the mind. *Ambulance* has always been a go-to word that does that to him, and he murmurs a string of them at the tiled floor.

He whispers the word *divorce* but its sourness doesn't change.

He has a bit of stomachache but not in the way that can be relieved here. The cigarette, tilted up so it burns with less smoke, is the reason he's hiding. Lately it's struck him that if Gwen doesn't know he still sneaks these things, there's a point in there somewhere. There's an elephant in their room.

Their twenty-fifth anniversary is in two days. They've mentioned it only a couple of times, and he can't even remember the context, the wording that was used. He thinks they were in the little studio she made for herself in the attic, where she only half-listens to him at best.

The laughter of children swells suddenly into the restroom, one shrill excited scream shearing through, then fades again to a distant riot. Lorne imagines the heavy door easing shut on its pneumatic elbow. He considers pitching his cigarette into the toilet, anticipating that angry hiss, but takes another drag instead.

A man of forty-nine smoking in the boys' room, tempted to stay in here and wait the party out. He shouldn't have another, though. His wife won't come looking for him for a while, but he has to make sure he doesn't reek when she does. He forgot his pocket can of air freshener.

Normally, when he really wants one, he would sneak off to a secluded hideout while his wife's busy telling someone about her new piece, slip around two sides of a house, down into someone's woods or the shed out back of the rec center. But heavy blowing sheets of rain, an hour of them now, have ensconced him in this public stall with the last half-inch of his cigarette.

For a moment, a vision opens in him, and he thinks of seeing early stars glaring between quilted clouds in an August afternoon sky, an afternoon far removed from the one outside. But even through the sudden clarity of the image, the room around him comes into a greater focus. Its acoustics sharpen in his ears, and he realizes he is waiting for the next noises to follow the opening of the door.

The squeak of a rubber sole. A throat clearing. Teeth parting in a zipper.

He hears nothing but the dimness of the party beyond. Some kid must have pushed the door open, then, and seeing it was only the restroom passed back into the fray.

Lorne has already forgotten the name of the birthday girl. Cara? Coral, that's it. The youngest of their friend Kay's brood. Coral. It's a precious name, the kind millennials fall for, but he admits to himself that the waft of fifties nostalgia has a nice feel to it. He relaxes a degree, puts his head in his hands, the ember of the cigarette close to his fingers now.

He's never cared for children. Never liked the way their screams when they play together sound so much like terror. To be a parent is surely to always have that shock-brief moment where your baby is being torn apart by wolves on the other side of the playground.

He has never liked the sheer drama of them, either. The crust in their nostrils, the constant needs and wants and everything with extra vowels shoved in to emphasize the life-or-death severity of the moment. And this is only what he has observed, before getting to go home and hide himself away in the garage with a Scotch and, in better days, a few Camels.

He shudders to think of that delicate quiet broken, but Gwen is beyond That Age. Thankfully. He once would have said she was enough for him, before she started painting. Before he started, belatedly, paying attention.

What about now? Now, here in what must be his midlife crisis, he still doesn't wish for children. He only wonders if they should have something to drown out the tired sounds of marriage.

The door of the stall next to his creaks, a soft and careful movement. It is an alarming, piercing noise in its smallness, but still he could almost pretend he hasn't heard it, until he sees two shoes under the wall for half a moment before they spring up and out of sight.

They are not a child's shoes. The silence falls again, just the distant surf of the party, which has receded, perhaps. The waiting thickens, Lorne only knowing someone is standing on the next toilet.

He won't give up his last drag, though, he sucks it through the wet filter then reaches down and grinds the butt out on the inside rim of the bowl, just above the water, keeping his eyes pointed up at the top of the thin metal wall. He has enough time to feel cheated out of the hiss of water eating the ember.

Something appears just over the wall, creeping up. It's a hand, in a white glove. It reaches higher and is joined by its mate, two pale spiders wriggling their legs upward. One hand makes a fist and lowers; the other raises itself and does the same. They repeat the motion, grabbing the air, clenching, pulling the air down toward their owner. Lorne sees it as the climbing of a rope, and soon a face begins to show itself at the top of the wall.

The forehead is painted a blind white beneath curls of orange hair. The eyes are a blue that the August sky of Lorne's imagination couldn't match, oddly pitiless eyes holding the reflection of the fluorescents like those daytime stars. Stars are painted around the eyes as well, north-south and east-west, black eyeliner diamond lines.

Lorne jerks away from those eyes, strikes the tiled wall to the right with his shoulder. "Jesus," he says, and laughs.

The gloved hands continue to climb the invisible rope, pulling the face completely above the wall. The rest of the face is also coated in white greasepaint. Two black circles punctuate the cheeks just below the southern tips of the stars, like the muzzles of revolvers, things Lorne could gaze into.

"Excuse me," Lorne says, "a little privacy here?" He aims for glib and falls short, his voice sounding trebly and frightened. The thought that Gwen would be filing this man away for a new piece won't leave his mind, and there's a wedge of anger to it. His fingers slip another cigarette out of his wrinkled pack, muscle memory, clinging to the routine of this motion he once performed thirty or more times a day.

The mime's face is still, and the hands have fallen back below the wall. The mouth, painted white to the point where the lips curve inward to darkness, parts. It parts slowly, in a way that magnetizes Lorne's attention, so that he must witness each segment of the lips' skin pulling away from its counterpart, the glue of tissue and paste and saliva tearing open. An unmentionable thread of white mucus clings to the left corner of the mouth, stretches to its tightest resistance, and snaps, draping across the lower lip.

Only then, unknown seconds later, does the mouth begin to collapse and expand into a great O, a bemused hole that doesn't change the eyes above it.

And Lorne simply leans back against the wall, watching a man that surely, simply, is here for a little girl's birthday party, yet he feels he is also watching a chrysalis unfold into some new nomenclature. He dreads the tongue that might emerge from that mouth, and wonders what color it would be.

One of the hands appears again, its index finger and thumb curling into a circle. They rub against one another, then straighten into a pincer and reach into the hole of the mime's mouth, disappearing to the second knuckles. Lorne pictures them grasping at the tongue, slimy with paint, but the hand pulls out and the fingers are empty, still shaped in a C, turning some unseen treasure back and forth as though gesturing for Lorne to admire it in the fluorescent light.

Those beautiful blue eyes, frozen in the long moments before a thaw, do not blink, or crinkle with amusement. The eyes don't leave Lorne's eyes. The mime tosses this non-object out and down to Lorne, who in spite of himself cups his hands to receive the gift, unable to quite deny or acknowledge the impact against his palms of some small weight.

Then the mime straightens himself, the thin white and black

striped shoulders appearing for the first time, and the hands flatten themselves against a barrier of space between their stall and Lorne's. They search, edging left and right along the border of air, pressing lightly forward.

The cigarette Lorne's not allowed to smoke falls from his hand. It strikes the gray tile at his feet and rolls under the door into freedom. Its escape jolts Lorne to his feet just as the mime's hands push through the air, as they slide down Lorne's side of the wall and the white face follows, the blue eyes wide and cold.

The stall door bangs the wall and Lorne's sneaker crushes the cigarette, scatters shreds of tobacco across the floor. He crosses the narrow room, snatches the door handle and bursts into the hallway outside the gymnasium entrance, its own doors wedged open by aluminum feet, the tidal excitement of the kids growing more substantial with every step.

The children and several adults are gearing up for a game of dodgeball. He sees Kay Powalski spread herself into an uncertain X, shifting her weight from one leg to the other, stretching. He sees Bruce Allan, his neighbor from Lampe Street until Bruce and Tamara divorced last year, shouting with false cheer at kids to line up.

It all has the momentary look of a painting, one of Gwen's with her hard putty-knife texture, but Lorne doesn't see his wife anywhere.

"Mr. Campion!" a kid yells across to him, a boy with a striped shirt—it takes a moment but it's okay, the stripes are red and white and too wide. The gym looks like a gym again. "Come play!"

Lorne has no idea who this child is, who he belongs to, why he would know Lorne's name or invite him to do anything. He considers approaching Kay, confirming that she hired a mime for the party, but the scene tells him no, the children braced with sugar rushes for dodgeball, unless—unless the mime performed just after Lorne crept off for his smoke.

At the back of the gym, finally, he spots Gwen. The new silver in her hair glints in the light as she pushes open the door into the charcoal rain outside. It seems to him that he can hardly remember the sound of her voice.

He traces the flaring curves of her just as he always has and hopes he always will. Another picture forms in his mind—her heavy breasts soaking in rain, how her chest would heave in the shock of cold water in the warm air. All the freckles clustered in that V. It's been too long.

He turns and looks behind him, but nothing fills the doorway that leads to the restrooms. There is only the dark hidden gleam of a water fountain. His left hand is clenched. He unrolls the fingers but there's nothing inside—nothing, but still he pulls a pocket of his khakis out before depositing that nothing in a safe space.

He walks along the fringe of the swarming children and follows his wife into the rain. Somewhere above them, reaching down to refract through each drop, are the glittering stars.

A Wake

Gwen has been quiet. Most of the words and their sharper edges have been forced into her paintings of late.

Her husband fidgets on the drive home, the wiper blades cutting into gusts of rain against the windshield. She and Lorne are still drenched, having walked around most of the rec center through flooded late-summer grass to get to the car, and she's seeing him as she usually does only after he takes a shower, his blond hair clumped into darker segments that show how dramatically his hairline has receded this past decade.

A moment ago he asked her something about a mime at the party, but she hasn't answered him yet. She opened her mouth to say, *Yes, the poor thing looked lost*, but realized that it wasn't at all her answer. *What do you mean, a mime?* is closer to the truth, but she did see something in the rain when she left the rec center, a bright shape fading around the corner of the building.

She waits to speak, though, letting the rope play out between her and Lorne for reasons she is tired of understanding. Almost tired of translating into whorls of color.

The rain has brought the soured cigarette smell out of his clothes. It's fragrant and awful, but she doesn't say anything about this, either. It strikes her that she's still in love with him when he commits his little sins. They bridge the gap between Good and Now in some way. She's spent the last two years—since his proclamation of going cold turkey—hiding her smiles when he finds reasons to spend a few minutes in the garage, coming back stinking of Febreze with a wrench and a flimsy excuse for needing it.

These moments have been harder this year, but she's needed them.

He turns left onto their street, at last, the percussion of rain on the roof like handfuls of grit. She realizes she didn't say goodbye to Kay, didn't stay for cake or to watch Coral unwrap the Erector set Gwen had gotten her. She simply felt it was time to leave. The nearest door caught her eye. She doesn't remember anything she could call an explanation. It's an unhinged sort of feeling.

In the driveway, she turns to him and makes herself say, "What did you see in the bathroom again?" while watching the water draw lines from his hair down his face, then gather at his jawline and fall to his lap. His hands have fallen there, too, palms up. He flutters the fingers of his left hand. The fingers of his right hand are folded, as though pressing something between them.

"A mime, Gwen," he says, turning to her, "white painted face, doing mime—you know, motions. Whatever you call them." His hands lift and press against an invisible wall, seeking a way around it. His right fist stays loosely clenched.

Gwen laughs. "I don't think Kay had a mime coming. Maybe. I don't remember. A funny choice, though, over a clown. Do you remember when it would rain and we'd wait it out in the car listening to the Cure or one of those sad rainy groups?" She's looking out the window again, at their house warped through the sheet of water. She hasn't said this much to her husband in weeks. "It was nice when sadness was kind of beautiful, and you could feel good about it. And we had to wait until the song was over, it was the rule. And the rain would quit."

Someone is standing at the far end of the house, by the corner of the porch, a smear picked out against the tall pine fence bordering the Ramiro house.

She peers through the window and watches the figure watch her, then it seems to—cartwheel away, around the side of the house, and she isn't sure she saw anything at all. Even now she could imagine another figure in the first's absence, if she wanted, inscrutable as the rain makes her yard. Would this new one turn a cartwheel too?

She looks back at her husband, almost reaches out to touch his cheek.

His hands are back in his lap. "I liked that rule," he says. "You know what the day after tomorrow is, right?"

"Of course I do."

"Just two days. You haven't mentioned it much." He sneaks a look at her, and years fall off his face.

"Well," and her breath goes thin, "neither have you. It's our silver. We're getting up there, hon."

"We are."

She doesn't say, *It's hard to get that old sad love song vibe after what you did in April.* "Let's go eat at The Standard," she does say, and smiles at the old joke, or tries to.

The first time she ever saw Lorne was at The Standard, three months after she moved to Atlanta, three years before they settled in Durham. They ended up at a corner booth until last call, and two hours after they parted ways, their first kiss still humming on each other's lips, the bar had burned half to the ground. An electrical fire. They slipped the word *sparks* into their origin story and rested on that anecdote's laurels for years.

She notices he's hard, the khaki tight around those rigid inches. Her hand twitches over toward his lap, a reflex of old habit, but he's lost in thought or memory. The yard is empty now, or still empty.

The uneasy light is like milk through the moonroof, swirling on their legs, and the rain won't let them go. There's no cure on the radio for it.

Gwen wants to say "Come on!" and rush into the downpour, feel it wash her because she hardly registered its texture outside the party earlier, but instead they stay where they are, and their silence grows layers. The rain will stop eventually because it's what rain does, or she will grow weary of waiting for it.

The Tired Sounds

Lorne wakes from a dream lost to him even while he was inside it. There was a moment in its passage, something he could almost slip into a pocket and bring into waking with him, but it too dissipates in the dark just as he fumbles at it, as elusive as whatever imaginary thing the mime gave him. Gwen was standing at a canvas, and he could feel paint drying tight on his face, but the rest is gone.

The nights are stretching further into the morning, the pink-edged black pressing at the curtains. With a powerful ease he imagines the mime under their bed, this very second staring up through the box springs and through the mattress into Lorne's spine, tracing the nest of nerves there. But what would a mime be doing under a bed? They create their own boxes of space in which to seek refuge.

The character of the bedroom's silence, its slow resonance, opens to him. He jerks his head to the left, horrified that Gwen has died during the night. He watches her breathe as sleep pulls away from him and the room's contents draw their shapes out of the gloom. His dresser is a low dark thing hulking across from the bed. A drawer is ajar, a pant leg hanging out like a pale tongue.

He shudders at the image, then looks at the top of the dresser, where there's an ashtray, a huge glass relic from the days when folks smoked wherever they pleased. It's where he keeps his keys, spare change that will end up sucked into a Coinstar machine, and other detritus from his days.

He remembers emptying his pockets last night, and his face heats with a low-grade shame at the idea of an invisible, intangible thing waiting for him in the ashtray. The idea that he saved it, placed it delicately aside for examination.

What would that gift be, if it were real? What could disorient him at the edge of morning? His mind has been clear. Most of his thoughts the last few months have been of a slow awakening. Of his senses and his sensitivities to them. He's been paying attention to Gwen, he reminds himself, and the emanations of their marriage. Figuring out how to fix things.

And with a sudden inspiration, he thinks of a new, better anniversary gift for her. It is obvious and perfect. The Victorian teapot hidden out in the garage, as gorgeous as she proclaimed it to be in the antique shop months ago, seems to become infected with verdigris as he lies here picturing it, its soft silver reflection wrapped in two old flannel shirts. Lorne can almost see it tarnish and dull, lost to another time. Another them.

He checks his phone on the nightstand—not quite six. He'll leave early for work. He'll take an early lunch or just leave early. It's not too late for early. Silver isn't gold. He dresses quietly, his skin taut in one of the first mid-September chills that always surprise him, year after year.

When there are only his keys and wallet to attend to, his hand pauses above the dresser, the empty half of the glass ashtray yawning up at him. He stands looking at the vacant, or not vacant, half of it for too long. What would Gwen think of him just now, frozen by something neither of them can see?

He groans and scoops it up and drops it into his left hip pocket. Turns to look at his wife one more time, wishes he could reclaim the nerve to wake her with a kiss. Instead he blows her a kiss that feels more like an apology, something that is breaking through a shell and striving to be born.

A Wake

Gwen listens to her husband creep around the room, peeks at the hint of him standing at his dresser as if lost in prayer, until a soft moan seems to spur him back into movement. He runs a hand through his hair, something he does when he's frustrated, caught in a torn moment.

She senses that he's getting dressed earlier than usual, but all she knows is it's nowhere near her own usual. Gwen is a deep sleeper now and doesn't rise until eight most mornings, when she makes her way into the studio and all those canvases she can't fill fast enough.

He kisses his fingers and puffs air at her before leaving the room. Maybe that warm little conversation they had yesterday was what they needed. A tiptoed step. She watches the line of light around the window grow from rose to an orange-yellow hint, forming a slow portal to something in the dark.

Brief kitchen noises, the pert chime as the front door opens, then she hears gravel pop and grit its teeth under the car tires, and he's gone.

Gwen turns onto her side, letting her mind fall back to far before Lorne.

She grew up in Vermont and misses it most upon waking. She misses rising early in the ice-floe mornings and carrying the first cup of coffee writhing with steam to the pond, a walk of less than two hundred feet. The texture of itchy wool thermals under her pajamas, under her parka, settling into a chair on the small lip of a dock. Unwinding from sleep as the sun slid above the horizon across the water, like a coin rejected from the earth. The almost tangible stillness in a green country she could believe had never dreamed of humans, and still was slow to acknowledge them.

She thinks of childhood, early womanhood, with a greater frequency now. Because she's getting older, but more because she isn't supposed to be a painter. Where did it hide as she grew into herself? Never once did she feel an urge to paint that pond, draw that sunrise fermenting the water's surface. She wanted to be a doctor at first, was somewhere near the top of her undergraduate class at Dartmouth, far enough outside the cum laude circle to leave the tang of regret.

But she drifted, after. She told herself she'd buckle down in med school, then headed out to Scandinavia to breathe the clean air of her forebears. A string of hostels and European villages threaded out across the pot-seeded pages of her atlas, little felt-penned pricks and daubs.

From '93 on she was a trust fund kid. The thought still could strike her with a profound shame. Even worse was that her focus hadn't kicked in until Atlanta, until perhaps that night at The Standard. It seems she needed Lorne to focus her—even define her, she has come to fear.

Painting has helped. She mixes these things in with her earth tones, clots them in bold strokes of her streaky reds. It thickens her bond with the old, slightly feral Gwen.

In '99 she and Lorne started Campion Financial and she found herself, as though fast-forwarded out of a lazy dream, essentially working for her husband. Never mind that the last of her share of the Burke nest egg had funded it. They were partners, they called her role "the important side of things," but the clients asked for him when the phone rang. Campion had been his name first.

She always saw herself doing—well, something. Something real, whatever that used to mean. But she tripped up and never found it.

Until, she supposes, she wandered into the art supply store down on the square that morning early last year. She still doesn't know why she drove over to Durham instead of going into the office. She always loved looking at paintings, would have gone to museums more often if she had any like-minded friends, or if Lorne wanted, but her knowledge was a shallow thing, something she never saw the point of deepening. Standing in the shop that day—she remembers her face scrunching up in confusion, smoothing out in fascination.

What followed was such a strange blur (months of blurs, her hands doing things they had only hinted at) until March of this year, when she decided to do nothing but paint. Clarity found her for the first time. Telling Lorne—she wishes that were a blur, too. The conversation didn't go well.

How she's gone from a glorified bookkeeper to a celebrated artist so quickly is still a vast enigma to her. It makes her feel like a fraud, and a dizzy one at that. An artist does not simply bypass amateur in her late forties and go straight to being talked about in those chatty little art circles.

She needs a calibration, a frame by which to view the transformation. Before, the family house in Monkton was always her reset button. Her affirmation that she still had one hand on the wheel. But there's no family left and the house was sold in 2015, effectively drawing the line of her life no more north than Virginia or so.

Something is under the bed, she realizes. Someone is under the bed. If only she rolls onto her other side, cranes her neck out, she'll see the ball of a shoulder, the rind of an arm, waiting for her down there with the dust.

She wants to know how real this feeling is, whether it's a certainty, so she lies still, thinking of Lorne's weird half-story of the mime at the rec center, thinking of the figures she probably didn't see outside the party and cartwheeling around the side of their house. She closes her eyes and places these things in a line. She feels watched but doesn't know how.

There are the small noises of someone wriggling out from under Lorne's side of the bed, as quietly as possible except for the errant knock of a heel against the floor. She goes stiff but won't open her eyes, she's astonished that she's keeping her eyes closed with an intruder in their home. The waiting is delirious and she wonders if Lorne felt anything like this in his bathroom stall.

There is the sense of movement but without the press and creak of footsteps across the hardwood. Chills crawl across her skin.

The bedroom door clicks shut and Gwen raises herself onto her elbows. The moment has passed. The visitor—the intruder is gone.

She places her feet against the floor, only for a second anticipating the circling of cold fingers around her ankle, and stands.

Still, she has to know who is in the house with her. She hears a soft crash from the hallway, the attic stairs being pulled down. Then another groan as they're pulled back up. Crumbs of mud trail along the floor, a faint smudge of white on the doorknob.

Outside the bedroom, the stairs are snug in their beveled frame in the hallway ceiling.

She passes them and goes into the kitchen. Nothing stirs in this part of the house, just the pooling of silence in recently vacated rooms. But the ceiling creaks over her head. The weight of a presence. She looks up as though expecting a crack to form there between two beams.

There is a heaviness in her chest, somewhere near her heart. The visitor can just wait. She decides to have a grapefruit before climbing up to the studio—or calling the police. The other half of yesterday's is still in the fridge, and she cups it in her palm, examines each sliver of meat. They're just sacs filled with acidic juice, thousands of them clustered in their chambers. Pink translucent maggots. A little hive, a microcosm.

Gwen lifts the grapefruit and buries her face in it, scissoring her jaws and digging. Tears burst from her eyes. In this moment she's so powerfully angry with her husband, with his idiot disregard for their relationship, the dynamic he steered them into and she enabled.

She gnaws her way into the feeling, mashing the pulp, her mouth flooding with saliva, then lets the mess fall to the tiles. The cloud over her vision slowly unravels. Her breath steadies. The sour fire drains from her sinuses and she spits into the sink.

"What the fuck am I doing?" She wipes her chin, not even sure if she's spoken the words aloud. Her husband has been putting in the work, never mind that he's fumbled at it. He's trying and she knows he regrets what he did. She has her own regrets.

She pulls the phone off the wall, holds it for a moment in her sticky hand. But then she returns it to the cradle, passes back into the hallway, pulls the cord to bring down the attic stairs. The picture window up there faces east, already spilling dawn light across the studio and down onto her face.

A distant rasping. It takes her only a fraction of a moment to identify it as a brush against canvas. She can feel her hair like live wires fanned across her skin, crackling, the brown and gray alike, the maroon straps of her top cutting into her shoulders. The tears still standing in her eyes. There's a faint, maddening itch around her waist from the elastic band of her pajamas pinching her through the night. Her curves have grown fuller.

She stalls by removing the rubber band from her wrist, bunching up the hair she's been thinking of getting rid of now that fifty's so close, and fashioning a quick ponytail. The square of light over her head continues to brighten.

In the beginning she painted stumbling, hackneyed blobs of impressionism: the furry teeth of the Appalachians, midtown Atlanta locked in a rare blizzard, scenes from their courtship travels that had been filed away. Intro to Art History was all the foundation she had to build on, really, and it was cobwebbed in her past.

But only in the beginning. Quickly, in the fall of last year, her work grew bold and outré. From "Picasso on designer drugs," as one wine-slurping hanger-on loudly proclaimed at an opening, to stark depictions of timeless paintings—such as Goya's iconic Saturn translated into his wife, the earth goddess Ops, in a maternity ward, a place Gwen has never been, a piece she titled *After Birth*—Gwen found her oils stretched across a gamut of expressions that were hardly traceable.

But what is she really *saying* with her work? She fears that this, too, comes from Lorne. As though she's speaking into the cavity that has opened between them, so that its contents, or its vacancy, can be examined. It is a hollow sound, an empty wind, like singing into a conch shell. It deepens the voice.

Suddenly she can't imagine her opening at the Shain down in Charlotte. How can it be less than three weeks away? *Artificial Pine*

Art, fourteen new pieces using only blues and earth tones, with one piece, *Dead People's Things*, expected to go for as much as eleven thousand dollars. A humiliating amount of money, a buzz that has already drawn phone calls from two galleries in Manhattan.

She takes hold of the stairs. Pulls herself up, emerges into the attic ready to see what has invaded their life. There's a flurry of movement at the window as the floor drops below her eyes. A handful of small rust-brown birds—robins, maybe—wheel around the oak beside the house.

The studio is empty, but the realization of this is slow to come. The seven-foot stretched canvas she's been saving as its purpose germinates is on the easel, turned vertical so that it towers like a cream monolith over her.

She lets herself acknowledge that such a tall canvas could never stand on the easel on its own, that someone must be behind it. She notes, too, more slowly, that she sees only the legs of the easel on the floor.

It is the canvas itself that draws her attention as she approaches it, and the crude strokes that have ruined it. A figure inside of a rectangle, both painted in a clumpy red-brown that glistens like fresh paste.

"Red Georgia clay," Gwen whispers. It isn't but it's close, her fingers come away streaked with a darker, grainier soil. And something else, sticky as mucus. Egg wash, from the tin on the workspace desk. This shape—it's the almost-finished outline of a person, a woman, judging from the bell of the head, where hair would fall to the shoulders.

She tells herself there's no reason to assume this nearly unbroken line would fit her contours, but there's nearly every reason. It's her house, her studio, her visitor, and the ponytail she's pulled her hair into is the only snag in the feeling.

A pair of small black boots sink to the floor behind the easel, scuffed, mud-caked. Gwen steps back from the canvas. She doesn't stumble. Her voice is almost steady when she asks, "Who's there?"

From the right side of the canvas—Gwen has been imagining herself painting her first Madonna with child on it, something malformed, like a zoomed-in Bosch treatise—a ridge of bright orange hair appears, long winding curls, within which rests the bleached sliver of an ear. A fan of fingers in a white glove stained with dirt lift and curl into a cup behind the ear.

Then an eye slides from behind the canvas, cold blue and wide, unblinking, at the center of sharp blades of black paint that form a cross. Its face is whiter than the glove, maybe whiter than the glove was before its fingers dug into the earth. The blaring shade of white she keeps at the beginning of her row of paints.

"What do you want?" Gwen says, and the mime's face leans farther out from behind the easel, the hand flattening into a pillow for the cheek against the striped shoulder. Those red curls tumble out and Gwen is sure it's a woman, Lorne was wrong, or did he even say it was a man?

She can't remember, but she sees the woman's plump mouth now, painted white and beginning to smile at her. The eyes glitter in their dark nests.

The two women stare at each other, locked in waiting, until the mime's body falls, an elbow cocking out to land gently upon an incline that isn't there, into a casual repose. A stained white finger points at the canvas then presses, erect, against the lips, then repeats these motions again and again until Gwen takes the first hesitant step toward the strange mud-painted outline. The mime's other hand appears with a paintbrush and tosses it at Gwen, who catches it and pauses.

The mime stands upright and shoves the easel over, her mouth drooping toward the chin. She steps toward Gwen. Another invisible wall is there, and her nose and mouth flatten against it. The gloves press against the wall and strain forward.

Gwen stumbles back and comes within a step of falling through the scuttle into the hallway below. But she catches herself and descends the stairs and shoves them up into their accordion.

She sits against the wall and hugs herself, staring up at the square of ceiling. Sour grapefruit juice stings the back of her throat again. "What do you want?" she calls up into the gaps around the panel, and thinks of that shape on the canvas, the edges of her skin already half-fitting into it in her mind. It had been more than just a box painted around the figure of a woman, but her mind couldn't grasp it.

She considers telling the visitor she's leaving, the house had better be empty when she gets back because she has so much work to do, she's calling the police. But she doesn't.

She realizes she still has the brush in her hand. It's little more than a twig with pine needles and stiff aluminum foil taped on. It's not a thing with any practical purpose. What use would a mime have for a paintbrush? Why does she feel no threat from this woman?

And the house has gone quiet, a deep silence as though the appliances have been unplugged, and she wonders what she'll tell her husband about this bizarre haunting they apparently share. The quiet spreads until she becomes a part of it. She makes herself rise, fetch her purse, and go out into the day and its lingering wet.

The Tired Sounds

Spores do their work in the damp and the dark, his father always told him. They build flowers, they construct little petals of architecture that bloom into cities under the microscope. Lorne can take a deep breath—the air is starting to get that clean spearmint taste of the fall—and bring who knows what into his lungs. He can release the breath in a cloud of apprehension or relief, and who knows what will remain a part of him for a time.

As a child, Lorne felt colonized simply by being in the world. He dreamed of metropolises spreading through his body. The monsters were never in his closet.

His father was a mold remediation contractor. He would tell Lorne these things while he looked forward to flood season, because wet basements meant work, and asking folks if they'd had anyone check between the ribs of their houses. From a young age Lorne knew he wanted a job when he grew up that didn't mean he had to want bad things to happen to people.

He's never figured out whether he went into insurance to help guard people against men like his father or to help those men get paid. Probably more of the latter, but he only knows he doesn't thrive when tragedy creeps into people's lives and takes their money just when they were starting to get ahead, turn a corner. He benefits when these things are still scenarios, little pieces of fear. When they never come at all.

Lorne sits in his office, leaning over with his elbows on the desk, not sure why he's thinking of his father. He pushes his keyboard off the blotter to expose the mostly blank calendar, September thirteenth circled in black and ANNIV written in blue. In the empty box of the fourteenth, the mime's gift sits unseen, and Lorne nudges the place where it would be if it were there, straining to feel a pressure against his fingernail.

The whole place has felt frayed at the edges since Gwen quit, and part of Lorne paying attention has been to make sure he understands exactly what that means. Martin is the junior agent, and a quiet younger guy named Julio answers the intermittent calls, full time since Gwen started painting.

Carla, his lead agent, is out with a client, for which Lorne is blessedly grateful. It's easier when he doesn't have to ignore her in person.

The big fight with Gwen happened right here in this office, and Lorne sometimes feels the vibrations from it still trembling in the walls and the floor and the wood of his desk. He imagines the spores of those words neither of them really meant continually being pulled into his lungs, to thread through his vessels and capillaries and linger in his thoughts.

The firm is suffering without his wife. It's not a grievous wound, it never was, and even less so now. She's pointed that out to him the two or three times she's even glanced at the numbers on the computer at home. It is pride, the pride that went before his fall.

He has tried to stare it in the face, so that he might see why his pride was damaged enough for him to end up at a bar that night, drinking whiskey that wasn't smooth, that didn't sit smoldering oaken in his mouth before easing down to warm his belly. And why he texted Carla of all people—though who else would it have been, with his social life?—tipping that lead domino over.

It took an eternity of eight more days for it to happen, all those days he could have turned away repeatedly, domino after domino, innuendo after innuendo. Never mind that it was a fumbling attempt that he gave up on halfway through, crying against Carla's shoulder.

And what he had done to Gwen's painting, before—

He nudges the space over September fourteenth. What is this thing that isn't? A lucky charm…he turns the possibility over in his mind, enjoying the pleasure of it. It's what he's wanted it to be from the start.

He's the type to not be physically able to leave a heads-up penny on the ground. For more than half his life he carried a St. Christopher token in his pocket, though he's never been spiritual, much less Catholic, and still isn't exactly clear on what St. Christopher was the patron saint of.

Lorne doesn't know if he can go through removing this un-thing from his pocket every night, depositing it in his ashtray while hoping Gwen never notices. Then slipping it into a fresh pocket the next morning. But he enjoys a talisman, and he could especially use a lucky charm.

Now he lifts it and moves it to the right side of the desk, next to his reading glasses. How would he ever know if he lost it?

He straightens in his chair, breathes out, and pulls the keyboard back over. Wakes the monitor up and Googles "renew our vows." He can't help but laugh. What if she says no? It's the few days after The Standard again, a lightness in his stomach, a sweetened dread, with the twenty-seven years between made to feel like a circle. A loop he has tread into the floor of their life, ending where they started.

But a loop can be made into something good—a ring, a beginning, a re-promising.

Julio knocks and tells him Ms. Glavine and Mr. Blyleven called, both semi-urgent. Lorne waves him off and turns to his computer. The search results are gone and the screen has loaded a web page for Decroux House, a white stone place half an hour south of Raleigh. It has a history in its seams, between the stones, that calls out to him from all those pixels.

He taps the phone number into his phone, slides the keyboard away again and writes the name of the place beneath ANNIV on the blotter. A coiled weight slips from his shoulders. He sighs in the lightness.

The blinds rattle two feet behind him, but he doesn't jolt from his chair. He takes his time turning on its pivot. Nothing is between the blinds and the closed window. He stands and pulls the slats out, but sees no smear of white paint. No one is crouched in the bushes outside.

It's hardly noon and there are still two days' worth of work to do. He shouldn't fob it off on the others. But he wants to call Decroux House and ask about their rates. Maybe even visit, see it with his own eyes.

He's thinking of invitations, any relatives Gwen has left that she'd love to see, cursing himself for the rashness of the timing. He's thinking of flowers and learning which bouquets would best represent the occasion. Working himself into the tux he hasn't worn in a decade.

He tweezes his lucky charm between his fingers and slips it into his right front pocket. His blazer, his shoulder bag, the spring in his step. The itch to go and do. Because he has to salvage his marriage, now that the scales have fallen from his eyes.

Out in the lot he sees right away the shape of a figure in the back of his car. Bright white hands pressing against something, the back of the driver's seat, maybe, or thin air.

Lorne stops with his keys hanging off an index finger. The fear and awe come back to him, the shock of that first hand appearing above the restroom stall only yesterday. He can't look into those eyes again, and he can't return the lucky charm.

He realizes he's whining, low in his throat, his fingers slipping down into his pocket to curl around what isn't there. A wind brushes through the trees, shaking the leaves and waking the silence he didn't quite notice before. The trees, a pruned wall of pine and Norway spruce, shiver around the arc of asphalt that hems the building in, seven or eight cars marooned.

"They sold trees," he whispers, and the words sound as beautiful as they always have to him. A familiar ache twinges.

The sound of his voice gets him moving. He's hardly started forward when the back door on the far side of the Accord opens and he can only glimpse the mime loping hunched into the trees. Black stripes on white, or white on black. A shock of orange hair swallowed into the green needles and the little corner of Durham grows still again. Mud gleams dull through the wet grass.

Lorne holds his breath as he reaches his car, pushes the back door shut. He slides into the front seat and scrutinizes the console beside him, the cup holders and passenger seat, saving the back of the car for last. He sees nothing out of place. The little door on top of his travel coffee mug is ajar, but he's mostly sure it was like that when he parked.

It strikes him that the car could be full of things he can't see. The floorboards could be littered with charms and crucifixes and coins that could never be spent. The thought shortens his breath, floods him with what feels like a panic attack, a thing that never left his life but hasn't intruded like this since college.

Will his world be refracted into what he can and can't see? He could have walked hundreds of streets and wooded trails with tokens, little treasures dangling from the sky on gossamer thinner than the naked eye, hanging just above his head.

"He pretended to give me something," he tells the cabin of the

Accord, the air that's stale with the scent of yesterday's rain, and perhaps a trace of greasepaint. "What else would he have done? Is a box he's trapped in really a box? No, and you've got nothing in your pocket but an imagination."

Saying this doesn't make it feel quite true, but it gives his lungs depth, it slows the prickling on his scalp that always felt like a cold fever when he was a teenager. He'd sit in his closet away from his three brothers, head between his knees, until it passed.

If the mime gave him something, it is important, but it should push him closer to Gwen, not veer him off into abstract waters. Their horizon is all he wants to care about.

The trees near the car rustle again, as though to disgorge what they accepted a moment ago. A smudge of dark emerges, a black cat flashing yellow eyes. It pauses to regard Lorne, then passes in front of the car. Lorne sketches an X on the windshield with a finger, repeating a gesture his grandmother often made when he was a child and she was still with his family—warding off bad luck, though she usually would draw it on the air. His hand falls to the top of his thigh, almost feeling a negligible bulge there in his pocket.

The cat runs across the lot, spooked, and vanishes around the side of the building. Lorne pops his key into its slot, starts the car. Before reversing, he turns and sees the white face peering out at him from the copse of trees, the orange fringe between branches. The black stars of the eyes watch him and tilt on some axis as the head nods slowly. Lorne is pierced against his seat, until Decroux House begins to ring through his head again like a mantra, a bell.

The face doesn't withdraw, but Lorne does, pulling the car back and forcing it out of his sight. He cranes around to check the backseat. There's a penny where the mime was sitting. It's on tails but Lorne doesn't know if the motion of the car caused it to slide and tip over.

He can't pick it up now, and he has to assume it's a bad omen. Or the mime telling him something, warning him.

THE TIRED SOUNDS, A WAKE

A Wake

Gwen loses herself near the Gothic thrust of the university. An idea has fallen over her as surely as the masculine gloom of Duke's vast chapel. It's a thought she's been fighting, and she already promised herself she wouldn't do it. She can't just rip the scab off the marriage. Not when it's fresh and still itching them.

The morning has grown strong, yesterday's rain steaming away. She puts the chapel behind her and finds a bench along a narrow quadrangle of grass, needing the sun on her, the warmth pressing against her scalp and burning along the part of her hair.

The idea, its reemergence, requires her to pause and relive the night she came home and heard Lorne up in the attic, the sound of smashing, her heart in her throat. She knew what he was doing while her key was still in the deadbolt. How could she not have? He never went up there, and their fight was still ringing in her ears.

The attic stairs had been pulled down, and a silence stretched out as she hesitated, clogged with his heavy breathing. His wheeze from all the years of cigarettes.

A final thump of something hitting a wall, and she climbed on numbed feet, knowing not only what he'd done but what he'd done it to. Telling herself to remember they had each transgressed, if in different ways.

The painting Lorne destroyed had been her favorite. No, more than something so trivial as her favorite, it was the piece that had told her she could endure, that her name might be spoken decades after she was gone. Such a strange, breathless thought to have. When she finished it, a last dab of deep red blood that bloomed in the priest's cheek, she stepped back and saw the breadth of her talent.

Students might one day study her, auditoriums full of them gazing up at her paintings projected onto white screens. They might want to take road trips to the museums that held her work, stand in front of it in quiet.

It was a long way from the unpainted, still pond behind the house in Monkton, her parents asleep as the sun rose, the whole of

Vermont under a quilt and scared to come out into the cold. A long way from The Standard.

She called it *A Wake*. Sooty black had claimed the negative space of the painting, playing at Goya's darkest hour and the mad despair that must have swallowed him whole in that Spanish farmhouse. She remembers the way her putty knife felt in her hand as she scraped that black nothing nearer and nearer to the focal point.

A coffin sat left of center in the picture, plain, pine, the kind of rough thoughtless wood that would give a bouquet of splinters to a sliding palm. Around its bottom was the suggestion of a hole in the earth, twice dug, coated in that black.

To the right stood the priest with a shovel raised in his hands as though to stab downward into the coffin. His face entranced Gwen, the resignation dulling the sheen of horror in the widened eyes, the open, almost writhing mouth, all framed by dirty gray mop strings of hair. And gathered around were five peasants, four women and a young boy kneeling, each soiled beige and contorted with a similar dread. They held candles aloft toward the figure in the coffin.

But they laughed, too, with teeth that were the slightest bit too pointed, and this had bothered her. It bothers her now, in the sunlight and the open. It felt and feels horribly occult, something that has never piqued her interest much.

The coffin had been empty for two weeks, both on the canvas and in her mind. The priest was attacking nothing but crumbs of grave dirt that littered the box. The vacancy there had been the whole point of the piece for Gwen, and part of her wishes she had stopped at her intended mystery, before she added Lorne. Yet most of her misses the anguish she got into his face, the raw death she had wrenched out of the maw of his mouth. She shivers in the heat.

Her husband, in the painting, was dressed in rags and a funeral shroud. Even the shroud was rough-grained, like a sheer sort of sackcloth. His knees were pulled up in defense, his arms a cross to ward off the shovel blade and his face peering out from their shelter.

His eyes, when she finally painted them, had looked straight at her, no matter where she stood in the attic studio, with a final question.

Her husband, that night in her studio, when she emerged through the floor, his chest heaved, his face was sheened with the sweat of exertion, his hand bled from a long gash on his right thumb. The broken frame, the hanging strip of canvas already curling. She couldn't look at him and so she looked down at the floor, the thick splinters strewn there as though from the coffin. Her heart had stopped and now thudded in her to catch up.

"What were you thinking?" he said, panting, and she knew he was waving the flap of canvas at her, wielding it, so she raised her head and let him almost hit her with it.

"It's just a painting, Lorne, I would never—" But she didn't know the rest of the sentence. Should she have admitted the obvious metaphor? That their marriage had grown stagnant and she kept blaming him for it, to the point where she couldn't even put herself in the piece at all? Those four women had been too round, too rosy. Too present. But she had never painted herself into anything. That was the only reason she hadn't taken her share of their fault. Wasn't it? The metaphor of *A Wake* grew cloudier.

"You're throwing our business away to do *this*?" he shouted. "To act out little fantasies where you, what, bury me alive? This is sick. We should probably talk about a divorce." But she was spared the monotony of why, and he was spared the kindling reciprocation of her anger, when he stormed past her and down the stairs.

All the sound dropped out of the air. The word *divorce* fell to the floorboards, leaden. She listened for the slamming of the front door. For a long time it didn't come. Until it did, and a heavy black line was drawn between them.

She's painted more since *A Wake*, better work, her skill burning with impatience from the decades she didn't know it. A few of the pieces in her upcoming show are technically superior and are lighted with their own almost preternatural voices. But that broken painting— her heart clenches in her chest, months later—had a rich and atavistic pull to it that would have started murmurs of conversation rippling across the gallery floor. All those black-tie moths would have swept toward such a bleak flame.

And she had *adored* it, with a deep shame and something like lust.

He's only brought up what he did to the painting twice, once in passing and once with a half-hour of tears that thawed her a little. In the latter he blamed his temper, which had still been running hot after her decision to leave the business.

Mostly he brought up his fear of burial, which she has always sensed has something to do with his father's obsession with mold. Both she and Lorne have the wish for cremation detailed in their wills. It was Lorne's idea because he can't bear the thought of being shut in a box and slowly eaten by nature.

But Gwen knows another reason for his anger. She has seen her husband's gravest secret—the half a novel hidden in his old desk in the garage, not only shut away in her least frequented part of their home but sandwiched between photocopies of old policies in a folder marked CANCLD 2002-3. She doesn't remember what she was looking for the day she happened across it five or six years ago, only that she pulled the folder out to check behind it and a sheaf of papers cascaded to the oil-stained floor.

The pages had not yet taken on the yellow of age, so she couldn't guess how recently he had written them. The old desktop PC was out there, Lorne could smoke out there, and he had little pieces of free time out there. *They Sold Trees*, the title page read, and something stirred in Gwen at that. It was an evocative, mundane sentence. It pulled her down onto his swivel chair in a powerful curiosity.

There was real talent, but the prose within could not come close enough to the odd power of the title. She hated herself for feeling such gladness that he had never asked her to read it. For a few minutes she considered hiding the hundred-odd pages inside the house for later, but decided to skim instead.

She read about a man who, to escape the idyllic malaise of his modern life, took to volunteering in soup kitchens and ultimately, it seemed, chose to be homeless and give up his family and the life he had built for them. American Man Finds Himself. At least in the first half. If there had been more, such as the titular trees that were sold, it was still somewhere in Lorne's mind. She imagined the title coming from the protagonist's childhood. Her husband is a Rosebud kind of man, after all.

But how strange it was, to learn that your partner of nearly two decades (with the rest to follow, it seemed then), the person whose nearness kept you warm in the bed even though he was the one who wanted the ceiling fan on, the only person you knew by heart, could harbor—or at some point had harbored—a creative drive.

Gwen, at the time, was far from cutting her own essence open and seeing what her blood looked like. There was no stirring of kinship that day. But now she understands, and she cries a little for him, in a different way than she teared up in the garage with those pages in her lap.

She found rejections slips in the folder, too, for short stories that weren't there, that had been thrown away, perhaps. She replaced everything the way she had found it, or close, meaning to ask him about his secret dream but somehow knowing already that she wouldn't. Surely it was something he would rekindle and bring to her, if it meant enough to him. Maybe he had found himself in some smaller way.

A Wake, then, must have been a perfect, gouging storm of disappointment and jealousy for Lorne. A reminder of his failure. Of her success, her ascent, her independence, her discontent with their relationship.

Still, regardless, even though, she wants it back. She wants to paint it again. It's been hanging in her mind ever since April as starkly as it would have on a gallery wall. But she needs to know if she would soften that look on Lorne's face the second time. If the priest might not hold a Bible now instead of a mud-stained shovel. Or if she might simply paint the empty coffin.

Concessions would leach it of any power it held in its original sorrow and horror. And she doesn't know if Lorne would let himself understand that, or if he should even try.

The visitor from this morning, Lorne's mime turning her attention upon Gwen. That vicious pointing finger. Is she being told to recreate the painting? To place herself in the coffin instead? Why is she sitting on a bench downtown while an intruder roams their house fourteen miles away? So many unfathomable questions, but this last one finally seeps into her, and she is finally afraid.

She takes her phone from her purse. Past noon. She has walked with her vapor thoughts trailing behind her for longer than she thought. Her message app is open and she taps Lorne's name, wanting to say something to him that will make a bridge between that little moment they had in the car and today. That little moment they almost had, rather, but it can be close enough.

I think your mime is contagious, she taps out, then stares at the words for a long time. Her thumb is poised over the send arrow. She feels someone watching her, and when she looks up there's a small cluster of people sitting on a blanket near the bunched trees behind the Rare Book and Manuscript Library building. They are not obvious in their watching, but there is something in their postures.

And at a distance to the right, a figure leaning on a cane is shading its eyes and peering nearly at Gwen, but the angle is wrong. The face is hidden in the shadow of that flat gloved hand. It is much too warm for the gloves, for the overcoat that might hold a white and black striped shirt in its shadow.

She deletes the text, replaces it with, *It stopped raining. We can get out of the car now.* It's letting him off easy, maybe, but she's tired. She sends it and gets to her feet. From the corner of her eye she sees the figure in the long coat approaching her, still a hundred or more yards away. The group of people by the trees are folding up their blanket. The blanket is striped, black and white.

Gwen hurries back the way she came, turns and passes the towering dirt-colored chapel, feeling the adrenaline dump into her blood. The back of her mouth tastes the way oil paints smell.

She cuts down a lane, passes under an arch. Such a sprawling campus this is, and she still has no real idea why she came here in the first place. She lets herself turn and look back.

The woman—she thinks so, a man wouldn't move so roundly—is closer than she was, and the cane is gone. Or there never was a cane; her hand is curled in a loose fist as though gripping one, rising and pushing down, and her body tilts to the right with every other step. Gwen still can't see the face clearly, but it's not pale enough to be painted, she thinks. Or hopes. But the long coat hangs further open now and she sees the stripes across the shirt.

Then from the right, a small knot of trees, three younger, shorter figures lope into her path, and Gwen runs. She doesn't stop again until the campus becomes a sudden forest and she plunges into its cool dark. There she lowers herself to her knees and gasps, the sprint stitching hot pain in her side.

There's no one following you, Burke. The rough bark of a spruce seems to dig into all the right pressure points in her back, and she begins to calm. Her maiden name. She's been calling herself Burke more and more lately, if only in her head. Ever since the gleam of posterity began to color the way she sees herself. Testing it, imagining telling Lorne, a great silence building in his eyes even as she says it, that she will be shedding his name for her work, too.

She peeks back the way she came but nothing moves in the gaps between the trees. But something tells her to stay where she is. She pulls her phone out of her pocket and calls Lorne. It rings several times but never goes to voicemail.

A Wake comes back to her as she waits among the first dead leaves. She'll use a smaller canvas this time so that it will be done before the opening. And she feels it deserves a smaller stage. People should stand closer to it before it disturbs them back a step. Just the thought of recreating the black void around the scene has her itching to stand up, brush herself off, and find her car.

She does stand, surprising herself—she didn't really mean to. She approaches the southern line of the trees, away from where she entered, and sees the figure in the coat in the distance, walking back toward the chapel.

Her phone goes off in her hand, the vibration startling her. She sees her husband's name on the screen and is relieved, somehow, that he called back. But her thumb won't move. The old anger is back from its brief absence.

At the edge of the trees, just before she steps back into the last hot day, another paintbrush is lying in the grass, still-green pine needles rubber-banded around a twig. Gwen stares out of the shadows at the retreating figure, past it to the smudge of the chapel in heat glare, wondering what men are entombed beneath the church.

The Tired Sounds

Lorne parks in the small gravel lot and stares at the modest grandeur of Decroux House. It sits back from the road in a pocket forest, speckled with birdsong and pieces of the sun falling below the brushed treetops.

The day has turned windy and he can hear its voice over the talk-show murmur on the radio. The bunched trees could extend into their own world, their own ecosystem and deep quiet, and Lorne imagines getting lost inside, even though he knows Highway 401 can't be more than a thousand paces away.

Decroux House itself is all mansard roof and chalky, weathered stone. It doesn't quite fit into rural North Carolina. There's a Puritan severity to its planed angles, but something about it says French beyond simply its name—he wants to use the term Romanesque but doesn't trust his shallow knowledge of architecture. It's plainer than a church, more austere, a farmhouse that would have needed hundreds of bright acres unspooling from it. Or was it an abbey once?

He loves every inch of it.

But it has to be perfect inside as well. The double doors are closed, and there are no other cars here. He wonders if it's open on Mondays. The gravel gives way to unkempt grass around both sides of the house, from what Lorne can see, leading only to a stone shed of some sort set back against the trees. He didn't call on his way down, too full of the hum of adventure, but even now he doesn't regret it. The simple effort of this is exhilarating him.

He turns the car off and picks up the stack of lottery tickets. It felt like a good test for the lucky charm, so he stopped at a gas station and chose ten scratch-off cards at random. The one on top is called I ♥ Cash.

He pulls a dime from one of the cup holders and begins rubbing it against the red hearts of the first ticket. He scratches quickly, the way he would have done it as a boy, and flakes of dull silver coat his fingertips when he's done. Neither of his numbers has a match. No two tickets are the same, but soon they've all disappointed him. He hasn't won so much as a dollar.

The disappointment is hot on his skin, and he has to take a deep breath so that he won't cry. Before it can begin to feel even close to a panic attack, he throws the lottery tickets back onto the seat and gets out the car, the wind cool against his sudden sweat. He bends over, hands on his knees, and feels better at once. This is only more proof that he should put the mime out of his thoughts. He's here, at Decroux House, paying attention and trying to do right by Gwen.

When he straightens there's a woman standing inside the house, staring out at him through the open right hand door. The lower half of her dressing gown is striped, horizontally, and it takes him a moment from this distance to realize the light is odd and the stripes are only shadows of some hidden objects—blinds from a nearby window, maybe—being cut onto her. They seem too inconstant to be part of the fabric.

He steps off the gravel and crosses the lawn toward her. A rash of grasshoppers, pale green and yellow and brown, launch from the grass around his shoes to announce his arrival.

The woman doesn't move or close the door. She's painfully thin under the sheer gown, with eyes that look wider and more watchful situated beneath hair that's shorter than Lorne's own. He sees an oxygen tank propped on a small cart beside her legs, rust flowering along the canister, and understands with an ache similar to the losing scratch-offs that the website must have had it wrong, this is a private residence.

A moment later, as he reaches the short porch, she fades back into the gloom. Lorne is standing at the mouth of half the horror films he's seen. Floor polish gleams inside the house, but the stripes that had fallen onto the woman's gown don't fall onto the floor as they should.

He breathes out with relief. A small brass plate beside the door reads – DECROUX HOUSE – *ring bell for service.*

He has to know if the place is available to him and Gwen, but there's no button around the doorframe. Just a rope above his head, knotted at the end and disappearing through a rough hole in the porch ceiling. He doesn't hear the quaint toll he was expecting when he tugs on it.

The floors might be freshly shining—unseen lights reflect down the hallway like blurred lamps in water—but the gloom holds everything else away from Lorne. There's the sense of mildew staining the walls, a damp rot he can almost smell. Things waiting for him.

He touches his right front pocket, suddenly unsure if that's where he put the mime's gift, and starts to move forward. A figure steps into the doorway. "May I help you?" an older man asks in a rich accent that, like everything here, is of a misplaced French. His eyebrows are raised toward a widow's peak in polite expectance, and below them the large nose flares its nostrils. A plain black pullover stands out like a void above creaseless white pants.

"Yes," Lorne says, staring at the man's pants for a moment, waiting for the shadows to lay themselves across the legs. But whatever light cast that effect must have been turned off, or the sunlight has weakened.

He tries again to force a sinister construct onto the man, realizing he expected something less normal, and in the same moment it hits him that he hasn't had a cigarette since yesterday afternoon. Since the bathroom outside the school gym. The thought shocks away the rest of his reply. This could be an extra anniversary gift for Gwen. It's amazing that he hasn't thought of it before now.

"May I help you, sir?" the man says again.

"I'm sorry." Lorne takes a huge breath. "I'm quitting smoking."

"Never cared for it myself. It's not a very corporeal thing, is it?" The man picks something invisible from his sleeve, a piece of lint or an unacknowledged treasure, and flicks it away. The corners of his mouth tick up in a brief smile, and he watches Lorne from beneath the lowered brow. A knowing expression.

"I'm hoping to reserve this place for, well, tomorrow," Lorne says, wanting suddenly to move this forward. "I know it's short notice, but I'm asking my wife to renew our vows. It's our silver anniversary."

"Well, in that case, do come in. *Félicitations à vous et les vôtres*, if you will pardon my French. I'm Étienne." He laughs at his little joke and sticks out a large hand, pale enough that for a second Lorne thinks it's in a white glove.

"Are you Mr. Decroux?" Lorne asks, shaking the given hand, the skin smooth and soft, and letting it pull him over the threshold. The interior is spare, old world, and deliciously clean. Not a spot of mold or decay. The high ceilings hold the light in the center of the house, dust motes floating in and out of the threads of darkness along the hallway walls.

"In a manner of speaking," Étienne says, but doesn't elaborate. Instead he steps briskly to the second room on the right and pulls shut another set of double doors that were ajar, just as something large slams against them from the other side. "Now!" He turns back to Lorne and gestures toward the smaller doorway closer to the entrance. "If you will step into my office."

They enter a small room made closet-sized by the shelves along three walls, full of worn books staring out with faded titles. In French, of course. The man steps behind a short crowded desk and sits, his old chair groaning in a high pitch under his weight. He laces his fingers tightly atop the desk.

"No computer," Lorne says, sitting in the single chair near the door. He needs to lose at least fifteen pounds, but the thin wooden frame takes him silently. "I like that."

Étienne purses his lips. "There is no need for modern noise in such a quiet place, yes?" His arms expand to take in the cramped space and his fingers close like beaks on the air. Then one index finger pops out. Its arm lowers with a strange grace and theatricality to press it against his mouth, then he seems to almost blush in embarrassment. He places his hands flat on the desk and leans a little of his weight into them.

Lorne waits while Étienne peers at the small ink-stained calendar. "Sorry again for the short notice, I—" He was about to say, *I've been paying attention*, but that won't do. "I, um—"

"Are quitting smoking?" Étienne smiles again. "It is a plausible excuse, my friend."

"No, it's just that I'm late having this idea, and I think it's just what Gwen and I need."

"Ah. Well. We serve more than the vows here in our home, you see. More than the white dress and the rice. We are in the business of rearranging. Finding the truth inside of the truth. We serve what will come. We take what is failing, and we give it the new eyes. Tell me, monsieur, have you ever moved the furniture in your living room, then stepped back and thought to yourself, why, this is how it should have been all along? No? This is rather the same."

The man is having trouble keeping his hands flat upon the desk. Lorne watches them wanting to move and gesticulate, and an uneasy bloom of cold opens in his chest. He reaches into his pocket—yes, it was the right front pocket—and pulls his little nothing out, lets it roll onto his upturned palm. Sweat beads and itches along his hairline.

He catches his host staring at his hand with a thin smirk and rolls his fingers into a fist. Outside the open door a slow squeak comes, then a boom and a rattle. Lorne looks into the foyer, the open mouth of the hallway, but sees nothing. The squeak might have been the cart holding the old woman's oxygen tank. The other sound, he'd prefer to politely ignore.

"Am I interrup—" Lorne begins.

"No, no. You mustn't think so," Étienne says. "Please pardon the noise. The future can be impatient. I see that tomorrow is free. All the day is. How strange! Wednesday and Thursday and the weekend are booked solid!" He tips his head back and laughs, clearly pleased with something. "Ah, but this is my little joke. We rarely make use of Decroux House. We have quite the discernment for our clientele. The pickiness. What time would you like?"

Lorne tries to think above the sound of the neighboring door rattling in its frame. "Let's do four p.m.," he decides. "Something about the light feels like it will be perfect then."

"Very well, Monsieur Campion," and with a flourish of his wrist, Étienne snatches a pen from an inkpot—a real, honest to God inkpot and the fountain pen to go with it—and jots something in tiny letters on the calendar. "The day is yours to spend as you see fit. Yes, even the room with the banging." Another sly smile. "Now, Brigitte will officiate. She is our lovely mademoiselle, and my own sister, very lettered and palatable, but as you can see"—with the pen he gestures toward the open door—"her health is failing at present. I shall reserve the house for you, and voilà." The pen falls and the writing hand returns to its prison on the desk's surface, alongside its mate.

Lorne rises from the chair, realizing at last that this man reminds him of the mime. The desire of his hands to shape the air. The drama crawling across the lined face. The French flavor of everything—even without Wikipedia handy, he's pretty sure the art form originated in France. A convergence of points that feel as though they always belonged together threatens to wrap around him, and he backs away to the door, full of an awe edged with panic. He breathes through his mouth.

"Oh, and one last thing," Étienne says, still seated, his hands still captive, "I am away from the house the remainder of the week. Our staff, though quite small, is here to attend to your every need. Your troubles will be over. Both the old ones and the new ones." He shows his teeth in a grin.

"Sure," Lorne says from the doorway. "Sure thing. We'll see you tomorrow. Well, we won't see you, but we'll see the house. You know what I mean. Do you take credit cards?"

"Ah, but we are not so modern as that. Payment can be resolved on your big day when you arrive in your best finery. And remember!" The smile drops off the older man's face before he continues. "You make your own luck in the world. You must trust what might grow from it." The face doesn't change, but there's a rigidity in the lines around the suddenly blank eyes.

Lorne laughs and turns, stumbling, for the front door and the swift fresh air outside. But the old woman is standing in his way, staring out the open door, as though still waiting for Lorne to approach the house.

"Excuse me, ma'am," he says, trying to edge around her, his knee knocking against the oxygen tank. "Brigitte?" He steadies the cart with a shaking hand, but the woman seems hardly to have noticed him. The dark stripes on her gown are not shadows but from the tights she's wearing beneath the sheer white cotton.

"Excuse me," he says again, and she finally shuffles a step to her left, turning her face farther away. Hiding from him. But her hand lifts from the cart handle and hangs there at her waist, open and waiting. Lorne stares at it. "Give it to me," Brigitte says in a low voice, part whisper and part song.

And Lorne's hand slips into his pocket. He thinks again of how he can't possibly know if anything is prized between the thumb and index finger he pulls out. He could act out giving this woman a hundred items and never know what any of this means. Snatch things from the air, from the damp under rocks, from the sole of his shoe, and it could all be nothing or something.

Suddenly he needs to see his wife. That's all he needs. To show her that he wants to touch her, and to witness her knowing that.

He starts to say something but the woman shakes her head, turning again and facing the doorframe. There are raw spots on her scalp, the daylight turning her short hair a wispy golden white. A missed whorl of white paint gleams behind the rim of her right ear.

"What do you want?" he asks. There's a prickle on the back of his neck, the skin tightening as though the strange thin man is behind him in the office doorway, his hands building things in the empty space between them.

"You have to use it," Brigitte says, or he thinks she says. But his urge to leave is fierce now, and he brushes past her and down the negligible steps. No grasshoppers are disturbed in his passage as he turns to look back at the old woman, whose head is dipped down now, like a bird's tucked under a wing in sleep.

Lorne senses movement behind her but sees nothing, just the sense of something rising up out of half-view, toward the ceiling, perhaps, and he's scrambling at the car door and then inside, holding his treasure clenched safe in a fist.

He backs up, turns, and accelerates onto the drab state road. Thoughts circling, the look on Gwen's face when he asks the big question both a balm and an ache in his gut. She could say no. After all they've been through, and here he is coming up with a romantic idea in the eleventh hour. She could say yes and it might be too late to find another venue. He's lucky to have found this one, even as it seems to have sought him out, to have been waiting for him.

The worthless lottery tickets in the well of the floorboard somehow soothe him. He glances down at them with a dangerous frequency, swerving onto the shoulder of 401 twice before his mind begins to clear. He'll see Gwen, he'll ask her, he'll keep paying attention until she has to pack him away in a nursing home one day.

But still threaded through this is something Étienne said. It's snagged in his mind and won't let go of him, and he thinks that it was intended to do just that. This odd man knows a lot about Lorne's current situation. *You make your own luck in the world. You must trust what might grow from it.* The first part is surely a message telling Lorne that the mime's gift was not a lucky charm. The lottery tickets support this.

The second part, though, that's what is pulsing in him now. He imagines sinking an index finger into the soil in the back yard, working it in circles to loosen the earth. Creating a new pocket, this one for a seed.

His phone buzzes from the passenger seat. He hasn't checked it since before he arrived at Decroux House. He fishes it out of his blazer too late and sees a missed call and an earlier text from Gwen, feels a childish flutter in his chest that reminds him of the old days. There's a gas station on the right, so he swings the car in and parks. He opens the phone and reads, *It stopped raining. We can get out of the car now.*

He mouths the words and doesn't know he's crying until a teardrop falls onto the screen. He reads it again. He says the words out loud. Everything feels right in this moment. This is the two of them finding their way back toward each other.

His throat is dry and he has to drink the cold coffee from this morning to wet it enough to call her back. After several rings it goes to voicemail. "Hey, you," he says, and gives a shaky laugh. It thrills him that he considers going into the menu and deleting that beginning so he can try again. If that doesn't prove the butterflies he has, nothing does.

He pushes on instead. "Headed back from an appointment. It was a little far out so I'm just going to take the rest of the day off and come home. I'll see you soon." He can't bring himself to say anything sweet or sappy. Gwen has always been those things, but she doesn't like them out on the surface.

His thoughts go back to Decroux House. They go back to the fact that even now, imagining a cigarette in his mouth, the heat of the smoke pulled down his throat, he doesn't want one. Part of him always wants a cigarette. He's told himself many times that he doesn't think he can ever really quit.

But in this moment, that little hollow is gone behind his

breastbone. That low-grade hungry want. He knows he should be peering closer at it, to see if it's full of something else. You don't start smoking at seventeen then have a cure switch flipped at forty-nine.

For now he'll see how long he can ride this out. He's going to quit and he'll confess to Gwen that he's been sneaking cigarettes, four or five a day, ever since he told her he'd stopped. She has to know he has one every now and then. She probably smelled it on him yesterday in the car after the birthday party, probably a hundred other times.

Strip malls and gaudy restaurants slide by in a soft focus. Stands of trees shake in wind that could almost be following along with Lorne, tugging the clouds north in his wake. He smiles at it all. A tight spot of imagined heat burns against his right leg, a thing waiting to grow.

It feels as though he is guided home. Lampe Street, Aster Court, a woman watering flowers by a mailbox, someone hidden in a long coat walking toward the main road. The driveway, Gwen's old blue Pathfinder. Months of dark marrow in his bones seeming to break apart.

Until he steps into the house and down the hall. He sees the attic stairs shut snug in their frame. All the other days before this one crowd around him, five months of them glaring and silent. He calls his wife's name and hears her steps approach him in the creaking floorboards, then pause.

"Gwen?" he says again. The steps retreat.

Lorne stares up at the square of fine light and realizes he never told that strange man at Decroux House his name. But the man had known it.

"I'll be in the living room, honey," he calls, much too softly for her to hear.

A Wake

"Things are in a rush now," she tells her studio. Her voice startles her. She didn't mean to speak.

She doesn't know how but the painting is half finished by the time the daylight begins to leak from the sky and she comes back to herself. Somehow she's pulling it off.

The priest is the only figure with flesh on its bones yet, more than a sketch. He stands with his grimace and his shovel, the empty coffin a surprised eye peering up at him. She's added something new, a crucifix by his feet, the rosary beads broken and scattered like crumbs. From the viewer's angle the cross is inverted.

Something happened when she came home, climbed up here. Something waited. She remembers moving the ruined canvas— the visitor had stepped all over it, tearing it in several places. But there's a rough blur pasted over the rest of the afternoon, occluding the imagery behind it—of touching, of almost being touched, the slashing paintbrush. Her thoughts feel different, knocked onto a neighboring band of frequency.

She tells herself she needs all this. It's the zone of creation, furiously bringing *A Wake* back from its grave. But her mind is tracing a far simpler shape.

On the small canvas the peasant women and boy are only thoughts for the moment, and Gwen is nervous about painting them, wondering if she'll end up in their dark rapture. And the coffin. It will be vacant overnight, and the morning will choose what to put in it. But she already is sure it will be Lorne again, how could it not be?

She's cold, up here in the attic. The room still holds the day's considerable heat. She can feel it on her skin. But the painting has chilled her. Two, three hours ago Lorne called up to her, home early and surely moved by her text earlier in the day. She hasn't acknowledged him yet and can hardly even face the simple fact of it.

He's probably sulking somewhere. And this is all just so tiring. Her hand reaches out, tentative, as though waiting for Gwen to notice and call it back, then shoves the easel over. The painting lands facedown. She doesn't rush to its rescue. What paint is wet can dry and stick to the floor.

Instead she grabs the largest canvas she has left, four feet by six, and leans it on the easel. She pulls her hands away slowly, ready to catch it if it tips, but it's steady. As long as she doesn't press too hard against it.

The two twig brushes are on the worktable, their tips blemished with black. They're impractical, of course, but she used them to add some thin texture to the putty-knife darkness of *A Wake*. She grabs both of them and a small tin of dirt that shouldn't be here beside her paints. She mixes in her saliva until she gets a good viscous paste, coats the useless brushes.

A deep breath and a line traveling down the left side of the canvas. A line smeared down the right. She stoops and connects them, stands on a folding chair and completes the box. Then all four lines again.

Trembling. Her scalp tingles, the hair wanting to lift away from it. Her nipples ache, chafing against the cotton of her top, a ribbed green daubed with white and red and black. There's a heat between her legs, pulling the warmth from the rest of her. An itch along the outline of her body, an inexplicable, delicious madness that wants only relief.

Her hand approaches the canvas again, poises to begin the final shape, but she hears the basement door closing two stories below her, the two beeps of the security system. She can just see the rim of light from the motion light as it clicks on. She is so thirsty. The rest can wait.

In the kitchen she drinks two glasses of water at the sink, filling them from the tap. She takes the third over to the window and looks down on the back yard. Her husband is walking in vague patterns through the overgrown yard, staring at the ground as he goes, and she has a sudden memory of him, as sour-sweet and strong as the grapefruit she attacked this morning.

Lorne snatching her as she came home one winter day. They'd been in this house a week, no more than two, and the walls still threw echoes back at them. Unpacked boxes in most of the rooms. He'd been waiting behind the front door as she came in, and he took her there against the wall.

She remembers the way the light slanted into the living room, sharp forbidding angles of January sun. Her face pushed against paint whose smell hadn't faded yet. She remembers loving that smell. Of course she did. She would figure out why later.

Maybe she'll raise the window, call down to him. Invite him up and try. It can be a way into talking about how scared she is of what's happening to them, separately and together.

Your mime was in our house, Lorne. In our house. Something chased me into the woods out at Duke—that wasn't quite right, but it was close enough. *My shape is somewhere, waiting for me to fill it. We have to do something.* And just what is he doing out there, passing in and out of the motion sensor, so that he's caught in a slow strobe light?

Yes, she'll go slip into something more comfortable, like they're in a movie and everything is just on the verge of fine. Out in the back yard Lorne lowers himself to his knees, pawing at the grass. He pauses. He looks up and sees her. She sets the glass down and turns the kitchen light out and watches her husband stand and step toward the house. Underneath her skin there's a twinge of pain, wondering if *A Wake* is ruined and whether she cares.

She wishes it would rain. If the sky would allow it, in this moment, she would go out to him before he could come in to her.

The Tired Sounds

Lorne goes out back, tired of waiting for Gwen. It felt important to talk to her first, before the planting, but she's wrapped up in her work again. Guilt creeps over him when he remembers that her big show opens on the thirtieth, just around the corner.

The last of the sun is raking its fingers through the distant tree line as he steps out of the basement. They have no garden, just grass that always borders on unruly as it slants down to the plank fence and the dried creek beyond.

He paces, catching the motion sensor's eye, the sheets of its brief light. Looking for a fertile spot, or maybe just the flattest space that will get sun and isn't too close to the house. He's standing beside the tiger lilies that came into the yard on their own when the light snaps on again.

In its weak reach he notices a vague shape flattened into the grass, something like a rectangle but less defined. They haven't had anything out here that would have sat in this spot, much less long enough to press the grass down.

But it's as good a garden as any, so he kneels down, digs a finger into the soil. Warmth is still baked into it. The sensation is pleasant but his gut still squirms at the idea of what lives under there. He moves his finger in a circular motion, widening the hole into a funnel shape, then pulls the mime's gift, the nothing, from his pocket.

With this seed, I thee wed, he thinks, and the thought gives him a sick shudder. He pulls his fingers apart above the hole, releasing, then lets spit drip out of his mouth before pushing dirt in behind it. The pocket is filled, and he pats it twice.

Something makes him look up and there is Gwen, standing at the kitchen window watching him.

From this distance she is unknowable. He wonders what she's thinking even as he notices something behind her, a figure crawling across the ceiling. The paste-white face seems to grin down through the window at Lorne as the limbs behind it scrabble toward Gwen, a spider about to drop onto its prey.

He shouts her name but it's dark, he needs to trigger the motion sensor. The moment he does the kitchen goes dark, and he's sprinting to the basement door.

A Wake

Gwen senses something above her. She drops to the floor and twists around so that she can look up. White hands, caught in the pale light that clicks on outside, are pressing flat against the air at the midpoint of the room. Something—someone—is drooping down toward her. She crawls into the hallway just as she hears the beep of the basement door opening, then Lorne's feet storming up the stairs.

She continues toward their bedroom, worming herself under the attic stairs, light blooming behind her and Lorne shouting her name. Then, as she rises and opens the bedroom door, a silence spreads out.

As though it has called to her, she lowers herself back onto her hands and knees and crawls under the bed. Lorne yells her name again, his feet thudding down the hall, but she doesn't answer. She squeezes her eyes closed, a ringing in her ears, an itch all along her sides.

He must see a sliver of her under the bed when the light snaps on. "Honey?" He stumbles down to the floor and peers under the frame at her. "What's wrong? What happened?"

"Nothing," she murmurs, unsure of herself. "Nothing in the kitchen."

"Gwen, don't be silly. I saw somebody on the—in the kitchen with you." His hair hangs down toward her in sweaty wings. The overhead light doesn't fall around his face and his eyes are wild and sunken in the shadow.

"Your mime," she says. Pushing herself to say that much.

Lorne raises himself but then falls into a sitting position. She can't see his face anymore but she can read it in the quality of his silence. "How?" he says. "You saw him?"

"I saw *her*. It's a woman. I don't know what she wants but it needs to stop."

"Tomorrow," he says, and lies down beside her, reaches in to take her hand. "I think I've figured it out. I need to ask you something." He tries to smile. "Tomorrow's our silver. I found a place, for the late afternoon. Will you do me the honor of renewing your vows with me?"

It is a strange question to be asked while under a bed. Gwen has enough room to awkwardly turn herself over and stare up at the box spring, knitting her silence into more and more complex patterns. She doesn't know what to say, or how to simplify it. She only feels that there's a space somewhere she needs to be inside. Something tighter, more precise than this one. What happened when she went up into the attic this afternoon, in that scratched-out portion of the day?

"We can have a reception party in a month or so," Lorne is saying. "After your show. Invite everyone over. It would be nice, don't you think? A new start?"

Her silence just goes on, her eyes peering up toward where she's slept every night for the last seventeen years. Eventually her husband pushes himself to his feet. She watches his loafers turn away from her and start for the hallway, and she says, just loud enough for him to hear, "Wait." Then, with more force, "Let's go to your little church or whatever. We'll talk on the way there."

His legs pause. "Thank you," he says. "Thank you, honey." And he leaves her under the bed, and she is more profoundly thankful for this than for his grand gesture.

The Tired Sounds

Lorne wakes on the couch in the living room. His face is tight and his eyes feel like they crack open. He swings his legs out and sits up, an ache in his hip and his neck, touches his face and brings his fingers away flaked and smeared in white paint. It's half-dried from his forehead down to the neck of his T-shirt.

He wanders down the hall, nearly limping, and into the bedroom. He has to see what she did to his face. Gwen is emerging from the bathroom as he arrives, and they stand face to face, frozen silent.

Her face is full of beautiful bones that make little hollows, the kind of sunken look he's always been astonished can be so strikingly beautiful along with the full curves of her body. But today her face is ghostly, sapped of vitality.

She reaches behind her and pulls a towel from the rack just inside the bathroom door, hands it to him. Lorne shuffles past her and turns the tap on. She painted his face with enough white to conceal all the color in his skin, with uneven black points around his eyes like shocked inkblots. He bends over and scrubs, squeezing his mouth and eyes shut as the paint sloughs away, thinking the both of them have gone crazy in a matter of days.

He drops the towel on the floor and returns to the bedroom. Gwen has only moved a few feet, near the bed, and she grabs his face and kisses him deeply, biting his tongue. Her nails press into his jawline, his temples. He kisses back, slipping his arms around her and crushing her against him.

It's been months, seven or eight of them. She's dry and brittle and it occurs to him to be gentle but the moment passes for restraint. He drags her onto the bed and halfway through she turns him over and climbs on top of him. Already there's a trickle of blood seeping from her and running down his thighs.

Complete silence, Gwen looking at him but mostly at the wall above, sinking onto him, moving in a swiveling circle. She comes at least twice and it's only shock that holds him back long enough for this. When she feels him spasm in her she stills, waits, then slips off onto the floor.

But not into the bathroom to clean off—he hears the attic stairs clatter down, her bare feet clomp up them, the stairs groan upward, the stutter of springs.

A Wake

Early this morning, after the shock of coating her husband's face in paint as he slept, she drew the outline of her body on the canvas. But it was wrong. Something in the shape, the flare of her hips. Or something else. Back in the attic now, with a sudden inspiration, she scoops his leavings out of herself and smears them around the contours of what she has drawn. Fine threads of her blood are caught in his pearlescent glaze.

Something is very wrong. Gwen herself is the loudest alarm bell. But she is calm for all the resonance. She walks around the studio while waiting for Lorne's semen to dry, standing in front of the only painting that hasn't already been wrapped and taken down to the Shain Gallery in Charlotte.

Für Hollow features a piano—decayed-looking and textured with gobs of paint, but majestic in spite of it—in an abandoned ballroom, huge windows dripping sickly light. A blur of a woman sits on the bench, howling at the vaulted ceiling. She only finished the woman in the last two weeks, erasing her a touch of paint thinner at a time. It's enrapturing but so prosaic to her now, and this brings a sharp regret for *A Wake*, which still is lying facedown behind the easel.

Time passes in an agony. Lorne moves around downstairs, running water in the sink, flushing the toilet. Creating circuits of motion murmuring throughout the house. At last, eagerly, wanting the itch and the compulsion to be gone, she lays the canvas on the floor so that her head will point toward the window and the gray morning light. It's no more than two muddy shapes, a childish scrawl. But she knows it's shaped just like her.

She sits on the canvas, gently, and then lies back, slowly, placing her hands at her sides, shifting an inch. The itch is gone, or placed elsewhere, Gwen can't know how much of this is in her head. "Gwendolyn Burke," she says, staring at the slants of the roof meeting fifteen feet above her. The single beam joining the two halves. A furry cobweb.

She thinks about Monkton, and the pond, until Lorne leaves, tires crunching along the gravel, and she gets to her feet. A trace of the feeling still whispers along the rim of her body, soft as a feather drawn up and down her skin.

It's still not right. Either she draws outlines of herself all over the house like future crime scenes, slipping into some bizarre midlife crisis, or she moves past this. She has a show that could change her life. She has a marriage to figure out. She has a wedding of sorts to get to.

The Tired Sounds

In the overcast light of morning, the space where he planted the seed—he has no idea what else he can call it—looks even more flattened, browning as though something has sat upon it for weeks. Something with the vague shape of a person.

But nothing has grown in the night. What is the gestation period for nothing to sprout into something? There is no precedent. And if he had asked the giver, there in that restroom stall, only silence and signs would have been offered as explanation.

For an hour he wanders the house in the strange, violent post-coital glow, glancing up at the ceiling, listening. He didn't intend to go to work. He wants to push everything to the side like he planned, to have a day full of import. Gwen is having some sort of breakdown, and there's a strong case to be made for his own as well.

But he has a good feeling. It follows him out to the car and out of the driveway. He sits there in the street for a minute. Everything is still and waiting. He reconsiders but since Gwen seems determined to spend the entire morning in her studio, he drives to the office.

Carla greets him as he comes in a little past ten, her face pleasant enough that no one would guess the strain that has been there. Lorne has been deeply glad for this. It could be much worse. She could have had feelings for him, and he would have betrayed her, too.

He offers to get her some coffee and she points at her full cup, still hot, threads of steam seeming to curl up toward the scoop of her blouse. She touches her dark tomboy hair just above the ear. Not flirting, but she smiles and enjoys the moment.

Lorne lets her think he's sharing in it. She's not even forty yet, trimmer than Gwen and beautiful in a way that takes months to really notice. But he's paying attention to something far more important.

He closes his office door, opens his planner to the current week, turns on the computer and navigates to his email. A busy man getting ready to knock out a chunk of a day's work. But almost at once he gets up and turns out the lights, then moves his chair to the window. He twists the blinds apart.

For an hour he sits there as the sun burns off the clouds and spreads across the parking lot. Shadows wither along the curbs. A painted face watches him from the trees, and he watches back. Another face appears, then another, slowly, melting into his view.

Let them look. He decides that he and Gwen are going on a second honeymoon after the opening of her show. Anywhere she wants. He can afford it, or he can afford to figure that part out later. Things are going to be normal and intimate and good. Better than they have been in too many tired years.

His phone buzzes on the desk and jolts him from his reverie. For a bad moment he pats his pocket for the mime's gift, searches the surface of his desk, scolding himself for trying to spot an invisible, impossible thing. Then he remembers it's not with him. It feels as though it's not his to have anymore, and a small sense of loss flashes over him.

Where is this place? When do we need to be there? her text reads, and he doesn't even pause to turn off his computer on the way out.

A Wake

She throws salads together and they eat in the dining room like civilized people. Lorne is smiling, eager, but she imagines the word *divorce* on the table between them, an amorphous thing full of legs and silent eyes. She doesn't want it to squat there, sluggish and myopic.

Their forks scrape the wooden bowls. Lorne asks her how the painting is coming along and she tells him she doesn't know anymore, but that she has enough to be pleased with the show.

Her agent called earlier but Gwen didn't answer. She hasn't listened to the voicemail yet. The important thing is that she will. The important thing is that she looks across at her husband, over the sloped back of the ugly thing crouched there, and smiles at him.

"One minute," he says, wadding his napkin and setting it aside. He almost runs out the front door, returns a minute later with a pale pink box with an ash-colored satin bow. She takes it from him, blinking down at it. She didn't get him anything.

"Happy anniversary, part one," he says, a bashful young man again, the same one that took five nervous minutes on the phone to ask her out after that first night at The Standard.

"Thank you, honey," she says, just above a breath, and it's the *honey* that gets her fingers moving, plucking the bow so that it slides onto her spattered jeans and drops to the floor. The *honey* doesn't feel like only a reflex.

Inside is the Victorian teapot she saw at Saddler's Goods, her favorite antique shop in Raleigh, back in another life. She stares at it, turning it left and right, the day catching in little glimmers along the plated spout and handle. It is beautiful and ugly and delicate.

She sets it on the table in front of her, pushes her salad bowl to the side. "I'll get dressed. You're sweet." She stands, hugs Lorne, then slips around him. When she turns at the hallway, he and the teapot are standing there, waiting.

The Tired Sounds

She said they would talk about things on the way to Decroux House. Lorne turns and glances at her every minute or so, the soft green dress she's wearing, but she just stares ahead, scratching the sides of her arms and rubbing her legs. He searches for the right words, or merely words that will bring her eyes over to him.

The mime is the last thing he wants to bring up, but he pictures her under the bed last night, pictures her walking out into a rainstorm outside the birthday party without checking to see where he was. He pictures her crouched over him in the dark, painting his face.

"So is the mime bothering you?" he says, almost putting his hand on her.

She pulls her head back, looks at him for a second. "No. Well, yes. She came into our house, Lorne. More than once. That's beyond just bothering." Her arms fold tightly around her chest.

Lorne breathes out. "Gwen, I'm sorry." It's hard to know what to say next, so he goes back to tugging at his collar, wanting to loosen his tie but not letting himself.

They're less than ten minutes from the turnoff when Gwen says, "Those times it would rain, and we'd wait it out in the car. We shouldn't have done that."

"I'll get wet with you," he says. "I really have been trying, or trying to try. For us. And I have another gift. I quit smoking. You probably know I never stopped all the way, but I don't even want one now."

She reaches over and squeezes his wrist, gives him half a smile. "Then I guess let's go get married." Her voice is almost a sigh.

A Wake

When they pull into the gravel drive, Gwen realizes she hasn't even asked what the place is called. The style is something European she doesn't think she's ever seen before. It's flat and white, the dark windows enough like eyes—or spots of black on cheekbones—to make the house look like a blank mime's face.

But she doesn't stiffen or tell Lorne to turn around.

The grounds are drab—no garden, no flowers adorning the doorway, not even a walk leading up to it. No cars, no signs of life. It's a museum with no effort put into it.

"How did you find this place?" she asks, looking over. His hands are still on the steering wheel.

"Saw it online." He actually laughs, and the air loosens with it, the tension not breaking but at least shifting a little.

"Famous last words, you know."

They get out of the car, closing their doors gently as if by agreement. The sky has grown leaden again, sifting the little warmth out of the afternoon. She takes his hand. She tries to remember the last time she did this simple thing.

"We're the only appointment today, according to the guy I met with," Lorne says. "You want to go—"

But he doesn't finish. Seven, eight, a dozen mimes come crawling toward them over the low peak of the roof, white and black striping the gray shingles under the gray sky. They strike a barrier halfway down and lower into crouches. For a minute nothing moves in the colorless scene, until the mimes begin feeling along the unseen wall.

Gwen turns back to the car but Lorne pulls on her hand. "Wait," he says. "Something is keeping them from us. Something has *been* keeping them from us. Maybe themselves. Maybe us. Let's go in."

The mimes stand up on the roof and group into pairs facing each other, leaning at an impossible, comical angle toward the front of the house. Each pair joins hands and Gwen realizes they're acting out getting married. She and Lorne watch them, Gwen doesn't know what else to do at this point, and after several moments the mimes lean toward one another and kiss, wide-eyed and chaste.

"I can't do this, Lorne," she says.

"Come on." He tugs her, and as she's done so many times in her life, she lets him. They pass through grass that needs an end-of-summer mowing and up onto the short porch. DECROUX HOUSE, a small plate on the wall reads. The front doors are unlocked, the hall inside dim and smelling of pine. "There's the old lady's oxygen tank," Lorne says, pointing at something standing beside another pair of doors, just outside a nest of shadow.

He walks across and pulls on the doors. They groan out toward him and everything out here in the hall and foyer becomes more visible, more detailed. From where she's standing Gwen can't see what Lorne sees, but he's frozen, his hands still on the brass knobs, his face slack.

"What is it?" she says, her hand pressed against her throat. The air is thin in her chest. "Lorne, what is it?"

He tries to speak. His jaw works and his throat flexes as he swallows. "I—Jesus Christ, Gwen, it's your art."

The Tired Sounds

There is music as the doors open, the groan of hinges turning into stringed instruments, low-pitched cellos. There is light, and too many things trying to catch it. He is trying to catch Gwen, to turn to her in the light.

A Wake

"What?" she says, stepping toward him, aware of how her legs are lifting higher than she thinks they should before coming down in slow pistons. Glancing down, past Lorne along the hallway, past the cylindrical tank on its cart, she sees a wooden coffin. A plastic tube snakes from the nozzle of the tank, down, across and under the coffin's lid.

A coffin. *A Wake.* For a moment she forgets what her husband has just said. The tube fills with a light fog that rapidly fades. Then fills and fades again.

But over Lorne's shoulder is a room, a sort of library, that changes the tone of the entire house, warm yellow-orange light flowing down from chandeliers in the high ceiling, and walls hung with, yes, her paintings.

Her paintings. *A Wake* hangs on the far wall, directly across from the doors, and Lorne is in the coffin again, peering from the shelter of his arms, pleading. It is a foul, brutally powerful thing, and once more she cannot believe something so raw and perfect could come out of her. Even from here she sees the broken rosary she added just yesterday.

Above it, a foot or so to the left, is the crude Gwen-shape she finished this morning with the blended glaze of her and Lorne's fluids. She's surprised to find that it belongs on a wall. Something accidental and atavistic pulses in those simple lines. She's tempted to suggest it to Amelia when she returns her call—if it's here, is it also still in the attic at home?

But these pieces, impossible though they are, don't hold her eyes long. There are other paintings, paintings that don't exist, can't exist, because she hasn't created them yet. Most of them aren't even glimmers of ideas in her mind, but they're unmistakably hers. No one else could have wrested them from a smear of oils.

She forces her eyes to her right, to possibly say something to Lorne, how can he not be looking at what's hanging in this impossible room, but he's over at a bookcase, browsing. So she turns back to this inexplicable wonder, counts each of them. Nine, all framed well, four that exist and five her instinct recognizes. There are paintings that can't be hers, good but different, but only three. Insubstantial in the warm light.

She walks to the left wall and gazes at one of "her" pieces, of a small round table, stark and muted at the same time, rather like the few Wyeths she's seen in person. The arm of a woman is draped along a chair beside the table just inside the frame. On the table there's a still life in a bowl, with one piece of fruit much larger than the rest, a cantaloupe, until she realizes it's the back of a human head. She thinks she recognizes the head, severed and turned away though it is.

But there's a depth here that goes beyond just photorealism, and an abstraction that goes beyond its own sake. It's like she skimmed a small flat stone across the surface of truth.

And in the bottom right corner, brownish-black, her name, Gwendolyn Burke.

The Tired Sounds

He finally pushes himself into the room, behind Gwen who has squeezed around him to gawk up at the walls. He gawks alongside her but only for a moment. Before he can say anything to her, he sees something conspicuous, in some subtle way, on a bookshelf to the right. The shelves are eight rows tall, nearly as many feet, but he is pulled to eye level, a smooth-jacketed book with the title *They Sold Trees* printed across the spine.

His heart contracts—his name, Lorne Campion, is right there below the title. He pulls it out, his hand shaking badly, and opens it to the copyright page—six years from now. Scribner. He flips to the back jacket. A photo of himself sitting in the garage in soft focus, looking over the photographer's shoulder. He looks handsome and, yes, writerly.

The shaking grows worse. There is so much to look at and read and touch and check right now. At least one more book has his name on the spine, but he's not allowing himself to look yet. He is close to fainting, a giddy tingle crawling all over his skin. He wants to sit down—there are two chairs and an overstuffed couch behind him—but he can't spare the few seconds.

He fans the pages backward, loving the whispered flutter against his thumb, loving the blur of the blocks of words as they fly by. There's an inscription on the title page, in his own handwriting, *To Etienne, who taught me to pay attention, and how useless words can be.*

The book beside *They Sold Trees* is titled *In Our Long Evenings* and, below that, *Stories*. To the left of that is another novel, thicker than the first. He pulls it out, tracing the title on the front cover with an index finger—*Remedial Mold Treatment*. An odd name, a bizarre context with which to echo his father. The copyright page tells him it will be published (was published?) in the unreal year of 2034. His name is in a larger print than the first two books. At the top, lightly italicized, are the words *NEW YORK TIMES BESTSELLER*. He barks a laugh.

This book has a loose, folded sheet of paper stuck in it like a bookmark. He slides it out and opens it. In cramped letters on the pale green paper, a long-fingered hand has written, *You may not remove any property of Decroux House from the premises. You may not transcribe. The more you read, the more you risk leaving something quite substantial of yourself behind. Now that you see what has grown from our gift, our sculpting of the air, you will see that one of you must stay here with us. Preferably your talented wife, as my sister is succumbing to her great age. We rearrange failing things, as I told you. We configure what is to come. We Give It Life With Our Hands. I could make statements of our intent, but really, the bargain, as some would call it, should be readily apparent. Sincerely yours, E.D.*

He turns to look at Gwen, who is at the other end of the room now, looking at that hideous painting of Lorne in a coffin, the thing he destroyed. The thing that helped start this whole mess.

If it exists here, what does that mean for his books? The painting is different somehow, smaller. His wife's hands are curled against her neck, as though she began to pray but then wondered what it was she was praying to.

A Wake

She's standing before *A Wake*, having just traced her fingers along the texture of the paint. This, too, is the original. She finishes it, then. She keeps painting and her talent continues to gush out of her.

What she wishes were in this room more than anything else is the pond in Monkton, the quiet golden morning—how amazing that she only thinks of painting it now, making it new instead of the past, when presented with the lack of it.

But the cold facts are seeping in, coated in strangeness. The questions. What is this place, yes, that's the obvious one. And how real is it? Half of what she sees she can believe, and the rest she can follow along with because of the first half. What details had to stand all in a row for this to come into a sort of existence? And—she means to turn to Lorne and ask this last question aloud—why?

Something catches her eye in the other direction. A tenth painting, one she didn't see before because it's closer to the floor than a painting should be hung, blocked from her view earlier by a leather wingback chair beside a table with a wax-shaded lamp.

It's dominated by creamy white, and it's without a doubt her own work, but she has to stoop down to its level to see that she—this other, future Gwen—has painted a bank of fluorescent light panels in a ceiling. A handful of desks, a wall of windows with closed blinds. It's their office. Lorne's office. Campion Financial.

And her husband is lying on top of the central desk, on top of Carla Koslowski, their senior agent, both nude but for a torn white wedding veil on Carla's head, their joined faces gaunt in a deep and violent kiss.

Gwen has painted the angle so that Lorne is raised and thrusting into Carla, a voyeur's angle, the harsh light gleaming off their union. Lorne has half-penetrated her, crudely. Carla's right breast is wadded in his fist.

Looking at it feels like an animal learning its cage door is ajar. Like watching the sky turn fluorescent yellow before a storm.

"Lorne?" She turns to him. He's still beside the bookshelf, looking over at her with a sheet of paper in his hand. The painting is too far away for him to see. She loves him, she really does. She often loves him so much. There is a throbbing in her head, a sense that she never wants to paint again, that she simply cannot bring herself to do it. Whatever hot midlife rage awoke in her last year feels unbearably weary, now, and is beginning to yawn in her chest.

"Your art," he says, and at first she thinks he's only stating the obvious, but then he lifts a book off the shelf beside him. "And my books. The one thing I always kept from you, that I tried to write a novel. I was embarrassed. But it looks like I finished it. And kept going." He glances at them. "Well, it looks like I *will* finish it. Not too long from now, according to the copyright."

She has no idea what he just said. "Did you fuck Carla?" she asks. Her mouth is coated with a rime of sour ice. The muscles in her face feel slack. The roaring fatigue.

"I—" He takes a step toward her, stops, tries to place the book back on the shelf without looking but it falls to the floor. He looks so young in the chandeliers' honey light. "Yes. Yes. I did. But only sort of. I tried to, it was a bad night, but I couldn't. But—Jesus, Gwen, we need to talk about what I found for just a second." He shakes a sheet of paper at her.

"I've been thinking about, dreading even the idea, really, of telling you I'm going to use my maiden name for my work." Now the inside of her mouth is full of dry heat. She pulls her hair back behind her, wanting it out of the way for this. "Now, though... we're getting a divorce, probably. But if we leave this place, right now, there's a very slim chance for us."

She turns and looks behind her, at *A Wake*, at Lorne's brown eyes begging and accusing in their agony. The priest putting a second end to him, the four women and the young boy gibbering with perhaps delight. She shines a light inside herself and it is cold.

The Tired Sounds

Her words tremble around him, and he touches the books again. He lifts them to feel their collective weight in his hand. He wants to memorize it, breathe all these words into his lungs like spores. They smell like hope.

Gwen already has her success. She has tasted it, enjoyed the sheen in the eyes that look at her work. Lorne wants so desperately to know the meaning of the words *they sold trees*. To end the shame of not being able to find out.

Leave Gwen here, walk out the doors and shut them behind him. Listen to the old wood judder as she slams against it, just as he heard something slam against it his first time here.

Drive home and open a blank page on the computer. Start finding out the reason he typed those three words on a different page years ago.

But what Mr. Decroux doesn't realize—though he seems to have realized a great deal—is that Lorne has been paying attention. Even though this not-yet Lorne told him right in the inscription, and he even told him something more: *how useless words can be.*

He slides the books, his books, back onto the shelf. This will end up being his true gift, he thinks. He doesn't know if it will mean as much as a renewal of their vows. Those vows will be dissolved now. But it's one last thing he can give her. He wants her very slim chance.

With another look at Gwen, he walks toward the doors and out into the hall. All the breath goes out of him as he crosses the threshold. He tries to welcome the old weight that sags back onto him.

A Wake

She lets Lorne close the library doors behind them, and the light goes back to a thin dinginess, the coffin on the floor the only true presence in the house. A soft hissing comes from the nozzle of the oxygen tank. The breathing tube fogs and clears, like a slow heartbeat.

Outside the roof is empty, the grounds swollen with quiet. Rice litters the lawn like dandruff. Gwen gets behind the wheel of the car without asking. Lorne hands her the keys and they leave. She retraces their steps back to Highway 401 and they listen to the hum of the car.

"It was only the once, after our fight, after I wrecked your painting," Lorne says, but his voice trails off halfway through, out of air.

She doesn't speak. The miles unspool in front of them. Her thoughts fan out into a flat plane of blank canvas, newly stretched on a frame, and she paints nothing on it. She only wants to get home. She has started to itch again.

The Tired Sounds

He's not out in the garage long. It's still their anniversary, and he wants to ask Gwen out to dinner, as absurd as she might think it is. She'll say no. Like so many men before him, he will pay for his moments of terrible weakness. He's earned it.

But he wants to do what he's come out here for with the assumption that he and Gwen will work through this. To give it the ring of honesty, and not fear. He slides open the middle drawer of his desk and finds the right folder, pulls the one hundred and thirteen typewritten pages out and looks down at them. He listens to the way he's feeling as though it has a frequency or a resonance.

Lorne has felt hatred for his wife this past year, because of the failure he's holding in his hands. Somewhere along the way he's admitted that it was actual hate, a hard kernel in their marriage. But now it doesn't stick in his throat. It doesn't swell into a knot. It's softened into a low-grade echo of some other person's fear.

He can still feel the heft of the hardcover back at Decroux House, the matte grain of the dust jacket like sandpaper worn thin. *They Sold Trees.* The pages were deckle-edged. He has always loved that. He must have requested it or had his mythical agent do so.

What he doesn't feel in the silence is the buzz of curiosity. He could sit down, turn on the computer, and open a Word document, watch the cursor blink at him in surprise on the blank white screen. But it's almost dark now, and the old lie of tomorrow is easier than it has ever been. Maybe this story could happen, he could learn who sold trees and why they sold them. Maybe it could be the blanket he hides under if the divorce grows teeth.

What if by leaving Decroux House, he left not just the book behind, but the possibility of writing it? It's what makes the most sense in this senseless week. But it's ironic, that he would lose his voice to the mimes.

His hand hovers over the trash can, then drops the pages on the desk.

A Wake

Gwen is in the kitchen, having wandered through the house looking for the box, something that's the exact shape of her. She's at a loss and itching madly. She painted for half an hour, just long enough for her hand to show her it still wants to do it. *A Wake* remains facedown, half-glued to the floorboards. Instead she started something that won't reveal its face to her for a while yet.

At the window, another glass of water, she looks out at the tree-crowded sky beginning to stain like blood in bathwater, down at where Lorne knelt in the grass yesterday evening. The patch of grass is paler than any around it, matted down as though by a more persistent weight than her husband.

It clicks for her. The contours of it, she didn't get a good look last night, and the angle is wrong from up here, but it clicks. Why the two paintbrushes made of twigs and pine needles? Did they come from one of their trees? She nearly runs down the stairs into the basement, opens the door and steps out into the back yard. The day has grown cold.

The dying spot of grass is shaped like a woman, because she knows to look for it. Arms against the sides, legs together, at a long, long rest. She wonders if Lorne noticed that, if that was why he was out here. She presses her hand against the grass, which is dry and broken, nearly white in the falling dark.

When she pulls her hand back, it knocks against the air.

She traces her fingers along a hard edge, down, across, and up again on the far side of the dead grass. Straight walls with clean box lines, wider at the top than the bottom. There seems to be no need for her to paint anything after all.

She steps onto the feet of the faded grass silhouette, turns herself around. A glance up at the kitchen window, feeling Lorne's eyes on her, but he's not there. None of the mimes is there. She sits, then lies back, bringing her arms to her sides and her legs together. Scoots up a couple of inches and her body goes numb and warm with blessed relief. She could cry from it.

The shape inside the shape fits like nothing she has ever known. It is a kind of heaven for her, and the first thing she sees is the pond in Monkton, the one image that has haunted her so well, spilling into the sky, this time the setting sun painting it for her since she never did.

She hears her parents calling her from the house behind her, which must mean their voices are coming from the earth. Her breath plumes out and spreads into a fog just in front of her face. Like the breathing tube under the coffin lid back at that awful house.

A coffin. The shape of a coffin.

"Gwen, you'll catch cold out there," her mother says, distant and muffled. Even farther away, deeper, her father laughs. The air changes, warms and thickens. She stares at the rough circle of condensation and panic sets in. The lid. The cover. She lifts her arms and they meet resistance. There's just enough room to fold them at the elbow so that she can press, then pound against the invisible barrier. Then claw. Then panic.

Hammering, feebly beating against the air but it will not budge. Lorne appears above her like a rising full moon, then just as quickly setting out of sight. But the sky is still that orange-yellow with its veins cut and dark blood swirling out. The shimmer of disturbed pond water. Her lungs hitch for air.

She sees Lorne again, more of him now, he's speaking but all the sound is gone from the world. He raises something above her. A shovel, he has it cocked back behind his head, its bright, dirt-tipped blade pointed downward, and there's a look of horror twisted into his face. She recognizes the look because she painted it into the mouth of a priest, the wrinkling back of thin lips, the gleam of widened eyes. What does her own face look like? There isn't space enough to cross her arms over it.

The blade falls in silence and strikes inches from her chest with a faraway crack. Again and again and again before Lorne pauses. Everything Gwen can see fogs with her hot breath. She looks up and to the right but Monkton Pond is lost in mist. So she closes her eyes.

The Tired Sounds

Lorne finds her out back and his first thought is that she's lying exactly on top of where he buried the gift, the seed. But Decroux is supposed to be finished with them, Lorne made his choice. Gwen looks peaceful but her pose is one he's seen before, in caskets at funerals he didn't want to go to because he would imagine where the deceased would be in an hour's time.

Then she begins to writhe and pound her fists weakly, just above her face. "Gwen!" he shouts, but she doesn't hear him, or doesn't acknowledge him. He bends, reaches down for her but she's encased in a box he can't see, something cold and unyielding against his hands, his prying fingers along its edges.

He steps away, looking around the yard. The grill under its tarp on the sad patio he built out of paving stones several years ago. The garden hose, coiled on its spool. There's a shovel in the basement, inside the door, and he runs for it, falling once and absorbing it with his elbows. He throws the basement door open and screams when the shovel isn't there, leaning against the wall, but then he spots it next to some boxes, fallen behind the rake.

Back in the yard, he lifts the shovel over his head, and is seized by a powerful fist of doubt. Will the barrier work both ways when he plunges the blade down? Is that old man in one of the trees bunched up against their property, watching Lorne about to lose everything?

He tries to think. But there is no thought, no precedent he can grasp at, so he slams the shovel down and it clangs mutely off the air two inches from his wife's heaving chest. The relief at this failure nearly buckles him to the ground. He slams the shovel down several more times but nothing happens.

The shock of the shovel hums through his arms, sharp pains that make him aware of the shapes of his bones. He can feel every cigarette he's ever smoked congealed in his lungs. He looks around again.

In the art of mime, how does one escape from the confinement one has fashioned? It's a question he hasn't thought to ask, hasn't had a reason to ask. He has assumed a mime is an autonomous thing, able to assemble and disassemble.

Does a mime make an escape for itself? Forge a secret latch from its pocket of ether? Would Decroux be able to tell him? Lorne remembers the nothing landing in the cup of his hands, the blue frozen eyes of the mime staring down at him from over the wall of the restroom stall. How did he not guess before? This is what they've needed since April. Probably going back five years or more.

He sinks the shovel blade into the earth, just beside her. He wiggles it free, sinks it back in. He levers out chunks of grass and dirt and flings them away, distantly aware that he must look like a man feverishly digging his wife's grave.

Soon he drops the shovel and falls to his stomach, works his hand under Gwen, feeling the rich damp of soil on his skin. It's only his arm that's swallowed by the earth, but his vision dims red and his lungs tighten.

His fingers grasp something, and he pulls out an earthworm. His arm plunges back in, up to the elbow. He doesn't know how he'll recognize its texture, how his fingers will encounter any hard edges it might have grown, and as he is not knowing these things, he feels cool metal suddenly in his palm.

A Wake

The air is thin. She can only drink it in sips. There are knocks against her back. She hardly feels them but they are insistent and regular, wanting in. Her eyes open, the fog has diminished with the air, she sees a swath of light reflected off water across the sky, soft ripples as the pond trembles in its bowl against gravity.

She looks for Lorne. She wants to say that she does love him, if it matters, of course it matters, but she can't find him. Instead there are two figures standing, just close enough for her to see their long narrow bodies, their white faces watching her. One could be her face. The other could be Lorne's, more beautiful than she painted it as he slept. She blinks and they are her parents, not a trace of paint on them, she blinks and there's nothing there, just the last curtain of deep blue.

The knocking stops below her. It turns into a scratching, a scrabbling like fingernails. She turns her head to the left and can just see the side of Lorne's face smashed against the wall beside her. His eyes are squeezed shut, straining.

Then he pulls away and is above her again, fumbling as though trying to grope her breast through the coffin lid, and she doesn't think of the painting she has so recently seen, of him and Carla, she thinks of their second date, when they started out on a nature walk north of Atlanta and ended up deep in the woods with sap-sticky pine needles clinging to their bodies, their clothes strewn between the trees.

It feels like what she might take with her, up into the water. She should have shown him Monkton Pond. Did she? She can't remember. Maybe in those first couple of years of them, before her father died.

There is a loud click and cold air almost sugar-sweet floods her. She gasps. Something is tearing at her left arm, but it's only Lorne pulling her up and out and onto the grass. A hole in the ground gapes at her. Her head rolls and she can still see the pond, she is tipping over into it, or it is pulled toward her and why did she never paint it?

She takes a breath. She takes another, fainter. Lorne is saying, "Ambulance, ambulance, ambulance," nearly mumbling, but it's all a mush that loses any sense, and a kind of cold ecstasy washes over her. Has it started to rain? A distant chill shock on her skin. Her vision goes from dark to a green-dark, and Lorne's face swimming down to hers, and it is dark, too, with no stars around the eyes.

She takes a breath.

A HEART ARRHYTHMIA
CREEPING INTO A DARK ROOM

The sun lowers until it's caught and torn on the mountains. I watch it through the window of our home office, thinking about how I have never been able to plan my stories out before I write them. They come in floods, lifting the surprised boat of my mind on their sudden waves, or they come stubborn as sap from a longleaf pine.

I have two weeks to write this one. From the carpet near my feet, my dog makes a noise in her throat for my attention. I nearly always give it to her, but these days I am supposed to be regaining my momentum as an author. "In a minute, bear," I tell her. In a minute she'll break me, and I'll be on the floor with her.

The story is for an anthology called *Miscreations: Gods, Monstrosities & Other Horrors*, and the loose theme is the Frankenstein myth. When Doug, the editor, invited me to write something for it, I said yes because I trust his vision and because I assumed life would have "turned around" long before now, the deadline drifting toward this streaked window and blocking out its view.

I was over halfway through a year and four months of no stories when I said yes. There was no room inside my cluttered, stressed head at the time, and so I told myself I would miscreate a monster later, there would be plenty of time. Plenty of sunsets.

(And life did end up turning itself around, to a degree. I started working for a new company, fixing words, tuning content to the right frequencies. My breath, most days, grew easier and filled the lungs more. But I didn't consider the creative rust, the clumsy decay that had set in. I assumed the exhaustion carried home every day on my shoulders would be no heavier than it had been in the past. I assumed the fear I had grappled with would break apart like a ghost, an exorcism, and would not seep into my heart. I thought my pride would have scabbed over.)

A scratched Bartók record is playing at a low volume, managing to sound like these American mountains, ancient things in a land we pretend is new. It's a concerto I found in a thrift store, and I've always felt it must have spent too much time in the sun. I picture a windowsill with open curtains, ambient heat seeping into a stranger's room. The record kept out of its sleeve by an inconsiderate listener. There's the mildest warp in the vinyl that causes the needle to rise and fall like a buoy on a black sea.

It could be a symbol, that this story will break into a wave of inspiration. Coupled with the saltwater static the needle reads in the scratches left by its former owner, the imperfection of the concerto moves me. The flaws bring me closer to something.

The Appalachians are flawed, from a certain perspective. They sit like old worn teeth coated in moss, rooted in the earth's jaw. I can see three eroded peaks from my desk, as their distant tree lines rake through the egg yolk of the sunset. The broken light turns from an aged yellow to a purpled orange, as though blood has swirled in. What will my monster be like? What will fill its veins?

My dog loves her neck to be scratched beneath her collar, around her neck. I lean forward and take care of this important task and my heart palpitates for the first time today—it skips a beat, pauses in some kind of fright, then stumbles back into its rhythm. I straighten in the chair, breathe deep in frustration, and look out the window for the fortieth time as the color of night leaks down. Calm leaks back into me with less grace.

I half-chant the list the ER doctor counted off on his fingers four months ago, afraid to lose the force of its litany: heart enzymes good, electrolytes good, no clots, blood pressure okay, rhythms textbook strong, no atrial fibrillation or arrhythmia. And the coda, lighthearted for a heart heavy with fear: Try cutting back on caffeine.

The dog puts her front paws up on my knees and stretches her nose toward me, concerned and offering comfort for her Boy. Her left ear never straightened, and I stare at how it flops over before closing my eyes.

I am as aware of the squirming organ in my chest as an owl is aware of the animal it snatches into its beak, the texture of warm flesh, the movement of the small bones down its throat. The owls are waking in the mountain foliage any moment now. The presence of my heart is as incongruous as a panicked fly trapped in a closed hand.

I spill similes across the carpet. I meditate for a minute, but meditation has always eluded me. It too comes in a rush or like sap from a narrow tree, never the holy middle ground.

My monster must be as inconstant as my heart. If it were a viola— another middle ground—in this Bartók concerto, it would be played vibrato, or perhaps in the spaces between the still lake of a legato and the skipping stones of staccato. It would corrupt the rhythm in a way that would need several measures to discern.

I lower myself to the floor and a rough, warm tongue greets my face. The opposite of a monster—though we call her a monster often—pounces on me, licking my nose, my eyes, my cheeks until I tell her that's enough.

(Later, a week after I thought I was having a heart attack at the office but wasn't, I canceled an appointment with a cardiologist after memorizing the ER litany, lovely excuses strung on a line, a comforting weight of words. I cut my coffee down to one cup a day and missed the other four terribly. The palpitations came less often, less thunderously. The panic attacks that erupted alongside them eased into manageable anxiety. The pair of hospital bills hurt, even with insurance, and I couldn't add to them just yet. It is too easy to ignore sickness in this country.)

My monster could be a heart attack—the fear of a heart attack, a heart attack that hasn't caught up with me yet—brought to flesh. The things I can't deal with. A disease of the heart walking upright, something I can see looming over me when my eyes open in bed, around a corner when I look behind me in the supermarket. A disguised creature parting the crowds toward me, its long fingers able to grasp my head full of excuses. It could reach me at any moment and with any audience, like the seismic stopping of a heart.

I picture its face as I begin to create it. I see it as so much like a man's face, with beautiful features and quiet, cold green eyes, a face to stare out of billboards. The beauty does something to my pulse, it sends a trill through the blood. But something is wrong with the face, soft and handsome though it is. It is slightly too large. And it is in the moment of beginning to slip from its anchor of ligaments and tissue.

If the face spoke—if it were not biding its time—the voice, like my heart, would carry an uneasy glissando that turns the stomach. It is an arrhythmia of nature.

It will come down out of the mountains, ancient and new as the land. It will follow me into the haunts of my world, its arms dragging behind it on the floor of the detergent aisle, in the gutters of the streets. Or else the long jointed limbs are folded into clothes for now, waiting to be freed. It will come after me like a spider in the end.

But for now it smiles at me from a distance. Its beautiful face slides into the corner of my eye.

The door sensor beeps twice as my partner comes home from work, and the dog, surprised that she didn't hear her Girl outside while distracted by my need, barks once and sprints from the office. I hear my partner's voice climb two octaves as they greet each other, reunited again. We are pack animals.

With the clatter of the dog's nails on the hardwood, my heart eases. It beats a sober drum. I put on my not-worried face, and it, too, seems poorly anchored by its ligaments and tissue. I stand and look out the window again and the sun is now just a stain on the mountains—for a moment it brings an early fall to their coloring.

How will my monster fit into this world? I must assemble it, give it sinews and lungs and something like its own heart, and it will give me a story. Tonight when the palpitations come, I'll pretend I am woken by the sound of scrabbling on the roof above us, though the dog will look at me with her eyes shining in the dark instead of giving a warning bark, and I know I'm always the last of us three to hear things, anyway.

Why do we create monsters? The mad Dr. Frankenstein, as we see him in films, wanted to play God. In the novel, he wanted to do so less theatrically. Horror authors answer this question differently: to frighten readers. It could be to make a buck, or it could be to hold a mirror up to the world, in more ambitious cases.

I've written creatures before that were for readers as much as they were for myself, if not more. I wrote them in the hope that what unsettles me would be a universal thing. But if I create a monster for myself, to coax toward the only heart it is made to haunt, to give voice to fears I won't allow to bloom inside a stethoscope or an electrocardiograph, how can I frighten others? How can I honor the trust placed in me by the editors of this anthology?

If the monster were to break free of this tether and appear on bookstore shelves, how could such a terror hope to translate? Perhaps the sign of a true artist is to make people afraid of things they didn't know they were afraid of.

But the reader has only to say—*This is a story about a writer writing a story. I am holding the book, so the writer lived to tell me the story. He even reprinted it in his second collection,* The Inconsolables. *From the start he is pulling back the curtain to show me the smoke and mirrors, the innards of his monster.*

(Sometimes, too, there's a tightness near my left shoulder, like the blood I need is trying to squeeze into my heart around an obstruction. I skim articles about angina and convince myself all the symptoms but the squeezing aren't present. It's only indigestion, I must be swallowing air as I eat. I remind myself the palpitations have improved. My partner reassures me, and the look in her eyes tells me she means it. Though I keep many of these thoughts from her and recite the ER litany to myself, familiar enough to hum under my breath as though it were the first measures of a concerto.)

Mid-mornings at work are the hardest. It's when my belly is full and indigestion—what I tell myself is indigestion and the only root of this pressure—expands inside me. But more than that, mid-morning is when I thought I was having a heart attack that day but wasn't. Mid-morning is a nudge for my palms to sweat, for my breath to become shallower than it needs to be, for my heart to gasp in my chest. Mid-morning is when I'm trapped in an office twenty traffic-clogged miles from home.

A panic attack is less likely these days, but if it's near, this is when its teeth will come out.

Today I go to the restroom in the office building and splash my face with cold water, looking up at the mirror in time to see a too-long arm retracting through the closing door, down near where the carpet begins in the hallway. I didn't hear the door open. There was no one here when I came in. A monster I made would do this exact thing, to let the protagonist know it is near and push the story a step further into horror and a heartbeat closer to confrontation. It's a reminder that the uncanny is insinuating itself into what has been mundane.

Since the monster is half-made, I spend my lunch break writing this list of components, the parts I will stitch together:

Organic and of the same atoms as my body. In another story, the protagonist would drive up into the mountains, wade through the dusk, and cut a palm open. Squeeze blood onto moss cushioning a dead oak, for the symbolism of it, the amateur witchcraft. In this story, my heart aches to be quieted.

12 appendages, long & pale & many-jointed for folding, the pair below the face ending in 10 growths that are almost fingers. In another story, the protagonist would have a terror of spiders. I do not—mine is of wasps, but I have no wish to build a creature from a wasp's blueprint, either. This would place my fear in the wrong box. The extra limbs remove it from any taxonomy I know, and will cause my gut to churn in unease, giving me another excuse to blame all of this on indigestion.

Hairless torso with distended belly & caved, sagging chest. In another story, the monster would have slept long beneath the mountains' quilt of nature and eons, waiting for the moon to shine through a hole eaten by a rare beetle in a leaf upon a certain tree. The line of moonlight would strike the earth at an ordained angle above the creature's open eye. The monster, the god has waited for this beetle to begin its hungry life. Somewhere a cult convenes, unaware that the benign moon has found something they have roamed the earth in search of. Its belly would be full of things that burrowed into the soil to offer themselves to it. In this story, it is the mere bloat of gas, and above it the breathless cavity searching for something to fill it. My worried heart.

No tail because this would suggest a demonic or religious nature. In another story, faith would be a consideration. Something to cling to, an icon to hold up to evil. Faith would carry more light than a chain of words spoken in an emergency room. In this story, the sermon is given behind a sternum, and the ribcage pews are empty.

9 feet tall fully upright, its many arms opening to embrace me. In another story, the monster would tower over the protagonist in the dark. It would snatch him up and bear him away to some unspeakable end. I don't know why the monster must be so tall, or why I feel the need for my horror to gaze upward. I suppose it's because awe tends to come from a great height, and I look up so rarely. But I will be left in my bed, I believe, in the end. Won't I?

A long withered neck, a stem holding the gorgeous, unnatural face of a 25-year-old Adonis, too large a face, careless brown curls draping the forehead, a wet plump mouth. In another story, such beauty would elicit worship, as it does in the cult that has been roaming cities and townships and poring over old books. In this story, I cannot fathom why this creature must be so handsome. Perhaps there is too much ugliness in the news and I can't bear to build more of it. Or it is the reverse—how much evil has crawled on the skin of this world with a pleasant pale face?

A voice box with no voice, the root of a tongue that never grew (my self-complicit silence). In another story, it makes an awful, awful noise, a burring clicking choking garble. But in this story, if I turned to my partner and told her my thoughts, if I used my own voice, perhaps the monster would have a tongue, or perhaps the monster wouldn't exist at all.

I can picture this thing clinging to the side of our house and peering through the top of the window, crouched in the vacant cubicle next to mine, bundled in the hatchback of my little black car. I can imagine it—I can almost feel this on my skin—creeping into our bedroom in the damp crease between night and morning. It's bent over staring into my face. Its eyes glitter with a distant beauty.

It drags the tips of its fingers through the sparse hair on my chest, above my heart. All of its legs are out and flexing in the dark air. And I can see my partner lying beside me, but not the dog—where is she? How could I bring the idea of something like this into the lives of my two loves?

But again, how could this creature scare anyone other than me? Many authors say they write for themselves, but it's not enough for my heart. I waste the rest of my lunch hour staring out a window, into a parking deck, and see something moving in the shadows between cars. I make it through the last few hours of the workday.

Traffic home is thick, an orange paste of taillights and sun glare, and my car is an oven. The air conditioning can't keep up and my blood pressure must be elevating. I worry about hypertension. I recite the emergency room benediction. My eyes keep darting to the rearview mirror, in case something is hiding in the space behind the back seat. But it's not ready yet. Neither is its maker.

We take it for granted our hearts will keep beating, and when they shudder out of their clockwork, we stare down at ourselves in disbelief. We feel our bones, the density of them, with a new clarity, we feel the tendons creaking between them. We feel the organs stammering inside of us. The spark of life glows brighter in a desperate confusion.

We are made aware of the machines of us, and we find we don't know them after all—the synchronicity of all these gears is suddenly frightening. And when we survive these interruptions, we build meticulous architecture with our minds and hope our hearts will settle into the new rooms. We exercise. We lock the bourbon away. We salt our food less. We let time pass.

On Saturday I take a nap and press my chest into the mattress when the day's first palpitation comes. My pulse lurches, then grows tranquil until I am lulled to sleep, then sputters again. Late in the afternoon, I buy a used elliptical machine from a local online marketplace, pick it up from the seller, and begin a cardio regimen for the first time in my life. I start slow, feeling my heart slam like an uninvited, furious fist on a cheap wooden door. I tape a note beside the display screen that reads WITH A HEAVY HEART.

The exercise seems to help. My heart thinks it's stronger and so it is. Sunday there are no palpitations, and we pull up poison ivy outside in the wet blanket of heat, our arms and hands covered in protection against these vines that are monsters, too, in their invasiveness. The mountains are hidden behind a screen of our pines and a neighbor's sprawling oak, a sluggish creek bisecting our properties.

We eat roasted chicken Monday night, dinner salads Tuesday, and I push my heart on the elliptical, a few more minutes each day. A drop of sweat jumps from my face onto the note, causing the AR in HEART to run, the ink blossoming from the paper. I hope and I worry that my monster is dying against this new determination.

Maybe the deadline for the story will become its own creature—it crawls behind me, ten days left, seven, three. Doug and Michael send a mass email reminding the solicited authors that they're looking forward to reading our takes on the Frankenstein theme.

I remember Doug telling me that we can interpret it loosely—war is a monster, I thought back then, the president is a monster, division is a monster, we made these monsters—and this looseness becomes its own little prayer I repeat. After all, I have committed to the fear of my own heart.

Evenings I sit in the office with my laptop and watch the sun drown in the trees through the window. The mountains like teeth, the sky a gullet, but the monster begins to swell in my imagination and my fear subsides in the blank face of such vastness—a cosmic Lovecraftian god cannot stir the creative hairs on the back of my neck as it once did.

The dog goes back and forth between the living room and the office, unhappy that her pack isn't in the same spot. "When I finish the story," I say to her, "just a little longer." She licks my face and later I take her out back so she can patrol the fenced yard in the dark, protect us from what creatures she would make up in her own mind.

We are caught in the rhythm of our workdays, there is something like peace, we watch our regular shows on TV. My skin doesn't grow hot with panic at the office, and nothing dark trails behind me through the herd of cubicles or the parking deck gloom. I begin to go long minutes without thinking of my heart, as it opens itself up to the future, locked in its steady voice: *believe, believe, believe—*

But, of course, this must be a horror story. Halfway through Friday evening's walk with the dog, the dark falling and the humidity reluctant to follow it, my heart stops beating. I stagger and count to what feels like three but can't be that long, until it swerves back into rhythm, runs pounding up a flight of stairs to catch up with the rest of me.

My partner asks what's wrong, a note in her voice that tears at me. I don't answer. "Was it a palpitation?" she says. I tell her yes, maybe the exercise isn't helping, and she tells me precisely the thing I need to hear. "You have to give it time. A week of cardio isn't going to be a miracle."

She's right, but ahead of us, in the overgrown lawn of the empty house where the road curves, I see the shape of my monster crouched in knee-high grass. A cloud of gnats writhes above it.

A nd it comes to me tonight, for the first time, after my partner has fallen asleep. As though it, too, has forty-eight hours to finish the story.

The bedroom doorknob clicks, and I hear the soft whine of a creaking hinge as the air we have been breathing escapes into the rest of the house. I listen to it creep into the dark, until the beautiful face slides over the lower rim of my vision, staring down at me. Its expression could be mournful or studious.

My heart trips beneath my chest, kick drums falling out of line, and the creature moves to my right, passing around my side of the bed. It is naked, with its appendages freed. Four of them unfold toward its head, and I still won't move my face to allow more of it into my sight.

But the dog is not making a sound—I jerk my head away from the monster and there she is, her head on her paws, her eyes open with a hint of streetlight gleaming off them. She hasn't shot to her feet with a volley of barks. Her silence tells me the story isn't real. Beside her my partner turns toward me on her side, her face soft in sleep.

I look back to my right and the creature isn't there. I wait to see if it is inside of me, twitching itself around the heart attack that has taunted me for months, long before I gave it a face. The dog stretches and puts a paw on my leg. Turning to her, I see that she has closed her eyes. A weight lifts from me. I muddy the story further by sleeping without dreams.

I have discovered what Dr. Frankenstein knew—that the trickiest part is the animation of the flesh, the flickering of the brain stem into sentience. And I have realized that 4,100 words into this, the deadline quickening like its own heartbeat, I have no tangible agency as a storyteller. These machines—the heart, the brain—are stimulated by electricity. What current can I hope to tap into, to bring the monster off the page?

My heartbeat has slipped three times today, and I am standing at a pine tree in the hills that crest up toward the mountains. I have pricked my right thumb and smeared blood on the dusty bark of the trunk, where a spigot might be driven in. But even if there were sap, it would have dried to a syrupy crust.

This story is due tomorrow. The creature will return to our bedroom tonight, and the final seizing of my heart feels like the only ending that's left.

My pulse judders a fourth time. A pressure builds near my left shoulder. I speak to the tree: "Heart enzymes good, electrolytes good, no clots, blood pressure okay, rhythms textbook strong, no atrial fibrillation or arrhythmia."

The words have gathered a sort of music into them, their constant striving toward the calm legato. They will keep me alive. The rough tongue of my dog will keep me alive. The arms of my warm partner will keep me alive. The old hum of the mountains will keep me alive.

The deadline will pass, the story won't end. Above me the sun burns through a sheer haze of clouds, its heat squeezing everything until it is forced under these green breakers again.

"Night, love," my partner says. She'll fade into sleep within a minute, so I kiss her hand as she rolls away from me. I hug the dog so long she tries to worm out of my arms. Though I'm tired from an extra fifteen minutes on the elliptical, I wait for the monster, counting the soft lines of light the blinds reach across the ceiling like fingers.

It clutches at the doorknob a few minutes past one, the hinge moans, and I see the shape of what I made filling the threshold of the dark room. Its shadow drops and the ends of its twelve legs scratch across the floorboards. My heart wheezes as the ambient streetlight catches the carved marble of its face, as it moves around the bed to me, as it rises up, limbs twitching out.

It leans down to me and it does have something of a voice, a crackling drone, arrhythmic with the straining root of its tongue. Then the static clears into words: "Heart enzymes good, electrolytes good, no clots, blood pressure okay, rhythms textbook strong, no atrial fibrillation or arrhythmia."

Its voice is awful. It plays back the litany in a decaying tone, a disintegrating loop that reveals how rushed the ER doctor was that day, how empty the rash judgment of my health was. How the staff simply needed the free bed once the surface level tests came back clean. The litany has been turned sour.

And only now do I notice it has no scent—I never gave it one. I think of the smell of my parents' basement the year it flooded, the moldy cloud that took months to get rid of, but the monster doesn't take the assigned odor into its skin.

I hear a whimper, a sound I would know before any music, and the dog is suddenly not on the bed. I slide up onto my elbows and see her crouched in the corner of the room, by the closet, her eyes wide enough to show the rings of white around the dark brown irises, staring up at the creature. She's terrified, and now I do smell something, the tang of her urine on the floor.

"What—" my partner calls out. "What is it?" And the monster's arm lowers to me, the growths that give it a hand spreading to grip my chest. The dog makes a noise that is terror and protection and heartbreak, my love makes a noise that is the low beginning of a scream, and I can't do this anymore. I can't bring this into their lives. It wasn't supposed to be real in this way.

I picture a man, my age, darker hair, murmuring the same assurances of an emergency room doctor. I sketch him in my mind with a blunt pencil, all in a moment. The replacement protagonist—David—reaches up and pulls the monster into an embrace. Its hand meets his chest, it pushes through the sternum and tears out his spurting heart. David's girlfriend—Ana—shrieks until the monster turns to her.

Then she is silent, and the dark thickens in the house. The night falls upon the night, and hides the twelve legs scrabbling out of the room, the crickets falling as quiet as Ana, the mountains poorly drawn silhouettes in the distance. A trail of blood follows the creature into the world.

There was never a dog in the room. David and Ana don't own a pet.

I have to send the story to the editors today, but my trick with David—drawing him up in an instant of panic, giving him rudimentary likes and dislikes and a familiar horror of what his heart is doing at every moment inside of him, channeling a kind of electricity through him—isn't the ending I wanted. It's an ending the reader is likely to feel cheated by. I fell back on the timeless author's trick, pitting an evil I created against an unwitting character I created.

David saved me. I was my own *deus ex machina*.

My dog comes over to the chair and tucks her head under my arm and lifts. She wants me to scratch her magic spot, so I do, grateful last night has faded from her mind. And my partner's—I swore she'd had a nightmare, nothing more, and she believed me just enough.

But the monster isn't finished with me—it wants blood, not David's pixels. When the book is published, the ink in David's veins won't be enough. I turn back to the laptop, this narrative with no resolution—

Unless—until the monster returns, the arrhythmia creeps into the dark room, and your eyes open at the creak of the door hinge. Your wife, partner, husband, boyfriend, dog, or child lies sleeping next to you, caught in their warm dreams. The face, beautiful enough to haunt us all, regards *you*. Its eyes glitter in what could be moonlight, if you want it to be. Its limbs reach out and flex along their many joints.

Again, you have only to say, *This is a story about a writer writing a story. I am holding the book, so the writer lived to tell me the story.*

But take a moment to imagine the organs filling your body. Focus on your heart, think of how you take it for granted that it will keep beating. Feel its rhythm, feel what happens when it stutters out of true, feel one of its valves close incorrectly, and gasp open again, feel the disbelief that the machine of your body has betrayed you.

Your heart has always been there, unnoticed in moments of calm. Focus on it until the calm slips. Feel it palpitate right now, and feel it gallop to reclaim the grace of its gait, fighting the abrupt illness of its rhythm. Feel the ugliness of it squeezing blood out and slurping blood in.

Take this moment to listen for your heartbeat, slow your breathing until you hear something behind you, crawling closer along the carpet or floorboards or blanket of pine needles.

I made David up, and in that fiction he canceled out the monster. It needs blood and squirming tissue to claim. David couldn't take my place because he wasn't real. But you are real, and I have pulled back the curtain to expose your heart.

THE TEETH OF AMERICA

[excerpt from *Rotting Pyramid: Tracing the Teeth of America Cult,* Dr. Linda Royal, University of Georgia Press, 2025]

The nine thousand wild acres between Hiram and Forsyth—between Georgia state roads 9 and 113 and 378, specifically—form a rough triangle, and the cult erected the pyramid in its center. They buoyed it in an ocean of scrub pine cut with hickory and misplaced live oaks, perhaps drawing on the power of a half-arcane symbology. Tennessee and North Carolina meet in a mountain seam just north. Hidden among the tallest trees, the pyramid decomposed for as many as four years, an organic clock winding down to apotheosis.

The estimated 136 people buried in the soil and red clay—all white males, per available data—were either victims or new archetypes, according to what is cherrypicked from local rumor[1] and certain archival material.[2] A circle of graves around the pyramid, a line of graves leading to it, each corpse sprouting into muddled, unclassified life. Today the wedge of forest is filled with ecologists, botanists, epidemiologists, and forensics investigators, among other branches of science.

Before its apparent dissolution in 2024, the Teeth of America is thought to have reached close to 200 members, including those that were buried. For several years, the cult recruited the majority of these online as Pale Cross,[3] an organization with no known status or physical headquarters. Membership in Pale Cross precluded an invitation to the Teeth of America.

The far-right and white nationalist leaning of its online content (primarily restricted to message board websites such as Reddit, 4chan, and 8kun, as there was no website of its own, even on the dark web) has contributed to a great stir of debate regarding the true intent of the group—whether to espouse the recently prevalent Aryan supremacy doctrine or to lure martyrs already steeped in it to a strange death.

The burials themselves further the mystery: antifascist murders or supremacist experiments in evolution? Both motives can claim righteousness. Both motives could even claim God, the malleable face of so many groups, as a benefactor, if one squints in the right way. These sociological impacts will likely ripple the surface of the conversation for some time.

[excerpt from "What the Teeth of America Cult Says About Our National Nightmare," Jonathan Diehl, *New South Magazine*, August 17, 2024]

Derek Albies doubts he will ever leave Hiram. The 19-year-old lifelong resident tells me he would have said this before the night of April 6, 2024, when he and two friends went into the forest that has been the subject of national fascination, and he would still say it now. Even after his brother, Hunter, was taken by the Teeth of America last year and planted in this Georgia clay.

"I've got my job," he tells me, referring to the polyurethane mold plant in Forsyth, a town that also borders the site of the "Rotting Pyramid." We're standing atop Noles Hill, which overlooks the beginning of those woods, the tip of the spearhead pointing at the world. This peak is perhaps at 40 feet of elevation, as the land here is a valley of sorts, a soft prelude to the Blue Ridge Mountains. "And there's my mom and dad and my sister, she's pregnant with her second. But I like it here, and President Trump got us disaster money. He's bringing the good days back."

Regional statistics do not bear out this claim, nor does the general tone of the town's residents. Fannin County has a growing unemployment rate (18% as of June of this year, far above the national average even during the height of COVID) following two decades of peripheral suburbanization. Atlanta is less than 100 miles south—a distance that once seemed greater—but life here is still decidedly rural, the population holding steady before and during the president's two terms.

And much like the Trump era, it is difficult to know how the area will make out in the aftermath of the Teeth of America.

Derek has an inordinate amount of gray hair for someone still in his teens. His crewcut glints in the strong sunlight. I ask him about the 6th of April, three days before the FBI raided this land and something far stranger than Waco or Heaven's Gate unfolded here. After several minutes of staring down at the woods, however, Derek says he can't open up about it yet.

[excerpt from *Proud Boys With Antlers: The Occult Evolution of White Nationalists*, Stefanie Morales, Riverhead Books, 2025]

The closest I came to interviewing a viable firsthand witness of the days leading up to the FBI raid was Anthony Belanger. He wouldn't answer or return my calls, but several weeks after the first draft of this book was finished, I received an email from him along with permission to reprint it here. Grammatical corrections, such as adding capitalization and paragraph breaks, have been kept to a minimum.

Here is how that night went.

Derek said his flashlight died soon as he went in the woods the night before so he chickened out. We laughed but he got real quiet all day at the plant worried about his brother. Then we caught him crying in the cafeteria and we said we would go back with him if he really thought Hunter was in there. I mean we were kind of friends with Hunter too.

We all brought lights, me and Derek and Robby, and they all cut out when we got in the trees. Phones too. You could hear the trees growing or something. It sounded like all the floors in my gramma's house before she died. Old wood all swelled like it was rained on her whole life and slow creaking. But the moon was enough and we went on.

Before long there were these mounds all in a straight line through the woods like graves. There were things coming out of them. Arms reaching up made of like mushrooms and bone and this jelly stuff but kind of none of those things either. But at the same time they were real arms with real skin. It is hard to explain. Everything smelled real green.

And that was what we had been hearing with the growing noises, them coming out. Then we saw some already mostly out and standing up. They were short. Spores were drifting off their skin and they had like deer antlers. Four or five each just coming out of their heads only in the wrong places.

We went on some more and these things looked less human but sort of more human too and what started off being like 4 or 5 feet tall was more like 10. Like house tall. A couple had those PROUD BOY tattoos on their arms just like on the internet but split open or covered in green stuff.

Then Derek yelled out Hunter and ran over to one. It did look like Hunter. I could remember one time he got in a fight with some

Mexicans and got his face busted from being outnumbered. He was yelling at them and he groped one of their girlfriends or something. So I had experience seeing him messed up. Of course he did not have a swollen neck and three white bones like antlers coming out of his face that time with the fight. But he or it or whatever did not react but just kept growing with that old floor sound.

I heard Derek screaming like his scream was turned on in the middle. I was feeling awful now. He pulled on his brother's arm and eventually Hunter looked down from high up and kind of grinned with parts of his mouth rotting off. There was like moss or pond scum in his mouth. He lifted Derek up off the ground and me and Robby went over and pulled him back. We ran like dumbasses in the wrong direction away from where we'd come in and the antler people kept getting taller at every mound.

It got darker too at first with the creaking and pieces of moon falling between the trees. We ran half blind but then we got to the pyramid and that changed. It was lit up in an ocean kind of way. Like what I had read about deep in the ocean when I was a kid the way fish have to have this weird biological stuff to live.

And the pyramid was alive. It was shaped like one of the ones in Egypt but it was alive and flexing like a stomach and it was dying. It had this awful stink cause it was decaying, parts peeling off like Hunter's mouth. The light moving all in the holes and full of maggots and there was a cloud of flies.

With the ocean light we could see some of those sort of human things around it but these ones were near as tall as my mom's house which is two floors. They had come out of the ground and were walking all slow with those antlers and extra arms or legs hanging off and skinny. The head of one was covered with eyes. They looked like the pyramid in some way that hurt to look at. Moaning a lot like with pain in their guts.

And almost worse there were naked guys crawling around on the pyramid and some of them pushing half into its walls. Those ones were still most of the way human.

There was this man sitting in front of the door of the pyramid but it looked like a mouth trying to say something more than a door. The man was bald and had the whitest skin. He had the blackest robe on. The maggots were piled up behind him in the door. He looked beautiful in some terrible way that makes me want to cry when I think about him.

He said he was taking the white race to its natural conclusion in self worship. I remember those were the words he used. He asked us if we thought the white man was a superior creature and if we liked to own the libs and did we think racism was over and would we like to join our brethren and become something more?

He laughed and pointed at one of the tall antler or tree or ocean things. I hardly remember Robby and Derek standing there. The air was hot and wet and got in the way of thinking.

Robby stepped toward the man and I just ran until I could not hear him laugh anymore. That's all I wanted was to not hear that bright laugh anymore. We came out of the woods on the Trickum Rd side but Robby was not with us. We called his name a while into the trees in between puking on the road.

He never came out. Derek's nose was bleeding. He had all these white hairs he did not have before. I looked in the mirror when I got home and I did too.

[transcript of "rotting pyramid speaks," YouTube video uploaded May 11, 2021]

[A grainy darkness in which the focus sharpens and dulls by small degrees, sometimes resolving into a pale face: the suggestion of eye sockets, a cheekbone, a mouth stretched open. The clip begins with 47 seconds of subtle wet sounds like eating or objects slowly stirring liquid or perhaps simply flaws in the recording. A persistent whining drone suggests a swarm

of flies. Then a voice, pitched low and threaded with a humming static, begins speaking.]

"The power of the mind is in and of itself occult. Confirmation bias and negative partisanship—willfulness—proved reality is only a fabric, and fabric can tear. It is a loose weave with rotted thread. We are at an apogee. The moon is at its furthest point from us. Maybe God is too, we as a moon in our own long orbit of whatever heaven is.

"I saw it everywhere. It clouded the air. It tasted like an ignored power. The hate flowing from mouths, breaking the hearts and even the minds of those who wanted the truth to be truth, and for kindness to be kindness. A plague made half of us crueler than ever. Facts became bolder, but lies rose up and became truth in such a profound, puzzling human moment.

"What was happening to us? Perhaps this was the tearing point for the fabric. People would not move from the lines their minds had drawn, and reality never stood a chance. How could it against such numbers?

"And I thought—it seemed like if the world can be a cult, the word *cult* can change with the world. And the word *occult* can change. Just think—can demons or what we call demons be made real if we choose to believe in them no matter what? Simple belief. If the idea of God Himself can be turned ugly across the centuries, if God Himself can finally be crushed in the teeth of His creation, the mind can do anything."

[The voice pauses. The white blurring face turns to look into the camera.]

"This is a new demonology. These are the teeth of America.

"And so it stood to reason that what I wanted to do was not just possible." *[A longer pause with continued wet sounds and a faint, panicked gasping in the background.]* "It was probable. I have given birth to my pyramid. To plant it with the worms. My edifice to new—gods, to use a word that doesn't fit. Something to wake us from our dreams."

[A hand appears, long and deeply white, more in focus than the face. Its fingers reach out and seem to caress the screen. The clip ends here.]

[excerpt from *Rotting Pyramid: Tracing the Teeth of America Cult,*
Dr. Linda Royal]

Little is known regarding the leader of the group. Presumably a
white male, he is known only as "Rotting Pyramid" in a pair of
YouTube videos[4] that would later be linked to the cult. As these clips
were uploaded in 2021-22, a particular veracity is afforded.

His expressed motives for constructing the pyramid further
muddy the waters of understanding, but it is the author's belief that a
mode of nihilism—driven by an interest in the occult and mysticism—
might be as much to blame as either pole of the political sphere.

Scarcely more is known about the pyramid itself. Nothing
remained but flies when the first forensics team got their test tubes
ready; thus, studies of it have been restricted to its ghost in the
ecosystem, primarily in soil, insect, and plant life. Models extrapolate
a square base with a height of 28 feet, small as pyramids go but
looming large in a forested area of relatively modest trees. Traces of
brick dust have been recovered from the site,[5] but certain recalcitrant
compounds, such as chitin and ossein, are prevalent to much greater
degrees, bearing out video and eyewitness accounts of purely organic
material. Namely, meat and bone.

As of late 2024, law enforcement and government officials have
yet to declassify the bulk of available reports and have been reticent
even in the face of public health concerns. One Georgia Bureau of
Investigation officer briefly discussed on Twitter what first responders
encountered in the Hiram-Forsyth woods on April 9:

"These things were like Jeff Goldbloom [sic] halfway through
that fly movie / they were coming at us and falling apart at the same
time / lord the stink of it."[6]

The tweet was removed promptly, but screenshots survive in
online posterity. Between the GBI, FBI, and Fannin County Sheriff's

Office, a total of 16 agents and officers were killed over the course of the raid, which reportedly lasted three hours. Somehow the media outlets were kept away until it was too late.

There were no survivors among the cult members—those that had been "born" as new organisms were certainly already dying before the raid—and the burial sites, too, have yielded limited and/or baffling results as a whole. However, two dozen of these graves still contained their corpses (or pupae, depending on one's perspective), nearly all concentrated at a greater distance from the pyramid.

Along with those dead at the scene of the raid, these have given researchers the greatest rewards. The bodies were found within a range of decomposition depending on time of death, but each exhibited a contradictory state of deliquescence and growth— turning to a mush densely packed with plant compounds while also calcifying, ossifying, sprouting new appendages such as antlers and limbs. The remainder of the mounds had been split open and bore organic traces similar to those at the base of the pyramid.

Organic compounds not previously found in nature were identified, such as the twining of plant and animal DNA—the calcium and phosphorus of antler marrow fused with urushiol, the oil secreted by poison ivy; bird feather keratin threaded with chlorophyll, pine sap, and squirrel hair follicles; the glossy chitin of a southern pine beetle's carapace threaded with white-tailed deer hair; human semen in mosquito proboscises; human teeth with Virginia creeper root fibers.[7] For each of these genetic anomalies, there is another that spirals into further esoteric biology. The bonding of lithium and chromium to white blood cells into perhaps a new element,[8] as only one example, is a question that will be discussed across the periodic table and in anthropology symposiums for decades.

Through litigation, the Southern Poverty Law Center acquired DNA results from eight of the occupied burial mounds—each that was identified matched an American male involved in far-right or white supremacist movements.[9] From the violently patriarchal Proud Boys to the Aryan Brotherhood of Texas—not to mention three known cases of active Ku Klux Klan members[10]—the devotedly disaffected found their way to the North Georgia mountains. It is assumed they did not know the nature of their "evolution" until it was too late, but this is far from certain.

[excerpt from *Proud Boys With Antlers: The Occult Evolution of White Nationalists,* Stefanie Morales]

The following letter was sent to Tyler Wilhelm, a Teeth of America member and victim, in September of 2021 along with a hand-drawn map. I reprint it below with permission of his sister, Sarah, who was kind enough to be interviewed for this book.

Fellow keeper of the birthright of the Pale Cross! It is time to join your brethren and Become something more. You are proven kin with the Teeth of America. As you are the product of superior evolution, in intellect and in cunning, in godliness, we offer you the final step into this ascension. This is the destiny of our race. The rise of the white sun. You have one week to arrive. You need only BELIEVE as lesser souls cannot. You need only taste of the Pyramid. Journey well, brother.

There came a point—around the time of President Trump's reelection—that Sarah Wilhelm stopped reminding her brother that he had never stepped foot in the South and began fearing his obsession with the Confederate flag. What had started as a bumper sticker on the tailgate of Tyler's pickup truck—HERITAGE NOT HATE shouted a foot above his Pennsylvania license plate—now seemed to be with him all the time: "a haunted look in his eyes," she says.

It was an accelerated infection Sarah can trace in a clear line back to their father. The elder Wilhelm was a quiet bigot. His slurs were couched in softer words and oblique nudges, easy to brush off even when they should not have been. The voices of Rush Limbaugh and Sean Hannity began murmuring through his ever-present earbuds sometime in the 1990s, and Sarah can now see the slow poison in him, the graying of his skin along with his hair. A self-righteous exoskeleton hardened around him.

Tracking her father's infection is more difficult, with evangelical threads trailing back through the Republican Tea Party, the conditioning of Reaganomics, piercing the Civil Rights Act to anchor in the ugly hide of Jim Crow. An illness of resentment and entitlement, vague as its logic, festered in millions alongside him. It is the familiar story that has weakened the dynamic of so many American families in recent years.

The two Wilhelm children took their nurture and developed entirely different social constructs—Sarah working with nonprofits in the blue bubble of Philadelphia, Tyler trawling online message boards in the 96% white Blair County. Their mother died in 2004, after 9/11 twisted a new dial of white nationalism, before she could watch her husband's political rage begin to be more carefully curated by the voices in his ear.

Sarah remembers the QAnon T-shirt Tyler wore to Thanksgiving dinner in 2019. She remembers spittle flying from his mouth—some of it misting onto the carved turkey—when he defended the shirt to their Aunt Linda. And she remembers his manic nature when Donald Trump was reelected, how the new facets of his personality seemed to sharpen. The look in his eyes went from haunted to bright zealous sparks.

At some point, he branched away from their father, into the open militant arms of certain online communities. Less quiet, less subtle, more catalyzing. Sarah recalls a friend sending her a video clip of Tyler in the spring of 2020, one segment of a foolish worm coiled in front of the state capitol in Harrisburg to demand the state be reopened completely in the first months of the COVID-19 pandemic, when the death toll was climbing nationwide.

He was holding an assault rifle that would soon make appearances in his social media posts. One day she zoomed in on him in a photo she found on Facebook until it blurred into pixels to try to read a patch on his jacket, which had been identified in a comment as the insignia of the Patriot Front, a white nationalist/neo-Nazi group that coopts conservative dog-whistle talking points about "freedom."

A few weeks later, another friend of Sarah's witnessed him using the same rifle to break windows in Philadelphia storefronts, a tactic used by many far-right groups across the country to escalate protests against police violence into all-out riots.

Sarah lost track of Tyler after that. Her attempts to reach out to him went unanswered for more than a year.

On September 19, 2021, he shouted four words on Facebook—"THE WHITE MAN ASCENDS"—and vanished. Three years later, his personal effects—wallet, driver's license, cell phone—were found buried in the woods outside Hiram, Georgia, near the site of the Rotting Pyramid. Tyler had ended up in the Confederacy, after all, through the jaws of the Teeth of America.

Sarah looks back over all the brooding signs and tells me she's not surprised he joined the cult and sacrificed himself to become such a malformed, brief monster: "He wanted to be something more," she wrote to me in an email after our phone call. "Then more again. Something always more. It's how that letter hooked him. I think white nationalists—or maybe the people who *make* white nationalists is the better way to put it—all know on some level that the world is moving on without them, no matter how much power they have. That must be where the anger comes from. He wanted to be a weapon for a cause I don't think he ever understood."

As for why he was chosen for the cult, perhaps it was simply this lack of understanding, and the passion that could be stirred up in the space where wisdom should be, in a better world.

But Sarah Wilhelm also remembers Tyler pulling her around their cul de sac, the wheels of her red wagon rumbling as he took her in ever lessening circles toward the center, a spiral that ended in the Happy Dot, which Sarah would always draw with sidewalk chalk before they started. And then out again, in widening loops. Hours of this, Tyler almost ten years old, Sarah still four.

She remembers Tyler driving her to get ice cream the day he got his driver's license, then to Duncansville Park and its little pond everyone called a lake, where they skimmed rocks until the light failed.

These days she works with Life After Hate, on Tyler's behalf, imagining a story arc in which he was able to pull the poison out of his mind and help others do the same.

She doesn't speak much to her father. He spends his days slouched in his den watching Fox and One America News—*den* is the right word, she says, an animal's dim lair with an animal's musk, in which his face is painted by the violent light of a constant news cycle, where truth is what you demand it to be.

It has become difficult for her to draw fond memories of him out of her childhood. She has already mourned him. Eventually, she worries, it will feel as though he was the first of their parents to die.

[transcript of "rotting pyramid speaks" #2,
YouTube video uploaded October 25, 2021]

[A candle, nearly burned down and guttering, sits on a saucer before the camera. Grainy VHS darkness crowds around the flame. Wet sounds can be heard, shifting and squelching, punctuated by long groans. A dark mass fills the background, perhaps a building or a mound of earth, and pale naked figures seem to be crawling upon it. They are indistinct. The candlelight catches their movement, those surfaces that glisten with moisture.

After 84 seconds of the unsteady light, a pallid face pushes into frame from behind the candle, into the foreground, its mouth and eyes pockets of shadow. The head is narrow and bald. The mouth opens and breathes upon the saucer, and the darkness folds over. Only the blurred hint of the face remains. The voice that follows is low and distorted.]

"I have eleven of them now. They find me, they come into the trees, hate and dogma flushing their soft skins. Their teeth already loosening for me. They lay themselves on the dirt and leaves before me.

"I send them into the pyramid to gestate, and they go without pause, without question, almost without thought. I tell them their favorite lies and they make their own truths, to become their own new templates. They make their bodies into their own new temples.

"They emerge, eaten and cleaned, and I bury them in shallow earth, I nourish them like the worms that eat them, but it is their belief that rewrites their bones."

[A pause of 21 seconds, in which the face tilts up and seems to scent the air. It opens its mouth into an obscene hole.]

"It is no scripture of mine. I am but their guide and their minder.

"What, before, might have been conjecture is now evident. Already evident. The power of the mind is in and of itself occult. This new demonology. This new apogee. These teeth of America."

[Another pause. A long, liquid scream from a short distance. More screams rise up to join it, drawn out and watery. A match tears into light, the candle wavers again, and the white face fades into the background with the light, toward the dark mass. The bald head is disembodied above the candle—or the figure is wearing a black robe.

The light is lowered to the ground as two people—presumably people— creep around the sides of the mass, as though escaping the light. White arms snake out of the robe and it—he—can be seen pulling something out of the mass, something wet and humanoid with growths extending from the front of its face. It moans as it flops onto the ground. Static builds as the bald man drags the figure out of the camera's view.]

[excerpt from *Rotting Pyramid: Tracing the Teeth of America Cult,*
Dr. Linda Royal]

Alongside the medical and scientific expertise in these North Georgia woods—all the teeming -*ologies*—a certain measure of attention has been given to an occult element. Folklorists, theologians, and professors of esotericism poke around the site of the Rotting Pyramid with their respective two cents, not to mention a peripheral contingent of conspiracy theorists and psychics that sneak into the trees after the others have taken their notes and soil samples back to their cities and universities. The Church of Satan has sent its own dignitaries on this strange pilgrimage as well, though this has largely been viewed more as a political display than a pursuit of knowledge.[19]

These experts, though less demonstrably academic, are asking the question more baldly: What was the role of the occult here? Could it be credible? Have demonology and Judeo-Christian theology anything to do with the organic matter of the pyramid and these aberrant ritualistic burials? Could there feasibly be an evolutionary catalyst in play, some cosmic straw best grasped within a Lovecraft tale?

In his "Rotting Pyramid" YouTube clips, the presumed leader of the cult claims to have created a new demonology predicated upon a theory that "the power of the mind is in and of itself occult." Vindication and fear are currently spreading through the theological world. Taken at his word, and supplemented by the evidence this small army of PhDs has gathered over the past ten months (see Chapter Four), this theory—with its aversion to natural laws—cannot be easily discounted. From an anthropological or sociological standpoint, there is merit, no matter that biology screams out against it, in that way akin to denial, not outright refutation.

Once science is scraped away and too much unexplained tissue remains, there is a sense of the alchemical, as applied in mysticism tracing to the ancient Greeks and Anglo-Saxon Britons. Paganism meets chemistry. This transmuting of elements brings to mind a Philosopher's Stone with lungs and migrating cells, all infused with and animated by—as the cult's founder puts it—belief.

No operative doctrine of the Teeth of America has been uncovered or even guessed at. There are only the musings and vague manifesto of this man's strange amateur videos, and he has presumably gone to ground.

Still, lacking clear lineation, and in spite of the occult straining faith in these long years since the Enlightenment, one must at least allow these considerations: What is more occult than belief? How may the occult survive without it? And what *is* belief in this saturated 21st century?

[excerpt from "What the Teeth of America Cult Says About Our National Nightmare," Jonathan Diehl]

When standing on a summit, it's easy to imagine a battle below. You get the bird's and the general's eye view. From Noles Hill, I can almost see shell casings gleam in the V of the two blacktop roads meeting here at the point of the trees.

What was this battle for? To show racism as the monstrosity it is—literally, with monsters that we finally cannot look away from? I believe the evidence says so, vigilantism aside. If these were gods shambling out of the mountain valley, they were as ill-conceived as much of the United States' dark history.

But in an echo of Charlottesville in 2017 (as all too often since), it has been said that our nation lost honorable citizens on the law enforcement side on April 9th...and the white supremacist side. The calls for unity are as divided as ever, leading us to wonder what the point of it all was, if there is any atrocity that *can't* be repackaged in real time for an intended audience.

In white evangelist America, the dog whistles have been put aside for megaphones. God Himself is shambling, too, chewed up in the teeth of His followers, to paraphrase the leader of the cult that nested here. Maybe this was the point, that all gods are ill-conceived if they are subject to ill beliefs.

But when belief itself will not coalesce into truth, when it stubbornly bends even further away from it into something new, where does this leave us? The Teeth of America has given news outlets such as Fox and Breitbart more fodder for their anti-antifa ramblings—*how dare this liberal cult target white people*, the subtext seems to demand indignantly, as though violent nationalists are standing in for all white Americans.

Meanwhile, some militant "news" sites that make Breitbart seem pacifist cling to a belief that the still-obscure things that emerged from the woods this spring may have failed but still foreshadow the next phase of some kind of reverse eugenics, a coming dawn of evolution. New hate groups have bred in the wake. This has shown us nothing so much as that the era of Fake News marches on, mutating into its own unprecedented monster until the word *unprecedented* loses the last of its meaning.

Have we learned anything? And what was the lesson? Perhaps these Teeth should have taken a bigger bite.

I ask Derek Albies if his brother wanted to see the white race elevated to its former epoch, the sort of dominance that would no longer be questioned. Instead of answering, he tells me Hunter wasn't a bad guy. He was tricked by the cult's promises.

When I point out that the promises involved a deep embrace of white supremacy, he goes back to the mantra: Hunter wasn't a bad guy. He says this repeatedly, though he'll never quite look at me.

Perhaps Derek isn't far from the truth. Unlike most of the cult's victims, Hunter Albies wasn't a known affiliate of any hate group.

He was a local. His proximity to these woods, and his driftless life in an agitated, divided land, may be as much to blame. Derek looks down at the spearhead of trees, the sun picking out the white in his hair like a constellation.

And just last week, a grainy video was uploaded to Twitter by the anonymous handle @newdemon, a drone shot passing over a sweep of forest darker and more textured than the one below us. It is riddled with static. A black pyramid seems to loom among the trees for a moment, before the camera glitches wildly and cuts off.

"I guess we still think God is ours," Derek tells me. His voice is difficult to read. "We say we were made in His image. Why do all you reporters think you'll change that?"

He turns to go, back to Hiram, away from where the pyramid fell apart.

[transcript of "rotting pyramid speaks" #3,
YouTube video uploaded July 7, 2025]

[In the 95 seconds of darkness, a mass shifts in the background among trees, as though the camera was moved laterally and segments were edited together afterward, into an unsettling smoothness. But the quality of sound, the tones of dark, the tree species, the candles in the middle foreground, the squelching noises, the naked figures crawling on the mass—it becomes clear that all these elements are different as well as in different locations.

The camera's viewpoint retreats six times to show a towering pyramid, a blue-black sky framing its lines between tree crowns. These are six distinct pyramids in six forests.

A voice speaks throughout the video, pitched low and warped. At times the edge of the white face is glimpsed on alternating sides of the frame, the curve of a grimace, a smile, the rim of a wide eye.]

"And now your new President, begotten of the old, builds the wall higher. He takes literature away. He controls your bodies. Eight zealots sit on the highest court. We lock the old weak gods inside with us. We insist on lengthening the apogee. We strain the leash of heaven. We wear our hate in our mouths. Our hate grows in our bones and we call it godliness.

"Books have been written of my teeth. Billions of pixels are spilled to understand. But my recruits—my little gods—my growths—these are just the abscesses. The infections at the root. The journalists and the anchors and the writers and the scholars, they second-guess. They appeal to the better angels that are long chewed and swallowed and digested. They give ugliness the benefit of the doubt until all is benefit and all is doubt. They still have not seen."

[A pause in which a chorus of groans can be heard.]

"Let them see.

"*These* are the teeth of America. The rotting pyramids. Surely you did not think it would be just the single tooth rooted in the jaw of this land? These will decay, until you are pulled from the mouth of history."

[In an echo of the first video of the series, a hand appears, long and white. Its fingers reach out and seem to caress the screen. The clip ends here.]

WATCH YOU

IT TAKES SLOW SIPS

Forty minutes to drive eleven miles, and the daylight was souring over the trees behind the apartments. He had left in the dark and just made it home before the dark. For a moment he sat in his car and watched a white dog being walked in the park across the street, its fur almost shining. People were wearing coats now, but it was only September. It had gotten cold two weeks before his favorite season, the one with her name.

He had been standing all day. His feet ached through the foyer and up the stairs to 312. A long envelope the color of butter lay on the carpet, wedged a few inches under his door. COLIN was written in black marker ink that had seeped out in tendrils before it dried, causing the letters to blur. The pale red words PINE ARCH RESEARCH had been stamped within a beveled rectangle in one corner.

Neither name had an address, as though the envelope had been hand delivered. He picked it up and something shifted from one end of the package to the other with a hoarse whisper.

The light inside the apartment was like stagnant water through the blinds. His laptop and phone waited on the kitchen island, and a dryness spread through his mouth. He hadn't seen her face since before the sun rose. He couldn't get used to missing her, but leaving these devices behind was the only way he could keep a job. The job was the only thing stopping him from moving back to her early. Before the fall. Her name.

He said her name twice as though greeting the phone and then the computer. Autumn, her hair a yellow darkened to brown like a turning leaf, waves crashing against her neck. Colin liked to picture her in the tiny pottery studio she had set up in the house she rented, streaks of gray drying on her arms, dabs of gray in the hair she kept having to tuck behind her ears. Barely five feet of her on a stool, spinning clay through her delicate small hands. When she paused and looked up into the distance, through her walls, what hung there in her thoughts?

While his soup heated in the microwave, he tore a side off the envelope to postpone the comfort of looking at her. Two halves of a CD slid out onto the counter, each a wedge of iridescent mirror. He turned them over and saw **WA Y** written on one half in perhaps the same black marker from the envelope, **TCH OU** on the other. The disc had been snapped neatly into two useless pieces.

He couldn't make sense of the letters. He opened the microwave to end the piercing tone that wasn't loud but always dug into his head. When he pushed the CD halves together, **WA Y TCH OU** stretched in a line that was almost perfectly straight above the center hole. Careful lettering. WAY. TOUCH? It clicked and he saw WATCH YOU. The disc had been broken on purpose. Otherwise the Y and the OU would have been written below the rest.

Colin wondered what the point of the package was. He'd never heard of Pine Arch Research, and the person he had hired online wouldn't have traveled up here to deliver a package in person. But even as the thought rose, it fell away. Autumn was all that mattered.

He checked his phone and saw an email notification on his screen from mid-morning. He tapped to open her full message and smiled into the phone light washing up onto his face. *A man was following me last night. Outside my window and scratching at the door. You promised in court. Leave me alone!* He turned on a lamp and the kitchen light and sat down to eat the soup.

He typed out with his thumbs: *Are you okay?? You should maybe call the police. I told you I have this job in Durham until October. Why would you think that was me? It was just one bad mistake. I thought I'd left something at your house but wanted to know if you were up before I knocked, remember? Please be safe. I care about you.*

The soup was too hot, it couldn't cover the taste in his throat of days without sleep. He closed his eyes tight and felt the burning under the lids. He listened to the warm song of his blood pushing through him, cresting in his ears. Sometimes when his eyes were pressed shut this hard, the sound of his blood was almost the sound of mountains shifting far away.

He counted the number of times he had typed *you*, each one an intimate touch. He deleted *I care about you*. The words ached as they disappeared, but he had to build to it. He needed her to realize some things on her own. He sent the text and closed his eyes again.

What was she doing in this moment, as the sun bled away? He pictured her out for a walk, in a light jacket because it was a little warmer down in Atlanta, his message vibrating against her thigh. She stopped and a man with a dog curved around her, the dog's tongue hanging out of its mouth like one of the cozy socks she'd had in her dresser drawer. She slipped her phone out of her pocket and read his words. What did her face look like? Did it light up? Did lines crease her forehead? He would need to know before he was near her again.

He checked his social media accounts, but they'd been dormant for three months. It was as though Colin had died and no one had noticed yet. These profiles only existed now as doors for Autumn to open, to walk back through into his life.

She had changed her Facebook, Instagram, and Twitter passwords weeks ago, but he didn't think she had figured out he had them because he could still get into her email. He had been careful ever since he found the list in her desk the only night he ever spent with her.

He handled this last password like a delicate glass structure that could collapse in his lungs at any moment. Even his breathing changed when he was in her account.

There was nothing today that caught in his throat or twisted cords in his gut. No cute messages from Cory, and she had lost interest in Brandon in July. She was working on herself, just like he was.

He logged out and opened his own email. There were message replies from the forum where his friends lived. They thought his strategy was solid. They reminded him that "celibate" didn't need to apply to him anymore, so why should "involuntary"? There was a time when you took what you deserved.

He saw a money transfer request from username par000600606, the message *went out with some females, went home alone*, and a video clip of Autumn, sleeping, filmed through a gap between her curtains. It was ten minutes long, and at the end, the scene changed to a few seconds of a different house, a dark figure stretching up the wall toward a window, before cutting off.

Colin watched the clip again as he ate the cooling soup, even though it was grainy and the angle didn't show much, then sent the second half of the payment and asked par000600606 if he was available to follow Autumn the day after tomorrow. He needed more. He needed it to elevate. He needed her to need him when he returned.

He felt he could sleep now, but he sifted through her social media photos. There were only two new ones, and no men in them. One had the caption, *Still scared of the dating scene but #selflove is my hashtag*. He tapped the heart on a select few images.

She had blocked Colin everywhere not long after their one date, the day after she caught him fastening his pants at her window. He hadn't been careful enough. But he could still see her because the profile swooning over her pictures was a woman he had made up. An older woman who sold pottery online just like Autumn did. This woman was safe, she had watched from a casual distance at first and only last weekend started messaging her, praising her work and promising to order some pieces.

It takes slow sips to not waste a good thing, he thought his father had told him that once. But he was still there when the night was gone, looking at her face. He memorized it all over again, and the first pink light pushed at the blinds.

C olin came home and the sun was still hanging above the trees, clawing at the sky as it fell. Its blood caught in the low clouds. He was tired again, his senses were dulled by patience. For the first time since moving here and leaving his access to Autumn at home every day, his work performance was suffering.

The manager had asked if there was something wrong after he got another order wrong, and Colin had looked into the perfect sunlight through the café windows and come close to saying the restraining order was choking him at this distance. He shouldn't have moved this far away from her, four hundred miles was playing it too safe.

There was another envelope outside the door of 312, the same weight sliding across as he picked it up. He placed it on the counter as soon as he walked into the apartment. He had missed her so much today. It was difficult to remember the way she smelled. He went straight for the phone.

The home screen was empty, just the washed-out background image of Autumn asleep on that delicate, awful April night. Her windowpanes had been poorly cleaned. He was still bothered by the streaks getting in the way of a good view of her. But it was still her face.

The stamped PINE ARCH RESEARCH was smeared this time on the yellow envelope. His name seemed to have been written with less care, with fewer tendrils of ink soaking into the paper fibers because the marker had slashed the letters instead of dragging them.

The disc inside was whole, it slid out onto his palm with a corrupted image of his face staring up at him on one side and the words WATCH YOU on the other in a nearly perfect line.

He thought of the "par" initials in the username he had paid to follow her. Maybe they stood for Pine Arch Research. Maybe this was more footage of her. His laptop was just old enough to have a disc drive, and it dragged the DVD in with a sound like wasps caught in a jar. A video player appeared and he filled the screen with it.

It wasn't her face. It was his face. It was the dark of 312 and he was in bed, a camera was hovering over him. He lay in half-shadow and seconds sifted into minutes in the bottom right corner of the screen. There was no sound, he could almost hear the blankness in the speakers where the ambient noise should have been, or the breathing of the person with the camera.

After eight minutes he began to smile in the video. It was slow, only the corners of his mouth creeping up into a curve, as though he had been dreaming her face. Eleven minutes and his eyes opened on the screen. He couldn't tell if they saw anything.

Colin watched his body shudder, gentle like an old memory coming back. The camera stayed hanging over him, the person holding it must have been near his feet. Thirteen minutes and a dark smudge leaked out of his smile, into the darkness of the bedroom.

He thought it was blood, but too thick and deliberate in its movement as it lifted from his chin. The smudge grew. It stretched across the bed, up toward the camera, and swallowed the lens in its mouth.

And he stepped away from the laptop, because the smudge seemed to peel away from its screen, out of the video and into the kitchen. Like wet smoke, like a flaw in a photograph of this moment. It seemed to rise above the computer, but he hadn't turned any lights on yet. He wasn't sure.

Something landed on the back of his neck, it pushed into his hair at the nape, but it was gone before he swiped his hand across the skin. His eyes crawled around the room, up into the corners and across the walls, along the carpeted floor. He flipped on the kitchen light and brushed his fingers behind his head again.

He looked back at the laptop screen. He was still sleeping there, the smile gone from the corners of his mouth, and there was something dead about his face, until static filled the scene like a swarm of digital moths and the clip cut off.

A group of moths was called an eclipse. He thought about this as he switched on a lamp and sat on the sofa in its pool of light. The video and the thing that seemed to lift out of it. The feel of a heavy moth on his neck. The walls were still empty. He wondered what would happen if he replayed the clip.

He opened his phone and was about to go online to see what Autumn had been doing today. Only she could calm him. But there was a sudden feeling at the back of his neck, as though the flesh was lifting away from the bone, and something pushed through the fold of skin. A pinch, the feel of suction, a numbness that ebbed through him.

Colin thought he jumped up from the sofa. He thought he screamed. But he was still seated, and he reached back and touched his neck. His fingertips came away stippled with a greasy black dust, a bead of blood clinging to his thumb. It was becoming hard to concentrate. A tired cloud seemed to spend minutes drifting over him.

He fought it because he needed to see her face. He typed her name into Facebook, but she didn't come up. He switched to a different fake account to be sure. The same thing happened on Twitter and Instagram. Had she locked down her privacy, was she taking a social break?

He went to her online pottery store, her Etsy shop, but the URLs wouldn't load. Other profiles appeared normally, people he had known before he met her. Other websites were functioning. She was even gone from LinkedIn. He noticed he was shaking. The back of his neck throbbed like the beginning of an itch.

Autumn's email account was still there, and his throat unlocked. He was able to swallow. But the inbox stopped two nights ago, with an unread message that hadn't been there when he checked yesterday. He hadn't deleted any of her emails. He was always careful now.

The subject line read WA H TCH IM, and he tapped on it.

The message was from pinedemon@z.z. Nothing in the body of the email, only blank space his finger had to drag up the screen to reach the bottom. Everything in her trash and spam folders was at least two days old.

He felt an awful drop in his stomach. He switched to his own email account. The message from par000600606 was still in the inbox, but the tiny video player was no longer embedded inside it. He should have downloaded the clip when he had the chance, grainy as it had been. He hadn't seen her face since before the sun rose, and now it was dark again.

But he didn't need to go online. He had his phone, the hundreds of images downloaded from her profiles over these last silent months. He opened the photo app, but it was a clean white sheet he swiped at in a panic, until he started seeing worthless pictures from before her. Above them, each of her photos was an empty square, the brightness shining up at him, too much light and too new, like spring or summer.

He stood and stared somewhere near the microwave for a long time. The cloud of fatigue settled into his pores. His phone fell asleep and he woke it up.

The background image was still there, but it was different now. With the screen held close, Colin saw that it had been altered somehow. Her window was dirtier and he couldn't see her face at all, it could have been anyone.

He looked up Pine Arch Research on Google and could only find a video of an indistinct figure outside a house at night, reaching a long impossible arm or movie prop toward a window. It was the house he had glimpsed at the end of the clip of Autumn sleeping, from the man he had paid to follow her. A different woman was pursued through trees, a different man tried to find her.

He didn't know what this could mean. It was from years ago. It felt like someone else's story. He watched the video until he was sure Autumn's face wasn't going to be in it.

The one thing he couldn't do was call her. She had changed her number before getting the protective order against him. If he called the new one, she would guess that he knew her email password. But he caved within minutes and it rang twice before a humming static filled the line. He redialed and the crackling started as soon he pressed the call button.

Where was she right now? Was she in trouble? He wanted to feel her heart slamming under his fingers. He wanted to calm her heart. He would have to quit his job and go back home early.

The night stretched ahead of him without her face, like a sickness. His eyes burned. His eyes ached. He tried to eat a can of soup and fell asleep on the sofa while waiting for it to cool.

The café windows poured light at him for hours. At lunchtime he felt something grip the back of his neck again, just under the collar. It pierced the skin. He reached his hand into his shirt, pulled it out to find a trace of black dust caught in his palm, a rill of blood in the seam between two fingers.

The manager came in to help with the rush and said Colin didn't look well. The café filled with chatter like a swarm of voices. An eclipse of one great voice murmuring.

In the restroom Colin looked in the mirror. He avoided his face when he could. It reminded him that Autumn had probably only taken him home the night they met because she'd had too much to drink. He had kept buying her shots, the kind of door that opened maybe once in a life.

He was used to the sunken flesh under his eyes, bruises from looking at her face all night instead of sleeping. It was difficult to remember waking up next to her that one morning, the way the light had come in between the curtains to swirl in the shadows like cream. Her smell mixed with his, and the quiet beatitude of the world.

He turned to check his neck in the mirror and saw something clinging to his back, in the corner of his eye. A shapeless dark thing. It shifted, it crawled to the other side of him. It was gone as he twisted in a circle and scraped at his back.

After the second mistake, the manager sent him home and told him to clean his fingernails. The drive was fast before rush hour. There was no envelope at the door of 312.

He called her and there was only the void of distorted rings at the other end of the line. Her face was still gone from the internet. There was such a profound tiredness, soaked in his muscles and his bones. The course of his blood had slowed in his head when he squeezed his eyes closed. He couldn't hear mountains out on the horizon.

He moved toward the laptop but then moved away from it.

The pinch came under the collar of his shirt again, the flesh pulling out and punctured by a tube or a blunt needle. The wet sensation of sucking, and small hands moving across his shoulders.

He tore his shirt off and the shirt beneath it. But there was nothing in the bathroom mirror. He tightened the blinds and sat down. The phone lay empty of everything beside him on the sofa.

Colin woke in the bedroom. He didn't remember coming in here, getting under the covers. A face was looking through the window at him, two eyes in the space between open blind slats.

For a moment he thought it was Autumn. He let the moment stretch into a floating island of moments. He didn't remind himself he lived on the third floor.

The eyes seemed too much like her eyes in certain pictures, when she was trying to look serious. He couldn't take it. He slipped out of the bed because he was too weak to stand. He had to crawl to the window and pull himself up with his hands on the sill.

The eyes were gone. When he spread the two slats farther apart, there was only the ghost of his own eyes in the glass. He thought he could see a trail of dark grime smeared along the wall and around the corner of the building.

The door of the apartment creaked open. It clicked shut. He waited in the quiet, watching his eyes watch him in the windowpane, until something came into the room and climbed up onto his back. He felt the pinch again, the dig in his neck.

He cried out in a high voice that was only breath and scrabbled a hand behind him. For a second he had it. It writhed out of his fingers and he felt the small weight of it sliding down toward his waist. Colin said her name, he put all of himself into it as he managed to get to his feet.

The laptop was still open on the kitchen counter. He woke it up but the video player was gone. The DVD wouldn't eject and there were beads of black paste around the mouth of the drive. He rubbed a finger down the screen and drew a line in the dark film coating it.

He opened a browser and searched for her, as though telling himself there was something wrong with his phone and not the reality of her. He would see her face in a few seconds.

But she was nowhere. He logged in as the woman potter and checked the Instagram messages, and only what he had written was there. Her replies were empty spaces beside empty circles. Search engines were no use, all he found were endless tributes to the season and empty, ugly Autumns with the same last name.

For a minute that felt like the last five months without her, Colin couldn't find his phone. He was weeping now. He remembered sitting on the sofa, and there it was, slipped down between two cushions. Her name was gone from his contact list now, her texts had faded from the messaging app. He struggled to remember her number, he could almost feel it leaking from his heart.

It rang six times before silence picked up, the distant sound of wind like a place outside of existence. He made a gap in the living room blinds and saw the trees in the park shivering. A man was crossing the street with the sleek white dog.

He felt a breath across his ear. He felt the nape of his neck bunch up. The tube slid into his skin. A wire of pain straightened down his back, numbness pulsing out in strands. He tried to go still as a warbling voice said his name in almost a whisper. What would it do if he let it, he wondered, if he didn't move. If he just stood watching the white dog in this loveless city.

It took a slow sip of him. His bones were like syrup, like the black paste beneath his fingernails, and he was folding down onto the floor. The voice spoke to him in crackles and gasps. He thought he heard it say Autumn was safe now, without him. She could sleep well again.

He thought he heard her name over and over again, an eclipse of names. Soon it was only wet noise instead of the perfect sound he had held onto for so long.

There was something he had not seen. He had forgotten what it was, that it was a beautiful face, that it had turned itself away from him. He had forgotten the face was hers. He had forgotten what name he had called when he needed a reason to go on.

There was only a remote impression of her still in his blood when he closed his eyes against the slanting blare of sunlight through the café windows. Leaves skirled past outside in a breeze, in the overture of fall.

Each day it took more of him. It drank the fact and the idea of her from him.

It let him watch the white dog on the leash in the park when he got home from work. It let him stand at the window with the blinds parted. It let him sleep through the night. The trees were starting to turn. But it took the color from even these things.

Colin carried two plates over to the small table closest to the door. He set them down and one of the women raised her face with a faraway smile. She didn't quite look at him, her eyes seemed to graze the line of his shoulders as though trying to crawl over onto his back to look there. Her hair fell in waves some would have called dirty blond but he called the color of the leaves starting to cover the world.

And for an instant—but the instant was gone.

He asked if they needed anything else. She shook her head and turned to the taller woman across from her. Their voices built their own secret murmur.

Back at the café bar he glanced into the antique mirror as he took a clean mug from the shelf. He saw a face rise up behind his shoulder. It was his own face but smaller, small enough to belong to a shape that could cling to his back. There was something dead about its eyes.

Its mouth opened, and a black growth pushed out over the tongue. He watched his face lower itself behind his head. He felt the pinch, and the tube going in.

IS THERE HUMAN KINDNESS
STILL IN THE WORLD?

1997

Jessie proposed to Rob in June. She joked that she was tired in her soul, thinking he was never going to ask. It had been seven years, she was thirty-four already. She got down on one knee behind a rest area north of Chattanooga, as he sat on a wooden bench. Poison ivy reached out of the trees.

"Yes," he said, "but wait a minute," and he half-sprinted out to his car and returned with two soft plastic figurines in the palm of his hand. Two ugly little cupids with bows and heart-tipped arrows, to bury in the soil where her knee had left an imprint.

"We'll protect this place, like something sacred," he told her. He seemed to always have some sentimental thing ready to fit the moment, trinkets he picked up at yard sales and thrift stores because he knew he would need them one day. That none of them were an engagement ring had never bothered her.

They talked about marriage often enough, and Rob once opened up about something his therapist had suggested. "I worry I'll die young and make you a widow," and his face filled with blood as he said it. Jessie had put her hand on the back of his neck and eased his forehead against hers. She had whispered to him, "I would have been a widow if I lost you the day we met."

"We'll wait," she said now, without a ring to slide onto either of their fingers. "We'll put our cupids somewhere else, another rest area and another bench. I don't want the poison ivy to spoil this. We'll know the right spot when we see it."

And it all—life and everything in it—just felt so light and absolute and suffused with normal potential. The kind where you don't think about it changing.

1998

Rob died at the end of February. A hemorrhagic stroke at thirty-seven, sprawled in a coffeeshop booth, everyone around him thinking he had fallen asleep. The rest of the year was a gray, wet smudge. Jessie quit her job and let their savings trickle away in the house they had bought. There were still boxes of books they hadn't unpacked, hers and his mixed together in the dust of their old apartment.

His funeral was exactly five weeks before their wedding day, and she would have so much trouble remembering the service later. The casket would be a blur. His face inside of it would be a wax mold that wasn't quite his face. Outside the church an older woman had been handing out pamphlets that read *Is there human kindness still in the world?* Thick white letters on a blue background.

It was Jessie's one really stark image of that afternoon. She hadn't taken a pamphlet, but the words would surface from time to time, a beacon and a benediction in the muddy sorrow of all those months. She didn't know how kindness fit into things, or if it would even be a mercy.

1999

Most of the year, Jessie haunted rest areas at night. She drove the dark interstates, creeping across the skin of the South with her talismans for Rob, a scrapbook and an old yellowed clock he would have loved, beside her on the passenger seat. These would have been her gifts to him for their first anniversary.

There were no clean edges to the thought. She just got into the car as the sun leaked out over the city, early in the spring, and started driving away from the smudge that wouldn't dry out. She went a hundred miles southeast and a hundred miles back, looking for signs that read REST AREA 10 MILES. Some weeks, she would stay in motels and strain the leash of her grief farther and farther from home.

Death was as present in the blank spaces of the map as it was in the creases of their house, but the reminders—a mound of earth piled on a shoulder, a broken deer, memorial crosses draped with rotting flowers—swept by in her peripheral vision, only there for an instant. She had to keep her eyes on the road. Trees swollen with spring tinted the nights green. Later, in the fall, their skeletons were easy metaphors.

It was more peaceful to mourn in motion. She cried less, or she cried as much as she should have after so many months.

She fed her thoughts to the road. She passed across the Florida Panhandle, along the sparse eastern wedge of Alabama, through the mountain seams of Tennessee and North Carolina, down into South Carolina, wandering in between through Georgia like a lost ant on a table. The ribbons of highways crawled with truckers and lonesome souls.

Never back roads. Never scenic routes. She stopped at each rest area, usually at night because she slept through the daylight now, retracing their steps to find the bench where they had finally agreed to bury the cupids. She didn't understand how she had forgotten which bench, which trip, which interstate.

But they had taken a lot of these little trips. Jessie could only narrow it down to parts of those six states, and all the stops strung like beads along the atlas pages. She and Rob had been fascinated with rest areas because they were where a person imprinted the smallest trace of their soul. "A personality can't linger here," he told her once, "there's only time for a brief exhaustion."

Jessie called them the least haunted places in America, until she began to haunt them.

They loved sitting on benches staring out at swaths of scrub pines and insubstantial oaks, gullies choked with undergrowth, as though they were national parks, old-growth forests, as the ceaseless surf of traffic noise sighed behind them. As though the benches themselves were destinations.

They were anti-tourists, anti-ghost hunters, a little too enamored of the irony, but they found the beauty in these spaces in spite of this. The ritual had been a metronome of their life. She found it somehow louder with only the one heart beating.

She would drive up the curving ramp and get out of her little night-colored Volkswagen and stretch the miles out of her back. As the year wore on, the crickets would often sing with an apocalyptic fervor behind the squat building, depending on where she was. There were more of them in North Georgia and around the Blue Ridge Mountains. In the fall there would be a great mouthful of silence cut with the rumble of trucks passing, one at a time in the dark.

Inside the building, she would absorb its transient energy for a minute, listening to the psychic absence. The blank slate. She would look through the travel brochures, if there were any.

There was always a bench somewhere out back, sometimes several, sometimes picnic tables, the silhouettes of leaning pines like quills in the earth. If a bench was roughly thirty feet from the rear entrance, she would scan everything around it, trying to remember, trying to place herself. She carried a slender spade to dig in the spots that sounded a chord in her.

She skipped the big rest areas, the state line welcome centers. The small facilities had always spoken to them in their single-minded hums. They existed in a limbo of anonymity, solely as way stations. They offered no segue or affirmation.

She waited until September to visit the rest area on I-75 in McMinn County, Tennessee, sixty miles north of the Georgia line, where she had proposed to Rob in the pine needles and patchy grass. She had forgotten where they buried the cupids, but she could not forget where she had first seen them. The poison ivy was worse this year. She fell asleep on the bench and woke at dawn, terrified of the light.

One night in October, she stood at the glass door in the back of a rest area south of Greer, South Carolina, and saw a gray shape sitting on a bench. The interior fluorescents and the single outside lamp near the roof could not reach it, so the figure was shaped like Rob for a moment, then another moment, until her eyes drew the shape more finely out of the gloom—it was heavier than Rob, a little broader. She had seen the pristine white pickup truck in the lot out front, parked between two of the longer slanted lines designated for RVs.

Just beyond the shape, in a shallow gully as the land sloped away, a pale face stared up at them.

It peered out from a curtain of shadow hanging over a stand of young pines. There was something wrong with the face, round and heavy and hairless, it seemed to have been watching her before she even arrived. Now the lower half of it opened into a hole. It was a bag, she said to herself, it was litter blown into a tree.

The figure on the bench turned as though Jessie had made a sound. A man smiling inside a beard, the farthest particles of the light above her glinting in the hair, on the teeth, making his mouth look wet. She thought the bench was too far from the door to possibly be where the cupids were buried, anyway. She pretended not to see him and drew back into the light.

In the ladies room mirror, she stared at the new lines that losing Rob had drawn in the skin around her eyes. Only Jessie could have seen them, they were more promise than fact for now.

She splashed water on her face, deciding whether to head home for the night or keep on and stop at a motel near dawn. She raised her head and peered into the mirror again, thinking of the round face out back in the trees, the plastic bag caught on a branch.

But it was the bearded man waiting for her out in the short hallway. He wrapped his fingers around her wrist almost as soon as she realized he was there, and the door whispered shut behind her. The entire world could have been stricken with emptiness, for all the good screaming would have done in this outpost in the folds of midnight.

The beard opened up again. "Your curls are so dark, and pretty dark eyes to match. Where are you headed?" His teeth were dry in this harsher light. "You're dark all over, I'd sure like to see if there's some pink somewhere." He shoved her back into the restroom, the door slamming open and again sighing closed.

Jessie clawed at his face and he pushed her with a snarl, an animal musk breathing off him, and pushed her again until she fell into a stall. Her back slammed against the toilet but it gave her an instant to pull the spade from her bag and stick it into him as he gathered her up in his arms. The tip pierced his belly, the momentum of his formidable weight helped ease it in two inches as he made a shocked barking noise into her face.

She squirmed out from under him and fled, to her car, the spade squeezed in her fist, her soul leaving a streak of itself behind to mark this place. A spark of exhilaration bloomed in her throat. It gave an unfamiliar throb in her heart.

She had been wrong. Something of a person could be imprinted anywhere.

But the next night she was back on the road, crossing rest areas off her list. She bought pepper spray and a modest folding knife. The last summer heat drained away. The nights grew crisper, and she came to learn the pale face in the South Carolina trees had not been an illusion, or a bag caught on a branch. A revenant or creature or angel or—her word for it would shift—was waiting for her, roaming the interstates as she was.

A week after the bearded man and the spade, a week in which Jessie stopped wondering how badly she had hurt him, she walked through rest area #34 on I-75, in middle Georgia, into the backside of the night. She sat on the bench. It wasn't the one she was looking for but a weariness pulled her down. She put her hands over her face. For longer than she should have, she wept into her palms, until she heard a rasping of pine needles and looked up.

The land here did not slope away but stretched back a few hundred yards toward a tangle of wilderness. It was almost a park.

The oaks and pines were spaced out, trimmed and residential, and a pale figure was passing between them. Behind each tree it would peek its face out, the same face she had seen watching her and the man with the beard.

At last it stopped between two trunks and stared openly at her, standing naked in the muddled dark. A man, she thought, too distant to be sure. Its limbs were short and one of the arms held something against a rounded belly. Jessie stood from the bench, the air cold and scented with pine and mint against her wet cheeks, and began to back away.

The nude figure moved toward her, pulling the rasping sound along with it, and she saw as it drew closer that its feet dragged across the ground in a perfect line, drawing grooves in the dirt, the toes pulling mounds of pine needles that fell away into bunches. Its legs did not bend or move. It glided toward her, coming into the rumor of light, coming toward the hemisphere of light that held Jessie.

It could have been an elongated baby, a thing stretched to the shape of an elderly man, old sagging skin and an infant's globe of belly. Sexless between its legs. Its head was too big for the tired body, wearing a baby's naive face despite all the years that seemed to hang from it in jowls. Red splotches stood out like bruises beneath the hollowed black eyes.

One hand lifted a bow, a curve of wood, simple as a smoothed pine bough. Jessie thought of the cupids buried somewhere in one of the six states she had been searching, she thought of them gestating in cool red clay and breaking open the shell of earth to be born.

The cupid's feet furrowed the topsoil toward the back wall of the rest area, passing between the last two trees. Its mouth dropped open and one short arm extended the bow. Its other hand plucked at the string, aiming nothing at her.

She ran to the back door and inside the building, the fluorescent bulbs washing her from the ceiling. Out front a short balding man stood near her car, next to a squat RV. Jessie looked back over her shoulder to see the empty front door, the night trying to quiet her again.

"Everything all right?" the man asked her. "Is someone in there, what's wrong, honey?"

"A naked man behind the building," she said, getting her breath back. "In the trees."

The balding guy looked around at the lot, at their vehicles and all the vacant faded asphalt around them. He opened a tall rear door, painted brown and white, and tried to get her inside. "Come on, I'll call the police."

She shook her head no, thinking of the other man's mouth opening like starvation in the nest of his beard.

"Now, now. It's all right. Nothing to worry about." He smiled, yellow and greedy. "You're a beautiful woman, I can see that, I'll fuck you good," and his bald spot gleamed in the arc sodium light from the long-necked bulb high above them.

"What did you say?" Jessie asked him. She took a step back.

"I'll fuck this naked dude up good," he told her, "just get in." And his fingers wrapped around her wrist in an echo of the week before, as his other fingers, this abundance of fingers reached out and squeezed her breast. He winked and his tongue slid half out of his mouth.

She pulled her pepper spray off the back of her belt and pressed a stream of it into his eyes. He wouldn't let go, he pulled her toward the dark cave of his RV, into the open doorway, coughing out screams of some thwarted emotion Jessie could not fathom.

But she had her knife, too, open and hacking at the arm that gripped her. He let go and she lashed at his face in a panic before crossing the gap to her car and escaping into the arteries of Georgia.

The man had fallen to the pavement in her rearview. She began to smile as she drove, her head aching with the impression that she was an angel of vengeance. Her heart fluttered with terror that felt more like awe. The terror was for the thing she had seen in the trees. The awe was for the idea that it might have been seeded by what she and Rob had buried.

The awe was also for the feel of her knife, the texture of its blade against the bone in the man's thin wrist. The texture slowed the terror. His blood browned on the small blade.

She had injured two predators now, two creatures who would think twice with other women losing themselves on the highways. And somewhere in her was the thought that she wanted more, she could drive through the dark and punish men like this when they opened their jaws at her.

Jessie saw the cupid once more and understood that each time she encountered it, another man would grab her, another man wouldn't keep his hands off her. For these men, love was forced, love was stabbed into women. Love was a stone you lifted up, you saw the worms and rage tunneling underneath.

Three days after Halloween, at a rest area as far into Florida as she had planned to go, the cupid was waiting. It stood behind a skinny old pine, its face a diluted moon looking out at the bench she sat on. Two shrunken wings hung from its shoulder blades, useless hollow bones strung with dead feathers. They could never lift its sagging weight from the earth.

She thought about walking out into the trees to ask it which rest area she and Rob had chosen to bury the plastic figures, and why she could not remember, when the door rattled behind her. She heard a thin twang of a voice. "What's a pretty thing like you doing in the middle of nowhere? Sitting in the dark all by yourself. Ain't you cold?"

A man with red hair halfway down his back sat down beside her with his wares on display, his pants open in a shocking V. He stroked himself, his hand slow and nearly elegant as it slid up and down in a cloud of orange pubic hair. "You like that?" He shifted toward her on the bench. "Ain't that why you're here?" His face was shining with acne.

Then he leaned over and his tongue was pushing against her mouth, his hand was pulling her hand toward the V. She tried to claw him and he punched the side of her head. A gray wool fog eclipsed her vision.

"You bitch," he hissed through his teeth. He hit her again, his intentions crossing beyond some awful amorousness into a dark and less retrievable thing.

But the cupid had given some part of her mind a way to get her knife ready, unfolded, and into the side of the red-haired man, who fell away from her screaming. She knew she might have really hurt him, she couldn't stop thinking about the way the knife had tugged upward, scraping a rib and pulling the cut wider, digging into him as he wailed. If she had punctured an organ, if he bled too much, if he was too far from the bank of pay phones inside.

S he knew that each encounter with a predator was more dangerous than the last, each chance to make it home alive dwindled to hard points of hunger in their eyes. Soon her luck would run out.

She stopped taking her night drives the week before Christmas.

What would Rob think, that she had never found the bench where they buried their sappy treasure? There was no time left to mourn, or roam the interstates as an avenging angel. The money was running out and she had to go back to work. It might have been the only reason she rebuilt her life.

2007

I n late September, Jessie's work sent her to Knoxville for a conference on helping women recover from sexual violence. Or she sent herself, it was her own nonprofit. Presenters spoke of small business loans, shelter security, new counseling approaches in underrepresented neighborhoods, lobbying legislators on the state and federal levels. They let themselves dream and worked to wrap the dreams around strong bones.

She listened and took notes and shared ideas over wine in the buzz that followed the panels. These were half-friends and colleagues lifting each other. She smiled and she missed her family.

On the way home her blood hummed with anger. The mountains were swallowed into the midnight of the rearview mirror, she passed south into Georgia on I-75, into the last hundred miles unspooling between Jessie and her daughter and husband.

The anger always came after sitting in rooms full of women who had been hurt, hearing their stories and hearing the statistics of what monsters did. The anger got in her throat. There was hope to thread it with, but the statistics never improved enough, the fuses of violent men felt shorter with every conference. In spite of their efforts, there seemed to be so little human kindness left in the world.

This thought made her remember Rob's funeral, the woman outside. She wondered what had been between the folds of each blue pamphlet in her hands, what the answer to its question was. Yes or no. The answer was usually God. It had seemed an awful thing, to preach outside a church when no one had come to worship.

"Let us mourn in peace," she said to the woman now, nine years later. Her voice nearly startled her in the silence of the highway.

Jessie sat with her anger recycling in the air of the car. She tried to pull the thread of hope through, tightening it, making a container, until she saw a sign creep out of the murk into her headlights. REST AREA 1 MILE.

Older emotions rose in her chest. She felt the heat in her face and told herself she was forty-four now, she was married to a sweet man. They had made a beautiful daughter to try to see a better world through. Ella had just turned five, every day she was a lens against the darkness, against the moments when Jessie wondered if there was human kindness still in her own body, and if she could build it inside of her daughter.

Rob had been a good man. Rough around the edges, his mind

strung with silver linings, illuminated by bright sides. And Jamal was a good man, it wasn't as though kindness was a finite resource. Was it?

She had met him just two years after Rob died. The year after the rest areas, the predatory men, the pale winged figure in the trees. She had still been tired. She had left too much of herself behind, and it was easy to fall into something resembling love again. It had felt to her body like falling into a chair in surrender, when all the adrenaline has bled away.

Her life had found real joy. Her vengeance had found softer weapons and routes.

REST AREA, the next sign read, with an arrow pointing up and to the right. She veered the car onto the ramp. The little brick building drew toward her above the curve, black trees stenciled themselves like veins over the roof, against the darkness and light pollution.

She parked and got out of the car and held communion with her younger self, and realized she couldn't remember the woman she had been before Rob's death and before her months of night driving. Not with enough clarity. That woman was an imprint in Jessie's mind, a tangle of sentiments and sensations, an artless ghost with nothing to haunt.

Behind the building she found a bench in a likely position. She bent over and scratched a finger into the soil, imagining a decade of erosion and rains and decay. She could smell Rob next to her, the last of their warm clean youth clinging to them.

She took out her keys and chiseled the ground open. This wasn't the right place, the figurines weren't here, but she looked up and then down along the slope of sparse woods. A thin creek lay stagnant a hundred yards off. Pieces of the moon gleamed on kudzu choking the stunted trees.

Two figures peered out of the vines at her, both of the dim and blanched faces now that Jessie had left that other woman behind.

They were too far away to speak to, they were far enough away to be swabs of moonlight and not creatures that had waited across a gulf of her life for some inscrutable purpose. But she asked them questions, anyway, "Why are you here?" and "What do you want?"

And she watched them creep through the kudzu, through dying vines and undergrowth, their pale bodies like things that had never seen the sun.

"Why would you show yourselves, after all this time?" she asked them. They rose and stood behind the same wide pine and peeked around its edges at her, close enough to see the dark holes of their mouths grinning.

Maybe their insides were still plastic, and they could not speak. Maybe they would have told her that love had watched over her, it had grown and wrapped itself around the bones she had needed. Or they were creatures wandering, simply as she had wandered, with no wisdom to give.

The door opened behind her, and the light from inside crept another few inches along the grass. A man's voice spoke into the gentle wilderness. "Are you okay?"

Jessie did not turn. "I have a gun," she told the voice. "You'll go back inside if you're smart."

She heard him say, "Jesus," and as the door sighed shut on its hinge, "Fucking bitch."

The cupids kept watching her, she kept watching them, trying to understand, but not for long. She was close to home and rest and light.

2023

She turned sixty in October. Ella drove down from school in Durham to surprise her, Jamal had planned a modest party to celebrate Jessie's milestone and her less modest work in getting the Violence Against Women Act onto the Senate floor and the president's desk last year. Key provisions had been left in the reauthorization bill.

At breakfast that morning, Ella had said, "Jeez, Mom, you're changing the world," and Jessie felt a ferocious strength. That old hope she and her half-friends and colleagues had held onto over the years was now a stronger cord.

No one had checked the mail that day. Between the guests leaving and bed, Jessie went down to the street and pulled out a credit card offer and a blue pamphlet that caught the breath in her throat.

Is there human kindness still in the world? it asked her in bold white letters, almost a shout. She opened it to see a grainy photo of a wooden bench, a small mound of earth next to a hole, like a toy grave. The bottom of a brick wall met the grass in the background.

In smaller type below the photo, *An Exhibition of Imprints, October 25, GA Rest Area #11. One night only.*

She looked up at the sky. All the stars were hidden under a gray skin of clouds. The moon like a forgotten bruise, even the injury that caused it only an impression now.

She prepared the garden against the toothless southern winter and stayed busy in her small Midtown office. There was fear inside of both days, but she did not pace the floors or wring her hands. She felt the fear in her mouth like the thrill of copper wires. She felt her old love for Rob.

There was the sense of a psychic energy, in which a structure has been brought back to its former architecture. Her life had momentum, she was deep into her second wind, the ghost of that other woman had been folded into the marrow of her experience.

Couldn't the answer to the pamphlet's question—the answer as it might be given by the inexplicable—connect that energy, those copper wires, to the time she had left?

Rest area #11 was south, halfway between home and the Florida state line, and the air seemed to warm and moisten toward summer as she drove, Ella back in Durham, Jamal snoring in their bed. She had left a note telling him she loved him, she was glad she had met him when she did, not because she believed she would not be returning to him, but because it would be cruel to assume.

The state opened up into a dead land once Macon was behind her, blank peeling billboards and fresh billboards plastered with the love of Christ. Even in the dark, these towns and spaces had withered on the vine of the map.

She came to the rest area without feeling ripples in any cosmic stream. There were no preambles or overtures. Only a simple green sign pointing her up a gentle bend to a brick building that looked like many others, one she had surely included in her year of night drives. A hundred and twenty miles ached in her joints. These muscles did not stretch lithely anymore when she got out of the car and arched her back.

There was nothing on the door, no mention of an art show, an exhibition of imprints. She went inside and passed through the endless fluorescent light, and out the opposite side, into the watery silence of distant cars. A cold breeze raked the silhouettes of trees. The sky was still ridden with clouds.

Enough light spilled across the lawn to suggest the mound of dirt by the bench. When she reached it, she saw the plastic cupids in the little grave, facing each other on their sides just as Rob had placed them. Her heart slowed and she used her foot to push the dirt into the hole, staining the side of her white shoe.

Her quest for them had been so long ago, that other woman suddenly felt so far away again, so she filled the little grave and stood on it, her weight compacting the soil.

The trees were empty across the moonless acre. She supposed she was standing on the faces that had once watched her. The door opened behind her with a brief groan and she turned to see it ease shut.

No shape pulled back into the light. She wondered where the exhibition was and followed the lure of whatever had pushed at the door. A bank of vending machines hummed, their lighted colors more desperate, more futuristic than when she had haunted these places.

She turned into the left hallway toward the ladies room and saw a door beyond it, half-open with one of the blue pamphlets taped to the beige paint. She waited in a different silence until something thumped inside the wall to her right. The sound repeated once, followed by a slow scratch that traveled down toward the floor, and Jessie went still for a long time before she let herself move forward.

The restroom was to her left, and the thump came again as she reached it, just on the other side of the right wall, keeping pace.

She tried to picture the narrow gap between the wall and the brick front of the building and what could be wedged inside of it. The cupids had returned to their grave. Now something dragged inside the wall, tracking her, with the same whisper her shoulder would make if she leaned against the thick paint as she walked. The presence gave a soft knock behind the drywall as Jessie reached the door of the exhibition and pushed it open.

It might have been a break room, or a large janitor's closet, emptied except for four plastic chairs in the middle of the space, vivid yellow, facing the right wall in a line. She saw a closed metal door across from her, another blue pamphlet taped askew in its center.

The chairs were occupied by men, their hands on their thighs, rigid and silent. She reached out to the wall they were staring at, spreading her fingers against it for support, and imagined she felt a hand press against hers on the other side.

For a moment she knew she would faint, as she stumbled forward and saw the seated men from a fuller angle. They were dolls, or mannequins, man-sized and as familiar to her as her daughter and husband, as much a part of her as Rob had always been.

Or the first three were. The last in the row was obscured beyond a waxy figure with thin red hair hanging in sheaves over the shoulders and down a blue plaid flannel shirt Jessie remembered the texture of, scratchy and hot, a sour stink she could still recall filling her sinuses. The shirt was matted in blood on the right side.

The face was bloodless, as though its body had pumped it all into the shirt, and dusted with violent acne above and below the fixed and stricken eyes. She could almost see the oil glistening on each pustule, the detail could not have been truer to life.

Its blue jeans were open, its thin white cock stood rooted in a bramble of pubic hair. She forced her gaze back to the doll nearest to her, the still face encased in a dark beard. The same shape in the frozen brown eyes, the sparks of violence deadened by what they saw. A gray T-shirt, a small tear in the belly like a parting of red lips, where her spade had punctured it twenty-four years ago.

A smaller figure sat between the bearded and red-haired mannequins, its balding head gathering up the fluorescent light in a wet gleam. Its widened eyes were painted full of burst blood vessels. An ugly gash extended from its nose to its right jaw, smears of dried blood below it. The right jacket sleeve was slashed twice near the wrist.

Jessie remembered spilling this blood. She had never been to a wax museum, but she could not have imagined this level of artistry. The low hum of the vending machines had not followed her into this room. She stood in a deep and awful quiet and waited for the dolls to stir to life.

They did nothing but sit, sealed in their moments of meeting Jessie. She stepped forward until she was standing before them, for judgment or lecture. She did not know the fourth doll. It was unknowable, with no features or clothes, it was a smooth humanoid mold of creamy wax or plastic. It was paler than the others, half-translucent.

She stared at the blank face and began to believe that eyes were watching her from just beneath its skin. If she moved closer, if she bent toward the mold, she would see the color of the eyes.

She would not touch it, or any of them, though her hands nearly ached with wanting to know what they were made of, plastic or rubber or some polymer in between. An inner logic, a part of her she could only listen to, assured her this unfinished effigy represented the fourth predator, the one whose path she had never crossed. The man who would have run out her luck in that year on the highways.

But her luck had not run out. She had gone on. Jessie stepped past them and went to the far door. The presence inside the wall went with her, thumping and scraping its shoulder along the hidden channel.

Nothing behind her was an answer, she knew the contributions of these men to the question of human kindness in the world. She knew the woman they had helped make. She pulled the door open and stepped through.

Five more dolls sat around a bare table, on the left side of a room of the same proportions and emptiness, in chairs of the same yellow plastic. But these were not violent men.

Rob sat at the table with the family he had never made, all of them arranged in poses of gentleness. Three children reached their arms out to the man and woman across from them, each as lovingly rendered as the predators had been, as on the verge of rising from its chair and turning to her.

She could not take her eyes off of Rob. She stood and absorbed the details of him, the ceiling light streaking his blue eyes, the light beading on his lips, the new lines drawn down from the corners of his mouth, the spreading gray in his hair, the scalp like a scar in the part. The skin under his eyes sagged.

But still his abundant youth was fixed upon him, he was still a boy in the rough body of a man. He seemed to stare at the wall to Jessie's right and not quite at the children. His mouth was opening into a laugh.

She thought this Rob was in his late forties, his brain had not ruptured in a coffeeshop, he had gone on with her. The whole of his face looked easy and delighted, as though love had watched over them all. A brushed silver band glimmered from his ring finger.

A minute passed before Jessie registered her own effigy at the table, smiling with her head tilted downward, but she had aged differently, more slowly. Her hair was a little shorter, its sprung curls had not begun to gray as they should have, three years younger than this husband.

And the children, the impossible creations, she saw Rob and she saw herself in the shapes of their brows, their cheekbones, the various mixtures of their coloring. She wanted to go to them and touch them but could not. A boy with a heart-shaped face, a strong-jawed girl, the eldest girl with a proud profile, Jessie's dimpled chin. Their living mother trembled and began to moan into the profound quiet.

There was a door, in the same position in the wall across the room. It must lead outside, she thought, surely the rest area could not extend any farther. She needed to leave, something was wrong. The gentleness of the artificial faces was tempered with anguish. It had begun to shape the corners of their mouths.

She thought she saw something in Rob's eyes. They did not shift or roll in their sockets but seemed to impart the desire for movement. They gave the faintest strain. The throat might have held the first vibration of a sound she couldn't bring herself to hear.

To reach the door she would have to move into his line of sight. She took her first steps into the room and a thud sounded inside the wall to her right. She stopped. She looked at Rob again, his dead plastic eyes hinting awareness, trying to slide toward her.

The children faced away from her new vantage. Jessie found herself reaching out to them, moving her hands across their backs. She felt the curves of wings under their shirts, the artificial flesh pliant, accepting the pressure of her fingers.

The face of the Jessie doll, ahead of her around the table, seemed to begin to lift up without moving. She had to know. She stepped forward and around and slid her hands down from the figure's shoulders, along the ridges of wings beneath a linen blouse she had never owned. This Jessie was so soft, its body carried a healthy fullness, nearly plump, that she had never quite known.

Just beyond, Rob waited for her to come to him.

"I'm so sorry I couldn't remember where we put them," she said. The shape of him blurred through tears.

But she could not touch Rob. Too much was rising up from the grave of her heart. She ran to the door and crashed through it into a dark breezeway littered with ambient light, glowing winks from the high halogen lamps and streaks of headlights on the interstate above the grassy slope. The sound of passing trucks was deafening as she bent over, gulping at the dirty air.

The door closed behind her, a soft and inconsequential click. She turned to see an aperture gaping at her in the wall, a cavity between the brick facade and the guts of the building. It was a foot across, too narrow to allow the thing that had been following her to emerge.

A voice spoke from the opening. "It's all right, there's nothing to worry about," it said. "Now, now," it soothed. It was her own voice. "You fucked them up good," it called out, "it's time to come back," and there was the noise of flapping wings, muffled in the cramped throat between the walls.

A pause, then a strained chorus of two octaves: "You are a strong woman!"

And another sound, the resonant snap of a plucked string. Pain stabbed beneath Jessie's collarbone, above her heart, and at once she felt a fraught desire to go back into the room where she and Rob and their children sat at the table. Her vision clouded and she turned to clutch the doorknob.

Then her hand fell away. She felt such hope for the world! It burned in her chest like her copper wire, and she backed away, toward the parking lot. A face approached the aperture, it came to where the thin light could touch it.

Powerful wings flexed over the shoulders, fighting for clearance. She saw the dark angles of a face and blind white holes of eyes. Somewhere in its contours she saw herself, as she had been. This imprint of Jessie might have kept on haunting these in-between spaces, hunting and growing fiercer with her strange grace. She felt such hope for her, too.

But she wanted Jamal, and Ella, and her second wind.

She staggered across the strip of grass and onto the asphalt of the lot, her car in a pool of blue light. Such a warmth was spreading across her chest, down into her belly like the rich burn of a red wine. Such a love for the world, such a triumph of hope thudding with the strength of the old anger. What sort of a kindness was this?

She looked down at herself, she swiped her hand below her throat, but there was no arrow jutting or blood leaking. There was no wound, only the sense of it. She wished she had reached out her hand and touched Rob, to feel the breadth of his wings, to remember the electricity of his skin.

Nothing pursued her to the car. She got in and backed out of the slanted lines, her phone out of her bag and calling home. The ring purring in her ear, it went on and on but Jamal did not answer.

She disconnected and drove up the ribbon of the ramp, around and onto I-75. She would have to exit the highway for a moment to access the northbound lanes. She called Ella, ringing and ringing, she waited to hear her daughter's voice saying she wasn't there, leave a message, but it kept ringing as though struggling to reach her. She had never gone as far as Durham in her year of night driving.

Love throbbed in her chest. A tight cord against her breastbone. A deep and cavernous love for the whole of her life. She called the landline at home again. She called her husband's cell as she got off the interstate and made a U-turn and got back on. She pressed the phone against her ear until it hurt, even the pain was sweet, if he would only answer.

"There's nothing to worry about," she said to the joy and the terror filling up the car. "I am strong, I am an angel of vengeance, my wings will lift my weight from the earth." Across the ringing and toward what waited at the far end of it, the first miles north unraveled beneath her.

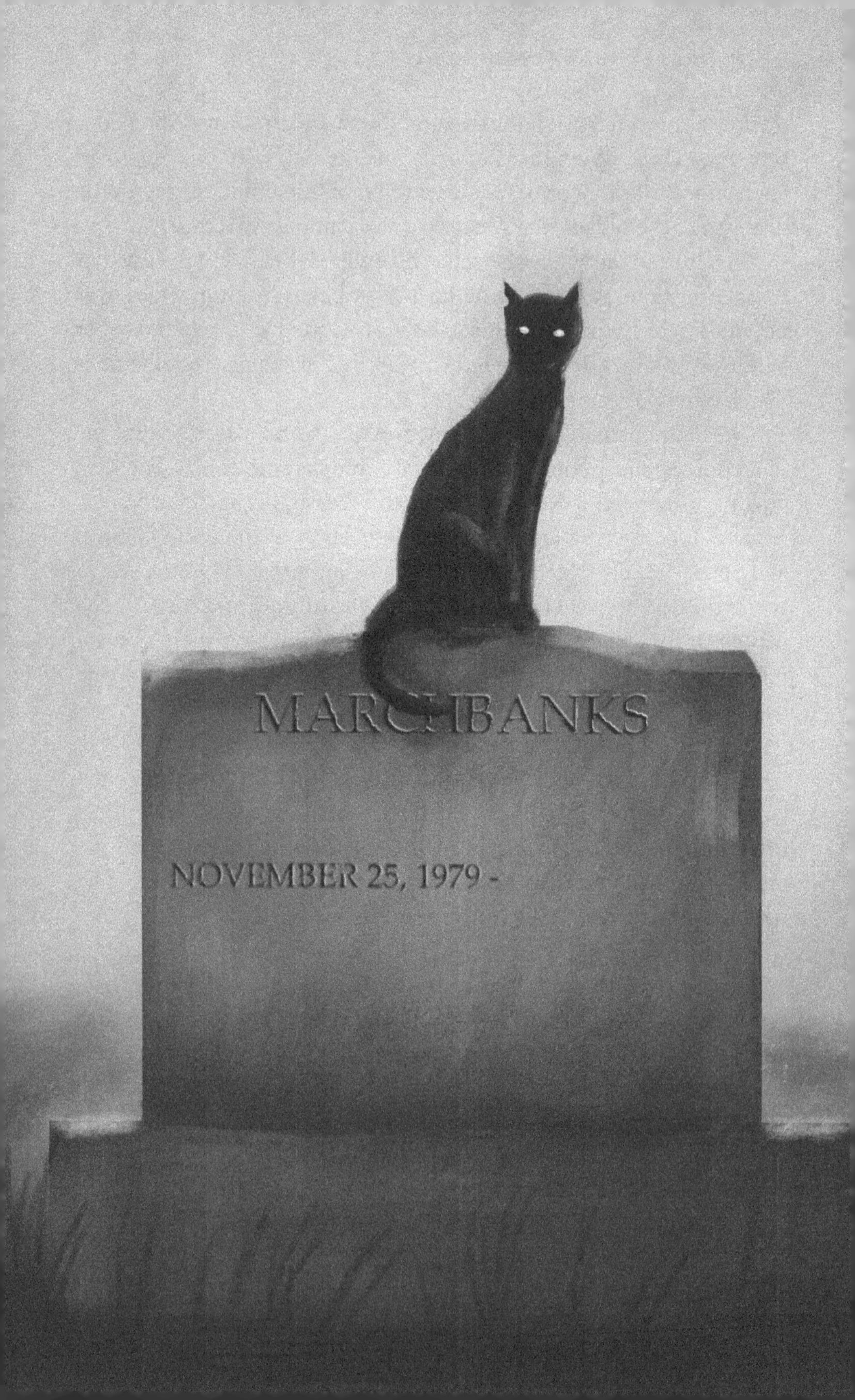
MARCHBANKS
NOVEMBER 25, 1979 -

AN ENDING (ASCENT)

Our graves will be a museum. A place where people come seeking a sense of what it was like to die, trailing through the rows of headstones until they find the youngest, the last of us. It could be they'll stop at mine.

I picture them standing there. It's not quite raining, there's a mist that settles on their coats in the moment of silence they give to me but mostly to themselves. Relief like a cold, pure breath released into the sky, if they've managed to keep the atmosphere clean. There are moments, plenty of them, I find myself hoping they haven't.

My story will be etched into the marble, slowly dimming in the seasons. I don't know what the second date will tell them. I only know the first, and it is the reason they will come.

November 25, 1979–

They'll count the days between my birth and the Age Line. Thirty-seven days. The weight of their voices, raw and respectful and relentless, saying, *He was so close.* They'll observe the old rites, while the novelty holds, stoop to lean irises or lilies against the stone. *That's less than nine hundred hours.* And they'll pull each other closer, as though against the damp. Looking out over all those monuments.

It's almost a comfort, this thought. I try to make it one. But only the slow rusting quiet will come when they no longer do, though we who remain cannot know the quality, the tone of that quiet, when the earth is left behind like a husk.

My mind circles back and back to these things, these pictures. Because I so recently stood in a graveyard, yes, and because I've returned to stand in the hallway of my home and listen to my wife and the lover she's taken, their laughter that already sounds young, the rhythm of the headboard tapping the wall.

I open the bedroom door and what I see before I close my eyes is the window looking out on the old cottonwood, the white sky cut into confetti through its branches.

A gasp, a scrambling within the sheets that pool around their bodies. "Caithlin." I say it again, louder but still numbed and too far from a shout. She's not even hiding it anymore, not in any concerted way.

Here are all the conversations we haven't had about the friendship she's rekindled with Terrence Dutil. Her late nights at the university, his visits to the house to help in the garden out back. How she carries her tether book from room to room, and in bed tilts the pale blue wash of its light away from me. All the clues arranged like careless furniture, and now that I'm here, forgetting to breathe, I admit to myself that I've been stepping around them.

"John, honey, I'm sorry, you weren't supposed to be home until tomorrow." Her words in a single blurred rush, running hot and cold at once. I keep my eyes clenched shut like a child's.

Terry says his own piece, but my mind is wet enough with resignation and I can't bear to listen. I rewind myself, step back into the hall, and let a throb of quiet cover the sound of Caithlin telling him to get dressed. Their murmurs of peaceful embarrassment, everything is out in the open now.

I stand in the family room staring half-lost into the video wall's screensaver, which is looping panoramic stills of our grandson splashing through Pacific foam, and I say, slowly, feeling every tick and tap of my tongue against my teeth, "I am the only one in this house who will ever die."

This anger, always at a slow burn. Knowing it is a selfish thing only dampens it so much. I flushed the antidepressants two weeks ago. Close to a hundred blue, government-sanctioned capsules. They had turned me into glass, a window I could only look through, and did little more than wrap the ache and hide it like a telltale heart.

Dr. Hinton recommended I connect with my parents and try to accept that I am of their era. Embrace my past, since it is no less primitive than my future. He has suggested many things since I was ushered out of my job at the accounting firm, most of them steeped in time. He preaches technology dissociation, foremost the surrender of my tether, all the networks and bells and whistles.

Go into nature, connect with where you came from, John. It's the only thing you can take with you.

But a few hours in Vermont and I found I could no longer abide the close green country folding around me. The cemetery outside Montpelier was held in a bowl of lush mountains, the grass too eager around my parents' graves and their parents' graves behind them. Their tiny beloved church a postscript there in the half-wilderness. I felt cloistered by the hunched forests, the peaks mossy above them, the air heavy with clean mint.

An old calico cat sat washing herself on a nearby headstone, her ear mangled and her mottled coat stretched tight over her bones. We watched each other, aged and crumbling things like the last beads on a broken rosary. Down to our last prayers.

I stood over my forebears and envied the ignorance of their deaths. They seemed to pull at me from the earth. Then I took a redeye back to Topeka, fleeing down the map to my adopted plains and a wife who has already replaced me, to live out my days with a sky in every corner.

I watch the photos surface and fade across the wall. They are like a balm but I don't think I can be here when Terry comes out of my bedroom, buttoning his pants, my wife drying on him.

It's already too easy a thing to hate Caithlin. I've been fighting it ever since the Amaranth Mandate. I get these thoughts, my hands with their first liver spots wrapped around her neck, wringing out all the millennia. See where immortality gets her then. That there's another man warming my bed can only push me farther out on the ledge.

Terry, tall and wiry as his brother. I remember him best as a boy of seven or so, crying tracks through the dirt on his cheeks, hurling his baseball glove because we wouldn't let him play left field when one of the guys didn't show. He'd sit on the fringe of chalk dust and make a keening siren noise until his older brother Tex, who was inseparable from me back then, would finally threaten him home.

I was usually the youngest outside of Terry, but only by a few months. We were ten, eleven, practically men on all those fine summer afternoons. Nobody knowing how tremendously lucky Terry was, that even then the rest of us stood, leaning forward with our hands on our thighs, shouting at the batters, on the wrong side of New Year's Day, 1980.

Another gif of my grandson surfaces across the wall. James raises his face to the camera, the sun winking peach and lemon off the lens, his smile so bright against the deep burnish of his skin. His sand-clotted hands hold a plastic shovel and pail.

I try to make what I see in his eyes worth all this. Then the series ends and the image changes to Caithlin and me last Christmas, reindeer on our matching sweaters and, for two more months, the same ceaseless future in our matching eyes.

Amaranth was introduced in the spring of '33. Exactly two millennia after the death of Christ, an irony epic enough to tremble the earth beneath its weight. People still talk about how the social platforms were overwhelmed, global servers crashing for the first time in decades, whoops of strident joy even on streets as isolated as ours. The pure delirium of it. The day history lost us from its clutches.

Caithlin's tether book sits on the coffee table, birthing headlines in its sleep. PONCETECH CEO DISCUSSES BAP MANDATE and SUICIDE RATES FALL 22% WITH AGE THERAPY glimmer in the air above the screen before I knock the book to the floor. Chalk it up to more of Dr. Hinton's dissociation.

Last month the US Bureau of Age and Population released three years of clinical findings and five more of rollout statistics, but I haven't made it past the second of its thousand-plus pages. We all know the gist of it by now, and I'd already let Caithlin talk me into renting space on a shrink's couch, where I memorize the texture of the ceiling in the gulfs of silence while the doctor sits in his early forties glow.

I only know what I learned of gene and cell research before the Mandate—what some of us call the Age Cleansing—was announced in February, when my mind snapped shut like a bear trap on it all. Before we millions were sent to pasture.

Humans have always been clocks winding down, our DNA disintegrating in an hourglass. Somewhere around 2025, breakthroughs in epigenetics and cellular senescence opened floodgates. AI soon joined the research, until the Prometheuses, those Titans in lab coats, isolated the telomere nucleotides that protect the ends of chromosomes. Replicated them, synthesized them, coated them with genetic chain mail.

And now they can replenish them without end. They've pressed their lips to the Holy Grail and slurped like children with sippy cups.

The important cells no longer die. Perpetual life. And that's to say nothing of age reversal and genetic regeneration on the horizon.

Or hybrid nanotechnology, which was put on the back burner once Amaranth hit its stride in clinical trials. Still, they claim brain transplants are less than sixty years from coming into vogue. Sooner rather than later, mortal injuries will need little more than Band-Aids.

It's Greek to me. I just round it up to forever.

By the time they unlock enough of those mysteries to do away with the Mandate, we Preemies will be gone, swept into the dustbin. A theft before the gift is given. And I cannot come to terms with it, no matter how many pills or perspective exercises Dr. Hinton pushes on me. I cannot because I had all those years of star-flung vistas in my eyes. The gleam of expectance.

The whole of humanity locked itself away at home to avoid car crashes and guns. Violent crime became a magnified sin. We started to hope racism and propaganda and the worst of the poverty might finally be conquered. Tether AI and social media platforms were regulated at last, in ways people could see were working. Wishful thinking, some of it, but we were trying. There was a reason to try.

We reassessed the sanctity of life, we were finally all on the same page regarding human rights, at least for a while, as we waited for the richest to line up for Amaranth, then the richer, then the rich. Until, at last, those below the poverty line—what we used to call the middle class—could sign up for the future. Tap on God's shoulder.

For eight years, all of us were told we would live forever.

Then came the Age Line. Anyone born before January 1, 1980, was told the rusting tracks ahead have a terminus. A ticket punched by the BAP. Some line in the biological sand has been crossed, and our genes have no way back to the tide of progress. Many of us closer to the Line could be receptive to Amaranth, but we are forced into retirement and grief counseling and the long shadows of our deathbeds.

I try to clear my head as Caithlin and Terry come into the room behind me, their eyes stirring the hairs on the back of my neck. This rage is an encompassing gravity, like stepping onto some bloated planet I will never see. It is a black wash of hurt with no possible container.

There is the faint squeak of her feet on the floorboards, her hand on my shoulder. "John." She says it with the voice she once used for Junior when he'd hurt himself playing. The one she now uses with our grandson.

I stare at the video wall like a semblance of a man, something carved from the veins of the limited earth, an uncaring marble. And I picture my gravestone again, Caithlin visits regularly and stands with her coat pulled around her, chin tucked down into the collar against the wind. It is always the blade edge of winter in the image. The shape of my name, here lies John Marchbanks, Sr., still with its stark contours as though the chisel has just left the stone.

She will not come to see me for long, and what is long for her, anyway? She was born in the fall harvest of 1982.

"John," Caithlin says again. Her hand slides up to my neck. I've tried to be happy for all my own, but how unfair it is, that I was born just thirty-seven days too soon—less than a moment for her, like plucking lint from her sleeve.

Caithlin, dean of her school for two decades and untold more, still with all her lovely grace, stern hazel eyes and silver threading through her hair like ore in red clay. She wears her first wrinkles as hard-earned trophies now. I can't imagine how she could stand to watch my face wither.

I don't turn around. I won't. Terry, dawdling, finally clears his throat and leaves, the front door clunking shut behind him.

"We should talk, honey," she says. "This is hard for me, too."

"Honey," I whisper. "Honey." I will not turn around. Her hand falls away and a moment later it opens the same door to follow her lover into their limitless day.

It's good that I don't keep liquor in the house. My father's old service Glock, balanced on my thigh, might not mix well with drink. So many of us are taking our lives while they're still ours.

I sit in my recliner watching James on the beach, thinking of the day I met Caithlin, the first morning of seventh grade, how even then she constantly tucked her red curls behind her ears. A life of her cycles through my mind, the better and the worse, till death do us part.

Junior lets himself into the kitchen through the carport, whistling out of tune. He rummages in the kitchen for a minute. I tuck the gun in a jacket pocket and drag myself away from the photographs fading slow and already wistful from the wall.

"Hi, Pop," he says, sticking a cup of leftover coffee in the microwave. He's got a good four inches on me—I'm sure he thanks his mother for that—and his hair's getting longer. His badge gleams from his hip, reminding me of my own father when he'd come home from his rounds and swap the badge for his creased Bible. I've never liked guns, even growing up in a house with them. Caithlin hates them, too, but here we are with a cop for an only child.

"Nice of you to drop in," I say. It's the first time I've spoken to him in I'm not sure how many days. I walk over to the window and look out over the wedge of backyard. The grass around Caithlin's garden is matted into whorls like thumbprints. The sky has nothing in it.

"I dropped James off at the soccer field with Nasim's parents," he says, "and I thought I'd see if Mom wanted to go. She said you were up in Vermont visiting Grandma and Grandpa."

"I came back early. I did my remembering and I did my expecting." A hawk appears and I watch it ride thermals out on the bleached rim of the morning, a thought breaking open that I now share more with the hawk than with my son. It thins a man's blood to let the mind go into certain truths.

"You want to ride over and watch him with me? He'd love that."

I go on staring out the window for what must be a full minute, trying to focus on the hawk but thinking of James's other grandparents, young and wealthy enough to get Amaranth over a year ago. They both work in climatology tech, where there's a lot of money.

Amaranth has made the world take carbon emissions as seriously as they should have been doing when Junior was a boy. Hell, when I was a boy. The timeline of living anywhere other than Earth is lagging behind immortality.

Junior puts his arm across my shoulders. "Dad," he says, "you're still keeping your appointments, right?"

I wave him off without turning. "Yes, yes, I never miss a chance to get talked down to. Doc says I'm moving into the acceptance phase. Like this is just some disease and the anger's over and done with. All this isn't right, Junior. I'm not even allowed to be tested. I asked Dr. Hinton what's it matter, then, if I die this Thanksgiving or ten years from now?"

"Dad, you—"

"Don't 'Dad' me. You're almost forty. You mean to say you'll remember me when you're a thousand and forty, when you're on some far-off planet with your alien concubines and android butler?"

"Pop, please. It's not like that." Junior sighs and sits down at the table. "There are ten billion people and not enough of anything for most of them. The climate's hanging on by a thread. Land's shrinking. They're rushing global birth regulations into place, but still they'd let you have this if the age of your genetic material could accept it. It's not like China where the age cap's an arbitrary fifty. No one can do anything. I'm losing my father, you know. James is losing his Papa."

"'Not like that.' How do you know what it'll be like?" Now I do turn around and face him, on the verge of shouting. "You get to be your own ancestor. You won't remember yourself as the kid who believed in Santa until he was nine years old. Nine! Or breaking your wrist the same day I took off your training wheels. And you won't remember *me*, not when your brain's plugged into some cosmos or other. Don't act like you will, John, to hell with you."

"I'm still just a person, though, like anyone. I love you, Pop. You're a part of me and I'll have you with me wherever I go. For however long. You told me that was important to you."

"Just let an old man die in peace."

I take his cup out of the microwave and pour the coffee in the sink. Press number 4 on the brew reservoir and the sound of beans grinding drowns my son out of my heart long enough for me to leave, light out for anywhere I don't have to look at the magnificent joy none of them can quite hide in their eyes.

I walk along the shoulder of Arden Road, away from town, seeking a calm that pulls like a magnet at the iron in my veins. A perfect Saturday morning, Kansas in early August, drawing heat into itself to bake the day into blindness. I listen to the shushed drone of an airplane across the stretched white canvas. The hawk is gone.

Up ahead one of Jeff Buckram's sons is pressure-washing the driveway. His little girl follows just close enough to catch the fine cloud of water that rises from the spray. The brightening blur of memory is everywhere since I stopped taking my medication, and I try hard to work my fingers through it, get some purchase and some anchor.

Dr. Hinton would cough and tap his pen against his knee. Baby steps, John. You can't let your future take your past, too.

I watch the Buckram boy and his daughter and wonder how James will think about his past. If he'll call it up on a screen or if it will simply recede into the background of his huge experience.

I can remember with an almost tangible ease my own warm lazing afternoons, rainbows flickering in a swarm of mist while my father washed his Impala. He was a short man, like his son, and had to stand on tiptoes to sponge the top of the car. My mother stood in the kitchen doorway with the telephone cord twined around her finger, her soft, dark head tilted to the right. I can taste how fine all those summers were.

Out to my left a horizon of wheat hems the outskirts of town, spread out as far as the curve of the earth. I have to stop and wait to see it rustle, so still is the day, frozen in time. As kids we'd machete through the wheat like knights errant, explorers, forming giant letters with our hacking until suddenly we were pilots rocketing our ships across the vast toothless mouth of the sky. Glancing down to see our proclamations, our hopes etched across that field, the letters clear even through the contrails and frayed puffs of cumulus we imagined clinging to our hulls.

And my family would spend a week every October in Vermont. The mountains like drowsy gods dressed in slow fire. I'd wait on the porch for my grandfather's '49 Harvester pickup to grumble long pipe clouds of exhaust up Wicker Ridge, the haunted creak of its door as he emerged and folded me in his arms.

He always smelled like cinnamon as he asked what I wanted to be when I grew up this year. Astronaut, it's always astronaut every time you ask, I'd tell him, and I can't help but think of that now, how I ended up counting numbers instead of stars.

Only one of my four grandparents was alive when I was a boy, so I put a lot of love into him. It is a wondrous and shocking thing, these last few months in particular, how much I miss him. Because I wonder how the memory of me will survive in my own grandson's heart. How long before I'm just a thumbnail file of a gray-haired man holding an impossibly small boy on his shoulders? Will he still see himself, where he came from, when he zooms in on my face? All these questions that aren't for me to ask.

My hand slips into my jacket and traces the crosshatched grip of the gun, and I remember the pledge Caithlin and I made as teenagers, to wait until marriage. I waged an honorable war with my body, lasting two years until a Saturday night in her parents' oak-paneled basement. The strange taste of a woman, alkali and berry, and time moved in a swift stumble to late the next year as I held John, Jr. in the crook of my arm. His skin a splotchy red, the afterbirth scrubbed clean, and I felt him rooted to me, and me to the future.

But what is that now? Roots only go into the earth, not away from it.

I could be in St. Louis or Lincoln or any of a hundred cities, holding an EXTEND AGE RESEARCH sign and begging military police to let us into BAP field centers. But petitions, protests, riots, even terrorism—these things do not rattle enough cages when the youngest hands shaking the bars are sixty-two years old.

More and more it is the churches that are bursting at the seams, though not with the young. Rows of gray heads bow in belated faith, the last of the great flocks. I wonder what my father would think of them.

But maybe I really am too old, because I *have* been walking toward town. I look up out of my woolgathering and see the Methodist church's steeple thrusting over the low trees. My parents missed one Sunday morning there in all my memory of them, but I haven't been in years.

Barre Park is around the next bend. Now that I'm straining for it, I catch a faint trickle of cheers way out at the edge of hearing. My pace is brisk enough and there is no stoop to my posture yet. The sound of children grows. I pass homes and farms bearing names I've known since I was brought here from Vermont fresh out of diapers. They're filled with good people, but most of them might as well be angels or vampires for all the commonality they have with me.

Still I notice the corners of my mouth tick up into something like a smile. It is a fine morning and I am in it. The heat hasn't choked the air yet and I want to watch my grandson play soccer.

Dr. Hinton likes to scribble my dreams into his notebook, so I started keeping what I see to myself. I don't have them anymore,

I say, his fancy pills mute them into white noise and I've resigned myself to the way of things. The doctor nods, lips pursed around a little "mmhm" noise. He taps his incessant pen.

But I do dream. Of blue-red skies and coarse, irradiated dirt sifting through my fingers like strange sugar. Places where sound carries forever and nothing is without heft or cadence. I dream of landscapes culled from the smudged pages of books I read in ancient childhood, worlds where cities must be torn down to make way for forests. Worlds where the rain will pick your bones clean in an hour. Clusters of moons in choreographed orbit. I dream of great terraform crafts lifting dust storms from arid planets, pumping our life into their wombs.

Incalculable distances in an eyedropper. Blooming nebulas swapping poetry. Star systems without carbon, forms of life stemmed from elements that require certain neurocoding to see, to fall in love with, their skins crackling with antilight. Immense and entire ecosystems that would fit in the metal wagon I pulled through long-ago Kansas streets, intelligent moss coating spiked stones like a diorama of my grandfather's mountain-shaded farm. I dream of the dreams I once shared with my friends, propulsion and reentry and streaking across pale skies over miles of gold dancing in our wake.

I dream every night, more and more vividly. Of my raised hand framing Earth and Sun between a thumb and forefinger, one inch and one moment. Homes in concert with heavens. Knowing when I return—if—my wife, my children and their children on and up and through the spire of history will not have changed a day. There is nowhere our consciousness is not. There is only ascent.

But whatever the colors of my dreams, in their ends they fade to the yellow of amber, to wheat in autumn, to the centers of daisies, and I open my eyes blinking tears. There through the parted curtains is the one star I am allowed to know, waiting for me.

Topeka proper begins here, the outlying church and a village's worth of restaurants and shops before you reach the business district and its heart cloven by the interstate. I climb up to the left shoulder and stand atop the park's shallow rise, under the great green bell of a sycamore, and watch James from a distance, he and his teammates blue-backed ants trundling in the grass.

Barre Park is small, just a vague crescent of trees holding two sports fields in its mouth. John, Jr.'s shiny Glide skims by and pulls into the lot farther ahead. I am glad I beat him here and spared myself the indignity of him coasting to a stop behind me on the road.

Part of me wants to stay on the fringe, but I'd like to see the boy get a good kick in. Whether it's a goal or as out of bounds as his grandpa, just solid contact where I can watch his face caught by surprise as the ball leaves his foot soaring and true.

So I step out into the sun and make my way over to the joining of the two fields, where the parents of a second team of children are congregated, sharing out water bottles and encouragement. James scans the grownups nearest him, his face lighting up when he finds his dad. He jumps up and spins in a circle, waving, trying to show off.

Nasim's parents are there, waving back. They will always be there, waving back, and I watch Junior hug his father-in-law, kiss his mother-in-law's cheek. They all laugh at something Ahmed points at in the empty sky. Even in August, Salma loves to wear inexplicable scarves. This one has all the colors of burning leaves. Of my grandfather's farm as I knew it.

"Well hey, Johnny," someone says from my left, and I know it's Tex before I turn. No one else has called me that since my mother died in '26. I think it was the end of spring the last time I saw him, right after the stem shot wiped him clean of pancreatic cancer, at least for a couple of years. He's lost some more weight from his already lean frame, his face all planed angles.

"Morning, Tex," I say, and shake his hand, which is smooth and dry as wax paper. An editor's hand, not unlike my own.

"It is for another few minutes. Until the heat gets us." He scans the crowd of children, squinting a little.

"I don't think it'll be so bad as that," I say. "Your granddaughter here?"

He shades his eyes and points out to the nearer group of kids, mostly girls. "She's right there," he says. "And what's more, Maisie's new little one came." He grins and nods toward the foreground and I see his daughter holding a fussing bundle, her head tilted down to block the sunlight.

"That's great, Tex. I know you're proud." I have to look away from all that thriving life because for a moment I'm sure I will collapse to the warm grass. It's been months since I could shut my thoughts off without the pills, cinch the anger, and without them something else is wanting to flood in, something almost from my dreams but yet unidentified. It feels like a kind of light inside cupped palms that haven't opened yet.

"What is it, John?" I feel his steadying hand gripping just below my shoulder. "Let's get you a seat."

"No, I'm fine. I'm fine. It's only—" I step back from the small crowd and he follows. We fade back until we're nearly within the first sycamore's reach. "It's dying, Tex. I don't want to do it. What's always made death peaceful, or close as we can get to peaceful, is knowing that everybody's got to go there. It was something you could reconcile. But now it's just me."

"Hey now, remember you got me in your boat. I never let you forget when we were kids that I was two months older, did I?"

"No, you didn't. I'm sorry." I look up into his pale eyes. He was always a tall one, even back then. "And I hate to bring up Mary, seeing as how she's gone, but she was born on the dark side of the line, too, wasn't she?"

"That she was." He smiles, but inside the smile it looks like he's losing her all over again. "Would've been by a few weeks, bless her heart."

I hear a sudden wail of pain, clear and high in the bright air.

One of the boys on the other field—not James, I notice at once—is holding his head and crying himself red-faced. As soon as his mother crosses the grass in a panicked shamble, his tears shut off and another kid kicks the ball back to him.

"It's a sad thing," Tex goes on, "and a cruel one, too. That Dickens line, about the best of times and the worst of times. The whole first page of that book, come to think of it. I read about a man over in Kansas City, killed his mother last week in her sleep. Said he was making it easier for her now instead of her constantly thinking about what she can't have. They're calling it an age crime, which makes it federal."

I pick my son out of the clapping parents. "He probably thought he had the authority to pass that kind of judgment."

"What do you mean?" Tex says.

I grimace in spite of myself. "They're all gods now, aren't they?"

"I wouldn't say that, no."

"But don't you want to live forever, Tex?" I run my fingers through my thinning hair, stomp at the ground in a near tantrum. "This planet's no more than—than one grain of wheat in all creation. Don't you want to see what else is out there?"

Tex looks up at the whitewashed sky then into the sycamore's dense boughs. As if he's giving it some real thought. "I don't know, John. The old world—the lily-white world, if you want to get down to it—is fading out. It's in better hands now, maybe. Besides, I never even made it from one end of my own country to the other."

"But what about having more of *here*?"

"Wouldn't it make you tired, though? You get full enough, I expect. I think all of them will, unless there comes another way of thinking about what life is. But I can't even wrap my head around that, so I don't try." He spreads his hands out, but not far, as though to emphasize the smallness of us. "I'll have what's left, then pushing the plate away won't be such a bad thing, will it? I'm trying to look at it that way, Johnny."

A swell of voices comes from the field. Parents are handing out water, packing up the kids' elbow and knee pads. A quick game, another team waiting their turn. I turn and look out across Arden Road to a strip of stores, and there like a bruise on the asphalt is Caithlin's purple Synergy. There's no other car in eastern Kansas like it and surely not one whose nose is pointed at Prairie House 8, her favorite brunch spot.

I watch a ripple of heat warp the air above the curve of the car's roof, picturing Terry's face beyond the restaurant window, younger already just from the pure confidence of life. His widower hands cut into his eggs, yolk pooling like the bed sheets did back at the house. Caithlin laughs, crinkles her eyes in that way of hers. I feel my father's gun adding dreadful weight to itself.

"My wife needs another man now to fill her up," I say, feeling a retaining wall crack somewhere deep, and it must be the shake in my voice that pulls my friend after me. I nearly stumble down the embankment to the road, Tex calling for me to wait.

I imagine some of that light leaking out as I cross the parking lot, my fingers opened into vague claws, phosphorous trailing like afterimages behind me into the crushing pressure of a black sea. In some part of my mind I've already erupted into the restaurant, but I stop outside of Errol's Sporting Goods and look into its wide streaked window.

I hear Tex come up behind me, breath ragged. It could be the light, that bright effusion, but my dreams appear to wake around me here on the beaten tar.

"John, what's got into you?" Tex says, tensed to grab hold of me. "That's her car, isn't it? What's she done? She's not worth it, whatever it is."

"That's your brother in there with her." But I can't take my eyes from Errol's window. For a moment one of my dreams, some cosmic straw I grasp at, seems to blossom there in its reflection. Just a hint, cut veins of yellow bleeding into charcoal dust. Strange stars waking. Something angry and wondrous I will never know.

"Terrence? And Caithlin?" Now it's Tex who jerks forward and my hand that restrains him.

"Just…" I don't know what I will tell him. Stars die in the glass and for the first time I look through the window to the shop behind it.

A faint "Papa!" comes from behind me, then a chuff of brakes. Just these two sounds that should never be heard together, pillowed in the quiet heat. I turn and run toward my grandson who stands in the road, bracing himself against the hood of a rust-colored hydrogen Civic. A breath from being taken from me.

As I reach him, Junior crests the lip of the embankment with a look of horror on his face, but the boy is a picture of wide-eyed calm as I scoop him up and press his cheek against mine.

"James, you can't be doing that. Don't run after your old Papa."

He says something into my shoulder, shy from being scolded. I glance at the Civic. A scared kid sits behind the wheel, not a dozen years older than James, and I wave him on before the temptation to do something else catches up.

Junior nearly runs after the car but thinks better of it. "Is he okay?" he says, turning his son's face toward his. "You know not to do that, James." He tries to take him but I turn and walk back into the lot, still squeezing, still awed. I both welcome and fear the thought of Caithlin and Terry coming out of the restaurant at this moment.

"Don't scare us like that, sweetheart," I tell James once we're on the sidewalk outside Errol's shop.

The boy pulls back and faces me, his eyes open and dry and clear. Those eyes have all the gentle darkness of his mother's. "But you were leaving, Papa."

You were leaving. I turn from those words so he doesn't have to see my own eyes, and in the window of the store there is only a five-year-old boy in his grandfather's arms, with the summer-dyed sky throwing them into relief. There is no way for me to ever mean enough to this child, not when there will be no end to his mind, and the life he will store in it.

"You've got forever inside you," I tell him, tapping his chest. "Right inside here. You're going to do a lot of wonderful things. Promise me you'll be very, very careful."

"I've got forever in me?" He tucks his chin down to look where my finger rests. "Forever like always?" Holding his smile back until I answer.

"Forever like always."

"And here, too?" He presses his palm exactly over my heart.

I glance back at the window and James follows my eyes. "See how it's like we're in a picture? That's the way it will be." I poke his tiny sternum again. "I'll be forever, too, as long as you keep this picture inside here with everything else."

He's confused but I watch him decide that what I've said must be good news simply because his Papa said it. As if to lock the truth of it in his mind, he nods to himself and finally grins. I give him one last squeeze before lifting him up so he can sit on my shoulders. "Mecha James!" he says, and I see his shadow spread its arms out. He's getting heavier and I'm getting older.

I carry him to his father and bend down so Junior can pull him off his throne. "Sorry," I say to him. "I never thought about him seeing me cross."

"It's fine, Pop. Come on, we'll take you home."

Something has taken hold of my mind, though, and I look over at Tex, who's standing off to the side, gazing idly at the restaurant. "You got your truck?" I ask my old friend, and he nods without turning. I gesture toward the shop. "You two go on, then. Tex'll drive me. I think I'll step in here a second."

"Well, thanks for coming," Junior says, and manages an awkward one-armed hug.

"I meant to walk in the other direction," I say. "It was an accident." I almost add that it was a good one, but instead kiss my grandson on the forehead, clap a hand on Junior's shoulder, and walk over to Errol's door.

"Bye, Papa." His voice is such a vessel, with such space inside.

"Bye, Names," I call across to him. This joke is going on two years old and he hasn't tired of it yet.

"Stop calling me Names!"

"All right, all right. I forgot. Goodbye, *James*."

I could listen to his giggles forever, in the way we meant that word before or after Amaranth.

It's cool and dim inside, and a bell jangles over the door with an awful quaintness. Errol's behind the counter that runs along the right wall, fishing rods hanging behind him like samurai swords. I laugh at the thought and he glances over at me.

"What can I get you, John?" he says. I once saw this man lose a tractor in a poker game and then his wife a couple of months later. Most of his hair followed along with them.

"Just browsing," I tell him, because I already see it, the thing that blazed in my mind between flashes of suns bleeding colors no one has named yet.

I heft one in my hand. God, but I remember the feel of it.

The bell rings again and Tex crosses the shop to the counter where I'm paying Errol. "What on earth are you buying a machete for?" he asks. The thundercloud of his face almost makes me laugh again.

"Because the gun in my pants is too easy." I look over and try a smile. "No, you'll see."

"I hope you're kidding about that gun, John," Errol says. "But the machete suits you. That outdoorsy look."

I want to ask him what year he was born but I can see him gauging the lines cut into my face, the beginnings of a droop in my cheeks. Something in his manner, the way he leans back toward the fishing poles, speaks of a taboo. He can't be much past his mid-fifties. I just tell him not to work too hard.

The day is still migraine bright when we step outside. I pull the Glock from my jacket and stare at it. "John, don't do this," Tex says, a waver of desperation in his voice. "Let me have him over to my place tonight and I'll talk to him."

We hold our breath in the pause and I can pretend the world holds its breath with us. Only the flat pressed sky is caught in the windows now, still waiting to be filled by clouds and the future. I can see neither my wife nor the deaths of galaxies shifting there. Caithlin, Terry, dreams, they're all transmissions severed by a line laid out across time, a cord so much sharper than history.

I put the gun away, let my breath go in a long stream. I am no arbiter of time. "Feel like some landscaping?" I ask him, pulling my hands apart so he can see I bought two machetes, each waiting in its canvas sleeve.

W e don't talk on the drive out of town, back the way I'd intended to walk earlier. The manicured grass climbs into bowed unkemptness along the shoulders, the road between threading out like an old film reel. I want to feel like I've never seen this movie before.

Soon the land unhinges and opens, the gold delta pushing us into the ocean of wheat. The road turning to gravel, then to dirt, and only the power lines remain to hum about humans. Once this was all like new snow that had never felt a foot break the crust of it.

I point and Tex wedges his truck as far off the road as he can. We ease our doors shut and I hand Tex a machete. "Do you remember?"

"Course I do," he says, and squints into the yellow light rubbing against the yellow land like it's all one gasp of sympathy. It resonates. Truly it does. "That was a long time ago."

"We'll be a long time ago ourselves." For a moment I wish James were here. He might have some unformed sense of this, even if his father wouldn't. Junior was never the imaginative sort, but I wish I'd brought him here when he was little, to walk in the ghosts of my footsteps.

Still, I could wring a couple of decades out of life yet. I could spend a few of those years passing through this ageless wonder with my grandson. But it is hard for me to picture that in all this light.

I like to think that for those before January of 1980 and those after it, this message Tex and I send will sound an echo of something, a grief wrapped inside of a joy, perhaps, and carry through the cold air of space. No one will read it, though, except a few curious souls from plane windows high above flyover country. It is a small wish, brittle and chastened, like singing into the wind, but in it is distilled what is left for me.

"What will we say?" Tex asks.

I tell him. Just one word. Maybe he sees the convergence, because he smiles and nods, and we walk into the wheat.

It is not like stepping into the past, least of all my own, though the past breathes always, rich and dusty. I fill my lungs with its smell, something that calls to mind old loved books and the wooden spoons that hung in my mother's kitchen like mute wind chimes. The smell of packed dirt is there, too, and somewhere on the rumor of a new breeze are horses and machine oil.

The wheat in August is still young even as it nears harvest, chest-high, and we are grown taller and aging, failing, when as children we could duck down and submerge ourselves with just the wide sky and its uncountable secrets to know us.

People here still cling to the wheat and its memory. In a way we're all old-timers. It has been a part of my life, an ambient background, since I was three years old, but I have never known intimacy with it. Not like the farmers. Not in the way a lumberjack feels the sweet weeping sap long after he has come out of the forest and washed. But I will call it home.

Tex is to my left angling off to make the first diagonal of our great W. He grunts with each hack of his blade. We push through the wheat, dry bristles whispering against us. When we were kids, there would be fifteen or more of us carving our message in the field. It will take two old men the whole of the afternoon, into the golden hour, chasing the sun down lest it put us out of our misery with heatstroke. There could be worse epitaphs.

The sound of crows on the air, thin and harsh. One caw pierces a higher octave and I see the hawk gliding, seeming almost to not move at all, like a scratch in a photograph.

I am thankful there are no threshers or even tractors out trawling. There aren't as many as there used to be. Our only companion held by gravity is a lone cottonwood sentinel in the distance.

The sky looms over us, on and on, now as limitless as my imagination tried to make it when I was a boy and it was two feet farther from my reach. May they keep it clean and blue and so wide. We pause often to catch our breath and swipe our faces with shirtsleeves. The sun slides to the patient west.

Tex and I stand back to back like duelers, then march forward as we shape the C, careful, aiming for grace and hoping for clarity. The O, the M, stalks crackling under our feet.

Finally I stand in the E and drop the machete, the deep ache of working the land setting into my bones, the muscles tight in my forearm. I press the gun against my chest and think of the man in Kansas City who freed his mother. I think of the eight years I tasted forever, turned it over and over in my mouth like exotic chocolate.

The idea of dying here in the flaxen light, doing it now with the earth's warm breath on my face, has the feel of liberation. A rush, to go a little sooner. After all, I was born thirty-seven days early.

But somehow I find that the number has become muffled by the wheat.

I let my mind go up and out and then down, peering from a cockpit or a bridge banked with glowing instrument dials. Mountains fall away to foothills and scribbled rivers and puddle lakes, arteries of concrete winding toward the heart where the wide honeyed vista unrolls. And far below, punctuated by two unseen grains waving their arms in childish vectors, is a shout in letters each stretching thirty feet long, a proclamation: WELCOME.

Still farther beyond, at a distance that was so recently impossible, abstract, God might glance down. What he thinks of this word I cannot say, whether he will step down to at last join the kin he made in his flawed image, or to grind them underfoot out of plain weariness.

I will not be here but I can try to hope, for Junior and for James, even for Caithlin, that if he exists out there, it will be the former. Either way, my friend and I have left him an offering at the doorstep, so that he can wipe his feet.

I pull back my arm to throw the gun far out into the wheat. But I stop, picturing my grandson wading through it. James will be old enough to hold a machete soon, if his Papa is beside him in this yellow-gold tide.

And what color is the wheat of other worlds? I don't know. I have yet to see it in my dreams.

STORY NOTES

"Vampire Fiction"

If this collection has a theme beyond the title, it is storytelling. Fiction about writers has clearly been troped to death at this point, but what about protagonists whose only narratives are interior? After all, our lives are stories we tell ourselves, whether we are authors, bakers, or candlestick makers. Every time we daydream, we make fiction. Every time we lie.

And so Fulton, in this new space between the quiet life and family he has loved and the unknown that will come next, becomes conscious of his childhood love of storytelling. I wanted to examine that thin crack between fiction and real life—and how much agency we have to make genuine decisions in that space.

The vampire game Fulton plays is familiar to me, as I invented a close variation of it at my own grandmother's house hundreds of times as a child, trying to scare myself before I understood why that was important to me. There were times it felt so close to real. I have veered close to the vampire in my past work, but here, at last, it seemed the perfect, endlessly creepy vessel to embrace with my whole heart.

And what even *is* a vampire? This is the root of why I find them so indelible.

"Holoow"

The Inconsolables is dedicated to Joe Pulver, a friend and author who is the reason "Holoow" exists. This story originally appeared in *Darker*

Companions: Celebrating 50 Years of Ramsey Campbell, which Joe co-edited, and while there's a lot more Campbell whispering in this story because I was actively paying tribute to him (start devouring his huge and peerless body of work if you haven't yet), there's a bit of that Pulver strangeness in the seams as well. (Joe's work makes quite a unique feast, too.)

Joe passed away after a lengthy illness in 2020. I only met him once, briefly at NecronomiCon in 2015, where I interrupted a conversation to introduce myself. I was still a baby writer, but he told me he'd heard he should pay attention to my work, and I fled shyly into the streets of Providence, RI. Joe was already living in Europe by the time I started emerging from my author chrysalis and gaining something of a "readership," but we struck up a lovely friendship online, swapping eclectic music recommendations and daydreaming strange collaborations that his health would ultimately prevent.

He championed my first collection, *Greener Pastures*, in its early days, which meant so much to me. He was a very special and singular human, full of light, and I miss him. I miss his *OVERmoons* and all his exclamation points shouting out the joy he found in life's smallest comforts and victories. You were loved, Joe!!!!!!! You are still loved!!!!!!!!!!!!!!

Which makes Claudette a little ironic in hindsight. With her character, I wanted to push back against my tendency to write sorrow-haunted protagonists, or rather to look at sorrow in a very different, selfish way: Claudette has led a life fully about herself, and it is only the part of *herself* she's lost that moves her to finally mourn. She comes close to understanding the emptiness of her life, doesn't she? But sadly, not close enough, and something else has to step in to show her.

"Holoow" draws its inspiration from two particular Ramsey stories, but I feel like a little mystery is good here, so I'm not telling which ones.

"Caring for a Stray Dog (Metaphors)"

Again, my fascination with bringing storytelling to the surface—what I might one day look back on as my Meta Phase. By filling the Lissa-shaped hole in his heart, by embracing the concept of metaphor, Kent is able to make sense of his mourning, his unmooring, his alienation from his wife, and the strange things happening to him.

When writing this story, looking through my laptop screen and through Kent's eyes, the storytelling elements of his life snapped into place with undeniable clicks. Kent needs those clicks. He needs the rules and the order of the narrative he has been forced to carry.

And school shootings and gun violence are such a difficult topic to write about. How dare I, or anyone. But Kent, in his sorrow, seemed to be calling out for such grief.

This is *also* an attempt to make amends for an older story in which two dogs meet an awful, awful fate. I get as upset as anyone when a pet dies in a book or film, so although that previous story needed me to be mean, I've felt guilty ever since. So I wanted to build a story around a dog and take care of that story dog as though she were my own Frida. (Frida is the very best dog. We're inseparable. She's starting to get a bit older here in 2023, and my heart is getting ready to break years too early. You can see photos of her on Instagram – @odandelo.)

"The Pine Arch Collection"

This has to be the most vividly dyed Easter egg in my bibliography so far, with its direct reference to Wes Cheung and the events of "October Film Haunt: *Under the House*" from my first collection. Readers have singled out "October Film Haunt" again and again over the years, to my immense joy, and I've taken that to heart.

"The Pine Arch Collection" is for all those readers, another love letter to the found footage subgenre I dearly love. It's also for me, selfishly.

"October Film Haunt: *Under the House*" uses a round-robin storytelling structure within an epistolary framework. Here, I wanted to imagine a chain-letter approach to low-budget horror filmmaking…and what if the chain is actually the villain? Not an entirely new concept in horror movie philosophy, but relying completely on emails seemed like an interesting way to play with the found footage "rules." A challenge, too: How can emails be scary?

So while my intent was to build a shaky-cam bridge back to the mysterious Lecomte's cult horror film, *Under the House*, I mainly just wanted to tap into something deeply creepy. This is where I most like to live, crawling along the floor with a face that is not quite my face.

The world of "The Pine Arch Collection" and "October Film Haunt: *Under the House*" will be returning soon, so if you've enjoyed either or both of these stories, stay tuned.

"The Tired Sounds, A Wake"

This novella was published by Dim Shores in a limited run of two hundred – print only – that sold out quickly. I always thought it would return in my second collection, but I like to think the people who have asked me if they'd ever be able to read it played a part in my decision, too.

I didn't put "metaphors" in the title of this one, but I did construct it around a metaphor: a mime haunting each side of a broken marriage, symbolizing emotional distance and conditioned silence in a way that's hard to miss. The obviousness of the mime attracted me, as did the fact that clowns have such a deep-seated place in horror lore, while mimes haven't had much of a voice. (Sorry. I'm a horror writer, not a comedian.)

Gwen's new fierce creativity, Lorne's old stifled failure, the wedge driven between them that feels like a gulf after so many years together with all their tired sounds and tired motions. What someone will sacrifice to save a relationship, what they should sacrifice, what they shouldn't. The boxes people put themselves into. And how, in spite of the difficulties and overfamiliarity in a long partnership, what each person does and feels can still fit together in their shared life, in ways they have stopped knowing.

Also, mimes are sublimely creepy.

"A Heart Arrhythmia Creeping Into a Dark Room"

If I do end up looking back on the last few years as my Meta Phase, "A Heart Arrhythmia Creeping Into a Dark Room" will surely be its ground zero, the one in which I was my own protagonist, writing a story about writing the very story the reader is reading. And it was written (miscreated) with such profound specificity for another book that to reprint it in *The Inconsolables* required some meta editing…well, it was an enjoyable headache to give myself. Hopefully you agree.

Yes, some of the elements here are autobiographical. I've experienced the threat of a traitorous heart. I've struggled to find the balance between not listening enough to my body (before) and listening entirely too much (after). It felt like a monster was being made inside of me, trapped behind bone, but it also felt separate from me, so when it came time to write something for the anthology *Miscreations: Gods, Monstrosities & Other Horrors*, the Frankenstein theme was already close to home.

In the unwritten sequel, the monster ended up getting me, in a way. But I escaped it again, at least for now. If you've come away from this story with a slightly keener sense of your heart and other organs swishing and pumping and churning in your body, my work is done. But not just to scare or unsettle you. Listen to the network of your anatomy and get a checkup if anything feels out of true.

"The Teeth of America"

A particularly terrifying realization of the past several years is how successfully propaganda and the internet have mated. We have nearly all of human knowledge at our fingertips, in our pockets, and yet millions of people will still believe things that are so clearly false, without stepping outside their echo chambers to learn simple facts. From QAnon to 5G vaccine myths to anti-LGBTQ+ legislature to the increasing bandwidth of white supremacists, the absurd has become reality for so many in this country.

And that genuinely scares me – this realization that wanting to believe something hard enough can give it the same weight as fact in the believer's mind. Belief can almost *create* fact. Belief can be powerful enough to feel occult, and so I wrote about it *being* occult. The thought felt as grim as nihilism, though, so I turned the tables on white supremacists and made them the victims.

But even then, I had to be honest with my storytelling, because what would that *really* change in today's sociopolitical climate? How would these events realistically be perceived in an alternative-facts world?

When Trump lost the election, the story was jolted into an "alternate history" category. Even so, the real world's sickness is very much alive and growing more malignant. I hope it is treated and torn out by the root in my lifetime, or at least during the lifetimes of the next, kinder generations.

Note: The nonprofit organization that Sarah Wilhelm works for in the story, Life After Hate, is real, and they do amazing work. With their help, people can walk away from white supremacist organizations and ideologies, rebuild their lives, and support others who want to do the same. They are high on my list of worthy charities.

"It Takes Slow Sips"

The word *incel*, which means "involuntary celibate," is never used explicitly in "It Takes Slow Sips," but this community, to use the term loosely, makes my skin crawl like little else in the world. An unstable mind identifying as such, commiserating online as such, is potentially a step away from mass murder (many incels idolize the killing sprees of Elliot Rodger and Alek Minassian) or single-minded stalking, as seen here in Colin.

You'll have noticed that the Pine Arch Research group shows up again here, as part of a triptych within this book (along with "Vampire Fiction" and "The Pine Arch Collection"). Additionally, this story's position right after "The Teeth of America" further highlights the idea of evil targeting evil. Could Pine Arch Research act for the good of the world? That might be a bridge too far, but it's a gray area that I find interesting.

Autumn is necessarily kept at arm's length throughout this short piece, but I enjoy wondering why Colin was targeted in the first place. Why those DVDs appeared outside his apartment door. And... who is that woman in the café at the end? Hmm. Should I tell?

"Is There Human Kindness Still in the World?"

This one shares a thematic connection with the title story from *Greener Pastures*: the lonely road at night. The blank spaces between points on the map and that state of being have resonated with a lot of readers. It seems to speak to cosmic horror without getting cosmic, in a distinctly wide-open American way. So I came back to it in a new light.

Dennis Etchison's wonderful story "It Only Comes Out at Night" reminded me of the strange nature of rest areas along interstates. Perhaps the loneliest public places in America, these way stations feel, to me, like a breeding ground for the uncanny. I thought about the idea that a rest area is too transitory for visitors to imprint any part of themselves on it.

Again, positioning was important to me here. "Is There Human Kindness Still in the World?" appears immediately after "It Takes Slow Sips," to rotate the camera and fill the screen with a woman who receives unwanted, monstrous advances from men.

Speaking of monsters, I also love what-if scenarios. What would a mime do as a monster in a horror story? What if white supremacy manifested as actual monsters in a horror story? As sweet and romantic and innocuous as Cupid is, the concept has always seemed a little creepy and malicious to me. Shooting love-infected arrows into the flesh of unsuspecting people to force affection? Removing agency from those who have to fight to have any in the first place? This new kind of monster played right into the story I wanted to write.

And Jessie is one of my favorite characters. I almost wish I had saved her for a novel. I'm so happy to have spent all these story years with her, watching her rise and change and grow fierce and stay the same. Her sorrow and her joy dug into me, and I needed to pause at my own rest area afterward.

"An Ending (Ascent)"

I was hesitant to include a story that isn't even close to horror – what, Wehunt writes science fiction now?? – but I knew this had to be the last piece. And as luck would have it, the word "ending" is right there in the title.

I don't know if I'll ever write a sci-fi story again, but the central premise here wouldn't let me go: What if the human race achieved true immortality, but some of us were too old to receive it? Those unfortunate ones would have to watch the light in the eyes of those around them, and it would stir up such an existential and profound complexity of emotions. And the world would change drastically, too, in nearly every way. I wanted to take a long look at that.

Greener Pastures ended with "Bookends," a horrific story that drifted toward real hope. Maybe it's a pattern now, that I like to try to lift the reader up at the end of a grueling journey. Part of me definitely knows that based on the way our culture is so divided and grim today, the setting of "An Ending (Ascent)" might be decidedly bleaker, but if we can't find hope in the future, we might as well give up.

If you waited the entire eight thousand words of this final story for a monster to appear, please accept my apologies. I hope you were glad in the end.

ACKNOWLEDGMENTS

The writer is still haunted at the end of the book. The exorcism – if that's what writing and publishing are – has failed. Wehunt knows something is wrong, or missing. He looks through the stories. Together they make a haunted house, of sorts, with his blood on the floorboards and walls. But the haunting is not there, in the stories, not for him. It's not in the story notes, where he parted the curtains of the windows in the haunted house.

It's here, in the acknowledgments.

The writer thanks Doug Murano, the only publisher he showed *The Inconsolables* to, such was his belief in Bad Hand Books. He thanks David G. Blake, who read these stories coated in their occult afterbirth. He thanks Daniel Mills, with whom he can talk about music, literature, and Vermont for hours. No ghosts there.

The first glimmer of what is wrong – the many others who have offered camaraderie, friendship, commiseration, wisdom, and cheer. There is not enough space here for their names.

He thanks the original editors of most of these stories: Joe Pulver (to whom this book is dedicated), Scott David Aniolowski, Sean Wallace, Silvia Moreno-Garcia, Andy Cox, Sam Cowan, Doug Murano, Michael Bailey, Max Booth III, Lori Michelle, and Richard Thomas.

He thanks the incredible authors who read the stories and offered deeply kind endorsements. Kristi DeMeester, Eric LaRocca, Matthew M. Bartlett, Sadie Hartmann, Andy Davidson, Clay

McLeod Chapman, Richard Thomas, Ramsey Campbell, A.C. Wise, John Hornor Jacobs, and Brian Evenson. He is so grateful.

He thanks Trevor Henderson, knowing he'll pull The Inconsolables down from the shelf to absorb Trevor's illustrations for the rest of his life. He thanks John Langan and his wonderful introduction. John has been kind and supportive over the years, and it's such an honor to have a master of the craft leading readers into these brief worlds. He thanks Todd Keisling for layout polish. He thanks his agent, Ron Eckel, an invaluable co-pilot on this author journey.

The writer thanks his partner, Natalia, as he does every day. He thanks their amazing dog, Frida. These two are his world, and he wouldn't be the person or writer he is without them – it's that simple. Of course they are not haunting him here.

He thanks his high school AP English teacher, Peggy Corbett, for helping foster the confidence he would one day feel – not then, not a few years later, but eventually – as he took that first step toward Greener Pastures, toward The Inconsolables and this haunted page, toward what comes next.

He thanks those who have read and shouted about his work. Adriane Lee-Wo, Tracy Robinson, BP Gregory, J.A.W. McCarthy, Sadie Hartmann (again), Michael Albright, Jonathan May, Matthew St. Cyr, Natasha Pavlitsevits, Konstantino Kellis, Timothy G. Huguenin, TJ Price, Micah Castle, and many others have lifted him up since the first collection, leading so many others to those pastures. Their passion is infectious, the writer's gratitude is endless. He wishes he had the space to list them all.

And these, too, are the hauntings, the restless wounds of the book. All these missing names, demanding to be here, crawling along the edges and through the pores of these acknowledgments pages. They ache. The writer hopes they know how much they mean to him. They are the reason he makes these stories up.

Thank you all. Keep haunting him if you must. You're worth it.

ABOUT THE AUTHOR

MICHAEL WEHUNT is a semi-reclusive creature living in the trees of Atlanta with his partner and their dog. Together, they hold the horrors at bay. He is the author of one previous story collection, *Greener Pastures*, and a forthcoming novel. His work has been a finalist for the Shirley Jackson Award, shortlisted for the International Association for the Fantastic in the Arts' Crawford Award, and published in Spain, where it garnered nominations for the Premio Ignotus and Premio Amaltea, winning the latter. He can be found in the digital woods of www.michaelwehunt.com.

CPSIA information can be obtained
at www.ICGtesting.com
Printed in the USA
BVHW072359310523
665165BV00001B/1

9 798988 128618